Books by
John B. Olson
FROM BETHANY HOUSE PUBLISHERS

---

*Oxygen**

*The Fifth Man**

Adrenaline

* with Randall Ingermanson

JOHN B. OLSON

ADRENALINE

BETHANYHOUSE
MINNEAPOLIS, MINNESOTA

Adrenaline
Copyright © 2003
John B. Olson

Cover design by Lookout Design Group, Inc.

Published by Bethany House Publishers
11400 Hampshire Avenue South
Bloomington, Minnesota 55438
www.bethanyhouse.com

Bethany House Publishers is a Division of
Baker Book House Company, Grand Rapids, Michigan.

Printed in the United States of America

Library of Congress Cataloging-in-Publication Data

Olson, John (John B.)
    Adrenaline / by John B. Olson.
        p.   cm.
    ISBN 0-7642-2819-6 (pbk.)
    1. Muscular dystrophy—Treatment—Fiction. 2. Muscular dystrophy—Patients—Fiction. 3. Graduate students—Fiction. 4. Biochemists—Fiction. I. Title.

PS3615.L75A66   2003
    813'.—dc21   2003013911

JOHN B. OLSON is the author of the Christy Award-winning novel *Oxygen* and *The Fifth Man*. John received a Ph.D. in biochemistry from the University of Wisconsin—Madison and did postdoctoral research in computational biochemistry at the University of California—San Francisco. He lives with his wife, Amy, and two children in the San Francisco Bay Area, where he works as a scientist at a company that produces scientific software for the pharmaccutical industry. You may visit his Web site at: *www.litany.com.*

ACKNOWLEDGMENTS

I am one of those rare writers who doesn't enjoy solitude. I never would have made it through this book if it weren't for the encouragement and constant companionship of a host of friends, advisors, and family members. In particular I'd like to thank:

Jonathan Reichenthal and Jennifer Abbu: who taught James and Jenny Parker how to live.

Peter Sleeper: the best friend a wisdom-seeking, fun-loving, advice-starved, encouragement-craving artist could ever have.

Michael Platt: for editorial guidance, encouragement, wise counsel, and for living my life before I had to.

Bill Olson: for planning, plotting, and scheming, and for extensive mouse-mongering research.

Ellen Graebe, Jan Collins, Kathy Marbert, Sally Olson, Peter Sleeper, Sherah Sleeper, Bill Olson, Judith Guerino, Nancy Hird, Robinette, Michael Platt and Amy Olson: for reading and editing and taking shifts in the bucket brigade.

Randy Ingermanson: a partner in crime and other good times.

Pond Dwellers: Jan Collins, Donna Fujimoto, Darrell Fung, Ellen Graebe, Judith Guerino, Heath Havlick, Nancy Hird, Kelly Kim, Sibley Law, Wendy Lawton, Kelsey Mitchell, Patty Mitchell, Carl Olsen, Amy Olson, Michael Platt, Jennifer Rempel, and John Renning, and Lynn "Kidfishy" Thompson.

Steve Laube and Karen Schurrer: for making this book happen.

The Third Element: Michael Platt, Craig Coengsten, and Julian Farnam.

John Bruce: for wisdom and spiritual guidance.

Leigh Nash and Matt Slocum: for singing to me while I wrote.

Lindsey Clarke, Casey Johnson, Kimberly Steele, and Pieder Caduff: for answers to technical questions.

Kim Lavoie: for the guided tour of the Cal chemistry complex.

Mom and Dad: for love and patience and never-failing encouragement.

Peter and Arianna: for being tireless, selfless, encouraging supporters who never fail to bring me joy.

Amy: who can step into any room and make everything better.

To

Peter and Ari

PART 1

BIRTH PANGS

"This was the shocking thing; that the slime of the pit seemed to utter cries and voices; that the amorphous dust gesticulated and sinned; that what was dead and had no shape should usurp the offices of life."

—ROBERT LOUIS STEVENSON,
THE STRANGE CASE OF DR. JEKYLL AND MR. HYDE

CHAPTER 1

PARKER

IT HAD TO BE A MISTAKE. James Parker sat paralyzed, watching as a jagged line plunged and leaped across his computer monitor. No. . . . It couldn't be. It wasn't possible. Ray had botched the experiment. Put a healthy control mouse in the wrong cage. That had to be it.

He tapped the Escape key and scrolled back through the data for mouse 87. If the data were from a control mouse, the line should have stayed at the same level throughout the—

His hands crumpled to the keyboard. The signal. It had started out flat. And then, halfway through the second day, it began to rise, jumping more and more as the mouse's movements grew more pronounced.

The computer screen went suddenly hazy. The mouse's movements? As in walking? Was it possible? He switched the display back to real-time mode. No doubt about it. The line was twitching like a coffee drinker on rage. Without taking his eyes off the screen, he flopped his hand across the desktop and hit the speed dial on his speakerphone. The phone picked up on the first ring.

"Hello?" His mother's worried voice.

"Mom, you're not going to believe this. I've got a moving mouse."

"James? Is everything okay? It's after eleven o'clock."

"Mom, I've got it. I've finally found a lead! I'm watching the motion detector readout right now. A five-month-old muscular dystrophy mouse. It couldn't even pick itself off the floor of the cage when we started the experiment. But now it's moving like crazy. More than the controls."

"Honey, that's . . . wonderful." Her voice trailed off.

"Mom, this is for real. The signal's way above the noise. And this batch of compounds—they came from the new docking studies." He scrolled over to the data for mouse 87. "I knew it! Adrenaline 355! Remember the adrenaline analogs I was telling you about?"

"That's great." Her voice sounded flat.

"I can't believe this!" Parker cried out. "You should see the motion indicator. It's pegging the top of the chart! Can I talk to Jenny? Has she gone to bed yet?"

Silence.

"She won't mind being woken up. You know she won't. She'd kill me if I waited till morning."

"James, I . . . Jenny can't . . ."

"It's okay. I won't get her hopes up. I won't be able to check on the mouse until tomorrow morning when Ray comes in—if he bothers to show up. Today makes the fifth day this month he's missed work. I ought to—"

"James . . ."

Something in his mom's voice sent a chill through his body. Jenny. Something was wrong.

"James, your sister is back in the hospital. Your father and I just got back. We were going to call you, but we—"

"The hospital?" His mind raced in a thousand terrifying directions. "She's going to be okay, right? Her heart's fine. They just got back the tests."

"She's in stable condition, but her heart's very weak. And it's only going to get weaker. Her muscular dystrophy is accelerating."

"But my experiment . . . adrenaline 355. It could help her. I know it could."

"Maybe." Her voice choked off. "Maybe it's God's answer to our prayers."

"I know it is. You should see the motion detector. It's—" Parker stared at the screen. The line had taken a sharp nose dive to the bottom of the chart. Flat line. Not even a squiggle.

"Parker?"

He checked the x-axis. The chart was still scrolling. It couldn't be the network connection. . . .

"Parker? Are you okay? Parker?"

"Mom, I've got to go. Something just happened. I'll call you in the morning, okay?"

"Parker, what's—"

"Love you. Bye." He stretched out a pronated hand and swatted an oversized button on his speakerphone. Dragging his arm back across the desk, he grabbed his joystick control and swung his wheelchair in a tight half circle. He jammed down on the joystick, and the wheelchair leaped forward, racing across his laboratory and out into the empty hallway of the chemistry building.

The adrenaline was working. It had to be. Something was just blocking the motion sensor. That was it. Maybe the mouse was moving so much it vibrated the sensor loose. There were millions of explanations. He stopped outside the elevators and jabbed at the Down button, toggling his footrests up and down as he waited for an elevator to arrive.

"Finally!" The doors slid open with a *ding*, and he guided his chair inside. "Come on!" He punched the *D* button for the lower basement five times before the doors finally closed. The elevator took a lifetime to reach the bottom.

"Come on!" The doors opened and he darted out into a dimly lit hallway. He sped through the maze of corridors, making his way toward the vivarium facility that housed his animal room. Raising his footrests all the way, he rammed into a set of swinging doors. No time to change into sterile scrubs. He guided his chair to the door of his animal room and inserted a key into the lock. Pulling down on the L-shaped handle with both hands, he pushed against the door.

No good. The air pressure inside the lab was pushing against him. "Hello? Anybody down here?" His voice echoed through the empty hallways. Inching his wheelchair back a little, he jammed down on the joystick and rammed into the door. "Hello? Anybody at all?" He rammed the door again. He was running out of time, and it was all his fault. After fighting so hard to get them to build an animal facility in the chemistry complex, he'd been too cheap to spend grant money on the door to his own animal room.

Holding the knob open with a trembling left hand, he spun his chair around and smacked his footrest into the door. The door popped open with a *swoosh* of escaping air. Before it could close, he angled his footrests into the gap, wedging the door farther and farther open. He was in!

Parker hurried across the animal room to the high rack of mouse cages that lined the back wall. A tangle of black cables cascaded down the front of the rack, connecting each cage's motion sensor to the monitoring station in the corner of the lab. He scanned the ID numbers on the metal tags hanging at the front of each cage. *Wouldn't you know it.* It was on the second row from the top. Too high up for him to reach without help.

He crossed the room and pulled two wooden dowels from the workstation. One short and one long. It had been over a year since he'd used the poles to pull an overhead cage out of the rack. He wasn't sure he could still do it. He positioned his chair beneath cage 87 and reached up with the long pole. Popping open the flag-like latch that secured the cage in place, he hooked the long pole under the lip of the cage and slid it out of its slot, inch after inch after painstaking inch. When the cage was almost halfway out, he reached up with the short dowel and wedged its tip into a circular slot in the bottom of the cage.

Almost there . . . He eased the cage farther out until the two slots at the back of the cage were exposed. Carefully transferring the long pole to the slot in the far corner, he was just about to pull the cage from the rack when it dipped sharply, twisting the dowel from his grasp.

Grabbing the long pole with both hands, he jammed it up into the base of the cage as the dowel clattered to the floor. For a heart-stopping second, he thought the cage was going to crash down on him. His arms trembled violently. If the cage fell, it could crush the life out of any chance he had to determine what had happened to mouse 87.

Parker tore his eyes from the suspended cage. The dowel lay on the floor about a foot away from his chair. Wedging the base of the long pole against the cushion of his chair, he leaned over, straining with outstretched fingers. No good. The dowel was a good six inches away.

"Dear God, please . . ." Parker extended his arm until his ribs ached, but it was too far away. If the mouse was still alive . . . If the adrenaline analog had actually given it strength, even for a few hours . . .

He sat up and clung to the pole with both hands, hugging it to his chest while above him, suspended by the force he applied to the pole, hung the life of his only sister.

DARCY

"Jason, no!" Darcy reached for the door of Jason's new Miata. "I really have to go. I've got work to do."

"But it's after midnight on a Thursday night." Jason leaned in closer. "The chemistry library's dark. Nobody's there. Let me give you a ride home."

Darcy turned to survey the dark buildings that made up the chemistry complex. "They just forgot to turn on the entrance lights. The stacks and carrels are probably full of students."

"Darcy, it's midnight. Trust me, nobody's there."

"No problem." Darcy pushed open the door and started to get out. "Lee-Hong works late. He can give me a ride home."

Jason reached over and caught her by the forearm. "I saw Lee-Hong this morning. He said he's never given you a ride. He doesn't even own a car."

Darcy slumped back into her seat, stealing a glance at Jason out of the corner of her eye. He didn't seem mad. Not really. Just a little confused. She flipped open the mirror on the visor and pretended to brush a strand of hair out of her eyes. Confused was good. She could definitely work with confused. She turned on him with her best whipped-puppy-dog expression. "I suppose if I were to tell you I've been working all night in the lab, you'd think I was an over-achieving, no-life geek."

"Of course." Jason's pale, overlarge eyes crinkled into a smile. "We're all overachieving geeks. We wouldn't be at Cal Berkeley if we weren't."

Darcy's face relaxed into an apologetic grin. "So you don't mind? I've got prelims coming up and I don't have a single result. Channing's ignoring me. She's ready to pull the plug. I know she is—"

Jason held up a hand. "It's okay. Things will work out." His features hardened into a frown. "But not tonight. You practically fell asleep in your curry."

"I know. Just two hours to finish up a gel. I'll call—"

"I also checked on the Berkeley Safe Walk Program. It hasn't been running for over two years."

Darcy could feel the heat rising to her face. She turned back to the mirror, trying to force herself to relax. She could just insist. Get out of the car now. Jason wasn't her guardian. She didn't have to get his permission.

"Darcy, I . . . It's late. Let me just take you home. I don't care if . . . I mean, we're grad students. We're supposed to live in hovels. I just got lucky."

Hovels? Darcy could feel the tension draining out of her muscles. She looked back at Jason and smiled. "Why don't you just drop me off here? If you saw *my* hovel, you'd have to fumigate me before letting me back in your car. Don't get me wrong. It's not that I mind fumigation so much, but sitting on plastic sheets gives me heat rash."

"Don't worry," Jason said, "I've got Scotchgard." He started the car, put it in gear, and pulled out onto the deserted campus street. "So, where's this hovel of yours?"

Darcy closed her eyes and tried to visualize a map of the city. Where *was* this hovel of hers? "I guess I know what I'm getting for Christmas—another flea-collar necklace and a pair of tree-shaped, air-freshener earrings."

"You're stalling. . . ."

"Okay, it's on Thirty-seventh Street." She'd seen the street sign once when she'd gotten lost her first week in Berkeley. The name was Thirty-seventh Street, wasn't it?

"Thirty-seventh?" Jason asked.

"That's right," Darcy said firmly. She'd been scared to death. The bullet-ridden street sign had made quite an impression. "Down Telegraph, on the right, almost to Oakland."

"See? That wasn't so hard." Jason turned right and sped down a dark narrow street. "Know what your problem is?" He turned and flashed her a smile. "You worry too much—over nothing. You've got to learn to relax. Chill."

"Well, your problem is you don't watch where you're driving."

Darcy braced her hand against the dash as Jason swerved back into his lane.

"See what I'm saying?" Jason was looking at her again. "Relax. We've got the road to ourselves." He glanced forward and pulled the car into a squealing right-hand turn. "All it takes is perspective. Perspective and a good set of tires."

"And a desire to spend Friday night alone," Darcy threatened.

"Okay. Okay." The hum of the engine wound down, and the car slowed to a reasonable speed. "I was just trying to get you to loosen up a bit. You know, seize the moment. Have some fun."

"Jason, it's late. . . ."

"I know, let me guess. You need to get up early tomorrow to work on your research."

She could almost hear the pouting in his voice. Why did he have to make it so hard? She looked out the passenger window as Jason turned slowly onto Telegraph Avenue. The car was barely crawling now. Another stall tactic? She rested her head against the window and watched the deserted sidewalks scroll silently past. Empty shops glowed feebly against the cloying darkness. Leather-studded mannequins cowered behind spray-paint-streaked bars. Blanket-wrapped cocoons huddled in the shelter of shadowy entryways, homeless pupae hibernating until their day of emancipation.

"Where is everybody?" She shook off the dark thought. "It's barely midnight."

"It's way too dangerous these days," Jason said. "Apparently *some* people have the sense not to walk home alone at night."

"Better be careful." Darcy allowed a little playfulness to creep into her voice. "*Some* people may get so paranoid they'll stop going out for Thai food."

Jason didn't respond. Had she gone too far? She glanced at him out of the corner of her eye. He was leaning forward over the steering wheel, peering ahead through a shroud of heavy fog.

"What—" Jason hit the brakes and the car skidded to a halt. Twenty yards ahead of them, illuminated by the fog-choked beams of his headlights, a mob of twenty to thirty people filled the street. "What do they think they're doing? They can't just stand—"

"Wait!" Darcy grabbed Jason's arm before he could hit the horn. The mob was shuffling toward them with slow, uneven steps. Blank faces. Glassy eyes. Their arms hung limp as they drifted from side to side, weaving a serpentine path up the litter-strewn street. A low keening whistle sounded through the chill night. An answering whistle.

"Glass-heads," Darcy hissed. "Get out of here. Quick!" She braced both hands against the dash as Jason threw the car into reverse and backed down the street. The glass-heads drifted after them, wide obsidian eyes staring sightlessly after the retreating headlights.

Jason swung the car around and slammed on the brakes. Then, shifting to Drive, he sped away.

"I can't believe this!" He took a hard left. "You've been walking home all this time?" The tone of his voice bordered on anger.

Darcy shrunk away from him. "They're not supposed to be dangerous, you know."

"That's not what I hear."

"And I suppose prisons give inmates glass because their prisoners aren't violent enough?"

Jason took another left, a little slower this time. "You still shouldn't be walking alone at night—especially not these days. Murder is still murder, whether the murderers are on glass or not."

"Okay, okay." Darcy threw up her hands in mock surrender. "I confess. I'm a geek. My life is so dull I have to walk home from the library just to get a little excitement." She watched Jason, waiting for a smile, a grimace, a shake of the head—anything to show he wasn't really angry.

"I'm serious. I don't want you out alone at night." Jason turned to look at her. His eyes were soft, pleading.

She swallowed the retort that had been forming on her lips. "Fine. I promise to be careful. No more walking the streets of Oakland . . . after tonight."

"After tonight?"

"You can't very well expect me to stay home and let you win." Darcy made a face. "As soon as you drop me off, I'm walking right back to the chemistry library just to prove people really are there." She stared Jason down, formulating a response to the objections she saw gathering in his eyes.

Jason shook his head and turned back to the road. Good. He was smiling.

Darcy relaxed in the padded leather seat and closed her eyes.

Time to keep her mouth shut. One more syllable of provocation and he'd probably blow.

"Here's Thirty-seventh." The Miata slowed to a stop at a dark intersection. "Which way do I turn?"

"Oh. Um . . ." Darcy leaned forward and gazed out the windshield. It was too dark to tell. "Right, I think. I'm not used to coming this way."

Jason swung the car into a wide turn and drove slowly down the center of a trash-littered street. Heavy mist formed sickly orange halos around unevenly spaced streetlights. Most of the warehouses appeared to be abandoned. She searched right and left for something that could pass as an apartment building. Maybe she should just give up and . . .

"Right here." Darcy pointed to a low building on their left, the only building on the street that had a light glowing outside its front door. "This is it. Hovel, sweet hovel."

"Wow." Jason stopped the car and stared up at the dilapidated building. "I had no idea. Now I understand—"

"Why I haven't let you take me home?"

"Why you spend so much time in the lab." He grinned at her and started to open his car door.

Darcy grabbed him by the arm. "Where do you think you're going?"

"To escort you to your hovel."

"I don't think so." She climbed out of the car and hurried around to push Jason's door shut. "Turn your back on this car for five seconds, and it will be stripped down to its hubcaps."

"Come on, Darcy. At least let me—"

"Good night, Jason. Thanks for the ride." She jogged toward the silhouetted building, her eyes fixed on the staple-pocked surface of the door. Stepping confidently onto the cement stoop, she gripped the rusted door handle and waited. Behind her, she could still hear the hum of the Miata's engine. What was he waiting for? She twisted the knob in both directions. Locked.

Turning around, she gave the okay sign and waved Jason away. "Go on. Get out of here," she mumbled under her breath as she dug in her purse for keys.

The car turned so that its headlights were aimed right at her.

Great. She pulled out her keys with a flourish and dangled them in the air for Jason to see. Then, after waving again, she pretended to insert a key into the lock and stepped toward the door. One more wave and . . . Jason was on his way.

Finally. Darcy heaved a sigh of relief and collapsed against the door. For a second there, she'd thought he was planning to stay the night. Now all she had to do was—

The hiss of distant voices sent shivers up her spine. Spinning away from the door, she dove for the cover of darkness. The whispers sounded again. A low keening whistle. It was getting louder. She crept along the side of the warehouse, searching up and down the shadow-blanketed street. Another pack of glass-heads. Two, maybe three blocks to the north. If she was careful, she could get past them. But it was going to be a long, long walk back to the campus.

CHAPTER 2

PARKER

PARKER STRETCHED OUT HIS HAND for the fallen pole. He'd tried every chair position possible and still the dowel lay five inches beyond his reach. He sat back up and checked to make sure the long pole was still jammed securely against the bottom of the cage.

"Come on, Jammy, think." Parker reached up with his right arm. The cage was too far away to use his shoes. What else did he have to work with? The wire leads running to the motion sensors? One of the other cages? Water bottles? Air filters? Mice . . .

"Yes!" He searched the cages within his reach, pulling out one cage after another. The mice all lay weak and helpless on the bottoms of their pans. "Come on! There's got to be a control somewhere!" He opened the top of the last cage and was rewarded by the scraping of tiny feet.

It was too far away to see inside, so he pulled off the metal bars that covered the bottom tray and lowered his hand into the cage. Tiny claws latched onto his sleeve, and the mouse started up his arm. "Oh no you don't!" He grabbed the mouse by the tail and pulled it from his sleeve. It dangled in the air by its tail, flailing around, trying to get at him with its teeth.

Parker guided his chair forward, positioning the left wheel so it was only inches from the fallen dowel. He lowered the struggling mouse, but it clung to the spokes of his wheel. "Come on little guy. I won't hurt you." He brought the mouse back up and twirled it around in a small circle—just enough to make it dizzy. This time when he lowered the mouse he made it past the spokes, all the way to the floor. The mouse latched onto the dowel immediately, clinging to it with all four sets of claws.

"Okay, hold on!" Parker raised the mouse off the ground and the dowel rose with it. "Just a little more." He swung the end of the dowel around so that it rested against the spokes of his wheel. "There you go, fella." Parker grabbed the pole and let go of the mouse's tail.

He heard the plop of a tiny body and the scamper of feet across the floor. "Thanks, little guy." Parker reached up and inserted the dowel into its slot at the bottom of the cage. Then, slipping the long pole off the front of his seat cushion, he lowered the cage slowly to his lap. "Yes!"

Parker stared at the cage in stunned disbelief. A small, half-inch hole had been bored through the plastic slats of the cover.

"No way." He lifted the cover with numb, fumbling fingers.

"Whoa." The cover slipped from his hands and dropped to the floor. The narrow metal bars that made up the inner cage had been bent—right where they dipped down to form a dish for the mouse's food. Dark flecks of what looked like blood stained the bars. Food pellets were scattered all over the floor of the cage.

The mouse was gone.

DARCY

Darcy shrank into the shadow of an old corner grocery, pressing her back against the rough plywood that covered half of a glass-toothed window. The rustle of dull footsteps scraped through the street ahead. What was this? Some kind of glass-head convention? You couldn't spit on the sidewalk without hitting at least three drugged-out mobs. And where were the Berkeley police? She hadn't seen a blue light all night. Maybe the *Daily Cal* was right. Maybe the police *were* dealing glass. They had to do something to support their donut habit.

She waited until the footsteps had faded into the rush of distant traffic before leaving the shadows of the building and feeling her way along the weed-choked sidewalks. The fog hung heavy over the city, screening her from the ghostly light of a pale blue moon. What was she going to do if Jason invited her to dinner again? She couldn't have him drop her off at the lab—not anymore. What if he insisted on driving her back to her hovel? She was tired of all the excuses, all the lies. Besides, they were never going anywhere—not as a couple. They were from two different worlds. Way different. He was an honest-to-goodness person and she was just a ghost. A wispy lie with all the stuffing scooped out.

She stopped suddenly and pressed herself against the base of a nearby building. Holding her breath, she searched the street behind her with wide eyes. A prickly weed scratched at her ankle. The air was stale with the smell of urine.

Nothing. Darcy took a deep breath and continued down the cracked uneven sidewalk. Jason. What was she so worried about? He wasn't going to ask her out again. Not after tonight. Why hadn't she just told him the truth? Surely it wasn't as bad as—

There it was again. The faint scrape of leather on concrete. This time she was certain. She spun around and searched the darkness. The more she stared, the more the shadows seemed to move. A patch of murky blackness across the street. An entryway behind her.

She forced her eyes away from the sagging structure. Ridiculous. Of course there were noises. She was in the middle of a city! Abandoning the idea of stealth, she broke into a slow jog. The campus wasn't that far off now; she could run the rest of the way. She kicked up the pace. The exercise would do her good. Dodging away from a dark doorway, she headed out into the open street. Shadow phantoms danced around her. The echoes of pounding feet. Lungs burning, ears pounding, she sprinted down street after terror-filled street.

Half a block from the edge of campus she stopped under a streetlight to catch her breath. She bent double, gasping for air, supporting her weight with her hands on her knees. What was that? She pushed herself up and held her breath. Strange noises floated on the gathering haze. Soft and sibilant, the murmur of whispering voices. She spun around. A shadow flitted at the edge of the surrounding light. Another shadow, drifting to her left. Another. Shuffling figures. Empty faces. Obsidian eyes.

Glass-heads! Darcy cut between two parked cars and bolted across the street. Left at a side street, right at the next, she ran blindly through the night. *Almost there. Almost there.* The steady chant burned in her brain. Sweeping the street behind her with tear-glazed eyes, she kept on running. They were still behind her. She cut through the narrow alley between the Hearst Gym and the parking garage. *Almost there. Almost there!* The chem building was only a few blocks away. If she could just make it—

Four pale figures drifted into the alley ahead of her—three men and a half-dressed woman. Darcy skidded to a stop and spun around. The alley behind her was rapidly filling with a sea of shadows and glassy black eyes.

She was trapped.

PARKER

"Yes!" Parker spun his wheelchair in a tight circle until the room around him was a blur of racks and yellow paint. "Yes!" He released the joystick and watched as the room kept spinning. He had done it! It had taken six years, but he had done it. Mouse 87 had escaped. It was the only logical explanation. It had to be.

The bars. . . ! He wheeled back to the workstation and examined the cage he'd disassembled. The bars were definitely bent. But what if it wasn't the mouse? What if a snake had somehow managed to . . . to what? Chew its way through the plastic cage? Slither into a room sealed so tight that even a bacterium couldn't get inside? Absurd.

But a mouse with muscular dystrophy chewing its way through plastic? Even a healthy mouse couldn't do that. Maybe a rat had gotten into the lab. No, it had to be the drug. It had to be. Parker pushed the cage back onto the bench and turned for the door.

If the drug worked that well without optimization, maybe he could convince a drug company to look at it. To fast-track it. And with the resources of an entire company behind it, maybe they could come up with something before Jenny . . .

He pulled down on the handle and tugged at the door. *Great.* Why hadn't he thought to wedge the door open? It had been hard enough trying to push the door open. Pulling it would be impossible. Extending his footrests, Parker rammed into the door. "Hello? Anybody out there?" He hit the door again. "Hello?"

He couldn't afford to miss any time in the lab. He had too

much work to do. Another synthesis. Another mouse study experiment. Analytical work. Dosing studies. Solubility. Toxicity. Clinical trials.

"Hey! Let me out of here!" He hammered against the door until his back and neck ached from the shock.

If only he had left the door open. If he had just—

No ifs, Parker reprimanded himself. Closed doors could be opened. 'Ifs' and 'whys' were the real prisons. *Come on, Jammy. Think.* Parker took a deep breath and let it out slowly. *One thing at a time.*

All he needed was a tool. A rope! He picked up the loose cable from cage 87 and looped it around the door handle. Tying it off to the arm of his chair, he swung the chair back and forth until the handle turned and the door *whooshed* open.

"Yes!" Parker drove toward the door while pulling back on the cable to keep it from closing. "Woo-hoo!" His voice echoed off the cinder-block walls of the empty vivarium corridor. "Parker does it again! Ladies and gentlemen, not only can he cure diseases, but he can also open a door. Woo-hoo!"

Parker sped through the deserted basement and stopped outside the elevators. It only took three tries to hit the Up button. "Hello? Anybody down here?"

An elevator opened and Parker rolled inside, jabbing at the button for the third floor. He couldn't wait to tell everyone. Adrenaline 355. Even the code name sounded right. Like a Ray Bradbury novel. Or maybe . . . Parker 355. Or Parkerinium. The elevator stopped, and the door slid open.

"Woo-hoo!" he shouted, loud enough for the entire third floor to hear. "I did it!" He rolled past his lab and stopped at the door to Sinclair's communal lab. The door's wire-reinforced window was dark. "Hello?" He checked his watch. It was only 2:30. Where was everyone?

Spinning around, he headed up the hall. "Hello! Is anybody here?"

He stopped and listened. Nothing. Not a sound. Surely, someone was still around. Someone working late. Someone like . . .

He wheeled to the end of the hall and turned left into the old unrenovated section of the building. His heart pounded in his ears as he guided the wheelchair forward across the cracked tiled floor.

Darcy Williams. She'd definitely be here; she always worked late. It was the perfect opportunity. He had to tell somebody, and she was the only one around. It was the most natural thing in the world.

He backed off the joystick, pausing at the turnoff that led to her lab. Maybe if he yelled from the hall, she'd come out to see what was happening.

No . . . too obvious. Nobody visited the old section of the building unless they were getting ice from the old vacant teaching labs, and he didn't have an ice bucket. Better to just burst into her lab, tell her he had to tell somebody his good news like he was too excited to think straight—which was true, wasn't it?

So what was he waiting for?

He fingered his joystick control. He'd just tell her about his experiment and leave. If she wanted to hear more, fine. If she asked, he'd even volunteer to take her downstairs and show her the cage.

Okay, Jammy. Think excited. He pushed down on the joystick and rounded the corner.

The lab was dark.

No. Parker stared at the closed door for several seconds. There had to be someone to tell. He rolled back to the new section of the building and punched in the combination to his lab. The door swung slowly outward and the lights flickered on. He went to his desk and grabbed his cell phone off its recharger unit. Staring at the names on his speed-dial menu, he hesitated.

No. He dropped the phone into the pocket of his chair and headed for the door. Another phone call—this time at 2:30 A.M.—would give his parents a heart attack, especially with Jenny in the hospital. He'd have to wait till morning. Maybe Ray would come in early. If he didn't show up, he was definitely going to have to train another lab assistant. He couldn't afford any more delays. Not now.

Parker turned out the lights and left the lab. The whine of his chair screamed against the silence of the building. Where was everyone? It was still early by grad student standards. Rolling into the waiting elevator, he punched the button for the ground floor.

A moment later the elevator door slid open, and he headed for the exit. Maybe he should call for a ride. He'd never thought twice about going home on his own before—even during the rage riots. But until now, he'd never had so much to lose. Mouse 87 . . . What if something happened before he could tell anyone? He hesitated at the door, wondering whom he could call.

No. Getting into an unmodified vehicle was a pain. It was easier to walk. He punched the door opener button and rolled outside. The night was cold and foggy. Before long it would be the rainy season, and then things would really start getting tough. Might as well enjoy the outdoors while he could. He switched on his chair's headlights and set out across campus. The direct route through the campus had four more curbs and two more step-ups than the perimeter route, but it was much safer. And if construction on the bridge was finished, going direct would be faster as well. He eased his chair down an uneven embankment and picked his way carefully across a gravel-strewn drive.

A woman's voice sounded, somewhere near Bancroft. He swung his chair around and stopped to listen.

The voice came again. Too distorted for him to make out the words, but there was no mistaking the tone. He guided his wheelchair forward. The least he could do was—

"Get your hands—!" A scream tore through the night.

Parker jammed down on the chair's accelerator, and the wheelchair flew across the debris-littered sidewalk. He rattled up a ramp and turned onto another sidewalk.

"Let go!"

Parker plunged toward the shrieking voice. There, between the gym and parking garage, he spotted a dark cluster of writhing figures. As he got closer he could see distinct shapes. Someone at the center of the group seemed to be fighting to get away.

Raising his footrests like a battering ram, Parker plowed into the mob with a brain-rattling crash. A heavy body slammed into his face and spun him around in a swirl of twisted shapes. *Crunch!* The side of his head smacked against the ground. Nauseating pain jolted through his body, filling his mind with a dark, expanding cloud.

CHAPTER 3

A BODY SLAMMED INTO DARCY, throwing her to the ground in a tangle of flailing arms and kicking feet. She pushed a hand out of her face. An elbow. Heaving a struggling weight off her shoulders, she lunged forward, crawling over the broad back of a beached glass-head. They were everywhere, picking themselves off the ground, looking around with sagging jaws, wide glassy eyes. She climbed to her feet and spun around to get her bearings. A whine. She'd heard a loud whine—right before they'd pushed her over.

A massive shadow lurched into her path and reached for her with groping hands. Lowering her shoulder, she threw her weight into the big man's gut and ducked beneath his grasp. Then, pushing off the ground with her hands, she sprinted for the street, blind to all else but the need to get away. The whine . . . The sound clawed its way through her panic. Something was wrong. She'd heard the sound before.

She cast a wary glance behind her. The glass-heads were milling about like ants around a stomped anthill. Something was on the ground. Something . . .

She slowed to a stop. A big wheel turned sideways. The high-pitched whine right before the collision . . .

That guy from the Sinclair lab. "Hey!" She started back toward the pressing mob. "Over here." Darcy waved her arms, but none of them noticed. They were pressing in on the wheelchair like a pack of wild dogs around a fresh kill.

"Hey, I'm talking to you!" Darcy hurled herself onto the backs of the glass-heads. One of them grabbed at her, but she evaded his grasp and threw herself into the crease he'd left exposed.

An arm wrapped around her waist and dragged her down from behind. She rolled to the side, wrenching herself free, but before she could stand up, another glass-head stumbled on top of her, crushing her to the ground. Another fell beside her and grabbed at her flailing fists. Strong hands locked around her ankles. A knee pressed down on her thigh.

"Let go of me!" She emphasized each word, giving her voice the tone of command. Why weren't they listening? They were supposed to respond to commands. They were supposed to be docile. "Let go of me—right now!"

Two hands reached down, cupped her under the chin, and pulled her head up until she was staring into empty, glazed eyes. A maniacal grin twisted the man's features. He flicked his tongue out at her, hissing like an asthmatic snake.

Darcy twisted her head to the side, cringing as his breath grew hotter on her cheek. The pressure on her jaw increased. Slowly her head was forced back up until his face was only inches from hers. She squeezed her eyes shut as a slimy tongue slid across her forehead.

"No!" Her terror erupted into a night-shattering scream. "Get away from me!" She smashed her forehead into the glass-head's face. Again. Again.

The hands dropped from her face. She lunged backward, swinging her head like a club. A weight rolled off her back but was replaced immediately by a heavier weight. Hands pressed in from all around her, grabbing her neck. Her hair.

"Freeze! This is the police!" The shout echoed through the narrow alley.

Lights flashed all around her, reflecting off darting bodies and glinting black eyes. The weights lifted suddenly from her shoulders and legs. Running footsteps. Hoarse grunts. Hissing breath.

Darcy rolled herself into a ball, pawing at her face with both sleeves.

"It's okay. I think they're gone," a gentle whisper sounded from behind her.

"What?" She sat up slowly and squinted against the flashing light.

"Quiet," the whisper cautioned. "They'll be back if they figure it out."

Darcy crawled toward the voice. *Figure it out?* The voice. The lights. They were coming from the wheelchair. "The police . . . Was that you?"

"Quick. I've got a cell phone in the pocket of my chair. Take it and call 9-1-1. You've got to get out of here."

Darcy crawled around the chair and kneeled beside the still figure that lay crumpled in its shadow. "Are you okay?" She reached out a trembling hand. He looked like . . . something was wrong. She didn't dare move him.

"Amazingly enough, I think I am." He sounded amused. "Now, get the phone. It's drilling a hole into my hip."

Darcy hesitated. "You're James Parker, aren't you? From the Sinclair lab."

"I usually go by Parker. Do I know you?"

"Probably not," she whispered. "I'm just a third year, but I work on the third floor too. My name is Darcy Williams."

Silence.

"Are you okay?" She laid a cautious hand on Parker's shoulder. "What can I do to help?"

"Darcy?" More silence. "Hi . . . uh . . . I . . . the phone is—"

A high-pitched whistle quavered on the night air. It seemed to be coming from the street.

Darcy searched the arm of the wheelchair under Parker's leg and plunged her hand into a canvas pocket. "Okay, I've got the phone."

"They're coming back. Get out of here!"

"How do you dial. . . ?" She felt for the keys and pressed the big button at the top. The keypad glowed with a dull green light.

"Too late. Get out of here. Tell Sinclair . . . No, tell my lab assistant that Adrenaline 355 worked. It'll cure my sister. Promise me—"

"Got it!" She punched 9-1-1 and hit Send. "Hello? This is Darcy Williams."

"Get out of here. They're coming!"

"I'm in the alley between the Hearst Gym and the parking garage on the Cal campus—right off Bancroft Way. We're being attacked by a gang of glass addicts. Send the police."

"Ma'am, I need you to calm down and . . ."

Murmuring voices sounded in the alley. Shuffling footsteps.

Darcy switched off the phone and grabbed Parker around the shoulders.

"Ow!" Parker didn't budge. "I'm strapped in. Don't worry about me. Just leave."

Darcy found the nylon strap around Parker's waist and traced it to a plastic buckle. The footsteps were getting closer.

"Run!" Parker hissed. "They won't bother me. It's you they want."

She squeezed the buckle and Parker's middle *whumped* to the ground. "Any more straps?"

"Just go. Get out of here!"

"Shhh." Darcy grasped him under his arms and pulled him from the chair, dragging him into the shadow of the gymnasium.

The murmuring got suddenly louder. A dozen or so lurching forms appeared under a streetlight. They could see her and Parker. Of course they could. She had no choice; she had to leave Parker behind. He was too heavy.

"Go on. Leave me!"

"No." She sat Parker down and regripped him from behind, circling her arms around his chest. Eyes fixed on the advancing shadows, she backed toward the campus, dragging Parker's trailing legs behind her. The glass-heads drifted closer. They could hear them. She had to make a run for it.

Her lower back burned and her arms ached, but still she clung to Parker. He'd helped her escape. Saved her life. She cut to her right and dragged him around the corner of the building. She couldn't do it. Couldn't hold him much longer.

Turning left and right, she searched frantically for a hiding place. A bicycle rack stood by a solitary bench. A dark leafy mound. Darcy dragged Parker to the low-lying flower bed and fell back into a tangled mass of vines.

"Are you okay?" Parker's whisper was barely audible above the rush of her gasping breath.

Darcy nodded, still struggling to catch her breath.

"I don't hear them. Do you?"

She held her breath and listened. The night was silent except for the whisper of distant traffic. The cold tingle of moisture seeped its way up into her jeans and shirt. The musty smell of earth and green.

"This is great," Parker whispered close to her ear.

"What? Are you hurt?" Darcy rolled onto her side. He had seemed so fragile. His arms felt like overcooked spaghetti. What if she'd hurt him picking him up? What if he'd broken a bone in the fall?

"Hurt? I'm fantastic! This is the best day of my life."

"Shhh." She ducked back down into the tangle of vines and listened intently for several seconds. Silence. No sound at all. Maybe the glass-heads had given up and moved on. "I don't hear them, but they could still be searching for us. We shouldn't take any chances."

"Fine with me." Parker sounded amused. "What a night! A ground-breaking discovery and the adventure of a lifetime!"

"Listen, I . . ." Darcy paused at the sound of a slow-moving car. "What you did back there. You could have been hurt. Most . . . you know, guys, would have walked on by. But you . . . even though you're in a . . . Well, I really appreciate it. A lot. I want you to know that."

"I'm just glad I was around. I don't normally . . ." Parker's voice trailed off. "Isn't it funny how things work out? I don't normally work so late, but I had an amazing breakthrough. The break I've been waiting for for six years. All my life, really." His voice faded.

Darcy frowned. What was this guy's deal? He saves her life, and now all he wants to talk about is science? "One more thing . . ." She had to say it. "The flashing lights. Yelling out like you were the police? Brilliant. Flat out brilliant. You even had me fooled."

Flashing blue lights reflected off the wall of the parking garage. Darcy sat up. "You turned your lights off, right?"

"Yeah, my emergency flashers are red and white. That's probably the real police."

"I'll check it out." Darcy started to sit up, but hesitated. Would Parker be all right on the ground? It didn't seem right just to leave him.

"Just be careful," Parker cautioned. "Stay out of sight until you're absolutely certain it's the police."

"You'll be okay?" Darcy picked her way through the flowers.

"I'm fine. Just remember to come back and pick me up. There's a fine for littering."

Darcy picked her way through the vines to the shelter of the building. So . . . she'd finally met James Parker. The legend himself. The cover of *Nature* and an article in *Science*—while he was still an undergrad.

She edged along the building, pausing occasionally to listen. He wasn't at all like she'd imagined. She certainly hadn't expected a sense of humor. The way everybody talked, she assumed he'd be a younger version of Dr. Sinclair—too brilliant to be bothered with mere mortals. And too incoherent for mere mortals to want to bother with him.

She peered around the corner of the building. Four glass-heads were shuffling toward the street. A tall, heavy-set police officer was right behind them. Anger bubbled up inside her. What was he doing? Letting them go? Didn't he know about the attack?

She stepped out after them. If he didn't haul each and every one of them off to—

The officer pulled something from his pocket, something that gleamed white between his shielding fingers. Darcy froze as he leaned in close to one of the glass-heads and slipped the white object into her pocket.

PARKER

Parker looked at his watch. 5:00 A.M. The police officer had been questioning Darcy forever. True, part of that time had been spent helping him into his chair, but still . . . How much time did it take to establish the fact that Darcy had been attacked?

He swung his chair around and pretended to examine the photos on Darcy's desk. The officer had tried to call an ambulance, but Darcy wouldn't hear of it. She wouldn't even let him give her a ride home. Instead, she'd insisted the officer walk her back to her lab. One of the photos caught Parker's eye. It looked like a guy, but there was too much glare to be sure. He stretched out his arm and casually bumped the photo so that it turned to face him. Definitely a guy. Long, greasy hair. Glasses. Good, he was wearing latex gloves. Probably someone from her lab. Definitely not boyfriend material.

He pulled his arm back in with a grimace. His rib cage felt like it had been run over by a fire truck. He probably should have gone to the hospital, but how could he agree to an ambulance after Darcy had turned it down? Besides, he was hoping to tell her about his experiment, maybe even show her cage 87. That is if Officer Let-Me-Rephrase-the-Question ever left them alone. What was it with this guy?

He turned his chair back around. The officer still had his recorder out, and he was still scowling.

"I told you." Darcy was leaning back against a cluttered lab bench. "My address is Latimer Hall, The University of California— Berkeley."

The officer wiped a forearm across his fleshy face. Patches of red blotched his neck and jawline. "Look, I just need a home address for my report. Not a school address. I need the place where you *live*." The officer held the recorder closer to Darcy, but she shrank away.

"I told you. I'm a grad student. If you want to reach me when I'm awake, this is the place. Parker, you tell him." She looked at Parker with beseeching eyes.

What was going on? She acted like she was afraid of this clown.

"Officer . . ." Parker looked to the badge on his uniform.

"Kelly. Dave Kelly."

"Officer Kelly, it's five o'clock and Darcy's been through a terrible ordeal. Don't you think we should continue this later?" He rolled forward to position himself between Darcy and the big man.

"A few more minutes, that's all." Kelly twisted his face into a smile. "I just need you to tell me again how exactly the fight started."

"I already told you!" Darcy's voice shook. "The glass-heads were chasing me. They cut me off and jumped me. Twenty of them to only one of me. There was no fight to it."

Kelly frowned, shook his head.

"I've already verified her story." Parker guided his chair forward. "What do you want her to say?"

"I'm just trying to understand. That's all." The big officer didn't meet Parker's gaze. He dropped his recorder in a pocket and eased his weight onto a lab stool. "People on glass aren't violent. They're harmless. It's a scientific fack. Maybe they were just curious?

Checkin' her out before moving on?"

"No way. They were all over her, trying to drag her down." Parker turned back to Darcy and was rewarded with a nod and a half smile.

"Then they weren't on glass," Kelly stated. "Folks on glass are physically incapable of . . . you know, that kind of attack. You sure they weren't on *rage*?"

"We're alive, aren't we?" Parker pressed in closer.

"Well, maybe they—"

"Enough maybes." Parker stared hard at Kelly. "We've told you everything that happened. You've got your data. You can analyze them later."

Kelly's eyes narrowed, and his whole body went suddenly rigid. He opened his mouth and snapped it shut again, clenching and unclenching his jaw. Finally he took a deep breath, held it, and let it out with a whistle. "Well . . ." He slapped his knee and pushed off the stool. "It's late and I guess we're all tired. You sure you don't want a ride home?" He looked past Parker to Darcy. "Seems to me if you was attacked like you said, you wouldn't be so anxious to walk home by yourself."

"Unfortunately I have work to do." Darcy walked to the door and held it open.

"I'll bet you do." Kelly sauntered out the door. "Lady works the night shift."

Darcy shut the door and leaned against it as Kelly's footsteps echoed down the empty corridor.

Weird. Very weird. He looked to Darcy, expecting to find her as puzzled by Kelly's behavior as he was.

"Can you believe him?" Darcy stormed back to the lab bench and plopped down on a stool. "He practically called me a liar! Like *I* was the one who attacked *them*."

Parker followed her across the room, watching her carefully. He'd expected a reaction, but not this reaction. What was she so worked up about?

"Something's definitely up with him. Him and those glass-heads." Darcy's eyes flashed. "Did you hear the way he defended them?"

"Is that why you weren't answering his questions?" Parker asked gently.

"I answered his questions. He just didn't like my answers. He kept trying to change them—make me say something I wasn't really saying."

Parker didn't know what to say to that. It didn't make sense. None of it did. Except that Darcy was distraught and tired and needed to get some sleep. They both did. It probably wasn't the best time to bring up his experiment.

"Kelly is definitely into something shady," Darcy said. "I saw him give one of the glass-heads something that looked like a packet of drugs. We should report him."

"You actually saw him?" Parker's eyes went wide. "How do you know it was drugs?"

"I saw something white. What else would it be?" Her face flushed.

"It could've been anything." Parker shook his head. "A Kleenex . . . a driver's license. . . . Maybe he was handing out tickets. You could hardly expect one officer to stuff twenty glass-heads in his squad car and haul them off to jail."

"I know what I saw." Darcy crossed her arms in front of her chest. "I think we should report him. You saw the way he kept asking me questions—while the glass-heads were getting away."

Parker thought a second. "Maybe Kelly was just . . . you know, stalling."

Darcy's mouth dropped open as understanding dawned on her face. "Giving the glass-heads more time to get away. You may be right."

"No, I mean . . . you know, maybe he was just . . . flirting."

"Flirting?" Her face wrinkled with disgust. "More like intimidating. Trying to threaten me into silence."

Not possible. Parker started to tell her but stopped short. What could he say? It was obvious Kelly was attracted to her. He'd seen it in the man's eyes. Bullying her was probably Kelly's way of acting on that attraction. A lot of guys had trouble acting normal around pretty girls—even girls who didn't act like they knew they were pretty.

Darcy looked at him through tired, droopy eyes. Beautiful eyes. Not brown, not hazel either. They were almost blonde—the color of honey in sunlight.

A lump formed in his throat. He adjusted the back of his chair and raised his legs a few inches. Kelly, the glass-heads, his experiment . . . He should say something, but what?

"Thanks for not leaving me alone with Officer Kelly." Darcy slid off the stool and crouched beside Parker with her hands resting lightly on the arm of his chair. "I don't know what I would have done if you hadn't been here. I don't know what *he* would have done."

"I'm sure you would have been fine." Parker forced a smile.

"And thanks for rescuing me." Darcy took him by the hand.

He felt like the air had suddenly been sucked out of the room. He closed his hand around hers and squeezed hard. He wanted to tell her to squeeze too. After years of electric pulse stimulation therapy, his bones were fine. She wasn't going to break him.

A hesitant smile. She seemed a little uncomfortable and it probably wasn't the strength of his grip. She pulled her hand away—despite his best effort to hold on.

"Thanks." Parker's voice was husky. "Thanks for hiding me."

"You're the one that charged a pack of glass-heads." Darcy smiled and the whole room seemed to dim. She stood slowly and turned toward her desk, her thick hair shimmering in the fluorescent light. He couldn't decide if it was light brown with red highlights or dark blonde with a hint of brown. A leafy twig peeked out above her ear. Eight years ago he would have been able to stand up and brush it from her hair, but now . . .

He swallowed hard. She was looking at the clock on her desk. Almost 5:30.

"I really should get going." Parker broke the uncomfortable silence. "It's late. And you look . . . I'm sure you're tired."

"No." She turned and fixed him with an expression he couldn't read. "I'm fine. Really."

"Really?" Parker fidgeted with his controls, lowering and raising his footrest.

She nodded, stars of light glinting in her eyes. "Are you sure *you're* okay? I could walk you to Health Services."

"I'm fine." He took a deep breath. "But maybe . . . I could walk you home?"

She shook her head, sadly it seemed. Like she actually wanted to go. "I really do need to get some work done."

"I could wait. It's almost morning. There isn't much point in me going home now."

"Please, Parker. Go. I'm fine."

Parker started to argue, but something in her expression chased away his words. "All right." He turned hesitantly in his chair. "Have a good night."

"You too."

He rolled slowly to the door. Footsteps sounded behind him.

"And, Parker?"

"Yeah?" Parker spun his chair around.

Darcy opened the door and held it open. "Thanks," she whispered. "I really do appreciate . . . everything. If there's anything I can do, anything at all, just . . ."

"You're welcome." Parker grinned and rolled through the door. He turned once more to face her. "Tonight was epic. I got to meet you, and I made a major breakthrough in my research. Maybe I could come by tomorrow and . . . tell you about it?"

"Sure." Darcy's face clouded for a second, then she broke into a wide smile. "I'd like that."

"Okay. Tomorrow, then." Parker drove down the hallway in a jumble of swirling emotions. Darcy Williams. He couldn't believe it. No matter what the police thought. No matter what they said, he really had saved her life. He'd actually done it! Like a knight on a charging stallion. The Scarlet Pimpernel. Tarzan and Jane.

He stopped at the door of his lab. No, he really needed to get home. His morning attendant would be there at 7:00, and his bladder was about to burst. Glancing at his watch, he started toward the elevator. He could call his parents in forty-five minutes. Maybe Jenny, if she was awake. He felt the arm pocket for his phone and stopped. It was gone. Did Darcy still have it? Had they lost it in the flowers?

He U-turned and retraced his way back to Darcy's lab. He turned down the final corridor and stopped. The door of her lab was closed. The lights were off.

"Darcy." He knocked the chair gently against the door. "Darcy!"

Silence crushed down on him, grinding its heel into his soul. She'd said she needed to get some work done, didn't need to be escorted home. He turned slowly from the door and trundled for the elevators. Of course she wasn't there. What had he been thinking? She'd probably been trying to get away from him all night, only he'd been too dense to see it.

He stopped at the blurred outline of the elevators. What had gotten into him? He should be happy. Filled with gratitude. He jabbed at the hazy button. The fact that someone like Darcy had noticed him at all, that he'd gotten to spend three whole hours with her . . .

It was more than he had a right to even pray for.

CHAPTER 4

JASON

JASON COULDN'T HELP STARING at Dr. Blake's eyes. Eyelashes were such tiny things. It was surprising how bizarre people looked without them. Eyebrows too. Hair of any kind, for that matter. Word in the department was that Blake didn't have a hair on his entire body. Not since his grad school days in an o-chem lab somewhere. Apparently he'd woken up one morning and all his hair was gone. *Poof.* Just like that. Little wonder he got out of organic chemistry. The molecules in p-chem were all theoretical—no danger there.

Dr. Blake droned on and on about his research as Jason shifted on the hard wooden chair. Didn't the man ever come up for air? He was supposed to be interviewing professors to find a lab to work in, but so far, Blake was doing all the talking. Blake the Snake. That's what the undergrads called him. Jason nodded politely when Blake paused, hoping the Snake wasn't going to start quizzing him for feedback. Nope. The Snake kept on talking. The only feedback he seemed to require was the assurance his audience was still awake.

Jason threw in another nod and let his eyes drift about the office. Blake wasn't so bad, as major professors went. But density functional theory? Who could devote a life to searching for multiple metal bonds? Jason hadn't listened to the Snake for thirty seconds before deciding he'd rather devote his life to searching for Blake's lost hair. Maybe it wasn't the organic chemicals that got his hair after all. Maybe it was sheer tedium. Still, Jason had to join somebody's lab, and his list of available professors was shrinking fast.

Blake stood up and began writing on the white board beside his desk, throwing up one equation after another. Jason's eyelashes were starting to tingle. What was that? One of his eyelashes must have jumped overboard, preferring to pull itself out by the roots rather than to listen to another *psi sub i of r squared over lambda.*

"Dr. Blake?" Jason studied his watch until Blake looked up from his equation. "Sorry. I just realized . . . I've got five minutes to get to class and it's all the way across campus in Koshland Hall. Could we continue this discussion next week?"

A long pause. Jason could hear Blake's gears grinding as he downshifted back to reality. "Certainly," he finally said. "How about Saturday afternoon, say four o'clock?"

"Saturday afternoon?" Jason suppressed a smile. "Let me check my calendar and get back to you. Okay?" He hurried out the door and pounded down the stairs to the fourth floor.

"Oh, man!" He slumped against the wall and fished the PDA out of his pocket. So much for Blake the Snake. *Dr. Samuel T. Blake.* He scratched the name off his list. Nine down and only four more to go. If he didn't find a lab soon, he was going to have to start over and go through the list again. What were the odds that one of the professors might suddenly have sprouted a personality in the last couple of weeks?

He looked at his watch. It was finally 3:30. He had a quantum mechanics class at four, but he could easily blow that off. As far as he could tell, Dr. Gillespy was speaking an obscure dialect of ancient Scaramaic, so it didn't make any difference if he was there or not. Which meant . . . it was officially the weekend!

Jason ducked back into the stairwell and clambered down the stairs. Time to have a little talk with Darcy Williams. No more beating around the lab bench. This time he'd come right out and ask her what was going on. He'd driven by her so-called apartment building that morning. He'd been hoping to give her a ride to the lab, but a big guy in paint-smeared coveralls answered the door and said nobody lived there. Said the building was used for warehousing drums of Mel-coat. Whatever that was. He pushed open the door to the third floor and hurried down the hall.

This time he'd ask her straight out. And he wouldn't let her scamper away until she gave him a real answer. Maybe they could talk over an early supper. Or at least break for a snack.

"Hey, Darcy!" Jason rounded the corner and marched into her lab. "I need to talk to you."

"Don't do that!" Darcy whirled around with her hand to her chest. "What are you trying to do? Give me a coronary?" She turned back to the mirror mounted on the side of her bookshelf and ran a brush through her hair.

"Sorry . . ." Jason watched as the brush plowed long wet furrows. "What's up? You look like you just stepped out of the emergency shower."

"Just washed my hair." Color rose to Darcy's cheeks. "I'm kinda getting a late start this morning."

"Morning? It's almost time for supper." He spun her desk chair around and sat down. "Which brings me to my mission. Want to go grab something to eat?"

"Now?" Darcy dropped the brush into a desk drawer and pulled out a ring of keys.

"Why not? Have you eaten lunch yet?"

"Well . . ." Her eyes strayed to a cell phone lying on the corner of her desk. "To be honest, I haven't even had breakfast yet, but I—"

"Good. Let's go to that new Cambodian restaurant I was telling you about. I need to talk to you about something."

"Actually . . ." She picked up the phone and studied it a second before slipping it into her pocket. "Think you could wait a few minutes? Maybe come back in an hour?" She crinkled her face in an apologetic smile.

"Sure. No problem."

Darcy took a half step toward the door, then turned back with an impatient frown. She seemed antsy. Almost nervous.

"Finally break down and get a cell phone?" Jason stood up and stretched leisurely. Maybe she still wanted to play games, but that didn't mean he had to make it easy for her.

"Actually, it's not mine." The frown vanished and she turned toward the door again. "I was just going to return it."

Jason followed her from the lab and waited while she locked the door. She used to share the lab with two other grad students, Aggie Chai and Mita Bhaskar, but they had both left earlier that fall, Mita in September and Aggie in October. Since then Darcy had been working by herself in the old lab. "So is Channing taking on any more grad students?"

"I don't think so." Darcy started down the hall. "She says she prefers running a smaller group. Wants to get us all back into the same lab."

"Which means one of her grants didn't get renewed."

Darcy grinned. "A big one. NIH. She'll have another chance at it next year, though. If she gets it she'll probably change her mind about small labs."

"Yeah, but that'll be too late. I need a lab now." Jason slowed his pace to let Darcy catch up, but she kept walking slower and slower until finally she stopped.

"This is where I get off," Darcy said. "How about we meet at the library in fifteen minutes?"

"Fifteen minutes? I thought you said an hour."

"I just have to drop the phone off and talk to someone. It won't take long."

Jason looked up and down the hallway, not recognizing any of the labs. "No problem. I don't mind waiting."

She pierced him with an aren't-you-a-social-moron look. Then she shrugged and turned back up the hall.

Jason hesitated, but only for a second. He hated being a jerk, but after last night, the way she lied to him. . . . He followed her, pausing while she knocked on a door with a keypad and a button next to it. One of those handicapped entrance things.

The door swung slowly outward.

"Hi, Darcy!"

Jason couldn't see who it was, but the guy was obviously glad to see her. And surprised. He stepped closer to the door. A guy in an electric wheelchair sat in the doorway. Dark hair. On the skinny side. A look that belonged in a tuxedo, behind a grand piano somewhere. Jason had seen him around on campus but never knew he worked in the chemistry building. He'd always figured him for an art student. Fashion design or something.

"Parker." Darcy stepped into the lab. "I just wanted to return your cell phone." She held out the phone, but he nodded to the left arm of his chair. She stooped over and dropped the phone into a little pocket, bumping his arm slightly with her elbow. Definitely familiar, Jason decided. He would have expected a lot more uneasiness.

"Thanks." The guy—Parker—looked up at Jason with big, spooky eyes.

"Hi, I'm Jason Shanahan." Jason stepped forward and started to offer his hand but hesitated. Something about the way Parker held his hands—too bent at the wrists. The fingers somehow seemed too long.

Parker held out his hand, without fully straightening his arm or his wrist. Jason took the hand and pumped it gently, watching Parker's face for any sign of pain or discomfort. His eyes looked red. Puffy. His sleeve was soaking wet.

"Jason's a first-year chemistry student." Darcy sounded suddenly formal, like a housekeeper announcing guests. "Parker's in biochemistry." She glanced nervously at Parker. "Are you a fourth- or fifth-year student?"

"Fourth." Parker stared at Darcy with a wide, expectant gaze. "Are you okay? I've been worried—"

"I'm fine." She stood suddenly and took a half step toward Jason. "Sorry not to return your cell phone sooner, but I slept in this morning. Or maybe I should say afternoon." Her laugh sounded forced.

Parker backed up and turned his chair to face them. "Last night, after Officer Kelly left, I—"

"Parker, can we talk about that later?" Darcy nodded toward Jason. "It's really kind of . . . embarrassing."

Parker adjusted the height and angle of his chair with short, jerky motions.

Jason shifted his feet in the awkward silence. *Officer Kelly? As in police officer?* He thought about asking but then decided against it. Darcy was obviously uncomfortable. Maybe he'd been pushing too hard. She'd open up when she was ready. And if she didn't . . .

"So . . ." Darcy turned to face the lab bench that divided the narrow room in half. "Parker, you were going to tell me about a breakthrough?" She took a step toward the bench and froze. A pool of liquid glistened at the base of the cabinets. Broken glassware was scattered over the floor and bench top.

"My lab assistant hasn't shown up for two days," Parker explained as he rolled up alongside Darcy. "I've been trying to repeat the experiment, but . . ." His voice broke off.

"Want some help?" Darcy looked back at Jason with pleading eyes. "We don't have anything better to do, do we, Jason?"

"Uh . . . no." Jason stepped forward. He didn't mind helping, and Parker obviously needed the help, but things here were so strange. Something was definitely going on.

"I don't know. It'd be asking too much," Parker said. "After last night I'd think you'd want to get some rest today. Take it easy."

"After last night?" Jason caught Darcy's eye.

She froze, color rising to her cheeks.

"You were with him last night, weren't you?" It suddenly made sense. Dropping her off at the chem library, the Mel-coat warehouse. She was living with . . . Parker? No, not Parker, but probably another guy. Parker's housemate? Either way, it didn't matter. He turned slowly away and headed for the door.

"Jason, no. I can explain."

Jason turned back to Parker. "You were with her last night?"

"Yeah, but there wasn't anything . . ." Parker looked to Darcy. "I was on my way home last night at around three-thirty, and—"

"No problem. What Darcy does is her own business." His face was suddenly hot, like an internal geyser was starting to boil to the surface.

"Jason, I was just going to the library." Darcy took a step after him and paused. "Last night I suddenly remembered I—"

"No problem." Jason backed toward the door with upraised hands. "It was good meeting you, Parker." He walked through the doorway and headed down the hall. When he got to the elevators, he stopped and waited—just in case. But Darcy didn't follow.

DARCY

Darcy stepped toward the door as a steamy wave of shame prickled over her skin. What could she say? She hadn't lied—not really. She'd told him she was going to walk back to campus. If he didn't believe her, that was his problem. Wasn't it?

She turned back to the bench, ignoring Parker's uneasy glances. She was the one who should be mad, not Jason. He was the one treating her as if he owned her, as if he had the right to tell her how to live her life. So she'd been with Parker. Big deal. It wasn't as if she and Jason were dating.

She tried to conjure up feelings of anger. Righteous indignation. She really hadn't done anything wrong. He was pushing her, not the other way around. Guilt pooled like molten lava in the pit of her stomach. She'd lied to him, and he knew it. He knew about Lee-Hong, knew about the Safe Walk Program, probably knew about Thirty-seventh Street as well. Jason didn't trust her, and she had nobody to blame but herself.

"Sorry if I said something wrong."

Darcy spun around. Parker was right behind her, looking up at her with wide, storm-tossed eyes.

"I tried to explain," Parker continued, "but that only seemed to make things worse. Want me to talk to him? Tell him that you and I weren't . . ."

She crouched next to Parker's chair and shook her head. "It's not you. It's just that . . . It's something Jason and I have to work out ourselves."

Parker nodded, then looked away. When he looked back, a wistful smile had settled over his features. She read something else in his expression too. Sorrow. Long experience with deep, abiding pain.

"Are you okay?" Darcy caught herself reaching for his arm and dropped her hand back to the top of his wheel. "I've been worried about you. That was a pretty nasty fall you took last night."

"Me? I'm fine." He looked down at his lap.

"Seriously, what's wrong?" She touched his arm gently. "Did I hurt you when I tried to move you?"

"No, I just . . ." His eyes darted to the mess on the bench. "I'm just having research trouble. My lab assistant didn't show up yesterday. And he probably won't be in Monday either. I've got to get someone else, but it takes so long to train them. . . . There isn't time." Parker's features tightened. His eyes glistened.

Darcy opened her mouth to speak, but the words wouldn't come. Her brain was locked up, frozen in the agony of awkward indecision. *Think.* What was she supposed to say? She had to say *something.* Anything. "You've got plenty of time. You're only a fourth year, and I've heard you've got loads of publications. Good grief. You've even got your own grant."

"So?"

"So I haven't had a decent result in three years. And I've got prelims coming up."

Parker sucked in his breath. Darcy waited for him to speak. Her legs were beginning to fall asleep. A burning pain spread its way up her lower back.

Finally he let out a long sigh. "I want to show you something." He wheeled around and headed across the lab. Stopping at a low bench, he reached out for a plastic cage, the type used by animal labs for rats and mice.

Darcy rose unsteadily and walked across the lab on wooden, pin-prickling feet. She picked up the cage and was about to hand it to him when she noticed a small hole cut into the top. No, not cut. She held the cage up to the light. The edges of the hole were ragged, as if Parker had cut the hole with a triangular file. Maybe that was it. Maybe he needed help making a bigger hole. "What's it for?" She held the cage out to Parker, but he didn't seem to notice. His eyes were distant. Worry lines creased his brow.

"My sister's in the hospital." Parker's voice quavered. "It's her heart. She's . . . very sick." He blinked his eyes and looked away. "The mouse in this cage had the same form of MD we have. I created the strain when I was a senior."

"The cover article of *Nature*, right?"

Parker nodded. "For four years I've been trying to find something to help her. Anything. At first I tried it Sinclair's way—protein crystallography, NMR studies, everything we could think of. But all we came up with is a minor difference in the structure of our muscle fibers. Our myosin proteins have an extra domain. That's it. Except for some weak evidence that something's going on with the neurotransmitter cascade, I can't seem to find a link."

"See? That's huge progress. How many pubs did you get out of that? Three? Four?"

Parker turned and glared at her.

"Parker, I'm just saying that you—"

"When Jenny went to the hospital the first time, I started doing assays. Using combinatorial chemistry to synthesize as many compounds as I could and testing them against my MD mouse model. Everybody thinks I'm crazy—especially Sinclair. They all say I'm too biased, too emotionally involved. If I didn't have my own grant,

Sinclair would have forced me to give up long ago."

"So you're just synthesizing random compounds and testing them on your mice?" Darcy tried to keep the incredulity out of her voice. "Isn't that . . . you know . . . a little on the low probability side?"

"That's what Sinclair thinks too. Says I'm firing a shotgun in the dark. But it's not that bad. I've got the myosin crystal structure. And a few clues about enzymes in the neurotransmitter cascade."

"But what evidence do you have that the disease is even reversible? At least if you kept doing studies . . ."

"I know. I admit it. I was desperate. Grasping at straws too tiny for an *E. coli* to pick its teeth with. But"—Parker pointed at the hole in the top of the cage—"now I have a lead. A big lead. I just hope it's not too late."

Darcy turned the lid over. A large hole was torn into the filter paper lining. No, not torn. Cut. Nibbled? She could see a distinctive pattern—mouse-sized incisors. "Are you saying your muscular dystrophy mouse actually nibbled through the filter?"

"Not just the filter. He chewed his way through the plastic too."

"You mean the mouse made this?" Darcy poked the tip of her finger through the rough hole. "No way."

"Not only that—it bent the bars of the cage."

"A mouse . . . like you? With muscular dystrophy?"

"Worse. The disease had progressed so much the mouse could barely move."

Darcy stared at Parker, searching his face for a trace of the smile that would tell her he was joking.

"It's a derivative of adrenaline. An adrenaline molecule bound to alanine and an ADP analog. N6(2-methyl butyl)ADP." Parker's eyes flashed. "I'm not making this up. I've got motion sensor data that shows the mouse became more and more active until it pegged the recorder."

"So where's the mouse now?" Darcy looked back to the broken glassware on the bench.

"It escaped. I was monitoring the experiments when the trace went flat. Unfortunately, I was too slow to get to the cage in time. I couldn't find it anywhere."

Darcy stared at the rough-edged hole, trying to wrap her mind around what a discovery like this would mean. Especially for Parker.

"I can't believe it. And you just lucked onto it with combi-chem. . . ." She cringed at the ring of jealousy in her voice. What was wrong with her? The guy was in a wheelchair, for crying out loud. His sister was in the hospital. "I mean you work so hard and get all those pubs, and then you try combi-chem and stumble on to . . . Mighty Mouse. You've got to be totally freaking."

Parker shrugged. "I need to reproduce the results. I'm running out of time."

Darcy shook her head. A cure for muscular dystrophy? A mouse that could bend metal bars? This was huge. A discovery of double-helix proportions! She'd chew her right arm off just to be the dishwasher on a project like this—especially a project that could help save someone's life. She searched his face warily, trying to read his expression. Most grad students got pretty territorial when they were onto a breakthrough, but maybe . . . "Listen. I'm not trying to butt into your research or anything, but if you wouldn't mind a little help, I'd love to—"

"You mean it? You don't mind?" His smile was so bright it almost hurt.

"Sure!" A thrill of excitement tingled up Darcy's spine. He really meant it. He actually wanted her help. "It's not like *my* research is going anywhere. My organic chemistry's a little rusty, but I was pretty good as an undergrad."

Parker started toward the bench, then stopped and looked back at her with puppy-dog eagerness. "When can you start?"

"Now . . . if you don't mind."

"Don't mind?" Parker beamed.

Darcy felt the weight of the past three years slipping from her shoulders.

"Let me show you the structure. I've got docking models of how it might be binding to my myosin. And don't worry. I know you've got your own research. I'll try not to monopolize your time."

"Please. Monopolize away. This is way more important." She followed him across the lab, floating on an effervescent cloud. She couldn't wait to tell . . . Jason. A lump formed in her throat. She had really blown it this time. She'd have to talk to him. Apologize. Tell him the whole, humiliating truth.

But first she had to help Parker. No way was she going to miss out on an opportunity like this. If he really had created Mighty Mouse, she was going to be there to see it. Whiskers, cape, and tiny yellow tights.

CHAPTER 5

PARKER

PARKER FORCED HIS EYES to the cracked basement floor as Darcy strode ahead of him. She was so excited. So full of energy. She reminded him of . . . Jenny. Parker glanced up as Darcy passed under a flickering fluorescent light. She was so . . . incredible. She'd given up her whole weekend to help synthesize a new batch of adrenaline 355. Working in the lab with her had been wonderful. Maybe, after they injected the mice, they could go out to dinner together. Maybe they could even . . .

No! He forced his eyes back down to the floor. He couldn't go there—not even in his dreams. It wasn't fair to him and it especially wasn't fair to Darcy. He didn't have that kind of future. If adrenaline 355 didn't work, he didn't have any future at all. Two or three years. Four at the most. He had to assume it wasn't going to work. How many other leads had he chased down over the years just to learn that they were dead ends? He couldn't afford to let down his guard. Especially not now.

His parents had called that morning to let him know Jenny was still in the hospital. He'd told them about Darcy and their progress on the synthesis, and although they weren't exactly discouraging, they weren't encouraging either. As long as he could remember, they'd been preparing him to accept his lot in life. To be content with the hand God had dealt him. In contentment lay his happiness, his strength.

But how could he be content when he'd been called to find a

cure? Could he be content and strive at the same time?

Darcy pushed through one of the vivarium's swinging doors and stood aside to hold it open for him. Parker rolled inside, acutely aware of the smile that lit her face. She was so close. He could feel her gaze tingling across his skin. Taking a deep breath, he rolled back and forth over a sticky mat, concentrating on the arcs of dust and dirt his wheels left behind.

"Is everything okay?" Darcy was digging through a stack of boxes in the corner of the foyer. "You've been quiet all morning." She tore open a pack of disposable scrubs and tossed it onto his lap.

"I guess I'm just nervous." Parker fumbled with the scrubs. "I've been looking forward to this all my life, and now that the moment has finally arrived . . ."

"Do you . . ." Darcy nodded to the packet of scrubs in Parker's lap. "Do you need any help with those?"

Parker considered for a second. *If you don't use it, you lose it.* It was the first rule of MD. But still . . . Every second counted. The mice were getting weaker. "Maybe with the shirt. I usually cut it down the back and wear it like a smock. The scissors are in the desk drawer behind you."

"This one?" Darcy rummaged in the drawer while Parker hurried to work the gauzy scrub cap over his head. By the time she turned back around, he'd gotten the cap almost all the way on, but she didn't seem to notice. She was too busy cutting the back of his shirt.

"Here you go." She slipped the sleeves over his outstretched arms and leaned in close to tuck the smock behind his shoulders. The scent of her hair surrounded him. Wild flowers drenched in sunlight. It would be so easy to reach out and touch a silken strand.

No. He gripped the arms of his chair as she fitted a mask to his face. Her hand brushed his cheek as she looped the elastic bands behind his ears. "How about the gloves?"

"What?" Parker silently repeated the words. "Oh, gloves. I won't be touching anything so I won't need gloves. No booties either."

"But I thought we were going to do the injections."

"We are—if the mice are still alive." Parker turned away and guided his chair to the door of his animal room while Darcy pulled scrubs on over her clothes. "We've got eight MD positive controls that haven't gotten anything but saline placebos. The way I figure it, we can inject four of them with the new batch of adrenaline and still have four controls left."

"So aren't you supposed to wear gloves when you handle mice?" Darcy stepped forward and opened the door.

"Sure, but I'm not—"he stopped in the doorway and looked up at her—"I'm not certified to inject mice. I was hoping you . . ."

Darcy shook her head. "I'm not certified either. Don't you have to take some kind of test?"

"Yeah, but it's really just a formality—something to keep the animal-rights activists happy. I'm pretty sure it's open book."

"Well, I suppose I could try . . . if you tell me exactly what to do."

Parker could hear the hesitation in her voice. "That's okay. I don't want you to get in trouble. We'll find someone else. There's bound to be someone around here with animal-handling experience."

"What about your lab assistant? Didn't you just say you needed to call him?"

Parker shrugged. "This is the third day in a row he hasn't come in for work. I ought to fire him."

"I know!" Darcy exclaimed. "Jason's worked with mice. He was in molecular biology before he transferred to Cal. Want me to go get him?"

Parker winced at the eagerness in her voice. Jason. How many times had she said they were just friends? It was so obvious. Jason wasn't the kind of guy a girl could be "just friends" with. That was Parker's role. Good ol' Parker. Friend to many. More than friend to . . .

No. He was doing it again. To worry about what could never be . . . it was stupid—the surest path to misery. He had to focus on Jenny. She was the only thing that mattered now. Adrenaline 355 . . .

"Well?" She stared at him intently. "Are you sure you're okay?"

"Fine." Parker fished his cell phone out of his pocket. "I'll give Ray one more chance. He does pretty good work when he actually bothers to come in." He punched the number into his phone and counted off the rings.

"Hello?" Ray's voice. It sounded like he was hung over again.

"Hello, Ray? This is Parker. I'm just wondering what's been going on. Haven't seen you for a few days."

"Sorry, dude. I've got this killer flu. Thursday I couldn't hardly move without puking my brains out."

"You should have called. I've been . . . worried about you."

"I really meant to, but it's been so bad. I like slept the whole day Friday. Didn't wake up till Saturday afternoon."

"Right . . ." Parker didn't know what to say. Calling him a liar wouldn't accomplish anything. And who knew, maybe he really did have the flu. He sounded terrible.

"I still have a pretty high fever, so I'll probably be out a while—at least another day. So far it hasn't been safe to venture too far from the toilet—if you know what I mean."

"Okay . . ." Parker bit his lip. He ought to chew him out for not calling in. "Hope you feel better soon. Get some rest."

"Thanks, dude. Later."

Parker switched off the phone and looked up at Darcy.

"Well?"

"He's got the flu and won't be coming in, probably for a couple more days."

"Then let me call Jason." She reached out a hand for the phone.

Parker stared at her hand, running through the members of the Sinclair lab in his mind. Surely he knew someone who did animal work, didn't he?

Darcy's hand closed gently around the phone, and he was forced to relinquish it. He watched as she punched in a number. She didn't even pause to think. She'd obviously dialed it before. A lot.

"Hi, Jason, this is Darcy. Sorry I haven't been around. I've been working on an experiment with Parker in the Sinclair lab, and . . . well, we could really use your help. Could you give me a call? I also want to apologize . . . about Thursday night. Hope you'll give me the chance. Bye." Darcy punched a button and returned the phone to the pocket of Parker's chair.

"He wasn't there?" Parker's voice sounded more enthusiastic than he'd intended.

"He's probably in the library, or at his desk. I can run get him if you want." Darcy started toward the door.

Parker swung his chair around and followed her. "Darcy, wait."

"What's wrong?" Darcy turned. It was hard to tell with the mask, but she seemed to be frowning.

"Before you go . . . don't you think we should search for Mighty Mouse? It has to be here somewhere."

"I don't know what good it would do. Without water it's sure to be dead."

"But still . . ." Parker thought fast. "Figuring out how it died could tell us a lot. Dying of thirst is one thing, but . . . um . . . internal bleeding or . . . broken claws? That's completely different."

"Broken claws?"

"You saw the blood on the bars. Maybe it died trying to scratch through concrete."

"I suppose . . ." Darcy looked dubiously around the room.

"It could be in the cage racks or under the sterile hood, or maybe even behind the workstation."

Darcy picked up a long pole and swept it under the hood in a wide arc. "Not under here. It could take forever to search the cage racks. Maybe we should get Jason first and then search for the—" Darcy pushed the barrel of mouse chow out from the wall and gasped.

"What?" Parker tried to move his chair closer, but Darcy blocked the way.

"Parker, I'm so sorry . . ." Her voice was so faint he could barely hear her.

"What? What's wrong?" He pressed in closer.

"The mouse. It looks like it might have been taken by a snake after all." She moved aside to reveal a tiny heap of fur and bones. "Whatever it was, it was really hungry."

Parker stared down at the tiny corpse. The eye sockets were empty, the skull cratered and completely hollow. Thin gray-white ribs had been stripped clean. They reminded Parker of curved toothpicks sticking out of hors d'oeuvres of fur and bone.

He felt a soft touch on his arm. "I'm so sorry. Are you okay?"

Parker nodded. "It could have gotten out by itself. Maybe it escaped and got caught by a rat. Or a snake. There could be a thousand explanations."

"I suppose so . . ." Her voice sounded hollow. She got up from the floor and walked slowly to the door. "Do we still need Jason?"

Parker nodded slowly. No point putting off the inevitable. Darcy and Jason were going to talk sooner or later. Then they'd kiss and make up. It was only natural. That was the way of the universe. His destiny lay along a different path.

He followed Darcy out into the hallway, waiting as she pulled off her scrubs, balled them up, and tossed them like a basketball into one of the bins set into the wall. She helped him with his scrubs, and then they walked back to the elevators in silence.

"I was just thinking." Darcy pressed the button for the third floor. "The hole in the top of the cage is too small for a rat. And the idea of a snake living in the vivarium is just . . . ludicrous. Didn't you say you let a control loose in the animal room? Maybe that was the control. Mighty Mouse is still the best explanation."

Parker nodded.

"At any rate we should examine the mouse and try to figure out what . . . ate it."

We—as in Jason too. Parker played with the controls on his chair, moving his footrest up and down to drown out the silence.

The elevator *dinged,* and the door opened. He led her back to his lab, but she didn't follow him inside.

"Okay. We should be back in a few minutes." Darcy gave him an encouraging smile and rushed off.

Parker took a deep breath and entered his lab. Even if she didn't come back, she'd done a lot. More than he had a right to expect. He rolled out onto his balcony and stared down at the courtyard below. It was sunny outside. One last spurt of Indian summer before the dreary wet season started in earnest. Two older postdocs from the Owens lab were playing Hacky Sack, keeping the little bag in the air for longer than seemed humanly possible.

A heavyset man in a baseball cap sat on a bench watching the Hacky Sack players. His head jerked toward the building and immediately snapped down to study the newspaper in his lap as Darcy walked out into the courtyard. As soon as she passed him, the man stood up and tossed the newspaper into a trash bin. Something was wrong. The man's profile flashed briefly in a ray of sunlight as he looked furtively around the courtyard and started after Darcy. Even if he hadn't seen his face, Parker would have recognized that rolling saunter anywhere. It was Officer Kelly.

JASON

Jason swept into the biochem office. "Hey, Dolores. What's trickin'?" He smiled at a younged-up woman who was seated behind a vintage cubicle-dweller desk.

"Jason." Dolores's Botoxed face stretched itself into a tight grin. "How's the search coming? Any luck yet?" A makeup-coated hand reached up to press back frizzy, platinum-blonde hair.

"Oh yeah . . ." Jason let sarcasm saturate his voice. "The chemistry department's chock-full of professors I'm dying to work for. Hello, I'm Doctorer Ramachandran." Jason exaggerated Ramachandran's Indian accent. "Be pleassed to come join my lab. Whirrrzzz. Whirrrzzz." He cupped his hands into pinchers and swung his arms around in his best Robby the Robot imitation. "Fluorine chemistry is very safe. No thing to worry about here. Much fun. Whirrrzzz. Whirrrzzz."

Dolores laughed behind an expressionless face.

"It's really hard to feel sorry for the guy when you learn he lost his eye and arms in *four* separate explosions." Jason sat on the edge of Dolores's desk and slid himself closer. "Yeah, that's the lab for me. Science first—that's what I always say."

"You're the one that signed up with chemistry." Dolores leaned in closer. "You should have applied to the biochem department."

"That's what I'm meeting Forrest about. I'm hoping to work something out with Dr. Channing, but she's worried I don't have the right background." Jason looked at his watch. "Speaking of which—she asked me to show Forrest the bios of four of her students."

Dolores pushed herself up from her worn executive chair and swerved to brush past Jason on her way to one of the double-wide file cabinets behind her desk. "Did she say which students?"

Jason shrugged. "Ming Lui Wang, Theresa Scolari, Darcy Williams, and, uh, Lee-Hong . . ."

"Lee-Hong Chen." Dolores started pulling the files.

Jason slid off the desk and paced the small office, glancing at his watch as if he were late for a meeting.

"Well . . ." Dolores looked at Jason and frowned. "What time's your meeting?"

"Five minutes ago." He twisted his face into a sheepish grin.

"Oh." Disappointment rippled beneath her implacable mask. "Well, out you go." She handed Jason the stack of files.

"Thanks!" He flashed her another smile and headed for the door.

"Jason?"

Jason stopped and turned, forcing himself to relax into an expression of calm indifference. "Yeah?"

"Good luck."

"Thanks." One more smile and he was gone, racing past the door to Forrest's office and into the stairwell beyond. He clomped up the stairs, flipping through Darcy's file in the dim fluorescent light as he went. A quick detour to the fifth-floor copy machine and he'd be back to Forrest's office in three minutes. Of course, Forrest wouldn't know anything about the meeting. Good old absent-minded Channing. She'd probably forgotten to mention it to him. Polite laughter. A brief commercial for the biochem department, and he'd have the files back to Dolores in less than ten. Q.E.D. Quite easily done.

Jason's cell phone went off in his pocket, filling the stairwell with a mockery of Wagner's "Flight of the Valkyries." He shouldered through a heavy metal door and answered the phone. "This is Jason."

A long pause.

"Hello?" He could hear movement on the other end.

"Um . . . this is James Parker, from the Sinclair lab. Is this Jason Shanahan?"

"Yeah?" *James Parker.* Jason frowned. The guy in the wheelchair? Why would *he* be calling?

"Is Darcy with you?" Parker sounded out of breath.

"No. I haven't seen her since—"

"Jason, listen. I think Darcy might be in trouble. She went out looking for you over an hour ago and hasn't come back."

"Looking for me?" Jason threw open the stairwell door and started back down the stairs. "What kind of trouble?"

"A guy was stalking her." The voice was almost lost in a crackle of static.

"Stalking her? Are you sure?" He tried to sound skeptical, but he could feel a dozen other weirdities clicking into place. Of course someone was stalking her. It explained a lot.

"Positive. I know who the guy is too. I watched him hide behind a newspaper and then get up and follow her when she walked by."

"Did you call the police?" Jason pounded down the last few steps, taking them two at a time.

"Yeah, but they didn't believe me." A static-filled pause. "The guy stalking her *is* the police."

"What?" Jason pushed out onto the fourth floor and headed for his desk at a fast jog. "I don't think I heard you right."

"The guy stalking her is a police officer. The same one that helped us with the glass-heads the other night."

"What glass-heads?" Jason swung around a corner and into the vacant lab that served as his office. "What are you—?"

James Parker sat in his wheelchair next to Jason's desk, staring up at him with round, startled eyes. Guilty eyes.

Jason stepped toward his desk and glanced at its cluttered surface, trying to remember whether he'd left his thermo notes open or not. He took a deep breath and slowly swung the stack of files around so that the names faced away from Parker. "Would you mind telling me what you're doing at my desk?" He knew he was being harsh, but for some reason it irritated him that Parker had seen him running with the files.

"Looking for Darcy." Parker fumbled with his phone. "The ladies in the chem office told me where your desk was."

"The chemistry office?" Jason watched Parker uneasily. He seemed to be having trouble with his phone. Should he offer to help, or would that just make him uncomfortable? "So . . . what's this with the police and Darcy?"

"I don't know." Parker managed to slip the phone into a pouch by his leg. "The guy's name is Kelly. Darcy thought she saw him giving drugs to the glass-heads."

"I'm going to ask one more time. What glass-heads?"

"Didn't she tell you?" Parker's eyes widened. "She was attacked by a pack of glass-heads. They bruised her up pretty good. I just assumed you—"

"When?" Jason already knew the answer, but he wanted to hear it anyway. "It was Thursday night, wasn't it?"

"Yeah, pretty late. Friday morning, really."

"Where was she when it happened?" *Thirty-seventh Street* . . . An image of a rough guy with paint-splashed coveralls flashed across Jason's mind.

"Next to the Hearst gym. There were about twenty of them. I tried to help, but they . . . knocked me over. If Darcy hadn't—"

"So what were you doing with Darcy?" Jason had to know. If he came across as a jealous boyfriend, then so be it. Maybe it would make this Parker guy think twice about what he was doing.

"I wasn't doing anything." Parker's eyes flashed. "I was walking home and heard her screaming for help."

"*Walking* home?" Jason stared hard at Parker.

Parker nodded. "Okay, maybe she wasn't screaming. It was more like yelling. I went to check it out and found a whole mob of glass-heads surrounding her. So I just sort of ran into them. This chair's been modified. It'll do nine miles an hour. And when I raise my footrest—"

"Was anybody with her? Did she say what she was doing out so late?"

Parker shook his head. "She said she was headed for the chemistry building. She seems pretty stressed about her research."

"Tell me about it." Jason frowned. Darcy had told him she was going to walk back, but he'd assumed she was joking—because that's what she'd wanted him to assume. But why? Why have him dump her off in the middle of nowhere if she knew she was going to have to walk back to campus? Unless she was meeting someone. Someone who lived nearby and could give her a ride.

"So do you have any idea where she could have gone?" Parker's voice rose in pitch. "Any favorite hangouts? Friends? Would she have tried to find you at your apartment?"

Jason considered for a second. "My house is way up on Hill Road. She wouldn't have gone there—not without a car. Besides, I'm hardly ever at home. She usually just calls me."

"She tried, but you didn't answer."

Jason nodded. So far his story fit. He had switched his phone off during the Ramachandran interview, such as it was. He should have left it on. Darcy's call would have been a great excuse to cut the misery short.

"Any other ideas where she could be?" Parker sounded desperate. "Where does she live? What's her phone number?"

"She's usually in her lab." Jason turned and headed for the door. An electric whine followed him out into the hallway. "I don't even have her home number. For a while, I thought she might not have a phone, but now . . . I don't know what's going on with her. I didn't see her all weekend." They walked to the elevators in silence. If he could just ditch Parker, he'd be able to get Darcy's address from her file.

"She was helping me with my research," Parker said apologetically. "My lab assistant is out with the flu, and Darcy . . . volunteered to help."

Jason looked back at Parker. What could he be working on that was important enough to pull Darcy from her own research? They rode down to the third floor and headed for Darcy's lab. The door was open. "Darcy?" Jason stepped into the room and looked around. Nobody home.

"Her backpack is on her desk," said Parker, "so she couldn't have gone home."

Jason didn't know whether it was a statement or a question. Had he ever seen Darcy carrying a backpack? He couldn't remember.

"Check the sinks. See if they're wet," Parker called out from the back of the lab. He was fumbling with the handle to a windowless door marked with a yellow radiation sticker.

"That leads to an old hot room." Jason said. "Nobody ever goes in there anymore." He grabbed a couple of paper towels and swiped them across the bottom of the sink. "The sink's dry. She probably hasn't been . . . Parker?"

"She's not here." Parker rolled out of the hot room and glided across the floor of the lab. "Where else would she be?"

"I don't know. Maybe getting something to eat?" Jason followed Parker from the lab. "She's got a major Bongo Burger addiction."

The whine of Parker's chair jumped half an octave, and Jason had to bump up his pace to a slow jog.

"What did she want to talk to me about, anyway?" Jason had to raise his voice to be heard.

"We need your help with—"

"Hey, guys! Wait up." Darcy's voice. Running footsteps came from behind them.

Jason whirled around. "Darcy! Where have you been? What's all this about—" His mind went suddenly blank. Darcy was blinking back at him with watery squinty eyes. "Are you okay? Parker said someone was after you. Something about the police."

"The police?" Darcy looked past Jason to Parker. "What's going on?"

"Did you talk to Officer Kelly?" Parker rolled alongside Jason.

"No." Darcy's eyes narrowed. She seemed confused.

"After you left the lab, I saw him pretending to read a newspaper down in the courtyard. As soon as you passed him, he got up and followed you."

"Are you sure?"

"Positive. He wasn't wearing a uniform, but I got a good look at his face. Where were you going anyway?"

Darcy shrugged. "I was looking for Jason. I went out to see if his car was in the lot."

"Was that all?" Jason searched Darcy's eyes. "You didn't take another trip to Thirty-seventh Street?"

"No. I've been looking all over for you. I checked your desk, but you weren't there." Darcy looked up at him accusingly. "And you didn't answer your phone."

"And you never saw Kelly?" Parker rolled forward.

"No. What would he be following me for?"

Parker wheeled around and headed down the hallway. Jason looked to Darcy for an explanation, but she ignored him and instead took off running after Parker.

"Darcy, wait!" Jason shouted. "What's going on?" He jogged after her, following her inside Parker's lab.

"There he is," Parker was out on the balcony at the back of his lab. "This time he's reading a magazine. See?"

Jason stepped out onto the narrow balcony. A big man in an Oakland Raiders cap sat on a bench reading a magazine. So what?

"Are you sure it's him?" Darcy spoke in a hushed voice.

"Just wait," said Parker.

Jason waited for what seemed like an hour. He had to get the files back to Dolores. If she talked to Forrest before he did . . . "Come on! It's just a guy reading a magazine. What's the big deal?"

Darcy and Parker ignored him, staring down at the man like two vultures eyeing their next meal.

"You're not going to sit and watch this guy all day, are you?

What did you want to ask me about?" Jason tapped Darcy on the shoulder. "Darcy?"

"What? Oh." She glanced briefly at Jason and then turned back to the courtyard. "Parker's lab assistant is sick, and I've been helping him with a very important experiment." She paused, biting her lower lip. "I know you don't like animal work, but we really need to do some injections. It's just mice."

"Sorry." Jason shook his head. "I don't do animal work. Not anymore."

He started to turn away, but Darcy caught him by the arm. "Jason, please. It's really important. The mice have muscular dystrophy. They won't even be able to struggle."

Jason looked down at the floor, shutting out the plea that shimmered in her eyes. Why should he help Parker? Even a blind man could see Parker had a crush on her. And the guy was in a wheelchair. How was he supposed to compete with that?

"Darcy, it's not that I don't want to help. It's just that . . . I can't. You've never had to shave a mouse. Never slipped and had blood spray across the wall while the poor mouse died, writhing in agony in your hands. You've never—"

"You won't have to shave them. Just give them a few injections." She looked to Parker for confirmation. "Right?"

Parker nodded. "It isn't that bad. Darcy could do it herself, only she isn't certified."

"Sorry." Jason shook his head and looked down at his watch. "I can't. I've got a meeting with Dr. Forrest to—" His cell phone rang out, causing them all to jump.

"This is Jason." He stepped back into the lab, turning his body to keep them from being able to hear.

"Jason, this is Dolores. I just got a call from Dr. Forrest, and he's—"

"Could you hold on a second?" Jason crossed the aisle and turned on the water in one of the lab's many sinks. He set his phone on the bench and rinsed his hands, drying them noisily on a paper towel. He picked up the phone again. "Hello, Dolores?"

"Jason, what's—"

"Sorry about that. Just had to make a pit stop. Could you tell Dr. Forrest I'll be there in a few? I've been . . . dealing with a bad burrito."

"Jason." Dolores sounded worried. "Dr. Forrest just called. He's on his way to the airport and says he doesn't know anything about a meeting with you, and he doesn't know anything about Channing's files."

"Channing didn't set it up?" Jason caught Darcy's eye and winked.

"Set what up?"

"She told me she'd set it all up. Does he want to reschedule? I really need to talk to him."

"Oh, he wants to talk to you, all right. First thing after he gets back."

"Okay. Great!" Jason waved at Parker and Darcy and headed for the door. "I'll be right there with the files." Ending the call, he hurried for the door. "See you later, Darcy!" He ran to the stairs and up to the fifth-floor copy room. He'd have a lot of explaining to do—to Darcy and Forrest—but no way was he going to turn in Darcy's file without photocopying it first.

CHAPTER 6

DARCY

DARCY SAT ON A DECK CHAIR on Parker's balcony, staring out into the gathering night. Kelly was gone. He'd left the courtyard hours ago, but she couldn't shake the feeling he was out there somewhere, searching for her. The library, the lobby, maybe even her own lab. He was out there, and he wouldn't rest until he found her. No. Not *her*. Darcy frowned. Kelly had followed her all the way to the parking deck, and she'd been alone the whole way. He could have talked to her at any time. He was after something else. Something that didn't have anything to do with police work. But what?

She turned away from the courtyard. Parker was sitting back in his chair watching her through heavy-lidded eyes. She looked down at the cement deck, but her eyes kept drifting back to his. What was he thinking? She smiled at him and looked back down again. She had such a hard time reading him. Other guys were easy. They were all basically the same story. Same plot. Same character. But Parker . . . After years of *Captain Underpants,* she felt like she was finally getting James Joyce.

"Okay, I give up." Her voice shattered the silence. "What are you thinking?"

"About you."

Darcy's gut tightened. She pulled her knees to her chest and sat back against the chair. "What about me?"

"Something's bothering you. Something besides Kelly."

She let her feet slide onto the floor. At least he wasn't making a pass at her.

"If you want to talk about it . . . If there's anything I can do to help, I'm here for you, okay? I hope you know that."

"I think I do. . . ." Darcy looked into Parker's eyes. They were soft and warm. Giving. Maybe that was the difference. Most guys were vampires, biting into her with their eyes and sucking her dry until she was a cheap, dirty skeleton of herself. "I . . . The other night . . . when you ran into the glass-heads." Darcy couldn't find the right words. "Why? Why did you do it? You could have been killed."

"Because"—Parker seemed taken aback—"you needed help."

"Is that the only reason?" She watched him closely. "Just because you're a good guy."

He seemed genuinely confused. "What do you mean?"

"Parker, when you charged the glass-heads, did you even know it was me you were rescuing?" She held her breath, waiting for his answer.

"No. I just heard shouts. Somebody in trouble."

She nodded, turned to face the courtyard. Of course he didn't. It didn't have anything to do with her. That was just the way he was. The kind of guy that risked his life to help strangers.

"If I'd known it was you . . ."

Darcy looked back at Parker. His eyes were smoldering beneath a knotted brow.

He shook his head. "I don't know what I would have done."

"What are you saying? If you'd known it was me, you would have let them have me?"

A puzzled stare.

Darcy looked out into the night. She could hear Parker fiddling with the controls on his chair.

"Darcy, I don't know why it's so hard for you to hear this, but you're a wonderful person. Sweet, caring, intelligent . . . beautiful. I don't want to make you uncomfortable, but I have to say it. I feel so . . . privileged . . . just to be able to sit here with you. To have had the chance to help you. It's the best thing that ever happened to me. Even if I had died, it would have been so worth it."

Darcy turned to study Parker's face. "I don't know what to say. You obviously don't know me very well."

"Maybe not. But I know you a lot better than you do."

She shrugged and stared again into the courtyard below. A misty fog had rolled in from the bay and was gathered about the campus lights, soft and insubstantial, like tangerine cotton candy around little lamppost sticks.

The *whir* and *click* of Parker's controls diffused the silence. He was leaning back in his seat. Confident. Comfortable. Totally at peace. She leaned back in the deck chair and let her eyes drift back to his face. The shadow of a smile touched his lips.

"Maybe he was just trying to get up his nerve to ask you out."

"What?" Darcy sat up suddenly. "Who?"

"Kelly. Why else would he be following you?"

Darcy shook her head. "He's the kind of guy who's immune to rejection. And he's definitely not the type to shy away from confrontation."

"Well, maybe he's just trying to finish his police report. Maybe he was following you to get your address."

"I told him where to find me. I'm in the lab all—" An icy dagger slid down her spine. *All day.* The only reason someone would need to know where she lived at night was if he couldn't get to her by day.

The Dark Man.

It was crazy, but nothing else made sense. Who else only ventured out under the cover of darkness? Who else was insane enough to blackmail a police officer? Insane enough to hunt her down? Kill her with his own two hands?

Darcy jumped out of her chair and headed back into the lab.

"Are you okay? Darcy?"

She ran to the door. "I've got to get out of here."

"Darcy, wait." The sound of Parker's chair followed her across the room. "What's wrong?"

"It's late. I've got to get home."

"At least let me walk you. It's too—"

"No!" She turned on Parker, grasping for excuses. "I'll be fine. I just remembered . . . something I have to—"

A clunk sounded at the door of the lab. The rattle of keys. Darcy whirled around. A man-shaped shadow moved against the door's translucent glass. "Hide!" Darcy whispered as she dove behind the farthest lab bench. Crawling down the aisle, she searched for an open cabinet, something big enough to crawl into—anything.

The lock slid back with a snap and the door squeaked open. Parker's chair whined. He was still by the door. He hadn't had time to hide.

"What are you doing here?" Parker's voice rose in surprise.

"Dude, you about scared me half to death." A stranger's voice. Definitely not the Dark Man. Not Kelly either. "It's almost eight-thirty. What are you doing here?"

"Working late tonight. We had a huge breakthrough."

Darcy climbed to her feet. A tall, gangly man in a lab coat stood at the door. He turned toward her and his eyes went wide.

"Dude." He swept a tangle of long greasy hair out of his face and looked to Parker with a twisted smile. "Way to go, bro!"

Parker frowned at the man and angled his chair to face Darcy. "Darcy, this is Ray Diekelmann, my extremely tardy lab assistant. Ray, this is Darcy Williams—a good friend of mine."

"Hi, Ray. Glad to finally meet you," Darcy said.

"Nice . . ." Ray stood leering at her. His skin was so pale it almost looked blue. In fact, his eyelids and lips *were* blue—the cold, clotted blue of a day-old bruise. And his eyes had that haunted, sunken look, the look of an old black-and-white photo—the kind found hanging in a holocaust museum.

Parker rolled to position himself between Darcy and Ray. "So what are you doing here? I thought you were sick."

"Dude, I like feel bad about being gone so long, but I was sick bad. I mean really bad." Ray walked over to one of the benches and eyed the pans of dirty glassware standing near the sinks. "I started feeling better some, so I thought I'd get a head start on the dishes."

Parker followed Ray to the sink. "Go home and get some rest. We've got a big day tomorrow. One of the MD positive mice may have started walking."

"Cool." Ray seemed ready to collapse, but not from excitement. He was obviously still sick. Deathly sick from the looks of him.

"If you still feel up to it tomorrow morning, all I need is for you to give four mice injections, okay? We'll call that a day's work."

"Sure." Ray picked up a pan of glassware and carried it to the sink at the end of the lab. "I could do them now if you want."

"Are you sure?" Parker's face lit up. "If you're too tired, we could do it tomorrow."

"Just four mice, right?" Ray set the pan down on a bench and shuffled toward the door. "Come on. Let's get it done."

Parker followed Ray to the door, then stopped and turned back to Darcy. "Aren't you coming?"

Darcy considered for a second. She had totally overreacted when Ray came into the room. Maybe she was blowing the whole Kelly thing out of proportion. The Dark Man wasn't after her. No way would Kelly be working for a crazy street person. It didn't make sense. "I don't know, Parker. I really do have some stuff to deal with. Maybe tomorrow. I could drop by in the morning. Maybe help check the mice?"

"Sure." Parker flashed her a ten-megaton smile and backed against the door to hold it open for her. "I can still walk you home if you want."

"That's okay. Go on with Ray. You've got history to make." She watched as Parker rolled to the elevators, then she turned and rushed off in the other direction, stepping lightly across the tile floor. Even if Kelly wasn't working for the Dark Man, she didn't want to stumble into him in a dark, deserted hallway.

Stopping at each intersection, she peered cautiously down each side passage before continuing on. Good. The short passage leading to her lab was empty, her door still shut. She inserted her key into the lock and eased the door open. So far so good. She switched on the light and gasped. The floor was littered with books, papers, and glassware. Every drawer in the lab had been pulled out, every cabinet left hanging open. She stood in the doorway, too shocked to move. Waiting, listening . . .

Nobody. Whoever had trashed the lab was gone now. She stepped inside and locked the door behind her. She was safe for the moment, but she'd have to lie low for a while. Which meant putting her research on hold. A lump of lead settled in her stomach. *Parker.* If he got hurt because of her . . . No, she wouldn't allow it. She'd have to stop working with him. She'd tell him in the morning. The last thing in the world she wanted was for Parker to get caught in the crossfire. This was between her and the Dark Man, and she wanted to make sure it stayed that way.

PARKER

"Are you sure you're all right?" Parker wheeled across the animal room floor to the computer station and started punching in his password. "Darcy?"

"What? Me? I'm fine. Really." Her eyes darted back to the door. She seemed nervous, antsy—like she couldn't wait to get out of there.

He turned his chair to look her in the eye. "Sorry I put you off this morning, but I'd just checked the mice and it was still too early to see activity." He looked at his watch. 4:15. "They've had nineteen hours. More than enough time to start moving around."

He brought up the monitoring software, and Darcy leaned over his shoulder. Eighty perfectly straight lines traced across the screen. Flat-line. Barely even a squiggle. For all the motion the sensors were picking up, the mice might as well have been dead.

"Tell me you've got the gain too low." Darcy tapped the *G* key and turned the gain up all the way. The noise level increased, but the signal remained flat.

Parker sighed. "There's gotta be something wrong with the sensors. This is California. Even the buildings move more than this."

"I can check." Darcy moved to the cage racks. "What's a good cage?"

"Sixty-five."

She counted down the cages, pulled one out from the rack, and opened it up. "He doesn't seem to be moving at all, but his eyes are open. Is this one of the controls?"

" 'Fraid not."

She balled a gloved hand into a bunny-eared fist and reached into the cage. "Little Bunny Foo Foo hopping through the forest, scooping up the field mice and bopping them on the head."

A huge spike appeared on the screen. "Okay, the sensor's fine." Parker double-checked the injection time. They'd had over nineteen hours. "Either the mice are too old or . . . the drug's a dud."

"They're only a few days older than when you injected Mighty Mouse. Does it really make that much difference?" Darcy closed up the cage and put it back in the rack.

"It shouldn't."

Darcy cast another glance toward the door.

"Maybe we should go get something to eat and come back later." Parker tried to keep the disappointment out of his voice. "It's possible they just need a few more hours."

She shook her head, sadly, it seemed. "I wish I could, but I've got other stuff I'm supposed to do. I'll probably be gone for a while."

Other stuff. Like washing her hair or ironing her socks. Where had he heard that one before? "So will you be able to come by and check the mice tomorrow?" he asked. "Ray gave them another dose this morning. Something might still happen."

Darcy stepped toward the door. "I wish I could, but . . ."

"But what? It'll only take a few minutes." Parker followed Darcy to the door and waited as she opened it partway and peered outside. "Have you seen Kelly again? Is that what's bothering you?"

"Kelly's not the one bothering me." Darcy opened the door all the way. "He probably just gets his kicks following co-eds."

Parker rolled out into the corridor. So who *was* bothering her? He started to ask but decided against it. The answer was all too obvious. His experiment was a bomb. She was probably regretting all the time she'd wasted on the synthesis.

"Aren't you coming?" Darcy turned around and waited.

"No, I'm going to stay here awhile, try to figure out what went wrong."

"Wrong? Nothing went wrong." She walked back and crouched next to his chair. "They just need more time. You'll get it."

You'll—as in me, myself, and I. All by myself. The word stung, but he wasn't about to give up. "Maybe something went wrong with the synthesis. If we redo it tomorrow morning, Ray can do another round of injections in the afternoon."

"Parker, I'm sorry." A wave of emotion swept across her face. "I . . . I'm not going to be able to help anymore. I want to. I really do. But there's this guy . . ."

"Yeah?"

She lowered her eyes, twisted a strand of hair around her finger. "I did something . . . something bad. Something that ended up hurting him. And now . . . I guess I need to lay low for a while. Wait for the storm to blow over."

Parker nodded, a miserable smile plastered on his face. Jason Shanahan and the *thing* she needed to work out with him. He knew the answer to the question but he had to ask it anyway. "So what does that have to do with me?"

"With you?" She screwed up her face in a confused frown. "Nothing. Nothing at all. I just don't want you getting caught in the crossfire. That's all. If you got hurt because of me, I . . . I don't know what I'd do."

Gee, thanks. Protect me from getting hurt by stabbing me through the heart. "Don't worry about me. I'll be fine." Parker eased his chair toward the exit.

"Parker, wait." Darcy stood up and followed along beside him. "I'm really sorry. I hate that this happened. Things were going so well. I was . . ."

He pushed through the swinging doors, letting his footrests scrape across their painted metal surfaces. "You were what?"

"We were just getting to be friends. I really want that—for us to be friends."

"Me too." He didn't look back at her. "Friends." Pushing down on his joystick, he sped toward the elevators, leaving Darcy behind.

James Parker. Friend to many. More than a friend . . . to none.

JASON

Jason waited outside the door to Channing's office, flipping through the photocopies of Darcy's file. Something was wrong. He'd been through the file dozens of times but still he couldn't put his finger on it. He turned to her undergrad transcripts. *Biochemistry, Physical Chemistry, Advanced Physical Chemistry, Organic Chemistry 1, 2, and 3.* She'd made straight A's all the way through the fall of her senior year. He flipped back through the papers to make sure. All A's. Not a single A- or B+. And then, boom. Three C's and a D her last semester. Right before graduation. It didn't make sense. She'd made A's in o-chem and p-chem. How could she get a C in Philosophy 201?

True, she'd already been accepted to grad school, but Darcy wasn't the type to slack off just because her grades no longer counted. Something had happened. Something big.

He checked her transcripts from her first two years as a grad student. Back to A's again. And if he knew Darcy, they weren't just regular grad student A's. Most likely they were the highest A's in her class. Darcy was nothing if not competitive.

So what had happened her senior year? And what was the deal with Darcy and the police? Jason went back to her admission info.

Home address: 1153 Elwood St., Sacramento, CA. A street that didn't even exist—at least nowhere around Sacramento. He'd checked every town and unincorporated area within a hundred miles. And her parents—they were listed on the form as Don and Sue. Just like that. No titles. No last names. Just Don and Sue. Of course their phone number had been disconnected. And although the operator at PacBell was ever so polite and ever so sorry, he couldn't get the slightest scrap of information out of her.

Jason flipped to the back of the admission forms. It was amazing Cal had even accepted her. For all he could tell from her admission packet, she might not even be a real person. He'd read characters from novels that had more reality behind them. Of course, she'd been an undergrad at Cal, and even though it was not the grad school's habit to admit Cal undergrads, the fact that they all knew her had to help with her acceptance. They probably hadn't checked up on her at all. Or had they? What if something suddenly changed her senior year? What if she'd witnessed a crime and was part of the witness protection program? What if her name wasn't even Darcy? Maybe she was a spy, planted on the campus to uncover—

"Waiting for me?" A pleasant-looking woman in her late forties pulled a massive ring of keys from a worn leather backpack and reached for the office door.

Jason stepped back out of the way, folding the sheath of photocopies in half so the writing faced inward. "Dr. Channing?"

"Gretta, please." Channing smiled and threw open the office door with a *jingle-jangle* of keys.

"Gretta." Jason followed her into the well-lit office and waited as she took a seat behind a gray metal desk and started rummaging through a stack of journal articles. The room was filled with aquaria, nine or ten in all. Big ones. All of them filled with algae. He searched the murky water for any sign of animal life. Apparently Channing preferred pond scum to fish.

He turned back to Channing, who was now reading one of the papers. "Gretta, my name is Jason Shanahan. I'm a friend of Darcy Williams."

Gretta looked up from the article and stared blankly at him for several uncomfortable seconds. "Oh yes." She smiled warmly at him. "How is Darcy's research coming along?"

Jason shrugged. "I'm sure you're much better able to answer that than I am."

"Of course." Channing smiled and looked back down at the papers on her desk.

"Dr. Channing . . . Gretta, I'm a first-year chemistry grad student and I know you're in the biochemistry department, but I have a master's degree in cell and molecular biology, and I was wondering if we could work something out where I could do a rotation in your lab."

Channing frowned. "Actually, I've been trying to limit the number of students in my lab lately. I tend to prefer a more intimate working relationship with my students. It's so much more fulfilling."

"That's why I think I'd like your lab so much." Jason smiled. "I have a full NIH fellowship, so lots of chemistry professors are interested in me, but I think your research might be a better fit with my background in molecular biology."

"An NIH fellowship . . . in molecular biology?" Channing stood and walked out from behind her desk. "You may be right. That really could be a good fit."

"If we could just convince Dr. Forrest," he added. "My undergrad degree's in chemistry and he's convinced that all your students have biochem degrees."

"Nonsense." Channing's eyes drifted out of focus. "Plenty of my students have chemistry degrees. I'm sure of it."

"So, Gretta, all we'd have to do is compare my course work to that of your students and his only objection would be answered."

"I'm sure that won't be necessary. If I have no objections—"

"Would you mind scheduling a meeting with Forrest?"

"I'll call him right now." Channing reached for the phone.

"Can't," Jason said. "He's at a conference and won't be back until next week—and he doesn't check voice mail. Think you could remember to call him when he gets back?"

"Of course." Channing jotted a note on a Post-it pad and pressed it to the desk next to her phone. "What did you say your name was?"

"Jason Shanahan." Jason reached across the desk and wrote down his name and phone number on another Post-it note. "If anything comes up, Darcy'll know how to get in touch with me. Speaking of which . . ." He carefully placed his note on Channing's desk so that it covered Channing's note. "Do you have Darcy's home number? I think she's visiting her parents and I really need to get in touch with her."

"Yes, of course." Channing opened an olive green file cabinet and pulled out a file. "Here it is." She read him the number. The area code was Sacramento, but it was definitely different from the number listed on her application.

Jason copied the number onto the Post-it note with his name on it and pulled both notes from the desk. "Thanks a lot, Gretta." He pocketed both notes and headed for the door. "I look forward to working with you."

Three minutes later he was behind his desk, punching the Sacramento number into his phone.

"Hello?" A lush feminine voice sounded on the other end.

"Hello, is this Sue?" asked Jason.

"Sorry, she just left on an errand. Could I take a message?"

"Yes, please. This is Jason Shanahan. I'm a friend of Darcy's."

"Darcy Williams?" The voice sounded confused.

"Yes, who is this?"

"This is Diane."

"And you're Darcy's sister. . . ?"

A long pause. "Listen, I don't know what's going on, but we've already said as much as we're going to say. If you want more, you'll need a subpoena."

"No, wait," Jason said. "I really am a friend of Darcy's. I was hoping to speak to her mom. Could you give me an idea when she'll be back?"

Another long pause.

"Hello? Are you there?"

"Is this some kind of a sick joke?"

"No. Please. I can explain. I need to get in touch with Darcy, and I—"

"Darcy's at Berkeley now."

"I know. I'm calling from Berkeley. I'm a good friend of hers, and—"

"If you were really her friend, you'd know her mother is dead." A sharp click sounded in Jason's ear and the phone went dead.

CHAPTER 7

PARKER RELAXED HIS EYES, letting the incoherent scrawl of the lab notebook diffuse and wander across its chemical-stained pages. It didn't make any sense. He'd been through Ray's notes a hundred times, and he still couldn't figure out what they were doing wrong. He and Ray had repeated the experiment twice—and still no Mighty Mouse. Mouse 87 was a fluke. It had to be. If he were smart, he'd cut his losses and have Ray start synthesizing new compounds, maybe try some different adrenaline derivatives.

He pushed the notebook onto his desk and spun his chair around to face the door. No. He couldn't give up. Not yet. Adrenaline 355 was the closest thing to a miracle he'd ever seen. He couldn't just walk away from it. Not until he had a logical explanation for what happened to mouse 87. A logical explanation that didn't involve snakes and rats that could teleport through twelve-inch concrete walls.

He wheeled through the door and was halfway down the hall before he realized what he was doing. Darcy. He hadn't seen her in over a week, and he still couldn't get her out of his head. She obviously didn't want to see him. She'd made it perfectly clear she didn't want him rolling into her social life like a monster truck in a demolition derby. He spun his chair around and headed back to the lab. What had he been thinking? She wasn't just a flirt at MD summer camp. She had a real future ahead of her. Getting married, raising kids. A real career. Besides, she'd probably already gone home for Thanksgiving.

Parker stopped at his desk and fought with the pages of the lab notebook. Darcy deserved better—someone confident, capable. Someone like Jason. Someone who could brush his teeth without the aid of an assistant.

He pushed at the pages with his arm, bowing them up until he could get a hand between them. The whole Mighty Mouse thing had been a big mistake. He never should have let down his guard. His parents had always taught him—

"Parker?" Darcy's soft voice whispered shivers up his spine.

He turned and caught sight of her, standing, small and fragile, in the doorway.

"Are you busy? I could come back later."

"No, please, come in." Parker raked a hand across his hair. "I was just . . . thinking about you."

Darcy stepped hesitantly into the lab and slid onto a lab stool to face him.

"What's that?" He nodded at the computer diskette she was flipping over and over between her fingers.

"Notes on the adrenaline synthesis. I hope you don't mind, but I typed them up—in journal format. Thought they might come in handy." She bit her lip and studied Parker with a frightened expression that made him uneasy.

"Thanks, I . . ." Parker didn't know what to say. "You really shouldn't have. I know how busy you are these days."

"Not at all. I've been . . ." Again, that frightened expression. "I couldn't work on my research, so I thought I might as well do something useful. And I've been thinking about Mighty Mouse. A lot. How's the experiment going? Any luck reproducing it?"

Parker shook his head. "You'll be the first to know—I promise you that. You'll hear the screams."

"Did you try looking at other peaks in the HPLC?"

"That was the first thing we tried. That and a hundred other experiments. I don't know what else to try."

"Is Sinclair in town? You should ask him."

"Already did—long distance to Amsterdam." Parker shook his head. "And Flemming and Hagen and Quade and Pulvermacher and Jennings. They threw out a few lame suggestions, but I could tell they didn't believe me. They were just humoring the poor crippled boy. They never come out and say it, but they all think I'm biased. Too emotionally involved. I'm pretty sure Pulvermacher thinks I'm mentally retarded. He raises his voice and talks real slow. Sometimes I wonder if Sinclair doesn't think so too, not that he's ever around. He thinks my grant was based on pity and politics. He practically came out and said it once."

"No way! I bet he never had a paper in *Nature*—especially not one he wrote when he was an undergrad."

Parker grinned. What was happening? Five days in hiding and all of a sudden they were having a real conversation? "Maybe not," he said, "but I'm still stuck. And given the outlandishness of my claims, I can't blame him for not taking me seriously."

"Why don't you ask someone else? Someone who doesn't know you have MD?"

"Like who? I'm not exactly an unknown in my field. My grant generated a lot of publicity."

"So use my name. I can help you write up the results, and we can use my e-mail address to send it out."

We? Parker started to argue, but something about Darcy's eyes made him suddenly uncertain. She looked so interested, so eager to help.

"I've already got the first three experiments down." Darcy tapped the diskette with her index finger. "Catch me up on the new stuff you and Ray have done, and we can write it up and send it out tomorrow."

"Tomorrow's Thanksgiving," Parker said.

"I don't mind. I wasn't planning to do anything anyway."

"But I was. I'm going home for Thanksgiving."

"Oh . . . right." Darcy's face suddenly flushed. "Of course."

"I . . ." Parker raised his footrest and adjusted his seat back. "Would you like to go too? My mom's a great cook. She makes enough food to feed an army."

Darcy shook her head. "I haven't been invited; I wouldn't want to intrude on your special family time."

"It wouldn't be an intrusion at all. My dad would kill me if he learned I'd left you here alone on Thanksgiving. Do you play bridge?"

"Not really. I've played hearts . . . a little."

"Don't worry—you can be on Mom's team. She'll teach you."

"But I really can't. You go and have fun with your family. I'll have the write-up all ready to go when you get back." Darcy stood up and Parker followed her to the door.

"Are you sure?" He looked up at her and waited, giving her plenty of time to change her mind. "My mom makes a mean sweet-potato casserole. Marshmallows, molasses, lemon . . . She even puts a few sweet potatoes in it."

Darcy looked down at the floor and shook her head.

Parker maneuvered closer, lowering his seat so he could look up into her face. Her eyes were moist. She looked as if she were in pain. "Are you okay?"

"I'm fine." She turned back to the door. "I'll have everything written up by the time you get back." She swept out the door and started down the hall.

"Darcy?"

Her head came up and she stopped, but she didn't turn around.

"My dad will be here at eight if you change your mind. We really would like to have you."

She nodded slowly and kept on walking.

JASON

"Just a second, Jason." Dr. Forrest motioned Jason to a scratched wooden chair that faced his old Steelcase desk and turned his attention back to the phone he held wedged to his ear with his shoulder. Jason slumped back in the chair and waited as Forrest barked orders into the receiver. "Make sure there are two laser pointers on the podium. Last time the batteries went dead halfway . . ."

Jason let his eyes wander to the pad by Forrest's computer monitor. *1:00—Lunch with Antonia at Chez Panisse.* After reading the message upside down, Jason wondered what Forrest's wife's name was. Somehow he doubted it was Antonia. Below the message was scrawled a number. It looked like 1836; or was it 1830? If things went south with Forrest, he might have a try at the number. One could never have too much leverage, especially with Forrest still mad at him for painting the chalk trays in the lecture hall with sodium tri-iodide. The man had no sense of humor. How was he supposed to know the contact-sensitive explosives would leave a purple stain?

"Well, Jason," Forrest said as he slammed down the phone and leaned back in his oversized executive chair, "I understand you had a meeting with me while I was on my way to Brussels. Dolores tells me she gave you some admission files for the meeting. *Confidential* admission files."

"Yes, sir. I take it you were called away at the last minute?"

"No." Forrest's voice took on an icy tone. "Actually I've had the IUPAC Congress on my calendar for several months. And funny, but I don't remember requesting those particular files."

"Actually the files were Channing's idea. She wanted to prove to you that my background wasn't that dissimilar from her other students."

"I'm sure she did." Forrest leaned suddenly forward and fixed Jason with blazing eyes. "Drop the nonsense. Tell me what's going on right now or I call security. Why the sudden interest in Darcy Williams?"

Call security? "Interest in Darcy Williams?" Jason feigned surprise. "I've gone out with her before, but I don't understand. I'm interested in Gretta Channing. I know she's biochem, but I really think I'd fit in with her lab a lot better than any of the chemistry labs. She thinks so too. That's why she set up the meeting."

"What meeting?"

"The meeting with you—Monday afternoon."

"Poppycock!" Forrest pulled out a staff directory and thumbed through its pages. He picked up the phone and tapped in a number. "Hello, Gretta? Dave Forrest. . . . Yes, I'm sitting in my office with Jason Shanahan, and he claims that . . ." A long pause. "What do you mean you forgot? . . . So you told him you were going to set up a meeting? . . . The backgrounds of your students? . . . Really? . . . Then I'm sure his background is just fine . . . No, I can check the records myself. . . . Really? . . . Well, no problem. We've all been busy. . . . No problem. Bye." Forrest hung up the phone and looked at Jason with a scowl.

"Is it okay, then?" Jason fought to suppress the smile that tugged at the corners of his mouth.

"Is what okay?" Forrest growled.

"Can I do a rotation in Channing's lab?"

Forrest stared at Jason for several seconds. "So you don't know anything about Darcy Williams?"

"What do you mean? I already said we went out. She's easily the prettiest girl in the department. Likes Thai and Vietnamese food. Doesn't have a car on campus." *Okay, Jason, let's try a flier.* "And one of her kisses will curl your toes for a week."

Forrest let out a deep breath and leaned back in his chair.

"So what's up with Darcy?" Jason let his eyes appear to drift to the window. "Is she in some kind of trouble?"

The change in Forrest's expression was immediate. "Why do you ask that?"

"That crack you made about calling security. If I wanted to ask her out again, that would be okay, wouldn't it? I mean, there's no law against students dating, is there?"

Forrest laughed—a hard, strangled-sounding laugh.

"Is that what this Channing rotation is all about? You trying to get with Darcy Williams?"

"Have you ever seen her?" Jason let his voice take on an over-awed tone.

Forrest shook his head. "Do yourself a favor and let it rest. Darcy Williams is . . . out of your league."

"No problem." Jason allowed himself to smile. He'd leave her alone—for at least the time it took him to get through his thermo class. But after that, the two of them were going to have to have a little talk.

DARCY

Darcy sat bleary-eyed in front of Channing's old laptop. So far, so good. It had been a week and she still hadn't seen any sign of the Dark Man. She had overreacted. That was all. It was probably just a random break-in. An undergrad frat boy looking for undenatured ethanol. Even if it had been the Dark Man, he'd probably given up by now. The man's brain was scrambled. He couldn't make his thoughts walk a straight line for a minute, much less a week. Everything was going to be fine. She could drop off her write-up at Parker's lab before he left to visit his parents.

She glanced down at the right-hand corner of her screen. Almost 7:00 A.M. She had to hurry. Maybe she should just skip the discussion section. Nobody said the write-up had to be in the form of a research paper. Parker just needed something to pass around for comments. She drilled out a few observations and listed possible explanations for what could have gone wrong: the snake/rat theory, synthetic impurities, a genetic abnormality in mouse 87. Then, hitting the Print button, she ran across the lab to the printer and snatched up each sheet of paper as soon as it hit the tray.

Darcy grabbed her duffle bag and ran from the lab. Halfway down the hall she stopped. Parker couldn't see her like this. She hadn't taken a shower in days. Retracing her steps, she ducked into the back stairwell and clambered down the stairs. It was already 7:20. She had to hurry. Bursting through the metal doors at the bottom of the stairs, she raced across the campus to the gym. The locker room was usually busy by 7:30, but this morning it appeared deserted. Thanksgiving. Everyone on campus seemed to have somewhere to go.

It took five minutes flat to shower and dry off, but blow-drying her hair took forever. She was late. Parker would be leaving in ten minutes. She threw open the locker door and selected a pair of khakis and her favorite cobalt-blue sweater from the pile of clothes that lay neatly stacked on the homemade cardboard shelves at the bottom of the locker.

She got dressed and threw on a little makeup. Then, glancing at her watch again, she sprinted from the locker room. It was possible she still might catch Parker before he left. He might want to read her paper on his way to San Francisco. Maybe he'd want to look at it before he left—in case she needed to explain anything.

By the time she arrived at Parker's lab, it was 8:17. His door was still open. Maybe it wasn't too late. She collapsed against the wall outside his door and tried to catch her breath. Her hair had to be a mess. She pulled a mirror from her purse and inspected the damage. It was worse than she'd thought. Using her fingers as a comb, she frantically attempted to calm down the flyaways and resuscitate the limp spots. Oh well, it would have to do. She put the mirror away and stepped through the open doorway. A tall man sat at Parker's desk. He started to turn. . . .

Darcy spun around and ran back through the doorway. As she

swung herself around the doorjamb her legs were suddenly cut out from under her and she fell forward, right into Parker's lap. She tried to twist to the side, to arch her back and push herself up by the chair's backrest, but the more she struggled, the more she seemed to be hurting him.

Hearty laughter broke out beneath her. "Darcy?" More laughter. "I'm happy to see you too."

"Parker, I'm so—" Footsteps sounded from the lab as she struggled to her feet. "Come on. We've got to get out of here!" She hurried down the hall. Why wasn't he following her?

"Darcy, wait!" Parker called after her. "Did you meet my dad?"

"Your dad?" She stopped in her tracks. How could she be such an idiot?

"Yeah, come on. I want you to meet him."

She turned slowly. Fortunately, Parker was too occupied with adjusting his chair to notice how embarrassed she was. She followed him sheepishly into the lab. With luck his dad hadn't seen her running from the room.

"Hey, Dad, this is Darcy Williams."

"Not the Darcy you were telling us about." A tall, distinguished-looking man in his early to mid-fifties studied her intently. "I thought you said she was pretty." The man's voice was stern, but bright blue eyes blazed at the focal points of a hundred smile lines.

Darcy shot a look at Parker, but he just rolled his eyes.

"Son, that's like calling the Mona Lisa adequate, like calling a politician shallow. This girl isn't pretty. She's spectacular, exquisite, dazzling, pulchritudinous." Parker's dad turned to Darcy with a mischievous grin. "Where are you from, Darcy?"

"Sacramento." Darcy felt heat rising to her face. She glanced back at the door.

"That's a pretty good drive. You heading home for Thanksgiving?"

"No, I was planning to—"

"Excellent!" He crossed the room and stood between her and Parker. "Darcy, do you play bridge?"

She laughed. "What is this, some kind of a conspiracy? That's the same question Parker asked."

Parker's father turned to his son. "Doesn't play bridge, does she?"

Parker shook his head.

"Excellent! She can be on your mom's team." He laid a big hand on Darcy's shoulder and guided her to the door. "We've got a twenty-four pounder in the oven right now, and two trays of stuffing! Darcy, are you a corn-bread stuffing girl or one of those regurgitated white bread vomit eaters?"

Darcy smiled and let herself be led away, wondering if Parker's father was ever going to get around to an actual invitation. Not that it mattered. He didn't seem the type to take no for an answer.

"Hey, Darcy!" Jason came running up behind them. "Where have you been? I need to talk to you, okay?"

"Actually I was just going to Parker's house for—"

"It's important." Jason took her aside, lowering his voice to a whisper. "I talked to a friend of yours in Sacramento. Her name is Diane. Sound familiar?"

Darcy's stomach twisted. She glanced over her shoulder to see if Parker had overheard.

Parker's dad whispered something to Parker, who then nodded back. Stepping forward with a big smile, Parker's dad extended his right hand to Jason. "I'm Bruce Parker, James's father."

Jason shook his hand. "Jason Shanahan."

"It's a pleasure to meet you, Jason. Tell me, do you play bridge?"

CHAPTER 8

"...AND FATHER, THANK YOU that Darcy and Jason could share this celebration with us. Amen." Bruce Parker finished the prayer with the tone of an unspoken dare.

"And thank you for the Cockfield cranberry pies," Parker interjected. A feminine giggle sounded from across the table.

"And Father, forgive Jammy, because he knows that cranberries are an abomination to your creation. A—"

"And the cranberry sauce." This time the voice belonged to Janice, Parker's mom.

"Amen!" Bruce's voice was tinged with anger now.

Shocked, Darcy opened her eyes and looked up at him. He was glaring down at a giant scoop of cranberry sauce that had magically appeared on his plate. Janice sat at his right with an exaggerated expression of innocence plastered thinly over a huge grin.

"Everybody help yourself." Bruce reached across the table for a big tray of corn-bread stuffing. "We don't hold to ceremony here. Just as long as you keep one foot on the floor."

Darcy helped herself to turkey, sweet potatoes, and a large helping of green beans with slivered almonds. When the corn-bread stuffing came around the table to her, she noticed that only one serving was missing. She held the pan for a second, feeling the weight of everyone's eyes on her. Then, passing on the tray with a sly grin, she reached for the bread stuffing.

Bruce groaned. "Another traitor!" He had to pause while

everybody else laughed. "Darcy, I had such high hopes for you."

"Welcome to the family, Darcy." Janice bustled around the table and plopped a sizable wedge of cranberry sauce on her plate.

"Note the traditional can-shaped mold," Parker said.

Janice moved to Parker and leaned over his plate, cutting his turkey into bite-sized pieces. Darcy looked down at the table, pretending not to notice. The last thing she wanted to do was embarrass Parker on Thanksgiving Day. She realized with a start that she'd never actually seen him eating. For that matter, she'd never seen him do much of anything besides drive his wheelchair and type on the computer. She looked up from her plate to discover Bruce's kind eyes resting on her. A tender smile touched his lips, a look of such understanding, such . . . love.

A curtain of shimmering tears clouded her vision. She turned her eyes to the ceiling, but it was too late. Hot tears spilled over her lids and streamed down her face. "Excuse me." She choked out the words as she pushed back from the table and rose to her feet.

Unseen hands settled on her shoulders. Janice's soft voice. "Are you okay, dear? Are you ill?"

"Fine. I just . . . Please . . . where's the bathroom?"

The hands guided her to a small bathroom near the dining room.

"Thanks." Darcy shut the door behind her and sank to the floor. The tears were punctuated now with short hiccoughing sobs. She tore a wad of toilet paper from the roll and buried her face in it, letting the sobs flow through her, rocking her like a cork on a storm-tossed sea. The concern in Bruce's eyes burned inside her. The dinner, the laughter, Janice cutting Parker's food with the love and tenderness, the tenderness of . . . a mom. A spasm caught at her chest and held her breathless. She could see her own mom watching her fry her first egg. The memory was clearer than it had been in years. She had been so beautiful. So kind. Everyone always said she had her mother's eyes.

When the tears had finally run themselves dry, Darcy got up from the floor and switched on the lights. Puffy, tear-stained eyes stared back at her above a Rudolph nose. She brushed a piece of tissue from her lip and dabbed at her face. A little more eye makeup and a little more time would have to do. She didn't have any other choice.

A burst of laughter sounded from the dining room. Bruce's hearty voice rose above the others in a booming laugh that brought a smile to her face in spite of her appearance. *Here goes . . .* She pulled back on the door and stepped into the hall. A chair scraped against the floor and footsteps made their way toward her. Janice's face etched with motherly concern. "Are you okay, Darcy? Can I get you anything?"

"I'm fine. Everything was just so . . . beautiful. You remind me of . . . my parents. They died when I was twelve."

Janice stepped forward and Darcy dissolved into her encircling arms. She buried her face in a soft shoulder, vaguely aware of a soothing voice. She shut her eyes, letting the words wash through her senses. *"Darcy, dear, dear, precious child."* It was her mother's voice. For the moment she was not alone.

JASON

Jason rode in the back of the minivan, jammed between Darcy and one of the windows. Under normal circumstances it would have been a nice opportunity, except that Janice Parker sat on the other side of Darcy, draping an arm around her like a mom on the way to summer camp. The two of them had been inseparable since Darcy's little visit to the bathroom. The whole thing was bizarre. He'd never seen Darcy lose it like that. Something was going completely berserkers in her life. It had to be. If only he could get her to open up—to trust him. He was good at fixing problems—the hairier the better.

Jason had overheard Janice talking to Darcy about her parents while they were in the kitchen scooping ice cream. It was tough to lose a parent; he knew firsthand how that felt. He'd lost his dad when he was thirteen. It was the blackest year of his life, but eventually he'd learned to cope. Darcy had to be dealing with something else though, something besides her parents. Something that involved the police, glass-heads, and walking to the university in the middle of the night. But what? Whatever it was, she didn't want to talk about it. She'd been hiding from him all week. Probably working on her little Parker project. He didn't get it. All of a sudden she'd gone from being a competitive workaholic to being an eagle-scout social worker on steroids. What was going on with her? And this thing with the police. . . . Maybe she'd been sentenced to five hundred hours of community service. That, at least, would explain her eagerness to visit Parker's sister in the hospital.

The boot of impending awkwardness pressed its heel into his gut. Parker's parents were great, the dinner wonderful. Even getting creamed at bridge by Darcy and Parker's mom had been fun, but Jason could think of a lot more uplifting ways to spend his Thanksgiving than visiting a complete stranger on her deathbed. He hated hospitals. Always had.

When the van pulled up in front of the hospital, Jason stayed seated while Bruce unhooked Parker's chair from the tie-down cables that held it in the passenger seat position of the van. He deployed an automatic ramp, and Parker rolled out onto the sidewalk. Janice followed, reaching back to help Darcy down the ramp, as if Darcy were the cripple and not her son.

Jason got out and followed at a distance. They were already halfway to the hospital entrance. If they forgot about him and went on up to the room, maybe he could wait for them in the lobby. He stopped and retied both of his shoes. When he stood up, Parker was waiting for him at the sliding glass doors. Oh well.

"You're really going to like Jenny," Parker said as he rolled alongside Jason, guiding him to the far bank of elevators. "Everybody who meets her likes her. We used to call her The Catalyst in high school. She makes everything more fun."

Jason nodded, wondering how Parker could be so calm about his sister dying. Maybe if you had long enough to prepare, if you knew it was inevitable. . . . Still the whole thing felt wrong. Twisted. The way the Parkers talked about their daughter. They treated her suffering like some kind of a party. A freak sideshow. Jason followed Parker into a private room and stood by the door, hanging back while Parker introduced Darcy and him to Jenny and three nurses—he didn't catch their names—who lounged by the bed and giggled behind their hands. Like the whole thing was a big joke. They were still snickering when they excused themselves and filed out of the room.

Darcy and Mrs. Parker sat down on two of the vacated chairs while Parker rolled to the other side of the bed. Jenny—what little Jason could see of her beneath an oxygen mask and a blue knitted stocking hat—looked pale and very thin. She lay perfectly still in the hospital bed, barely a wrinkle beneath the sheets. She had long arms and long, delicate fingers, much like Parker's, but her eyes were her father's. Even from across the room, Jason could see the fire sparkling beneath their blue depths.

"So what's so funny?" Parker flopped a hand onto the bed next to his sister's.

"I have no idea." Jenny's voice was barely louder than a whisper. "I told them I wanted turkey. But all they brought me was this." She motioned with her eyes to the IV bag hanging at her left. "Turkey pee."

"Jenny!" Mrs. Parker's severe frown buckled at the edges. "You be nice."

"Me be nice? They're the ones that taped three hours of *Days of Our Lives* and then left it running on my TV. With the volume turned up and no remote in sight."

"Ouch!" Parker lowered his chair so he could be eye to eye with his sister. "I take it they found out."

"Found out about what?" Mr. Parker asked.

"Nothing." Jenny's eyes sparkled mischievously.

Jason stepped closer to the bed, waiting for the explanation he could see building.

"It was nothing!" Jenny sighed dramatically. "All I did was have Dr. Kincaid help me write a love note and sign it *A Secret Admirer.*"

"Go on. A love note to whom?" Parker coaxed.

"To nobody," said Jenny. "It was none of his business, and he didn't ask."

"So . . ."

"So I had Miss Gallimore fill in Jill's name." Jenny watched her brother out of the corner of her eye. "Jill and I are friends. I happen to love her dearly."

"And then you had Hailey write another anonymous message, and Dad addressed it to Dr. Kincaid."

"Can I help it if Hailey and Dr. Kincaid have distinctive handwriting?"

Mrs. Parker shook her head. "And Debbie was involved too?"

"Debbie and Duane and Lauren Dohr and Charles Halaby and Colette Mertens. Did I mention that Charles and Colette are dating now? Strangest thing."

"You're lucky they didn't put the tape on a continuous loop," Mr. Parker growled.

"I'm lucky they . . ." Jenny's eyes grew wide as they fell on Jason. Her delicate features seemed to be lit by a soft internal light that made her . . . Jason almost gasped out loud. Even through the plastic mask she was incredibly beautiful.

Jason stood awkwardly at the foot of her bed, wishing he hadn't abandoned his post by the door. Parker frowned severely at him.

"Jenny?" Parker's voice was filled with concern.

"So you're Jason." Jenny didn't take her eyes off him. "Jammy told me about you."

Sweat prickled at Jason's hairline. Parker probably hadn't told her why he couldn't work with mice. That he'd dropped out of the cell and mo. bio. program just to get away from them. It wasn't fair. She probably thought he was—

"You're a lot different than I pictured you," Jenny's voice was even softer than it had been before.

Jason swallowed hard. "How did you picture me?"

"Not gorgeous."

Relief washed through him, making him laugh out loud. "Parker failed to mention that little detail about you too."

DARCY

Darcy sat in the back of the minivan, watching tattered fog phantoms drift in sheets across the deserted bridge. A deep emptiness that no slice of pumpkin pie could ever fill ached inside her. Parker's parents were wonderful. She'd never wanted so much to belong someplace.

Janice had practically adopted her on the spot. Bruce had talked Parker into taking the van back to Berkeley so they could drive down for a weekend visit. *They*—meaning her and Parker. He was so kind to her, so loving. But then, he didn't know anything about her. He didn't know who she was. What she had done. All he knew was her need.

And he didn't know she couldn't drive. Not legally. She would have said something, but Jason had jumped in and announced he'd be happy to drive. Whether he meant that night or the next weekend, she didn't know. She hoped he meant the former. She liked Jason, but he was a bit too much in a family setting. She knew she was being selfish, but some things she just didn't want to share.

Darcy let her eyes drift to Parker's profile. With such extraordinary parents, it was easy to see where he got it. Good-looking, super-intelligent, a heart of pure gold. If only . . . An image filled her mind: Jenny lying in a hospital bed. Still and frail, barely able to speak.

Parker . . . How much longer before he'd be just like his sister? The air thickened around her, pressing down on her with a nauseating weight. Not again. It wasn't fair. It was too much to bear.

She gazed out the window, trying to scrape the thought from her mind. She should have realized. She knew what muscular dystrophy was. Parker had said Jenny was in the hospital for her heart; and the heart was just a muscle after all.

The girders of the Bay Bridge rushed past her in a blur.

Parker's parents . . . What must they be going through. And yet they'd showered so much attention on her. She felt so selfish, so shallow.

Darcy pressed her head to the window, letting the vibrations of the engine rattle through her brain. The sound of her name broke into her thoughts. Jason and Parker were talking about her. Something about the experiment.

"You can't use Darcy's name on the message." Jason's voice. "If Mighty Mouse turns out to be real, it could be huge. But if it isn't . . . well, you wouldn't want it to turn into a cold-fusion debacle."

"So whose name do we use? Yours?"

"John Pyramid. He's a full professor visiting Cal from the University of South Africa. He's just now starting a new muscular dystrophy research program."

"What makes you think he'd be willing to help?"

"Because he doesn't exist." Jason laughed. "It's perfect. They'll have to take him seriously. He's a full professor in South Africa. All we need is a Cal e-mail account, and I can get that easy."

"No way. You can't just make up a professor."

"Tell that to Nicolas Bourbaki."

"Who?"

"Only one of the most influential mathematicians of the last century. He didn't exist either, but that didn't stop him from writing over a dozen books." Jason paused, waiting for Parker's response. "A group of French mathematicians just made him up. Started publishing under his name."

Silence.

"Don't you see? We could do the same thing. We're already halfway there. My dad made John Pyramid up as a practical joke while he was at UCSF. Actually got the department chair to assign him to a committee. It's not that hard. The professors here at Cal are almost completely autonomous. We could resurrect him easy."

We? Darcy frowned. Since when did Jason become part of *we?* Last she'd heard, he didn't want to have anything to do with Mighty Mouse. He was too mouse-o-phobic, too profoundly sensitive to sacrifice a mouse's feelings to save a human life. Of course, he didn't have a problem with massaman pork or ginger beef.

"We can e-mail Darcy's write-up tomorrow afternoon." Parker sounded excited. "Then we can start work on reproducing the original experiment using the reaction mixes without any purification. You sure you don't mind helping with the mice?"

"As long as I don't have to do any shaving."

Great. Parker's going along with him. Of all the stupid ideas. Darcy slumped against the window and watched the dark city streets pass by. A brown street sign flashed in the headlights. They were already in Berkeley.

"Hey, Darcy, we're almost there. Where do you want Jason to drop you off?" Parker called from the front.

Darcy's stomach tightened. "Just drop me off at the lab. All my stuff is there."

Jason stopped the van in front of the chemistry building and turned in his seat to watch her.

"Go on up and get your stuff," Parker said. "We'll wait for you."

"Thanks, Parker. Tell your parents I had a wonderful time. They're the sweetest two people on the face of the planet."

"Even my dad?"

"Okay, the orneriest and sweetest." She climbed over the wheelchair ramp and stepped onto the curb. "Don't bother waiting. I may decide to work a few hours before I turn in."

Jason pierced her with a dark look. She bit her lip, waiting for the argument.

"I need to talk to you," Jason said ominously. "Tomorrow."

Darcy nodded and hurried to the entrance before either of them could say anything else. They watched her until the glass door of the chemistry building swung shut behind her, then the van pulled forward and they drove away.

She took a deep breath and let it out slowly. What a day. She hadn't expected a turkey sandwich, much less a Thanksgiving feast in San Francisco. A guilty pang tickled at the back of her mind as she made her way through the deserted building. Okay, maybe she had hoped, but she'd never imagined Parker's parents would be so . . . so much like Parker.

She unlocked the door to her lab and poked her head inside. Good. No uninvited guests. She felt her way across the room and slipped through the back door into the vacant hot room. The lab was dark, perfectly still. Rummaging through the contents of a drawer under a counter, she pulled out a flashlight and switched it on. Nothing seemed out of place. The old library-style ladder was just where she'd left it. She rolled it along a metal track built into high glassware cabinets and scampered up it.

Pushing up on the ceiling tile just above the ladder, she switched off her light and pulled herself up into the space above the suspended false ceiling. Lowering the tile back into place, she felt around in the darkness and switched on a small clip-on lamp. Its ten-watt bulb cast a sickly light on her surroundings. A hot pot, a small microwave oven, cardboard boxes full of dishes and books and dirty clothes. A ragged sleeping bag spread out on a four-by-eight-foot plywood deck. Home sweet home.

She crawled out onto the deck and plopped down on her sleeping bag as images of Thanksgiving dinner flooded back to her. Janice cutting up Parker's food. The sympathy and sorrow in Bruce's eyes. Jenny, lying helpless and weak in the hospital bed. She was only two years older than Parker. Two years! She buried her face in her pillow, pressing its folds to her eyes.

Just when she'd finally found someone. A place where she really and truly belonged. It wasn't fair! Why did everyone she loved have to die?

CHAPTER 9

"JASON, I DON'T GET IT. I thought you wanted to work with Channing." Forrest slammed his palms on the desk with a loud smack. His typical acid grumpiness seemed to be spiced with more than a little hot sauce this morning. Jason let his eyes slide to the notepad by Forrest's computer, wondering if Antonia had dumped him.

"I do—eventually. But there's still a month left in the semester. Couldn't I rotate in Pyramid's lab for a month? He said it was okay."

"I already told you." Forrest pushed Jason's folder across his desk. "Visiting professors can't take rotation students."

"But it wouldn't have to be an official rotation. I've already finished my rotations for this semester."

Forrest slumped back into his chair with a sigh. "Then why are you bothering me with it?" He stared at Jason, a look of triumph lighting his eyes.

Jason let him bask a few seconds in his victory before reaching to pick up his folder. "I guess no reason." He smiled sheepishly and headed for the door. "Thanks."

Closing the door gently behind him, he slumped against the wall. *One down, four to go.*

"Tough meeting?"

Jason jumped. Kendra Wilson, one of the department secretaries, was working her way toward Forrest's office. She was one of the busiest bodies in the department. Jason fought back the grin that threatened to give him away.

"Forrest is in a royal mood." He pushed away from the wall, turning sideways to let her pass. "I guess he finally found out."

"Found out what?" Kendra's eyes lit with sudden interest.

"Haven't you heard about Antonia and that visiting professor, John Pyramid?"

"Antonia Gomez?" Her mouth dropped open.

Jason shrugged. "It's just a rumor. Nothing official." He walked slowly down the hall while giving her time to chew on the bait. Spinning around, he asked, "So how long's Pyramid supposed to be here? Do you know?"

"I'm . . . I don't remember."

"If Forrest's mood is any indication"—Jason flashed her a conspiratorial grin—"it won't be long."

Kendra nodded and grinned back. He could tell by her eyes that the hook was already set—deep.

Okay, step three. Jason ducked into the copy room and pulled a few forms from his admissions folder—request for keys, computer accounts, a mailbox. It only took a few seconds to copy the forms, but whiting out his blocky, uneven print took almost an hour. Everything had to go—everything but the authorizing signatures at the bottom. When he was finished whiting out the documents and going back over the lines with a ruler and black pen, he photocopied the forms and filled them in with a black Sharpie in John Pyramid's flowing, elegant script.

"Not bad." He held up the documents to admire his handiwork. "John Pyramid is quite a guy. I can see why Antonia likes him."

He slid the fresh documents between the pages of a phone directory and pounded the edges on a nearby worktable until they were good and dog-eared. Then, tucking them into a folder, he headed down the hall. It was almost too easy. If Dr. Frankenstein had had access to the machinery of modern-day bureaucracy, it would have saved him a lot of digging.

He dodged a herd of undergrads and slipped into the chemistry office.

"Hey, Dolores. Here's my life story." He sat on her desk and held out his admission folder.

"Thank you." Dolores took the file and returned it to the file cabinet at the back of the room.

While her back was turned, Jason stuck Pyramid's documents under the staff directory next to her phone. "Do you know Rama-chandran's office number?" He wandered over to Kendra's empty desk.

"Just a second." She turned back to her desk.

"Never mind. I've got it." Jason grabbed the staff directory off Kendra's desk and headed for the door. "Thanks, Dolores." He thumbed through the directory as he walked. *Antonia Gomez. Rm 301B, Materials Science Building.* If she spoke Spanish, the game was on.

"Hi, I'm Jason Jackson." Jason breezed into Antonia's office and plopped down on a chair facing her desk.

"Hello." Antonia eyed him with dark, dazzling eyes. Though her skin was quite fair, the style of her makeup and her black lustrous hair gave Jason cause for hope.

"I heard you spoke Spanish, and, well . . ." He looked around the room for a few seconds. "I was wondering if you could do me a favor."

"Maybe," Antonia's tone was dubious, but he could tell she was curious.

"You see, I met this . . . girl. And she doesn't speak much English." He looked down at his hands, as if he was too embarrassed to meet her gaze.

"Yeah." He could tell by her voice she was starting to warm to him.

"And I was wondering if you could help me write her a note in Spanish." He looked up at her and was rewarded with a smile.

Jason dictated a long note, not too mushy, but mushy enough to elicit several coos of delight. At the end he had her close with a simple *Te amo* and asked if she had a spare interdepartmental enve-lope. She pointed to a box on one of her shelves, and he selected an envelope that had her name displayed prominently on the last line.

"One other thing," he said with an apologetic smile. "Could I use your phone?"

She hesitated a second, then pushed the phone over to him with a frown. This was his last favor. Quickly he punched in the number for the chemistry department office. "Hello, Kendra? Jason. I'm in the Material Sciences building right now and need Juanita Perez's office number."

He heard the phone rattle and then an exclamation of irritation. "Dolores, do you have a staff directory?" He could barely make out the muffled voice. "Just a second, Jason . . ." Distant office conversation. He couldn't be sure but he thought he heard the name Pyramid. Dolores must have found Dr. Pyramid's paper work. More conversation. This time he definitely heard Antonia's name—several times.

The hook was set. Now all he had to do was mail Antonia's note to John Pyramid and the fish would be flopping all over the boat.

PARKER

Parker bumped his chair against the open door to Darcy's lab. "Darcy, it's me, Parker. Can we talk?"

No answer.

"Darcy?" He rolled inside and looked around.

Nobody.

Rolling up to her desk, he placed one of his business cards on her chair. As if having his home number was going to help. He hadn't seen her for almost a week, not since Thanksgiving. The first couple of days he'd told himself she'd been working on her prelims, but deep down inside he'd known the truth. Something had happened at his parents' house. It was the first time she'd seen him try to feed himself. The first time she'd gotten a glimpse behind the mask of confidence and self-reliance he always wore in public. She'd finally put two and two together and realized the other half of the life he lived. And after seeing Jenny, it didn't take a genius to extrapolate a few years into the future. If he even had a few years. He turned away from her desk and headed for the door.

She hadn't dropped by the lab, hadn't returned his calls. Not even to ask about the experiment. That was what hurt the most.

How could she not want to help after meeting Jenny? Everybody loved Jenny. How could she not even care?

He rolled into the open elevator and stabbed at several buttons before getting the fourth floor. Even Jason seemed to care. Somehow he'd come through with John Pyramid's e-mail account. He'd even helped Parker send out Darcy's write-up. Every scientist they could think of—every big name in the field. So far the suggestions Pyramid had gotten back weren't very promising, but at this point, every little angle counted. Ray was in the lab right now, synthesizing a batch of adrenaline 355 with D-alanine instead of L-alanine. The chance of getting the mirror-image molecules mixed up was infinitesimal; however, it was worth a try. They'd run out of every other possibility.

He drifted through the crowded hallway and into Jason's temporary office. Jason was sitting at a desk behind his computer.

"Hey, Jason. Have you seen Darcy?" Parker pulled up beside Jason and waited for him to finish typing.

"Not for a while. She's pretty busy preparing for prelims. What's up?"

Love you, John. Parker's eyes went wide as Jason signed the message and hit the Send button. "Nothing really." He raised his chair. "I haven't seen her since Thursday and was just . . . wondering if she was okay."

"She's fine." Jason leaned back in his chair with an amused smile. "She sometimes does that. Gets so involved in her work that she forgets to come up for air."

"I've been checking her lab. She's not there."

"You should check the library," Jason said. "Sometimes I think she lives there."

Parker nodded. Jason's e-mail program—it was logged into Pyramid's account.

Jason followed Parker's eyes back to his screen. "Oh, yeah." He double-clicked on a new message. "Pyramid got another response. Two responses."

"Anything useful?" Parker maneuvered his chair closer.

"Not in this one." Jason scrolled down the message. "But Johnston wanted to make sure Pyramid knows that *separate* has two *a*'s."

"Oops."

"No biggie," Jason said. "Pyramid's from South Africa. He's always had trouble with the word *separate*."

Parker leaned back in his chair.

"Wait a second." Jason sounded excited. "Check this out." He clicked on the next message and stood aside so Parker could read it.

The message was from Dr. Greggory Pylant, one of the movers and shakers in pharmaceutical chemistry.

Parker scanned the first few lines.

Dear Dr. Pyramid,

We are pleased to inform you that your paper, *Adrenaline Derivative Induces Muscle Regeneration in Gambol-type Muscular Dystrophy Mice,* has been accepted for publication as a note in the *Journal of Applied Pharmaceutical Chemistry.* . . .

"Oh no."

"Oh no?" Jason hit the Reply button. "This is great!"

"But he can't. It's not even a real paper."

"Pylant disagrees."

"And John Pyramid doesn't even exist," added Parker. "We've got to write him and explain—"

"But Pyramid *does* exist." Jason started typing a reply. "As soon as Pyramid's paper comes out, scientists all over the world will be falling all over themselves to reproduce that experiment."

"But we can't—"

"Why not? We can't withdraw a paper we never submitted. Besides, the paper's all true, isn't it? Pyramid admitted the experiment wasn't reproducible."

"That's the whole point. It's stupid. You can't publish something that isn't reproducible."

"Pylant says different." Jason kept on typing—thanking Pylant for accepting the paper.

"But it's under Pyramid's name."

"So? You said yourself it's stupid. Do you want it under your name?"

Parker didn't know what he wanted. Maybe Jason was right. Maybe it was Jenny's one last hope. No, he couldn't publish under false pretenses. It would be deceptive. A lie. "Tell you what," he said. "Let's write Pylant and admit that John Pyramid is nothing but a hoax. Maybe he'll still be willing to include the paper."

"Too late." With that, Jason hit the Send button. "You already said nobody'll take you seriously. But they'll take Pyramid seriously."

"Come on, Jason. Be serious." Parker reached out a hand for the keyboard, but Jason pushed it away. "Write him back. Tell him Pyramid doesn't exist!"

"But he *does* exist." Jason grinned. "You've got Jenny to thank for that."

"Jenny?"

"Jenny's love letters gave me the idea. I—"

Parker's cell phone rang out with a loud chirp. "Could you help me with that?" Parker pointed to the inside pocket of his chair.

Jason eased his hand inside the pocket. Removing the phone, he pushed a button and held it to his ear. "Hello. . . ? Yeah, this is Jason." His face went suddenly slack. "I'm . . . so sorry."

A sick feeling settled in Parker's stomach. He could just make out the sound of his father's voice.

"Just a second." Jason held the phone to Parker's ear.

"Hello, Dad?"

"James, your mother and I are at the hospital. Jenny's taken a turn for the worse. The doctors say it's just a matter of time. . . ."

CHAPTER 10

DARCY

DARCY KICKED AT A DUSTY PILE of peeling bark and eucalyptus leaves. Her feet would smell like kitty litter for a while, but who cared? Channing certainly didn't. She'd been playing possum for over a week, and Channing hadn't even noticed. Channing didn't know you were alive unless you had a paper or two in the works.

Keeping to the cover of the trees, Darcy followed the creek bed east toward the back of the chemistry complex. A chill breeze tingled through her wet hair. It felt good to be clean again. She felt almost human. Maybe she could stop by and see how Parker was doing. It had been close to two weeks since her lab had been ransacked, and she still hadn't seen any signs of the Dark Man. He wasn't after her. She'd overreacted. It had been frat boys after all.

But even if it hadn't, she was done with the hiding. Parker had called her four times. His last message had been so sweet. *"No good news on the Mighty Mouse front. Just wanted to let you know that I'm worried about you . . . and I miss you."* She'd been so tempted to call him back. But what could she say that he'd believe? He'd never talk to her again.

Now that she was presentable, maybe she could go back and explain. Maybe they could pick up where they had left off—get back to trying to figure out what had happened to Mighty Mouse. She made her way through the walkway beneath the library to the sunken courtyard behind the chemistry building. The closer she got to the chemistry building, the more tightly the tangled mass of knots inside her twisted.

She would tell him everything. He would understand. He had to. And if he didn't, that was okay too. At least she'd know.

Throwing open the lower courtyard door, she marched through the basement hallways and climbed the back stairs. The whole building seemed to groan under the weight of a dark cloud. The Dark Man wasn't looking for her. It had all been a mistake, she told herself over and over as she walked down the hall toward Parker's lab.

The door was open. She could hear the clink of glassware inside. She took a deep breath. She could do it. She had to. *Tell him everything.* Darcy pushed her way into the lab.

Ray's gaunt form was hunched over the lab bench. His back was to her, but his head snapped to the alert as she walked across the floor.

"Ray, have you seen Parker?"

Ray shrugged, not bothering to turn and face her. "He left about an hour ago. I think he was looking for you."

Another twist to the knots. "Did he say when he'd be back?"

"Soon." Ray ejected a yellow tip from his Pipetman and pressed on a clean one. Darcy winced when he touched the tip with an ungloved finger. Didn't he realize he was contaminating it? She watched as he sucked in a few drops of solution. "Maybe he's gone back to his apartment. You know. To get help." The Pipetman trembled as he held it above a ninety-six well plate. He squirted the solution into one of the wells. As he was doing this, his hand shook and a blob of liquid pooled around the edges of the hole.

"Try putting the tip all the way into the well." Darcy handed him a ChemWipe to absorb the drop of liquid on the narrow plastic shelf separating the two wells. "If you keep the tips clean, it doesn't hurt to touch the solution inside the wells."

She watched with wide eyes as Ray kept on pipetting. He didn't record the mistake! The data from the well was invalid, and yet he didn't write it down in his lab notebook. If he'd missed the well . . . If the solution had spilled over into a neighboring well . . .

"Ray, I've got to talk to Parker. It's important!"

Ray shrugged again. "Hey, man. If he, like, had an accident, he might not be in for a while."

Darcy grabbed a pen and pad of paper off Parker's desk and wrote, *Ray missed well and didn't record. Spilled soln. all over the plate. Adrenaline 355 could be mixed with soln. from neighboring wells. Check all combinations. Darcy.*

Sticking the note to Parker's computer, Darcy ran for the door.

"You might check that other dude's lab," Ray called after her. "He's here all the time these days."

"Who, Jason?"

"Good-looking? Tipped, spiked hair?"

Jason. Darcy hurried from the lab and ran down the hall. She called out to a man in a suit who was just stepping into one of the elevators. "Excuse me. Sir? Are you going up?"

The man turned and nodded. His entire face was blistered with red scar tissue. Everywhere but a patch of clear, light skin around the eyes. As if he'd been wearing safety glasses when something exploded. Darcy darted into the elevator while the man held the door open for her.

"Thanks." She forced an uneasy smile and then lowered her eyes.

His jacket gaped open as he reached for the button panel. Under his arm, sheathed in a holster of worn leather, was the square black handle of a pistol.

One of the Dark Man's men? Darcy stepped to the back of the elevator, cold sweat prickling at her skin. The man smiled at her, a leering smile that turned south at a jagged patch of scar tissue at the corner of his mouth. She stared straight ahead, tapping her foot on the floor to mask her fear.

After a long, chilling ice age, the elevator doors finally opened again and the man stepped out. Of course he did. The Dark Man wasn't searching for her. He didn't even have men. She gave a weak laugh at her own foolishness and stepped cautiously out onto the fourth floor. The man was nowhere in sight.

Walking boldly down the hall, she made her way toward Jason's office. A voice sounded in the chemistry office as she walked by. The man with the gun was talking to the receptionist: "Excuse me. I'm looking for the lab of one of your visiting professors—a Dr. John Pyramid."

Darcy's whole body went limp. It was all she could do to keep from collapsing in a heap on the floor. With trembling muscles and a pounding heart, she turned slowly and walked back toward the stairs. The man was still talking as she passed by the office. He didn't seem to notice her.

Ducking into the stairwell, she pounded down the stairs. John Pyramid! Jason's imaginary scientist. Somehow, someway, the Dark Man had connected her back to Pyramid. Parker and Jason would be next. She had to warn them, tell them to lie low.

Or did she? She pushed out onto the third floor and ran down the hallway to her lab. What if she went into hiding? The Dark Man wasn't after them; she was the one he wanted. So long as she kept her distance, they'd be perfectly safe.

PARKER

"Woo-hoooooo!" Parker spun his chair in a tight circle until his hand slipped off the joystick and the chair coasted to a stop. "Yes, yes, yes!" He'd done it! He rolled back to the computer and double-checked each trace. Mouses 10, 18, 26, and 34 were showing definite signs of motion—huge Mighty Mouse motion! He checked the log to make certain. Sure enough, they were the ones that received mixtures of adrenaline 355 and 5-aminolevulinate. Darcy was right. The neurotransmitter analog had been in the well to the left of the original 355 sample.

Parker zipped across the animal room. Mouse 10 was within easy reach. He pulled the cage from the rack and was rewarded by the skittering of claws. Lifting off the plastic lid, he stared through the bars into the upturned face of a quivering mouse. The mouse hopped shakily to the side of the cage, sliding and falling and jerking around like . . . like an adult mouse that was just learning to walk. "Dear God . . ." Parker watched as the mouse continued to twitch. It was bursting with energy. Exploding with joy. "Thank you. God, thank you. Thank you."

He couldn't believe it. It was actually working. The mouse was walking. If everything went right, he himself might even be able to walk someday. Just a few months of refinement and then . . . toxicity, pharmicokinetics, clinical trials. It might take a couple of years, but—

The cage slid out of Parker's hands and clattered to the floor.

Jenny. His eyes clouded over, and the room went dim. It was too late. It was only a matter of days now. Even if a big pharma helped him, it would take months to refine the drug, years even. "Why?" The irony smacked him upside the head like a cruel universe-sized joke. He'd finally discovered a lead compound, and it was too late. His sister didn't have months. According to the doctors, she might not even have days.

Why? A high-pitched whine buzzed in Parker's ears. He pulled back on the tether he'd fixed permanently to the door. It didn't seem real. After all these years . . . *Dear God, please. Just a little more time. Until we can get this drug through refinement and testing. Just a little . . .*

No, it was no good. Even if they had enough time, what pharma was going to sink millions of dollars into a drug that helped such a small population? He'd been a fool. Doomed from the start. He'd been so arrogant, as if he could single-handedly thwart the will of God.

Parker hit the Up arrow and rolled into the elevator. All that time . . . wasted. Time he could have spent with Jenny. Talking with her. Enjoying her. But instead he'd locked himself away in a laboratory dungeon, fighting against the inevitable. Raging against the storm when he could have been warm and cozy inside and spending his time with a family who loved him. Now he was going to lose the one person in the world who truly understood.

The elevator felt suddenly hot. Thick air clogged his lungs. The doors slid open, and he burst out into the hallway. Darcy. He had to find her. Ray said she'd tried to find him the day before yesterday, but he hadn't been able to locate her anywhere. And then, after he saw her note, he and Ray had been too busy with the new experiment. He had to talk to her, tell her about the mice.

Pulling off his sterile mask and cap, he charged into her lab.

Darcy spun around at the door to her hot room. "Parker!"

"Sorry to barge in like this, but we've got to talk." He stopped his chair halfway across the lab. Darcy stood rigid against the door. She looked almost frightened.

"Parker, I can't. Not now." Her hand felt for the doorknob. "We can't be seen together. It's not safe."

"Safe? What are you talking about?"

Darcy's eyes darted past him. Footsteps echoed in the hallway.

The sound of voices. "Please, just go. There's no time to explain."

"But we got Mighty Mouse. You were right. It was just like you said in the note. We . . ." Parker faltered, suddenly confused by Darcy's expression. "What's wrong?"

"I'm glad for you. I really am." Her eyes filled with tears. "I wish I could see it, but I can't. It's not safe. For you or me."

"Why not? Is it Jason you're worried about? He and I already talked. I explained about the glass-heads."

She shook her head. "Please, just go. Don't mention Pyramid's name. Don't even admit that you know me."

"Sorry." Parker switched off his chair. "But I'm not leaving. Not if you're in trouble. Not until I've done everything in my power to make things right."

Darcy tensed and her eyes flew once more to the hallway. More footsteps. She stood frozen like a wide-eyed statue until the footsteps had passed. Finally she relaxed, took a deep breath and closed her eyes.

"Darcy, please. Just tell me what's wrong. I'll do whatever I can to help. I promise."

She opened her eyes and her face seemed to harden. "Parker, I didn't want to do this, but you leave me no choice." Her voice sounded mechanical, hollow. "Nothing's wrong. I'm not in trouble. I just don't want . . . to talk to you."

Stillness rang like chimes in Parker's ears. He couldn't speak. Didn't know what to say.

"I'm sorry. I don't want to be like this." Tears were streaming down her cheeks. "Ever since my mom and dad died. And my grandmother and Mrs. Simmons. Everyone I've ever loved. I just can't . . ."

"Can't what?" Parker choked out the words.

"Keep working with you."

"That's okay. We got Mighty Mouse."

"You don't understand." Darcy buried her face in her hands. "It's not the experiment. It's . . ."

Parker sat, staring with unfocused eyes. He felt like he was going to throw up.

"You and me. I just can't handle it. Being . . . friends."

The words hit him like a slap in the face. He switched his chair back on and made for the door.

"Parker, I'm sorry. I really am. I just need time."

Time? Time for what? To get used to the freak in the chair? Parker whirred down the hall, pushing the chair to its limit as blurred figures curved and dodged out of the way. He coasted to a stop at his lab door and spun around to check the hall behind him. *What did time have to do with it?* Jenny was the one who needed time. Didn't anyone care about Jenny?

The lab was dark. Somber as a morgue. He moved across the room and pulled open the refrigerator. Jenny was dying. He didn't have a choice. He couldn't just give up. Not now. Not when he had a real lead. He fumbled with a tray of Eppendorf tubes—the compounds he and Ray had synthesized for the last experiment. There it was. Adrenaline 355 and compound 39. He removed a bullet-shaped tube from the tray and crossed the aisle to his lab bench.

Either he followed through with his research now, or he admitted defeat and went home. He pulled a sterile syringe from the drawer of syringes and ripped open the pack. If he went back home to be with his parents, his life was over. The outside world would be shut out forever. All his goals. Everything he'd worked so hard to accomplish. Existence and existence and death. That was all.

Popping open the lid of the Eppendorf, he drew the clear liquid into the syringe and held it to the light, tapping it with his fingers to loosen any air bubbles that might be clinging to the sides. He pressed up on the plunger until a single drop formed at the tip of the needle and spilled down the side of the syringe. Then, turning the syringe in shaking hands, he injected the drug directly into his vein.

Existence and existence and death.

PART 2

Pyramid Scheme

"Think of me at this hour, in a strange place, laboring
under a blackness of distress that no fancy can
exaggerate, and yet well aware that, if you will but
punctually serve me, my troubles will roll away like a
story that is told."

—ROBERT LOUIS STEVENSON
THE STRANGE CASE OF DR. JEKYLL AND MR. HYDE

CHAPTER 11

PARKER

A WAVE OF NAUSEA TRAVELED UP Parker's body, leaving him suspended in a dry, retching gasp. White-hot light dazzled his eyes. *Water.* He squinted against the liquid brightness, searching for the laboratory sink. He had to have water. His body was on fire. He could feel the blood boiling in his veins.

His chair jerked across the floor, lunging and halting as trembling muscles clenched and released in a series of quivering spasms. A hand shot up from the chair's controls and struck him across the bridge of his nose. A haze of shimmering stars. Both legs kicked off their rests and landed in a tangle on the floor. They were possessed. His whole body was possessed by some flaming spirit. A demon from the pit of hell.

Dropping his arm back onto his armrest, Parker jammed the joystick forward, pushing his kicking and twisting feet across the glass-covered floor. A crash shook the chair. The sound of more breaking glass. The room surged around him as he pushed down on the joystick. Another crash. Another. His arm dropped into an abyss, sending a shock of liquid coolness coursing up it. The dim outline of a faucet penetrated the opalescent brightness. He reached for it, but his muscles locked up in a pushing, pulling, bone-wrenching tug-of-war. A sudden muscle spasm doubled him over and forced the air from his lungs. *God, please . . .*

A part of him lifted above the agony that twisted his body—an eagle soaring on the thermals of a burning plain. The world beneath him started to fade, rushed past him like the wind. Buoying him up. Sustaining him. Sharpening his senses and giving him strength.

A shout called out. Behind him, the sound of a creaking door. Parker forced his eyes open, tried to turn, but his body was too far below him to respond. His shuddering limbs had a will of their own.

Another sound. The scrape of dragging feet. The room suddenly dimmed as a cold shadow fell across him. Dark, loathsome, unimaginably evil. He tried to get away, scrabbling forward, tearing at the chains that bound him. The dark presence seeped into him, invading his thoughts. He could taste it in his mind—cruel, wretched, dripping with poisonous venom.

Parker fought to escape. He felt himself falling, the rush of wind in his ears. *Crack!* His head exploded in a starburst of red-hot pain. White stars receded to a shimmering pinprick of light. A high-pitched alarm screamed, piercing his ears. The shadow was after him; he had to get away. Had to find Darcy.

The darkness receded like a spent wave, leaving a marbled pattern of gray on beige. Dirty cracks in the form of a grid. Floor tiles. A hand swept before his face, and realization washed over him as the shadow returned. The hand was his. He was crawling.

DARCY

Darcy jerked awake, searching the darkness with wide, frantic eyes. The noise. She'd heard it again. And this time she wasn't dreaming. She lay rigid beneath the folds of her sleeping bag, straining to hear above the mad rush of blood that surged in her ears. A soft scraping noise. The *plink* of glass touching glass. Someone was in the lab. Just below her, near the lab bench. She could almost feel the person's presence filling the room like an evil spirit. Searching, listening, sensing . . .

The Dark Man. She lay so still she could feel the individual beads of sweat rolling across her skin. She breathed through her mouth in slow, shallow breaths, ignoring the burning cry of her lungs for more air. He'd stopped moving. He was listening. He could hear her. Could hear the pounding of her heart. A soft tap. A beaker or flask being set on the table.

What? What would the Dark Man be doing with glassware?

It was just Jason. It had to be. He couldn't sleep and was working on Parker's experiment—that had to be it. A few days ago he'd gotten keys to the hot room beneath her, set it up as Dr. Pyramid's lab. He claimed it was all part of maintaining the Pyramid myth, but she suspected it was nothing more than a thinly veiled excuse to spy on her. Whatever it was, he was making it almost impossible for her to get in and out of her loft without being seen. He'd almost caught her climbing down the ladder that morning. She was getting sick and tired of the whole Pyramid scheme.

Pyramid. The man in the elevator had been looking for Pyramid. What if he—No, it had to be Jason. A cabinet door squeaked beneath her. Then another. Of course it was Jason; he must be looking for clean glassware.

She rolled onto her hands and knees and moved quietly to the edge of the plywood floor. Suddenly a golden network of light traced upward through the ceiling tiles. Darcy froze. Why a flashlight? Why not just turn on the lights? She backed slowly away from the edge of the plywood. *The Dark Man.* He was searching for something. A clue to where she lived? An address?

Parker's business card! She'd left it on her desk. It had his name, his address. If the Dark Man found it . . .

The flashlight snapped off with a sharp click. A faint fluttering sound rose and fell like the crashing of a distant wave. Then silence. Dark, screaming silence.

Was he gone? She counted to a hundred. Still quiet. He had to be gone. She crept back to the edge of the plywood and lowered herself to her stomach to look through a gap in the tiles.

Nothing.

Holding her breath, she lifted the ceiling tile and looked down into the room. So far, so good. She stepped down onto the ladder and started to descend, pausing at each step to listen.

A thud sounded in her lab. The scrape of metal on stone. Leaping from the ladder, she hit the floor in a widespread crouch. A second thud, followed by heavy breathing, low and guttural. She scrambled for the cover of a vacant desk as the door crashed open. A rush of heavy footsteps. An animal's rasping breath.

Darcy huddled beneath the desk, pulling her legs tight to her chest as a dark presence filled the room. A dark shadow against an even darker room. The floor beneath her shuddered. *Crash!* The room was filled with a burst of blinding light as the lab door swung open and slammed shut again.

Darcy waited, trying to regain control of her racing heart. Had he seen the address? She stretched out her legs, biting her lip as life slowly tingled back into her feet. Slowly, careful not to bump the nearby chair, she scooted out from under the desk and tiptoed across the room. Pausing to listen at the door, she eased it open and stepped into her adjoining lab. Light from the far door backlit a jumble of containers and glassware lying across the floor.

He'd searched the whole lab. She was too late. Picking her way across the floor, she ran her hand across the surface of her desk. A slip of paper slid from the desk and fluttered to the floor. She picked it up and crossed the room to read it in the light filtering in through the glass in the door. It was Parker's card. His address and home phone number were printed right below his name. Had the intruder seen it or not? She had to warn Parker.

A scratch sounded at the door. A soft rattling moan.

Darcy whirled and ran for the back of the lab. Through the hot room, out into the hallway, she raced for the back stairs, sliding into the stairwell door with a crash. Footsteps sounded behind her. She pulled the door open and plunged inside. Half stepping, half leaping, she bounded down the stairs.

A door slammed above her. Pounding footsteps merging with her own. They were gaining on her. She hit the door at the bottom of the stairs at a run and exploded out into the hallway. Around the corner, bouncing off a wall, she pushed through a set of glass doors and into the back courtyard. No time for the library. They were still behind her. She darted across the courtyard, then sprang from a wooden bench up onto a low flat roof—the air-handlers for the underground building below.

Pressing herself flat against the icy metal grate, she waited for the bang of opening doors. Silence. Nothing but the sound of her breathing. No running, no gunshots, nothing.

Cold moisture seeped up through the soft fabric of her sweats. Her bare feet were freezing, but she didn't dare move. Finally she heard something. Shuffling footsteps, not from the chem building but from the other side of the courtyard, near the library. A fairly large group, judging from the sound. They were moving slowly. Searching.

She lifted her head and peered out over the edge of the roof. They were halfway across the courtyard before she saw them. A small mob, and they were heading straight for her. *Glass-heads.*

JASON

Jason placed a cup of freshly brewed coffee on his desk and settled back into his father's old chair. The picture window in his living room was sprinkled with a fine mist that distorted the lights of the bay below him. Long streaks of condensation ran down the inside of the window. It was getting cold out—a good night to stay inside and get some work done.

But first . . . He logged on to his computer and double-clicked on his browser. *John Pyramid.* He typed the name into a search engine. In the last couple of days he must have heard ten people talking about John Pyramid. The secretaries he could understand. He'd engineered just the kind of scandal they loved to gossip about. But when polyester-suited strangers started asking about a man that wasn't supposed to exist, Jason wanted to know why. And then there was Blake the Snake. Blake insisted he'd had a full conversation with Pyramid. Face-to-face. In person.

Jason hit Enter and scanned the list of entries, wondering exactly what he was looking for. Manuals on anger management, paperweights made of blue john stone, a bakery in Massachusetts—nothing jumped out at him. The list was actually pretty sparse. As names went, John Pyramid seemed to be rather unique.

But the Snake said he'd talked to John Pyramid for over an hour. And if that wasn't weird enough, Blake's description of the man—tall, brown eyes and hair, pale skin—sounded just like his dad . . . right before he died.

Jason entered his father's name into the computer. *William Shanahan.* The search engine pulled up over four hundred entries. He paged through the list, recognizing the occasional link to UCSF or one of his dad's old papers. He followed a link to one of the abstracts. *Identification and characterization of gene that controls aggression in mice.* Scanning the list of authors and contributors, he searched for a reference to John Pyramid. There had to be something. A link somewhere between his father and Pyramid. As a boy, he'd heard his dad use the name when he answered the phone— before the practical joke. The name had captured his imagination. For months afterward, he'd pretended his dad was a secret agent masquerading as a mild-mannered research scientist. John Pyramid. It was the ultimate alias. There had to be some reason his father had chosen the name. What if the practical joke had just been a front for something real? Maybe a project or agency that the government wanted to keep covered up?

Familiar childhood fantasies began to quicken, a hope Jason didn't even dare put a name to. No. This wasn't a comic book. His father was gone. He'd been gone for a dozen years. People didn't rise from the dead—not in real life. Not anymore.

Jason followed a link to another of his father's articles and then ran his finger across the list of authors. Still no mention of Pyramid. Of course not. There was no such person. It was all a product of his hyperactive imagination. There were no talking slugs in the sewer system of their house. He never got a live Tyrannosaurus Rex for his birthday. And there was no John Pyramid. He paged to the top of the article and read through the list of authors one more time. Marcus Foley was the first author, probably one of his dad's grad students. He'd been too young to remember any of their names. He checked the date on the paper.

Impossible. Jason shook his head in disbelief. He checked it again, then followed the reference back to the journal. It didn't make sense. The paper hadn't come out until five years after his father's death.

CHAPTER 12

DARCY DREW BACK FROM THE ROOF'S EDGE and scooted across the metal grate. One of the benches creaked under a heavy weight. The glass-heads had reached her hiding place. They were trying to climb up onto the roof now. Flipping over the edge on the far side of the narrow structure, she hit the ground running. A maniacal laugh sounded to her left. They'd blocked off the courtyard. The chemistry building was her only chance, but that meant stopping to unlock the door.

A shrill whistle sounded behind her. The babble of incoherent voices. They'd seen her. Abandoning stealth, she sprinted across the courtyard, heading straight for the doors. The courtyard behind her was filled with voices. There were more of them than she'd thought.

She slammed into the door and fumbled with her keys in the lock. "Come on!" Her fingers were so numb she couldn't get the key in the lock. "Come on!"

They were getting closer. She could hear the swish of fabric on fabric, could see their dark outlines in the glass.

The key slipped into the lock and she turned it hard. Pulling the door open, she darted inside and slammed it shut behind her. *Whump!* One of the glass-heads hit the door head on. Darcy ran for the stairs, expecting any second to hear the crash of broken glass. She churned up the stairs, past the first floor, the second, the third, then burst out onto the fourth floor and down the long hall, zigzagging back and forth between the doors that lined the walls. Locked. Locked. All the doors were locked. She ducked down a short corridor and pressed herself against a shadow-darkened wall.

Silence. She caught her breath at intervals, listening for sounds of pursuit. If the glass-heads broke through the glass, wouldn't that set off some sort of alarm? She'd hear it, wouldn't she? She waited for several more minutes, feeling more and more vulnerable in the open hallway. She had to find a better hiding place. Somewhere they wouldn't think to look. Various hiding places popped into her head, but she quickly discarded them. They were all too public, not nearly as hidden or comfortable as her ceiling loft.

Her lab was safe enough now. It had to be. The Dark Man wouldn't search it twice. If it had even been the Dark Man. Maybe it was just glass-heads. That would explain the lack of interest in Parker's address. Or maybe it was a thief. A frat boy searching for ethanol or clean needles. She made her way silently back to the main hallway and made a mad dash for the stairs.

The stairwell was silent. The whole building, in fact. If the glass-heads had gotten inside, she would have heard them. They were about as subtle as a herd of water buffalo. She slipped into the stairwell and crept down the stairs to the third floor. Easing the door open, she stepped through into the dimly lit hall. A strange noise prickled at her senses. Her imagination? She crept forward, straining ahead with every sense on the alert. There it was again. A faint flutter. The sound of breathing. Panting. She froze, started to retrace her steps. Whatever it was, it was just around the corner. Right outside the door to her lab.

The breathing deepened to a low, gasping moan. A human moan. He didn't sound dangerous, more like he was in a great deal of pain. One of the Dark Man's victims?

Darcy stepped forward and peered around the corner. "Parker!" He lay belly down on the floor, his face twisted toward her, twitching. She flung herself to her knees, searching the floor around him. "Parker, what happened?" She placed a hand on his shoulder and then jerked it away as something rolled beneath her fingers. His arm was popping and twitching like popcorn in a popper. Like something inside him was crawling around—trying to get out.

A dark puddle next to his cheek caught her eye.

"No!" She reached out to steady herself against the wall. "No. Please . . ." The corridor seemed to shift beneath her feet as she rolled him onto his back. His right cheek was slashed with three parallel cuts. *The slash of an animal. A big animal.* Her stomach felt it deep, an instinct too primal to question.

"Parker, can you hear me?" She brushed his cheek with cold fingers, and his breathing seemed to slow. "Parker, it's me, Darcy." She pressed a hand to his forehead, stroked back his hair. "Talk to me. I have to know what happened."

Parker's eyes fluttered open. He stared up at her with a faraway expression. A faint smile touched his lips.

"Hold on, okay? I'm going to call an ambulance." She started to pull away, but Parker's hand closed around her wrist in a surprisingly firm grip.

"Please . . . stay." His voice trembled with the effort of speech. "No ambulance. Please."

Darcy pulled her wrist out of his grasp. "What's happening? You're shaking like a leaf."

"It's . . . getting better." His face pulled suddenly taut. The muscles under his skin quivered with intense strain.

"Are you all right? What hurts?"

"Fine." His face gradually relaxed. "I'm fine. Adrenaline 355 . . . mixed with aminolevulinate."

Darcy drew back with a gasp. *He didn't . . .*

"I had to." He seemed to be reading her mind. "Jenny took a turn for the worse. She won't last much longer."

"You took Mighty Mouse?"

Parker's eyes narrowed. In concentration? Pain? "Please . . . I need water."

Darcy jumped to her feet. "I'll call an ambulance. You—"

"No! I've got to keep taking it. You have to synthesize more."

"Parker! It's killing you—don't you understand? We need to get you to a hospital."

"No hospital. Please. If this doesn't work, I'm dead, hospital or no hospital. But it's working. I was actually crawling. For the first time in years. Don't let them take that away from me. It's my only hope. Jenny's only hope."

"Crawling?" Darcy looked around the hallway. "Where's your wheelchair?"

"I was in my lab. Took the drug . . ." Parker's face clouded. "I thought someone was after me. I was trying to get away. I thought it was chasing me. Next thing I knew I was crawling." He closed his eyes. After a few seconds he opened them again. "I guess I was hallucinating. I must have been trying to find you."

"What happened to your face?" Dread sat heavy in the pit of her stomach. She wasn't sure she wanted to hear the answer.

"What do you mean?"

"Your face. It's . . . cut." Darcy bit her lip, not wanting to say the next words. "It looks like you were attacked by an animal."

Parker's face tightened, creasing his eyes with pain. His foot kicked out and his whole body went suddenly rigid. Then he started to tremble, even more violently than before.

"Hold on. I'll get you a blanket." Darcy unlocked the door and ran across the cluttered floor of her lab.

"Please . . . no doctors." Parker's quivering voice followed her into the hot room.

Stepping through the shards of a broken flask, Darcy climbed up the ladder and into her loft. She grabbed her pillow and sleeping bag, leaped from the ladder, and was through the labs in an instant. Parker was still trembling when she got back. He seemed to be getting worse.

"Here. I'm just going to put something under your head." She lifted his head and slid her pillow under it.

"Thanks." Parker's voice was almost a whisper, his eyes narrow slits. The lights seemed to be bothering him. "Please . . . water."

She threw the sleeping bag over him and ducked back into the lab. She could only find a beaker to hold the water. It would have to do. "Think you can drink?" She lifted his head and held the beaker to his lips. He took a long greedy gulp and started coughing. "Easy." She pulled the beaker away to keep him from spilling it. "Just a little at a time."

She tipped the glass toward him and pulled it back after a tiny sip. "That's it, just a little at a time." Her mind raced. Parker could have been hallucinating, but what if it were the glass-heads? Or the Dark Man? What if he'd attacked him, dragged him from his chair?

The guy from the elevator. She could feel her face burning with pent-up fury. To attack a guy in a wheelchair . . . it was inhuman. Beastly. And the worst thing was Parker thought he'd been crawling.

She looked down into his face. His breathing seemed to come easier now. He seemed to be falling asleep. She brushed a dark strand of hair from his forehead. Why did it have to be Parker? It was all her fault. If she'd just heeded the warning signs.

There was only one thing to do. She had to get out of town. Now. Find a way to pay back the Dark Man's money. The longer she stayed in Berkeley, the more she was putting her friends in danger.

But she couldn't leave Parker. Not like this. She tiptoed into her lab and picked the phone up off the floor. Good, it still worked. She punched in Jason's number and waited while it rang.

"Hello?" A groggy voice answered the phone.

"Jason, this is Darcy. Parker took the drug. He's practically in convulsions, but he doesn't want me to call an ambulance."

"Darcy, slow down. What drug? What are you—"

"Adrenaline 355. Mixed with 5-aminolevulinate. It was my suggestion, and now he's shaking all over and his face is all cut up and I think he's been attacked."

"Attacked? Where are you? Have you called the police?"

"At my lab. But please, don't call the police. Not yet. We have to figure out what to do. Parker wants to keep taking the drug. He thinks he can crawl now."

"Is he delirious?"

"No. I mean, I . . . I don't know. Maybe. I think someone dragged him out of his chair, but he doesn't remember any of it. He thinks he can crawl, and I . . . I just can't—"

"Darcy, just slow down and tell me what happened. From the beginning."

A groan sounded out in the hallway. Parker's breath was coming in heavy gasps.

"Jason, I've got to go now. Something's happening. I'll call you right back."

"Darcy, wait. I—"

She hung up the phone and ran back out into the hall. Parker had kicked off the sleeping bag and was shaking again—worse than before. She knelt down beside him and covered him back up. "You're going to be okay, Parker. We'll get through this together. It'll clear your system soon, and then you're never going to test drugs on yourself again. I won't let you. You're too good a person to treat yourself like a lab rat. You're—"

A door slammed. Somewhere on the third floor, near the elevators. She grabbed Parker under the arms and dragged him into her lab, pulling the door shut behind them. They were coming for her, and the lock wouldn't hold. Not for a second. She searched the room for a place to hide. Nothing. He was too big. She couldn't just stuff him in a cabinet.

Footsteps sounded in the hallway, heading their way. She could hide in the loft, but Parker was way too heavy to carry up the ladder. She had no choice. Tiptoeing back to the door, she picked up a ring stand with a heavy metal base. Holding it like a baseball bat, she crept to the door and waited. She might not be able to get them all, but the first person through the door was going to pay.

JASON

Jason ran up the stairs of the chemistry building, two steps at a time. Darcy was out of her mind. What did she think she was doing, testing drugs on Parker? If the grad school found out, she'd be kicked out of the program. Or worse, she could be arrested. Thrown in jail.

He threw his shoulder into the stairwell door and burst out onto the third floor. And what was she doing up with Parker in the first place? It was 3:00 in the morning!

He hurried down the hallway. The more he thought about it, the madder he got. This time she'd gone too far. Way too far. He rounded the corner and stopped at Darcy's door. It was locked.

"Darcy! Open up." He pounded on the door. "Darcy?"

"Shhh!" The door swung open and Darcy poked her head out. Eyes blazing, she grabbed him by the arm and pulled him inside. "What are you trying to do, announce our location to the whole building?" She locked the door behind them and leaned against it, a heavy ring stand grasped in her left hand. "Why don't you just put up billboards with big arrows?"

"Would you please tell me what's going on?" Jason's frustration lent a razor-sharp edge to his words.

"Someone attacked Parker, tried to kill him." Her eyes were puffy, brimming with tears. "He might still be in the building."

"Who?" Jason stared at her hard, daring her to dodge the question.

"I don't know. A group of glass-heads was chasing me. They could have—"

"Glass-heads? What is it with you and glass-heads? And what were you doing here with Parker at three in the morning? You're not leveling with me."

"I wasn't here *with* him. I was just working late. I don't know what he—"

A low groan sounded behind him. Jason turned. A worn sleeping bag was spread out on the floor in the midst of piles and piles of lab equipment. The sleeping bag moved, jerking and twitching like a break-dancing slug. Parker's face appeared behind a fold in the bag.

"Parker!" Jason hurried down the aisle and dropped to his knees. Parker lay writhing in agony beneath the sleeping bag. Dried blood covered his cheek. Knotted cords of tension creased his face. He was having some sort of seizure.

"What did you do to him?"

"I didn't do anything." Darcy's voice trembled. "He took the drug. I didn't have anything to do with it."

Jason grabbed Parker's wrist, feeling desperately for a pulse. "Did you call an ambulance?"

"He wouldn't let me. He made me promise."

"Do you have any idea how much trouble you'll be in if he dies?" Jason dug in his pocket for his cell phone.

"No!" A deep voice.

Jason stared down at Parker, stunned. It didn't sound like his voice at all. It was stronger, more forceful. He almost sounded angry.

"I'm not going to the hospital. The ambulance can't take me if I don't want to go."

"Parker, listen to me." Darcy was leaning over his shoulder. "You're shaking all over. You might be going into shock."

"I'm not going into shock." Parker's eyes were clamped shut. "I'm fine. Better than I've ever been."

Jason exchanged glances with Darcy. Clearly she was just as worried as he was. Parker did not sound like Parker.

"What do you want us to do?" Darcy's voice was strained, like she was talking to a stranger.

"Take me back to my apartment. I'll be fine. I just need to rest."

Darcy looked up at Jason, eyebrows raised.

"Parker?" Jason didn't know what to say. "You sound different. Are you sure you're okay?"

"Fine." Still the strange voice. "Take me back to my apartment. I need to get to my chair."

Jason looked around the room. His chair? "Where is it?"

"Back in the lab," Parker said. "I crawled here. I'm sure I did."

"Crawled?" Jason looked to Darcy.

"I'm getting stronger. I can feel it." Parker's voice was flat, almost monotone. "Just like the mice."

Jason started for the door.

"No!" Darcy cut in front of him. "Stay with Parker. I want to see his lab."

He shrugged as she raced from the room. He could hear her footsteps echoing down the hall.

"So . . ." Jason felt suddenly ill at ease. "Is something wrong with your eyes?"

Parker's eyes opened a tiny crack but then squeezed back shut. "It's too bright. Must be the drug." Again the deep, flat voice.

Jason crouched next to Parker, the skin prickling at the back of his neck. *Weird . . .*

A half smile crept over Parker's face. "The drug really is working. Darcy doesn't believe me, but I was crawling. I haven't been able to crawl in years. You've got to help me synthesize more. The instructions are in the lab notebook on my desk."

"Got it," Darcy's whisper was almost drowned out by the whine of the chair. "It was in his lab. There was broken glass all over the place—like there'd been a big fight."

Darcy stopped the wheelchair next to Parker. Jason leaned over and grabbed him under the arms. His body was rigid as a board. He didn't seem to want to bend. Finally he managed to get Parker in the chair by reclining it all the way back.

"Parker, you're skin and bones. How can you be so heavy?" Jason guided the chair down the hallway with Darcy leading the way. She searched from side to side, scanning the side corridors with nervous, darting eyes. A growing sense of dread was beginning to take hold of him. He wished she'd stop it with the horror-film routine.

Darcy held the elevator door while Jason guided Parker's chair inside. The building was silent as a tomb. It was starting to give him the willies. "You hanging in there, Parker? We're almost there."

Darcy jumped back as the elevator doors opened. She stepped cautiously forward, scanning the lobby like a soldier in enemy territory.

"Would you relax?" Jason followed her out. "Everything's fine. Isn't that right, Parker?"

"Hmmm . . ." His voice trailed off. He seemed to be falling asleep.

Darcy looked up at Jason with wide eyes.

"He'll be fine." He pushed open the outside doors and guided Parker up the long sidewalk. "I'm parked on the other side of the auditorium. There won't be room in the car for his chair, but I should be able to get him inside his apartment without it—assuming there aren't any stairs."

Jason ran around his car, opened the door, and hit the control to lower the top of the convertible. Then, running back to the passenger side, the two of them lifted Parker from the chair and laid him in the passenger seat. His muscles seemed to be loosening up. The shaking wasn't nearly as bad as it had been. Was he sleeping? Jason wondered if he shouldn't drive Parker straight to the hospital. But then there would be questions. Awkward answers. They'd probably want him to sign a release form. Show some ID.

"Parker, you'll be okay. I know you will." Darcy was leaning over Parker, smoothing back his hair. "Everything will be fine. Just no more drugs. Not till they've been thoroughly tested."

Jason walked around the car and slid behind the wheel. He started the engine and looked to Darcy. "Do you want to squeeze in next to him? It'll be tight, but it's only to Dwight Way, right?"

She shook her head slowly. A tear-stained cheek glistened in the moonlight. "Take good care of him. Dwight Way Apartments, number three. Oh, his keys!" She dug in a pocket of his chair and pulled out a plastic key ring with four keys. "Make sure he doesn't try taking the drug again. It could kill him." She looked down at Parker, cupped a hand around his cheek. "Bye, Parker. I wish things could have been different. I really do. It's just . . . Take care of yourself, okay? I'll . . . always remember you."

"Always remember you?" Jason cast a quizzical look at Darcy. "What's going on?"

Darcy turned and fled back toward the chemistry building.

"Darcy, wait!" Jason opened his door and hopped out.

A low moan escaped Parker's lips. He was starting to shake again.

"Darcy!" Jason watched her disappear around the auditorium. "Of all the—" He dropped back into the driver's seat and slammed his hands against the steering wheel. He couldn't believe it. She'd done it again. He slammed the door and threw the car into gear. Stomping hard on the gas, he took his frustration out on the rubber of his tires. This was the last time. As soon as he got Parker situated, he was going to hunt Darcy down and get the truth. Even if he had to beat it out of her.

Tires squealing, engine roaring, Jason raced through the deserted streets. There it was, Dwight Way Apartments. He drove up onto the sidewalk and pulled to a stop in front of a ground-level apartment marked with a large black three. "Okay, Parker. We're . . . Parker?"

Parker was still as death. The trembling had completely stopped. He didn't seem to be breathing.

"Parker?" Jason ran around the car and checked his pulse. Parker's heart was racing like Michael Andretti. He sprinted to the door of the apartment and fumbled with the keys in the lock. "Hold on, Parker. I'll get you inside where it's warm." Throwing open the door, he hurried back to the car and hauled Parker out. Gripping him around the torso, Jason dragged him inside to a surprisingly neat living room. Nice furniture, fresh-cut flowers. He dragged him to a back bedroom and hoisted him onto a bed.

"Come on, Parker, don't do this." He felt again for Parker's pulse. Still too fast. His forehead was on fire, dry as paper. "Okay, that does it." He walked around to the bedside table and reached for the phone.

A snakelike hand darted out and grabbed him by the arm.

"Huh!" Jason twisted around, flinging the hand from his arm. "Parker! You scared me to death." He stared down into Parker's squinting eyes.

"Please . . ." Parker's eyes pleaded. "No doctors. It's working. I can feel it."

Jason nodded. "Of course it is. You'll be just fine."

"I'm serious." A shaking hand stretched toward Jason and grasped him by the right hand. His grip was anything but firm, but still . . . He tried to remember the last time he'd shaken Parker's hand. It did seem stronger than before.

Parker's hand suddenly clamped down on Jason's, squeezing his bones together in a viselike grip. "Ow!" Jason started to yank his hand away, but the hand turned limp.

"It comes and it goes," Parker said with his new deep voice. "But I can tell—it's building. I *have* to keep taking the drug."

Jason nodded, too stunned for questions.

"I need you to synthesize another batch. The instructions are in the notebook on my desk."

Jason flexed the fingers of his right hand. A drug that made people stronger. It was more than just a cure for muscular dystrophy—way more. It could be huge. The possibilities were endless. If he could just—"I'll do it on two conditions."

"Name them."

"First, if it works, I want in on the patent."

"And the second condition?"

Jason's mind raced. "The second is . . . I want to be the one to tell Jenny."

The room seemed to stand still while Parker considered. Finally, a wide grin spread across his face. "Deal."

Jason reached out to shake Parker's hand, but then thought better of it. "Okay, then." He stood up and walked across the room. "When do you want me to start?"

"Right now."

CHAPTER 13

PARKER

LONG GOLDEN HAIR FLASHED in a shaft of blinding light. Bobbing, ducking, weaving through the rain-soaked forest, Parker ran after the girl. Strength surged through him, burning with the intensity of a wildfire. He gathered his legs beneath him and leaped into the air in an explosion of terrifying power. The rush of wind, the blur of scratching branches, outstretched hands ripped the forest to shreds, the steel talons of a savage bird of prey.

He hit her hard, driving her to the moldering loam. Wild eyes flashed. Screams of terror. A tremor coursed through him, erupting in a wild exultant laugh. Power. Freedom. He clamped a blood-stained hand across the girl's face and pressed back her head to expose an ivory white neck. Opening his mouth wide, baring powerful, razor sharp teeth, he—

"Nooooooo!" Parker screamed, and the forest melted away like a dark mist, leaving him wet and cold. Trembling. "No, please, God . . ." He raised his hands to his face. Blinding light streamed through his fingers. Squinting into the tear-distorted haze, he examined his hands. He couldn't be sure, but there didn't seem to be any blood. No, of course not. It was all a dream. The result of too many horror films. His mom always said they would rot his brain.

He rolled his head to face away from the light. A blue blur lay right beside him, startlingly close. What was it? Fear rattled through him, a vision from the nightmares that still haunted his thoughts.

He blinked several times, brought a hand up to shield his face. The object came suddenly into focus. A ripped lampshade, the lamp from his living room. He searched frantically around him. Stuffing from a torn pillow, crushed flowers, broken glass, a wooden leg from his coffee table. He was in his living room. Lying in the middle of the floor. What was going on?

Hazy images crystallized into jagged shards of memory. The mice, Darcy, his lab . . . He'd taken the drug. He'd been crawling. Had he crawled all the way home? Shielding his eyes, he searched the room. The place was a wreck—the proverbial china cabinet after the bull. Rocking himself back and forth with his arms, he scissored his legs and pushed himself onto his stomach. His clothes were soaking wet. He must have wet himself during the night.

Darcy's face drifted like a phantom across his mind. He'd been walking with her, carrying her in his arms. . . . His stomach twisted. It was only a dream. He hadn't done any of those things. Not in reality. He lay facedown on the carpet, trying to sort out the torrent of emotions that raged inside him. If it was only a nightmare, why did he feel so guilty? Dirty. He'd been on the drug, adrenaline 355. It was the drug—not him.

Mighty Mouse. He tried pushing himself up from the floor. His arms felt stronger, but there was something missing. Some connection he still wasn't getting.

He rolled onto his back and looked around. The lamps were broken, the coffee table destroyed, the curtains hung in shreds above a broken window. Dim light filtered through the fronds of an Australian tree fern, illuminating the broken shards of glass with the pink glow of early morning sunlight.

A loud knock sounded at the door. The jangle of keys. A surge of exultation rose up in him as the door opened and Carol, his morning attendant, stepped into the room. "Good morn—" Her musical voice choked off as she took in the room. "Parker! Are you okay? What happened?" She was at his side in an instant, checking his pulse, inspecting his neck and arms for cuts, broken bones.

"Carol, I'm fine. Just help me off the floor."

"What happened? Was there a break-in?" She ran her fingers along his ribs. "Does this hurt? Any pain at all?" Blonde hair fell across her face. The smell of perfume, fragrant and heady.

"I'm . . . fine." Parker's face felt hot. A burning sensation deep inside him. A glowing coal, long buried beneath a mound of cold ash. "Please. I need some . . . space."

"Let me get you to the bathroom where we can get you cleaned up." She reached around his shoulders.

"No!" Parker's hands clamped around her wrists. A feeling of power surged into his arms. "Please, get away!"

"Parker." Carol drew back, her eyes wide. "What's gotten into you?"

"I . . ." Parker turned his head to face the wall. "I don't know, I just—"

A loud ring sounded from his bedroom. Darcy?

"Carol, please. Could you get the phone? I'm expecting a really important phone call."

Carol looked reluctantly toward the bedroom. Her expression was turned down in a disapproving frown.

"Please?"

"Okay." She hurried off to the bedroom. "Hello? No, this is Carol Benjamin. I'm Parker's nurse. Can I tell him who's calling?" Carol walked back into the room and handed Parker the phone. "Jason Shaniman. He says it's an emergency."

"Hello." Parker spoke over what sounded like a bumper-car rally on the other end of the phone.

"Parker . . ." Jason's breathless voice. "I just wanted to check. Make sure you're okay. I stopped by earlier, but—" The other end *whumphed* as Jason did something with the phone.

"Hello, Jason? Are you still there?"

Shouting voices. Clicking and banging. "Sorry about that, but we've got a bit of a situation here. We're in the animal room, and the Mighty Mice are going crazy."

"We?"

"Me and Ray. We thought we should check up on the mice from your experiment."

"And?" Parker put a hand to his ear. Carol was bending over a pile of glass, placing the shards in a trash can.

"It's the Mighty Mice. They got out of their cages, and they—"

"I know. The first mouse got out too."

"Parker, they're killing each other. I found three half-eaten mice on the animal room floor. They're totally berserk—worse than Chicago street rats." A loud clang sounded over the receiver. A shout. "Parker, I gotta go now. Glad you're doing okay."

Parker dropped the phone as the connection went dead. *"Worse than Chicago street rats."* A dark phantom brushed his mind. The image of fingers outspread like claws, rigid and covered in blood.

"Okay now. Let's get you cleaned up." Carol's face. A touch on his shoulder, soft and warm, radiating heat.

"Carol, please. Get away from me."

"What? What's wrong?" Shell-shocked eyes. Perplexed lips.

"Please. Just leave me alone. You've got to get out of here. Now!"

DARCY

Darcy guided the wheelchair down the crowded city sidewalk. How did Parker keep the ornery thing on the road? She stood in the grass next to the chair, waiting for an elderly couple to pass. Then, easing down on the joystick, she walked the chair forward to the next clump of pedestrians.

She stopped at an intersection and looked up and down the cross street, studying it carefully before venturing across. The chance of meeting the Dark Man in the middle of the morning was almost zero. She had nothing to worry about. As far as she knew, he didn't have any men working for him. The man in the elevator was probably just a friend. A fellow escapee from the paramilitary loony asylum.

Nobody was going to see her. It was just a quick visit. In and out. A chance to check in on Parker and make sure he was all right. Jason had said Parker was fine, better than ever, but something about the way he said it made her uneasy. She'd feel a lot better if she could see him herself. Besides, she couldn't leave without a proper good-bye. She had plenty of time. Her bags were packed and waiting. She'd be able to make the bus station with hours to spare.

She stopped at the next intersection. Dwight Way. If anyone followed her to Parker's apartment . . . If anything happened to him . . . she'd never forgive herself. She turned and studied the road behind her. A couple of undergrad-looking guys were walking down the street, backpacks slung over their shoulders. A redhead in dark glasses, tall and confident and dressed for business. Something in retail from the looks of her.

Darcy crossed the street at a jog, pushing the wheelchair ahead of her. Parker's apartment was just ahead. Apartment number three.

Just then the door opened and a woman with long blonde hair stepped out. Tall and slender with long, perfect legs. She stared as the woman turned down the sidewalk and hurried to her car. What was going on? She guided the chair forward and double-checked the name of the apartment building. Dwight Way Apartments. There had to be some mistake. She pulled Parker's card out of her pocket. Apartment number three. Could the card be out of date?

Darcy stepped slowly toward the door. Maybe she was just a friend of the family's—one of Jenny's friends. Or maybe she was a doctor making a house call. That had to be it. If Parker was hurt, he wouldn't have any other way to get to her office. She brushed back her hair and checked her face in the mirror of her compact before ringing the doorbell.

"Yes?" Parker's voice sounded on the other side of the door.

"Hi, Parker, it's Darcy."

Silence.

"I thought you might like to have your chair. In all the excitement last night we ended up leaving it on the sidewalk outside the chemistry building."

"Darcy, I . . . thanks for bringing it. I really appreciate it."

She waited, kicking at a weed growing up through the sidewalk. "Could I come in? I need to talk to you."

A muffled crash. The sound of breaking glass.

"Are you all right?" Darcy tried the door, but it was locked.

"I'm fine. Just knocked over a trash can."

A trash can? Made of glass? "Parker, what's going on? Do you need help? I could get the apartment manager to open the door."

"No!" Parker's voice was deeper now—the voice from last night. "Darcy, please . . . things are kind of strange now. I'm not feeling myself."

"What did the doctor say?"

"I haven't seen a doctor. I really don't think there's any need."

"The nurse?" She felt bad about pressing, but all of a sudden she had to know.

"I don't need a nurse either."

She closed her eyes and took a deep breath. Not a doctor, not a nurse. That left family friend, the kind that visited at 10:00 in the morning. "Parker, could I just come in? I really need to talk to you. It's not exactly something I can shout through the door."

"Darcy, I . . . I want to see you. I really do. More than anything else in the world. But I don't think it would be a good idea. Things are . . . changing. I'm changing."

Changing? Darcy couldn't believe this was happening to her. How many times had she heard this before? "Parker, I want to be your friend. Can't we talk about it?"

"I want to be your friend too. But I'm having these dreams. Everything's so . . . I don't know how to say it. I just don't think I should see you right now."

Dreams? A misty haze clouded Darcy's eyes. "Parker, I know about the blonde, and it's okay. I can deal with it." She paused, waiting for Parker to say something. Anything.

"The blonde? What blonde?"

"Parker, I've got to go away for a while." Darcy could barely get the words out. "I was hoping to be able to say good-bye. You're a special person. I want you to know I . . . admire you a lot. You're one of the best guys I've ever known."

"Darcy, I . . . I don't know what to say."

"Can't I just come in, just for three seconds?"

"Please . . ." She could hear his voice trembling through the door. "Please don't ask. Not now."

Darcy turned away, cheeks burning as if they'd just been slapped. "Good-bye, Parker."

"Maybe we could talk tomorrow? Maybe get something to eat?"

Tears streaming down her face, she walked down the sidewalk and crossed the street. Without looking back.

CHAPTER 14

PARKER

"**WOULD YOU HOLD STILL?** You're worse than the mice." Jason held Parker's wrist to his chair and jabbed a needle into his arm.

Parker felt his muscles tense as the drug spread through his veins. The jolt of electricity. The surge of power. His body shuddered, muscles clenching and unclenching, gasping to life after an eternity of slumber. Wave upon wave of exultation crashed over him. He was alive. Free!

Gradually, a strange presence reasserted itself in his mind, alien yet inexplicably familiar, like a long-lost friend after a sojourn in a foreign land.

"Come on, Parker! Focus. Stretch and relax, stretch and relax. Just like we've been practicing." Jason's face appeared before Parker's dazzled eyes. "There you go." He slid a pair of sunglasses over his eyes. "Stretch and relax, stretch and relax. That's it—the shaking's getting better. Good. Much better."

Parker concentrated on Jason's face, willing his gamboling muscles into synchrony. *Stretch and relax. Stretch and relax.* It was working. Control was returning.

"Good. Excellent. It's really working!" Jason's excitement set loose another burst of trembling. "Come on, Parker. You can do it. That's it."

Parker felt the tension easing, a redlined engine dropping back to idle. "Okay. I think I've got it."

"Good." Jason looked at his watch. "Only a hundred and twenty seconds. Another record! Ready to try the tests?"

Parker shook his head, felt the muscles in his neck and shoulders leap into action like a high-performance race car. "A few more minutes. The storm clouds are still circling my brain. Wouldn't want you to get hit by a lightning bolt."

"Okay, what time did you pass out last night?" Jason was taking notes in a lab notebook. "Did you look at a clock?"

"I'm not sure." Parker closed his eyes, trying to concentrate through the swirling storm. He'd waited too long the night before and ended up losing consciousness in the bathroom, so last night he'd gotten into bed at 10:00—as soon as he started feeling funny. "I'm guessing some time after ten o'clock. Maybe ten-thirty, ten-fifteen?"

"I'll put you down for ten-twenty. That makes it fourteen hours and ten minutes before blackout. You've been holding fairly steady at around fourteen hours. It doesn't seem to be increasing." He stepped out of Parker's bedroom and came back in with a set of five-pound dumbbells. "I'm going to start you off with the fives today. No point even bothering with the ones or threes."

Parker watched as Jason added the dumbbells to a long line of weights at the foot of his bed. He tried to focus on Jason's movements. Slowly the winds subsided, leaving behind a dark fog.

"Have you seen Darcy?" Parker finally broke down and asked the question he'd been avoiding for days. "I haven't heard a word from her. I must have left a hundred messages on her phone, but she hasn't even called."

Jason shrugged. "I wouldn't worry about it. She's a major flake. Probably holed up in some library somewhere, hiding out from the world."

"I'm worried about her. The last time I saw her she sounded so strange. She wanted to tell me something, but she wouldn't say what. When she left, she made it sound so final. Like she was afraid I wasn't going to make it."

"When?" Jason set the dumbbells down and turned to face him with intense eyes. "When did you see her?"

"Four days ago. The morning after I first took the drug." Parker studied Jason's expression. He could almost see the gears turning. "What's going on? There's something you're not telling me."

Jason turned back to the row of dumbbells. "She did the same thing when I was about to drive you here. The good-bye-forever thing. Said she'd always remember you."

"Always remember . . ." Parker wheeled his chair around and headed for the door.

"Parker, wait. We've still got to do the tests." Jason followed him into the living room. "Come on. We need this for the paper. Darcy's not worth it."

"Not worth it?" Parker opened the door and drove out into the bright sunlight. New energy flooded through him. Freedom! He felt like he was stepping out of a tomb.

"Come on, Parker. Darcy's a waste of time." Jason was still behind him, following him up the sidewalk. "I know her type. Running away as soon as things get a little scary. She's bad news. Just let her go."

Parker shook his head. "It's all my fault. I should have talked to her. I at least could have explained."

"Okay, have it your way." Jason called out from behind him. "I'll be at the lab if you want to talk—after she runs and leaves you high and dry."

Parker drove out onto the side of the road and pushed his joystick to the limit. Blinding sunlight washed past him in waves of green and gold. *Darcy*. Why hadn't he let her in? Was it such a shameful thing to have wet his pants? He'd been knocked out on the drug. It could have happened to anyone.

Visions of bloodstained fingers crowded into his brain. A living room ripped to shreds. Sure, nothing had been torn up since that first day, but the nightmares hadn't stopped. If anything, they'd gotten worse. More disturbing, more vivid, real. It was like puberty all over again. Puberty on steroids. He slowed his chair to a crawl and pulled back onto the sidewalk. Maybe it was still too early.

He stopped the chair, hesitating between faith and doubt, left and right. Then, turning to the left, he eased forward on his joystick and continued toward the campus. He'd been working hard. Making good progress. He'd be fine. He was getting better and better at keeping the new emotions under control. Besides, he had so much to tell her. So much to show her. She was going to be blown away.

Parker crossed the street and headed up Sproul Plaza. He just needed to explain why he hadn't been able to let her in. Tell her about the Mighty Mice going crazy. The nightmares. She'd understand. He'd been trying to protect her.

The closer he got to the chemistry building, the more nervous he became. A tremor ran down his arms, making his fingers play an imaginary concerto on the arms of his wheelchair. *Stretch and relax. Stretch and relax.* He rolled across the lobby and into a waiting elevator. Up to the third floor, down the hall. A burst of adrenaline quivered through his frame. *Darcy.* The hallway seemed to dim.

The door to her lab was shut. He knocked hard, taking pleasure in the sting of his knuckles. "Darcy! Are you there?" Not waiting for an answer, he tried the knob and threw the door open. "Darcy?" He drove inside, took in the lab in a glance. Something wasn't right. The benches were too clean. The equipment all put away.

Wheeling down the aisle, he headed straight for her desk. The desktop was clear, the backpack gone. Where were the pictures? The mirror on the side of her bookshelf? The books?

"Darcy!" Her name echoed off the walls.

Throwing open a desk drawer, he searched one drawer after another. Her stuff was all gone. "God, no! Please bring her back."

He rolled into the hot room. Searched the entire lab. Nothing. No notes, no telephone numbers, no forwarding address. She was gone. Completely and absolutely.

And it was all his fault.

He pushed out into the hall and took the elevator back down to the first floor. Bitterness and self-loathing burned inside him. If he had only taken the time to listen to her. She'd been trying to tell him something. Why couldn't he have just listened?

Bursting out into the sunlight, he circled around the chemistry building, wandering down sidewalk after sidewalk after sidewalk. She was gone. He should have realized. That's what she'd been trying to tell him. He swerved off the sidewalk and crackled across aromatic strips of bark. Stopping in the shade of a grove of eucalyptus trees, he buried his face in his hands and gave in to the circling blackness.

"Parker?" A still, soft voice. Just behind him, to the left.

Parker looked up, wiped a sleeve across his face. "Darcy?"

Her face was lit with an uncertain smile. She knelt down on the ground beside him, leaned against his wheel. "I saw you leaving the chemistry building. You looked upset. I thought maybe . . ."

"I was looking for you. I thought you'd . . . gone away."

Darcy nodded and looked down at his wheel. "I thought I was going to, but I couldn't. Not without saying good-bye."

"But all your stuff. I checked your lab. Everything's gone."

"All packed up and ready to go." The shadow of a smile touched her face. "But not gone yet."

"But why? Where are you going?"

"Someplace that's . . . not here. It's kind of complicated, and you're going to have to trust me on this. It's best that you don't know. Better for you and better for me."

Parker searched her eyes, saw the determination, the finality and . . . was there something else as well? "I'm really sorry about Sunday morning. I wanted to let you in, but I was afraid I might hurt you. I was still on the drug, and I didn't know what it was doing to me. I'd torn up the apartment. Had really terrible dreams."

"Afraid?" Her voice held a note of skepticism. "You weren't too afraid to let the blonde in."

"The blonde?" It took a second for Parker to figure out whom she meant. "My morning attendant? She let herself in. Jason called and told me about the Mighty Mice, and I sent her right back out. She wasn't inside but three minutes."

Darcy's eyebrows gathered in a frown. "What about the Mighty Mice?"

"He said they were totally berserk. Jumping around and killing each other like wild beasts."

"And you thought you"—her frown deepened to an expression of disbelief—"were going to do the same thing?"

"Kind of silly, huh?" A rush of warmth surged up Parker's neck. "You have to remember, though, the drug was totally messing with my brain. I wasn't thinking clearly. I hadn't gotten used to it."

Darcy nodded. A tender smile stole over her face. "I'm just glad you're okay. I was really worried about you."

"Sorry. I was worried about me too—for a while. But I'm better now. Better than ever."

She looked up into his eyes, studying him for several seconds. Her mouth opened and closed as if she wanted to say something. A tiny chink in her armor seemed to be opening.

Parker leaped at the opening. "Are you sure you have to go? Couldn't we just talk about it?" He took a deep breath. "If you left now, I'd have to live with soul-crippling regret for the rest of my life."

"What regret is that?"

"That I'd never gotten up the courage to ask you over for dinner when I had the chance." He searched her face, found the faintest trace of a smile. "Would you please? Let me fix you dinner? Tonight?"

She was considering it. He could see it in her eyes.

"Come on. Just one night. What could it hurt? Wherever you're going, it will still be there tomorrow, right? It can wait. You know it can. You wouldn't want me living with soul-crippling regret, would you?"

"Parker, you're so selfish. Some things are just more important." She shook her head, sadly it seemed. "Like the soul-crippling regret I'd feel if I missed out on your cooking. Did you ever consider that?" Her face lifted in a mischievous smile. "I'd love to have dinner with you. Just name the time and tell me what I can do to help."

DARCY

Darcy ran down the sidewalk, sweeping the dark streets with her eyes. For a second she thought she'd heard something. The faintest scrape of a shoe over cement. It was probably just her imagination, though. If someone had tried to follow her from the chemistry building, she would have lost him long ago. Nobody could have made it through the alley and over the fence without her hearing him—even the Dark Man, with all his paramilitary mumbo jumbo and midnight maneuvers. Before the accident, she'd seen him several times, slinking along dark alleys, running like G.I. Joe across Telegraph Avenue. He'd been far from silent then and he'd only be noisier now.

She turned at Parker's building and hurried down the narrow walk that led to his apartment. Deep breaths, nice and slow. She had to get hold of herself. Stepping up to the door, she rang the doorbell right away, before she could change her mind.

"Come in. It's open!" Parker's muffled voice.

Darcy tried the knob. "Parker?" She pulled back on the door and a cloud of spice hit her in the face, burning her eyes and tickling at the back of her throat.

"What are you cooking?" She called back to the tiny kitchenette. "Pepper spray?"

Parker was locked in heated battle with a frying pan on the stove. Wielding a spatula like a sword, he stabbed at the hissing pan, a valiant knight subduing a fire-breathing dragon. "Sorry. Tactical error." He turned slightly in his wheelchair. "Word to the wise. Never chop fresh jalapeños in a food processor." He nodded toward the sofa and faced off against the stove. "Have a seat. I can't leave these onions or they'll over-burn."

Darcy nodded and continued to watch him cook. His hands were still shaking. Why hadn't she noticed before? It had been five days and he still hadn't recovered from the drug. Could it have done permanent damage? Surely he would have said something, unless of course he blamed her. If she hadn't abandoned him, he never would have tried the drug on himself. She wouldn't have let him.

"Can I do something to help?" She stepped into the kitchen, wiping her eyes as a fresh blast of spice hit her in the face.

"Burning the onions?" Parker grinned and waved a wooden spatula at the sofa. "I think I've got it pretty much covered."

"Seriously, what can I do? Put me to work."

"I intend to. I'm leaving you the hardest part—next to having to actually eat my cooking. Go ahead. Have a seat. I'll let you know when it's your turn at bat."

"Okay . . ." Darcy turned, looking around the room. It didn't look at all like what she'd expected. Fresh-cut flowers filled several large vases in the living room. Matted Renoir prints, a matching sofa and chairs, pillows in blues and greens. And everything looked new, even the carpet.

A chirp sounded from the kitchen. "Hello, Mom?" Parker held his cell phone to his ear. "Can you hold just a second?" He turned to Darcy with an apologetic smile. "Go ahead and have a seat. Dinner's almost done."

Darcy lowered herself onto the sofa, and the scent of new fabric puffed up around her. It really was a new sofa. She ran her hand across the carpet. The carpet too. Why would he remodel his apartment at a time like this? She watched as he stirred a pot on the back burner. She could see the reflection of a creamy sauce in an angled mirror mounted under the fume hood. He seemed to be doing fine. Apparently, she'd been worrying for nothing.

"What do you mean, you got the time wrong?" Parker dropped the spoon on the counter and switched off one of the burners. "How am I supposed to cook it eight minutes less? . . . I don't have time. She's already here."

"Okay, okay." Parker turned to Darcy and rolled his eyes. "Mom says hi and wants me to tell you she's a better cook than I am and we should both go to San Francisco for something edible." He held the phone to his chest. "Between you and me, I think she's sabotaging my meal on purpose. She's been on my case to bring you back ever since Thanksgiving. I think she likes you better than me."

"Of course she does." Darcy forced a smile. His mom had been wonderful. What must she be going through now? "Maybe we should—if it's burned that bad."

"Bad? It's burned to perfection." Parker uncovered a pot and held it to his nose. "In some parts of the world, smoked rice is a delicacy."

Darcy's eyes shifted to the other pots on the stove and countertop. She would have liked to see Parker's mom and dad again, but he'd gone to so much effort. Besides, who would drive the van? "Tell your mom I'll take a rain check. Okay?"

"Mom?" He held the phone back to his ear. "Darcy says she likes my cooking way better than yours. She's still trying to recover from your Thanksgiving dinner. Had to have her stomach pumped three times."

"Parker!" Darcy charged the kitchen and reached for the phone. "Let me have that."

"Oops. Gotta go. Time to check the vindaloo. Bye." Parker switched off the phone and stashed it in his pocket. "Mom sends her love." He looked up at her with a mischievous grin. "And Dad says you owe him a rematch. He's hurt you haven't visited yet."

"Of course he is. He likes me better than you too." Darcy felt herself starting to relax. Shakes or no shakes, he was still the same old Parker. "So, what can I do to help?"

"I could use some help checking the vindaloo." Parker opened the oven and looked inside. A foil-covered casserole dish took up the entire middle rack. "Could you pull that out and set it on the counter?" He handed her two mitts and arranged three hot pads on the counter.

"Sure." Darcy put the mitts on and pulled the glass dish from the oven. "I know I'm a pig, but don't you think this is a little much for the two of us?"

"My mom's recipe. She subscribes to the one-meal-a-week school of cooking. She and Dad will be eating turkey till Christmas."

"And cranberries. I know how much your dad likes cranberries." Darcy set the dish on the hot pads and peeled back a corner of the foil. A blast of steam hit her in the face with a spicy, vinegary smell that made her mouth water. "This looks good. What did you say it was?"

"Chicken vindaloo. It's Portuguese-Indian-Dakotan," Parker said. "Jason mentioned you like spicy food."

"Dakotan?" Darcy quirked an eyebrow.

"Dad perfected the recipe. He grew up in North Dakota."

Darcy nodded. *Chicken vindaloo.* The name sounded familiar—like something out of an Indian fairy tale. "Okay, now what? What do you need me to do next?"

Parker poked a potato with a fork. "Nothing. It's all done. Help me serve the plates and we can start eating."

Darcy glared at him. "I thought you said you needed help."

"I did." Parker pulled a pot off the stove and started scooping rice onto two plates. "If you hadn't pulled the vindaloo out of the oven, we would have starved. I couldn't have managed it at all. It was hard enough getting it in when it was cold. You should have seen me. I looked like a Chinese acrobat."

"Well, if that's all you need, feel free to call on me anytime." Darcy helped him scoop baby asparagus onto the plates.

"Really?" Parker held her with wide, piercing eyes. "I thought you had to go someplace that's not here."

"I guess that depends on the meal." Darcy smiled and stared boldly back. Something about his eyes. The way he looked at her, like she was more than just a midnight snack. Was it the MD that made him so different, or was it just him?

"Are you serious?"

Darcy jumped back, suddenly aware of how close they had drifted. "I'm sorry. What were you saying?"

"Are you serious about staying?" His voice was little more than a whisper.

"Well . . ." She turned to face the counter and took a deep breath. "Let's eat dinner first. If I only have to get my stomach pumped twice, then maybe we can work something out."

"In that case, want to go out to dinner tomorrow night? I'm pretty sure you'll still be in town." Parker rolled up beside her and started splashing the asparagus with a salmon-colored sauce. She leaned against the counter and watched him serve a mix of what looked like lentils and chick-peas. His hands were still shaking, but his eyes were steady and radiant. Silence thickened around her. She stepped back to take it all in. He was gorgeous. How had she not seen it before?

"How tall are you?" The question was out of her mouth before she knew she was even thinking it.

"Five-foot-one, sitting up straight." Parker stared back at her with an intensity that made her blush. Did he know what she was thinking?

She cracked open a tiny pot and peeked inside. "This looks good. Did you make it from scratch?" Picking up a spoon, she added big blobs of mango chutney to their plates.

"Six-foot-three."

"What?" The lid of the pan slipped from Darcy's fingers and landed with a clatter on the stove top.

"That's how tall I am standing up." Parker's voice sounded behind her. "Why do you ask?"

"I don't know. You just seem tall, that's all." Darcy settled the lid back on the pan. "This is a ton of food. I hope there isn't anything else. The plates won't hold much more."

"There's a salad on the table. Could you help me with the plates?"

Darcy picked up the plates and followed Parker to a small round table with candles and a white tablecloth. She set the plates at each setting, feeling suddenly awkward. "You know, this fancy crystal is pretty intimidating for someone used to eating ramen out of a Pyrex beaker."

"Sorry." Parker looked down at the table. "I was afraid the meal wouldn't turn out, and I guess I . . . overcompensated."

Darcy sat down in the chair opposite Parker. She looked down at her plate, waiting for Parker to make the first move.

"Father God, thank you so much for this food. Please help it to be edible."

Darcy looked down at her lap as soon as she realized what Parker was doing.

"And thank you especially for the chance to share it with such a good friend. Amen."

"Amen." Darcy waited for Parker to take the first bite. "Did it work? Is it edible?"

"It's a miracle." Parker laughed. "Even with Mom's attempt at sabotage, it's a one stomach-pumper meal."

Darcy tasted the vindaloo and grabbed her glass of water. It was a little spicy, but the flavor was incredible. She tasted the asparagus and the raita and chick-peas. "I'm impressed. This is really good. I'll take dishes out of the oven for you any day."

"Careful, I'll take you up on that." Parker smiled. A piercing look that made the color rise to her cheeks.

She took another bite of vindaloo and stole a quick glance at him. He seemed to be managing fairly well, even with the tremors. Thanksgiving dinner was probably just a bad day for him. "So, what's the next step in your research?"

"The next step?" Parker looked puzzled.

"I've been thinking . . . just because Mighty Mouse didn't pan out doesn't mean you're not close. You could do some docking studies. Start testing derivatives of the original adrenaline compound."

Parker shrugged. "I guess I haven't thought much about it."

Haven't thought much about it? Darcy couldn't believe her ears. Surely he wasn't giving up. Unless . . . "Parker, is Jenny . . . okay?"

He nodded. "Actually she's a lot better. She was in ICU for a while, but now they're talking about moving her back home."

"Really? That's wonderful. Why didn't you tell me?"

"You weren't around." Parker's tone wasn't accusing, but Darcy felt guilty just the same.

"I'm sorry," Darcy said. "I didn't mean to abandon you. It's just that I . . ."

"Go on."

Darcy felt her face heating up again. "Nothing. I'm . . . really, it's nothing."

"Darcy, it's okay." Parker reached across the table and took her by the hand. His hands were warm—almost hot. Their trembling reminded her of the rumble of her dad's old Mercedes diesel. He leaned in close, looked her in the eye. "Tell me. What were you going to say? I can take it. I'm a lot stronger than I look."

"It's not about you, it's . . ." Darcy's voice caught in her throat. She couldn't tell him, not now, she just couldn't. But what could she say? "Parker, I . . . I guess with all the pressure and Jenny in the hospital . . . well, I don't do death very well. After my mother and father died, then there was my grandfather and grandmother and Mrs. Simmons. It seems like everybody I've ever been close to has died."

"And you were worried I was going to die." Parker's voice was gentle. Something about it reminded her of her father. The way he talked when he held her on his lap.

"It's not that. I was thinking about your sister."

Parker shut his eyes. After a long pause, he nodded. "We're all going to die. In a way, Jenny and I have been lucky. We both grew up understanding and accepting our mortality. We never had to go through the pain of the 'immortal stage.' The reality of death puts life in perspective. Concentrates it. Distills it. I love life. I learned early on to appreciate things that most people never even notice. The thrill of watching an ant walk across a sidewalk. The glory of a beautiful woman's smile. Even pain. Everything has a reason."

He looked up and stared at her. His eyes shown like twin moons, electrifying the air between them. He bore his burden with such grace. It was so unfair.

"I . . ." Her voice shook. "I admire your attitude, but pain's a hard one for me. I just don't know."

"What?" He squeezed her hands. "What don't you know?"

"My grandmother was a good Christian lady. Sweet, kind, loving. But before she died she developed Alzheimer's." Darcy closed her eyes. She could still hear her grandmother's shrill voice. "All of a sudden she was a terror. Where's the soul in that? In the end chemistry won out. It always wins out."

Parker held her gaze for a breathless minute. "Don't you believe in God?"

She looked down at her plate. She could still remember what it felt like, the happiness, contentment—the warmth of her father's encircling arms. "Sometimes I wish I didn't, but I don't seem to have a choice."

"But why? Why would you not want to believe in God?"

"There's no way you could even understand. He's not out to get *you*." She looked down at her plate, searching for the words. "Let's just say that I believe in God, but He doesn't believe in me. Not anymore. I haven't exactly been giving Him a reason to."

"That's impossible. I'm not God, and I . . ." His voice faded into a look of such sadness. She had to look away.

"Darcy, you're a biologist. You know how important pain is. It's what keeps us safe. It drives us away from what's bad for us—toward what's good for us. But if you think God's out to get you, you'll always run in the wrong direction, back into more pain. Maybe that's why life has been so hard for you."

Darcy shrugged. "Or maybe I'm just being punished."

Parker shook his head. "Life doesn't work that way. Don't you know how the story ends? It's *happily ever after*. Everything working together for good. Diseases, Jenny going to the hospital, getting attacked by glass-heads . . . In the end it's all good. Like the MD. I always believed God made me smart for a reason. I was so confident I was put on earth to invent a cure for my disease. I was so sure He'd lead me to the answer."

Was. Past tense. A lump formed in Darcy's throat. Tears blurred her vision. He sounded like he was giving up. After six years of research he was finally quitting. She clung to Parker's hands, pressed them to her lips. "Parker, I'm so sorry. Sorry I wasn't there. I won't run away again. I promise."

"Darcy, it's okay."

"No, it's not." She could feel tears stinging her cheeks. "Parker, I want to be here for you. I can help with your experiment. Even if I have to drop out of the biochemistry program."

"Darcy, listen to me. I'm fine. I've been taking the drug."

"You what?" Darcy pulled away. Swiped a hand across her face.

"Ever since Saturday night. Adrenaline 355 and aminolevulinate. I've been taking it."

"Parker, no. You can't. It's not safe. You could be . . ."

"It's okay." Parker braced a hand against the wall. "I wanted it to be a surprise." A faint tremor ran through his body, and his face tightened with concentration. Slowly, he rose up out of his wheelchair. His legs bobbed and pulsed beneath him, but not from weakness.

He was standing.

CHAPTER 15

PARKER

DARCY'S LAUGHTER THRILLED THROUGH Parker's senses. The room was awash with her presence. Beautiful, intoxicating, dazzlingly bright. Words bubbled out of her with joyful abandon, dimpling the corners of her mouth with an ironic smile. Silliness tempered with thought. Joy anchored by a slender thread of serious purpose that he couldn't begin to fathom.

A tendril of hair fell across her cheek. Burnished bronze against a pool of liquid gold. She glowed in the candlelight. He ached to reach out, to smooth back the hair, to trace a finger across the contours of her face. The ache grew in intensity. Deep, bone-crushing pain, working its way back from his fingertips. He could feel the darkness stirring inside him, seeping through cracks in his consciousness, groping, spreading, polluting the golden light with cloying blackness.

Darcy's face filled his vision, vivid and startlingly close. The sound of his name. She was repeating it over and over. He could feel the softness of her breath. The tingle of her hair on his cheek. *His* cheek.

"Are you okay? Parker?"

He reached up with his hand. The tingle of cascading light flowing across his fingertips. Gently, reverently, he touched the strands of hair to his lips. Its clean freshness blew through him like a spring breeze. Cold, bracing, pushing back the darkness like the early morning dew.

"Parker, answer me. What's happening? Do you feel sick?"

He squeezed his eyes shut and took a deep breath. *God, please. Help me.* He rapped his knuckles against the arm of his chair, focusing on the pain. "I'm fine." He opened his eyes and tried to smile. "Just fell asleep for a second. It's not you—it's the drug. It's great for about thirteen hours, but then I crash hard. I don't think my body's used to all the exertion. I'm exhausted."

"And here I am rattling away like a ditzy airhead. Sometimes I can be so clueless." Darcy stepped back, leaving a sense of loss and emptiness in her wake. "I should let you get some rest."

"No. It's okay, really. I was just a little drowsy. Too happy and content."

Darcy shot him a hard look. Her wide eyes reflected golden flames beneath finely arched eyebrows.

"Seriously, this was the best night of my life. I've been . . ." A lump formed in his throat at the smile that spread over her features. "For years I've been looking forward to this day—to being able to walk again. It's been my life's work, my dream, my calling. But now that it's finally happened, it barely seems to matter. Everything else pales compared to being with you."

Parker's breath caught in his chest as he watched Darcy's face, searching for traces of embarrassment or displeasure. Her eyes took on a faraway expression and her lips parted. He'd blown it. It was too early. He shouldn't have said anything.

"Parker." A soft smile suffused her features. "That's the nicest thing . . ." Her voice quivered. "That's the nicest thing anyone has ever said to me."

"Sorry if it's not what you wanted to hear. But it's true. I had to let you know."

"Thank you." She took a step toward him, hesitated. Her hand stole to the side of her face, brushed back her hair. "I—"

"I know you need to get home." Parker turned his chair to face the door. "May I walk you?"

"No, I . . ." Darcy's expression seemed to freeze, then slowly, as if she were locked in a great internal battle, her features softened and she nodded her head. "Thanks. I'm going back to the lab but I'd . . . like the company."

"Oh no. It's late." Parker looked at his watch. "I'm sorry. I totally forgot about your prelims."

"That's okay." Darcy grabbed her jacket off the sofa. "I haven't given them a second's thought. Dinner was so nice, you drove them completely from my mind."

Parker rolled to the door and held it open for Darcy. He watched her step outside, wondering if she'd noticed how easy it was for him to turn doorknobs now. She smiled shyly at him as he caught up with her and started in the direction of the campus. She walked quietly at his side, keeping to the edge of the sidewalk to give him room to maneuver around bumps and holes in the cement.

"So how far can you walk?" Darcy finally broke the silence.

"This morning I walked to the bathroom and back without falling once." He looked up at her for a reaction.

"Amazing." Her eyes were wide with excitement. "I can't believe it!"

"I have the strength to go farther," Parker blinked his eyes, trying to push back the exhaustion that was stealing over him. "It's just a matter of balance. The muscles in my legs want to fire in bursts. If I lose concentration for a second, I end up jumping around like a grasshopper."

"Think it's the same thing that causes the shaking?"

Shaking? Think it's the thing? Parker repeated the words over and over in his mind, trying to make sense of them. *The jumping and shaking.* "Probably," he answered. "Both seem better. I think I'm learning to control it. Maybe my brain—"

"Shhh . . ." Darcy stopped suddenly with upraised hand.

Parker turned with a gasp. Her face glowed by the light of a misty moon. She looked so good. An angelic being straight from the presence of God. He was unclean. Wretched through and through. He could feel the darkness seeping into his skin. Burrowing deep inside him. Finding refuge. Sanctuary. A dark cathedral filled with blood-red pews.

" . . . hear me? Parker?"

"What?"

"Come on. We've got to hurry." Darcy was several steps ahead of him.

Parker hurried to catch up with her. "What were you listening to?"

"It seriously wasn't anything." Darcy's words were clipped. "I guess I'm just paranoid these days."

Glass-heads. Parker urged his chair forward. Faster. *"I thought I heard something, but it was just a car."* Darcy's voice crept out of his memory.

" . . . but now I don't know what to do." Darcy's face twisted and stretched. A drop of food-coloring in a glass of water.

Parker pounded his knuckles against the plastic arm of his chair. Pain was an anchor. He had to hold on. A shadowy darkness pressed down on him. Choking, suffocating, overpowering him with its vastness.

"What do you think?" Darcy was walking beside him. They were already in the middle of campus and coming up on the chemistry complex.

"What do I think?" Parker tried desperately to recall her words. "Actually, I . . ." A sudden awareness warned him to silence. "Actually, I think we should talk tomorrow. When we have more time." The words spilled out before he'd decided what to say. "Want to mcct in your lab? You helped me with my research. Now I'd like to . . ." Blackness. The words left him. *Return the favor.* He tried to form his mouth around the words, but . . . She was so beautiful.

"Okay." Darcy smiled. Her lips were moving but she wasn't making a sound. Moving. She was moving toward the glass doors, a light blur against the dark, retreating, getting smaller.

The plan! He was supposed to stand up and give her a hug before saying good-bye. He tried to run after her, but blackness pinned him to his chair. A soft moan sounded in the shadows. A dark presence flickering at the edge of his awareness. The white blur gradually faded. Smaller and smaller until all was black.

DARCY

Tattered ribbons of fog streamed across the light of a full moon, painting Sproul Plaza in a wash of shifting shadows. Dried leaves skittered across the sidewalk, clamoring in angry protest against the cold, intolerant wind. Darcy looped an elbow through the straps of her gym bag and draped her towel over her head. The towel was still damp from her shower, but at least it blocked the wind. A little. She folded it in thirds and pulled it tighter over her ears.

A muffled noise spun her around. The plaza was deserted. Of course it was. It was just the wind. It was late. She'd taken a lot longer at the gym than she'd intended, but dinner with Parker had left her way too keyed up to sleep and way too vindaloo-smelling to meet him in the morning without first taking a shower.

Parker . . . He had finally done it. She still couldn't believe it. It was like a real-life fairy tale, complete with fairy godmothers and superhero mice. And she'd been so worried about him—the rat. All that time she'd been torturing herself and he'd been getting better. She should be furious, but all she could think of was him standing proud and tall at the table, a broad smile lighting up his face like the Fourth of July.

She still couldn't get over the difference it made. He seemed so confident, strong and self-assured. All that from a slight change of perspective. Looking down at the world rather than looking up. And looking up at him felt good. It wasn't so much that he was better looking now. His looks hadn't changed. But he was more . . . What? Imposing? Impressive? No, it was more fundamental. He was more . . . *masculine.* She didn't like admitting it, but that's what it was. Strong. Slightly threatening.

Soon he'd be able to walk, do his own research, play sports, drive a car. Everything was changing. She could already feel it. He was turning into a . . . guy. The thought about made her sick to her stomach. Not that he wasn't a guy already. That wasn't it at all. He was just so different from most other guys. The way he talked to her, showing genuine interest in what she was feeling. The way he looked at her. Give without take. Sight without bite.

If only he could stay like he was. Sweet. Innocent. But that probably wasn't possible. She could already picture him walking across the campus. A sea of mascaraed eyes would follow him everywhere he went. Everywhere he turned, he'd be swarmed by dozens of insatiable co-eds. They'd eat him alive.

Darcy jogged up the steps past Sather Tower. Not that she wasn't happy for him. She really was. But it wasn't fair. No one had even looked twice at him when he was in a wheelchair. No one but her. But now, even if she ever wanted to be more than friends, how could she? Parker would think she was just like the others, that she'd never been able to see him past the chair.

She ran up the hill, following University Drive up to the chemistry complex. The hulking buildings loomed ahead like a dark stain against the eastern sky. Dark? That was odd. Not a single light was on in any of the buildings. All the good little grad boys and girls were home and snug in their beds. Where she would be if she hadn't made such a complete mess of her life. She looked at her watch again. Parker was supposed to meet her at nine o'clock. She should get some sleep.

She slowed to a walk at the entrance to the underground auditorium and turned left toward the main entrance of the chemistry building. The walkway was uncharacteristically dark. The lights that normally burned in the lobby were off. Was there a power outage? She fumbled through her gym bag, feeling for the spiral coil attached to her keys. Something crunched under her feet. Broken glass? She hopped aside and her feet landed with a grinding scrape. More broken glass. What was going on? She squatted down and examined the ground. The walk was covered with shards of splintered moonlight. Too flat for chemistry glassware. A broken window?

A muffled crash sounded all around her. Darcy sprang to her feet, searching the gap between the two buildings. Had the sound come from inside the chemistry building or was it behind her? Either way, it was probably best not to wait around to find out. She stepped toward the doors, groping for a handle. Her right hand found a glass wall, but her left hand passed completely through the door, tipping her off-balance. A shard of glass cut into her shin as she caught herself on the metal frame of the door. The glass had been shattered.

An angry cry pierced the night, shrill and inhuman. Darcy leaped through the door, lifting her legs to clear the jagged shards of glass. The elevators. She ran for the twin points of light and pressed both buttons. Another cry, a strange laugh. The lobby exploded with the crash of shattering glass. Darcy tore across the lobby, scrambled up the stairs. If only the elevators would open!

A resounding boom sounded behind her, hollow and metallic. Something hitting the elevator doors. Suddenly the stairs dropped away from her, and she fell crashing onto the landing. Before she could climb to her feet, a loud thud sounded on the steps below her. No time. She rolled to the side and pressed herself against the wall, huddling in a tiny ball, fighting to control her gasping breath.

Footsteps on the landing now. A gravelly wheeze, a wolfish growl. A dark shadow moved past her. Massive, filling the landing. *God help me!* Darcy held her breath. *Help me. Please, don't let it hear me.*

It was right next to her. Undulating, constantly moving. She could feel air wafting against her cheeks. Sudden movement. A fluttering sound and another crash halfway up the stairs. Darcy hugged her knees to her chest, trying to smother the fire that burned in her lungs. Another crash, higher up. Another. Whatever it was, it was almost two flights up. She opened her mouth wide and took a gentle, shallow breath. Her lungs still burned. She needed more air. Needed it soon.

The crashing on the stairs stopped. Suddenly she could hear herself breathing in desperate, trembling gasps. Another thud, this time it was closer. Darcy sprang up and clambered down the stairs. She ran blindly across the lobby and slammed into the opposite wall. Trailing her hand across the smooth surface, she felt her way to the left. Where was it? Had she missed it in the dark? The ladies' room should be somewhere—

A loud smack sounded behind her. Somewhere near the bottom of the stairs. She felt frantically along the wall. Heavy footsteps. It was getting closer. There! Darcy's hand closed around the door handle. Slowly, she pulled it open. One inch. Two inches. Antiseptic air felt cool on her face. Three inches.

The hinges emitted a high-pitched squeak, and the hall was filled with the flutter of sudden motion. Darcy flung open the door and darted inside. Throwing herself to the floor, she army-crawled across cold damp tiles. The stalls should be right ahead of her. Where were they?

A boom shook the room. Another. It was trying to break the door down. Darcy lunged forward and hit her head. Something smooth and cold.

A splintering crash. The shriek of twisting metal. Darcy could hear the breathing again. Footsteps echoed in the bathroom. She pulled her legs up under her and crouched next to the cold porcelain of a toilet.

The stall surrounds shuddered as a large body brushed by. A loud clang and a heavy panel slammed down on the top of Darcy's head, driving her to the floor. Something was on top of her, pinning her down. She twisted onto her hands and knees, tried to crawl out from under the debris. Suddenly a massive weight crushed down on her shoulders, pressing her to the floor. The panel on her back shook. She could feel its weight shifting. A sudden surge and it was gone. Behind her. It was attacking another stall. With what? A sledge hammer? She wriggled her way out from under the wreckage, keeping close to the toilets that supported the heavy boards.

The sound of destruction echoed all around her. This was her chance. She crawled across the floor, angling toward the rectangle of lesser darkness that marked the bathroom entrance. Keeping to her hands and knees, she made her way out into the lobby.

A bestial roar sounded behind her. The sound of breaking glass. Darcy leaped to her feet and ran. Through the lobby, out the door, she raced down the sidewalk and out into the night.

It was after her. It could hear her. She fled up a walkway and dodged around a row of cars. Veering off the sidewalk and leaping a flower bed, she ran for the dark, wooded section of campus. Footsteps sounded behind her. Breathing all around. She had to hide. A dark flower bed. A bush at the base of a tree. Still she kept running. Her chest burned. She couldn't breathe, couldn't see through the fog that swirled inside her head. It was there, somewhere. Waiting, observing. She could feel the weight of its eyes. Waiting until she couldn't run anymore. Then it would pounce. From behind that gate. From the shadow of that door.

Darcy's ankle twisted and she went down, collapsing in a heap on the sidewalk. Searching the street behind her, she rolled onto the street and into the shadow of a parked car. It was behind her, somewhere. She crawled under the car and waited, letting her mind go numb with the wash of oxygen in her lungs. Gradually her thoughts began to clear. She had lost it—back at the chemistry building. She was safe. It couldn't have followed her.

She crawled out from under the car and climbed to her feet. She walked painfully to the shadow of the nearest building and turned to survey the neighborhood. Nice trees, upscale flats. A rustic brown apartment building. She was in Parker's neighborhood! How. . . ?

Edging along the side of the apartment building, she crossed the street at the corner. There it was. Parker's place. She limped to his door and pushed the doorbell.

"Parker! It's me, Darcy!" She beat against the wooden door with her fists.

Slumping against the door, she slid down its polished surface. Either he was sound asleep or he couldn't get up. Either way, it was going to be a long, long night.

CHAPTER 16

PARKER

A SUFFOCATING SHADOW MELTED AWAY, black and icy, like an early winter wave on a broad and desolate beach. Gleaming sand burned white-hot in the early morning sun. A flock of dark gulls. The lingering echo of a high-pitched scream.

Parker squinted against the shimmering light. Its brilliance stabbed through him. Head, neck, hands—his whole body throbbed with pain. He turned away from the light, and a dozen tiny needles poked him in the face. *Grass?* He forced his eyes open. A wide grassy lawn. He was lying facedown in it. He tried to move a hand, but his arm flashed out in pain.

What was going on? His hand felt stiff and hot, like it was in some kind of a cast. Gritting his teeth against the pain, he brought it closer to his face. His knuckles were swollen. Dried blood covered the back of his hand. *Great.* He'd had an accident, had fallen out of his wheelchair. Somewhere.

Shielding his eyes, he searched the surrounding area. Shrubs, grass, trees. The rim of a cement sidewalk shone in the sun at the top of a shallow rise. He was on campus. But how. . . ?

Darcy. He'd been walking her home and . . . he must have had another blackout. That had to be it. But where was his chair?

He dragged himself toward the sidewalk. His arms and legs ached, but at least he could move them. Even after the drug had worn off, he could still feel its effects. He was getting a little stronger. At the top of the hill he held himself up off the ground and looked around for his wheelchair, turning himself from one side to the other. It was nowhere in sight. The realization left him feeling weak and sick.

He flopped back down on the grass. Someone had stolen his chair. Thirty thousand dollars down the tube. It might be weeks, months, before he could get a replacement.

Footsteps approached from the left. Someone walking on the sidewalk. A tall guy in a leather jacket. Parker pushed himself up onto his elbows. "Excuse me. Hello. Sir?"

The man kept walking. Parker watched him go, too stunned to call out after him. He'd obviously seen Parker. He had gone out of his way to pass by on the other side of the walk.

A few minutes later and another guy walked up from the other direction. He was wearing a blindingly white shirt. "Excuse me, but do you happen to have a cell phone on you? Someone stole my wheelchair." Parker blurted out the words while the guy was still ten feet away.

"Sure, I guess." He eyed Parker warily before handing him his phone. "Do you know how to use it?"

"It's just like mine." Parker took the offered phone and dialed Darcy's number. "Don't worry, it's a local number." He waited five rings and hit the Clear button. "My friend's not there. Mind if I try another number?"

"No problem." The man seemed to relax a little. "Mind me asking what happened? Looks like you got pretty banged up."

"Fell out of my chair." Parker turned his arm to examine the scrape on the back of his hand. A ragged cut marked where his hand had hit the sidewalk. He'd probably run off the edge of the walk and been dumped out. He punched in Jason's number and hit Send. "To be honest I'm not sure I know exactly how. I was on my way home last night and blacked out. When I woke up it was morning, and—"

The phone picked up on the other end. "Hello?" Jason sounded angry.

"Jason. It's Parker."

"Parker? Do you have any idea what time it is?"

"Listen, I'm sorry to call so early but I need your help."

Parker gave Jason a quick rundown of his situation, leaving out any mention of Darcy or the drug. The guy in white stared down the sidewalk, but Parker could tell he was hanging on every word. When Parker finally hung up, he handed back the phone and the man hurried off, claiming to be late for a meeting.

Parker stretched out on the ground, shutting his eyes against the glaring light. His hands and arms throbbed. His back ached. What had he been thinking? If he had passed out on the road, if a group of glass-heads had found him . . . He was lucky he hadn't been killed.

Things were happening way too fast. Darcy, the drug, Jenny. He felt like his life was flying out of control. He needed to slow down, to stop and think things through. He needed another dose of the drug. Just one more to build his strength, to clear his mind. Yes, he needed the drug. With his chair gone he needed it now more than ever.

Parker heard Jason's stumbling footsteps while he was still twenty yards off. Unshaven, blurry eyes, hair poking everywhere but up, he looked like a '70s rock star. He broke into a shuffling jog when he saw Parker. "I hate to break it to you, partner, but I've seen prettier morning faces at my grandma's nursing home. You look terrible."

"You should talk," Parker said. "At least I have an excuse."

"Are you hurt?"

"I ran off the sidewalk and took a pretty bad spill." Parker held out his hand to show Jason. "Serves me right for not wearing my seatbelt."

Jason was silent for several seconds. "So how am I supposed to get you back to your apartment? I'm not going to be able to carry you—not the way you've been packing on the weight."

"Get the drug. I've got a vial in freezer two. Syringes and needles are in the second drawer down from the hood."

"Why didn't you tell me before? I could have swung by the lab and saved a trip."

"There was a guy here listening," Parker said. "I know it's a pain, but believe me, I'd be happy to do it myself if I could. I'd be overjoyed."

"Sorry, I didn't mean to—"

"It's okay . . . partner. Thirty minutes after taking our drug, I'll be walking back to my apartment with you."

"Really? You really think you can walk that far?"

"Maybe, with a little help." Parker pushed up on his elbows and nodded back to the base of the hill. "I crawled all the way up the hill. And that was *without* the drug."

"In that case, hold on and I'll be right back." Jason set off for the chemistry building.

Parker squinted after him, then, patting his pockets with both hands, he felt for his sunglasses. For some reason his eyes were still light sensitive, even when the drug had worn off. He wondered how long the effect would last if he stopped taking the drug—not that he was considering stopping. All things considered, wearing sunglasses was a small price to pay for living to see thirty. Even the blackouts.

"Hey, Parker! I found it!"

Parker swiveled around, shielding his eyes with a swollen hand.

Jason was walking next to the sidewalk, pushing Parker's wheelchair in front of him. "It was just around the corner of Gilman. Tipped on its side next to the construction trailers." He stopped the chair. "Think you walked all the way here? That's at least thirty yards."

"Maybe." Parker shrugged. "Let's get some Mighty Mouse in me and see what I can do."

Jason helped Parker into the chair and they walked around Gilman. Jason's step was light. Springy as a cat's. "How many people do you think have muscular dystrophy? A hundred, maybe two hundred thousand worldwide?"

"Any form?" Parker waited for Jason's nod. "Over a million in the United States alone."

"Wow! If they take it every day for the rest of their lives, at ten dollars a dose that's—"

"Sorry to burst your bank account, Jason, but we don't know if the drug even works on any form but mine and Jenny's." Parker pulled alongside Jason to watch his expression. "Our form is extremely rare now, thanks to the miracle of in-utero genetic screening."

"Aren't your parents doctors? Why didn't they. . . ?" Jason's face froze. He looked away. Finally, after a long silence, he looked back. "Sorry about that."

"No problem. Just wanted you to be clear on the economics. If there was an incentive for drug companies to work on it, I wouldn't have had to do it myself. And I certainly—" Parker pulled to a stop. Four police cars were parked outside the chemistry building. One of them had its lights flashing.

Darcy. Parker sped up the hill, swerving recklessly around a cluster of startled pedestrians. The entrance to the chemistry building was blocked off with yellow tape. Thirty or forty students stood behind the yellow barricade, watching a gaggle of uniformed officers whose primary activity seemed to be watching the students watching them.

"Excuse me." Parker pushed his way through the crowd. "Excuse me. I've got to talk to the police."

A burly officer in an overly tight uniform stepped forward to intercept Parker before he reached the tape.

"Officer, a friend of mine was working late last night in the chemistry building. Darcy Williams. Do you know if she's okay?"

The officer shook his head. "I'm sorry but I'm going to have to ask you to stand . . . uh . . . please stay behind the line. The detectives will make an official statement as soon as all the information is in."

"But is she all right? Do you know if anyone has been hurt?"

The officer dismissed Parker with a wave.

Parker was just about to protest when Jason stepped in front of him, strode up to the tape, and ducked under it. "Sorry I'm late." He called out to the officers. "I got here as fast as I could. I'm Jason Shanahan from the chemistry department. You needed information about the research projects here?"

Two of the officers looked at each other and pointed Jason to two men in suits, who were talking just outside the shattered door. Jason stopped to talk with the officers. One of them led him to the suits. They talked for several minutes. Occasionally Jason jotted down a note on his PDA. After shaking each man's hand, he turned and made for the barrier.

Parker caught up with him at the edge of the crowd. "Jason, what'd they say?"

Jason didn't turn around.

"Jason."

"No one was hurt," Jason said in a subdued voice. "At least they don't think so."

As soon as they rounded the corner, Jason slowed his pace.

"Sorry about that, but those guys make me so mad. You'd think they were still in junior high the way they gloat over their little secrets." He turned suddenly, and Parker had to yank back on his joystick to keep from slamming into him.

"They think it was animal-rights activists." Jason's voice was strained. "In addition to the lobby, five labs were destroyed. They wanted to know about the research going on in those labs." His eyes were wild, his face pale.

Parker swallowed back the lump forming in his throat. "Which labs?"

"Two teaching labs on the second floor. The other three were on the third. Yours and Darcy's . . . and Pyramid's."

Parker sped along the city sidewalk at Jason's side. "What do you mean he had a conversation with Pyramid?"

"I know it doesn't make sense, but that's what Blake said." Jason shrugged. "The man said his name was John Pyramid and he was doing research on the Mighty Mouse receptor. Asked the same kinds of questions we've been asking ourselves."

"What did he look like? Could it have been Kelly?"

Jason shook his head. "Tall, wiry, brown eyes and hair. I only saw Kelly one time from three stories up, but I can't imagine anyone calling him *wiry*."

Parker tried to process the information. "And you say strangers have been coming around looking for Pyramid? Why haven't you ever bothered to tell me this?"

"I'm telling you now, aren't I?"

"Are you sure they're not internal, maybe from another department?"

"Positive." Jason nodded vigorously. "I've seen them. The admins have seen them. They've been sending them to Pyramid's lab."

"So now, out of the blue, someone breaks into the chem building and tears up our labs." Parker eased his chair down a ramp and crossed the street toward his apartment building. "It doesn't make sense. Why would anyone want to sabotage our research?"

"Maybe it doesn't have anything to do with your research." Jason stepped in front of Parker and proceeded down the narrow walk that led to Parker's front door. "Maybe it doesn't have any-thing to do with you at all."

"Then how do you explain all the people looking for Pyramid? The fact that our labs were specifically targeted?"

Jason stepped aside to let Parker get to his door. His eyebrows were turned down in a scowl as if waging an internal war. From the expression on his face, he was losing.

"So?" Parker stopped sorting through his keys and waited.

Jason frowned and shook his head. "I hate to say this. I really do. But have you considered it might be Darcy?"

"No way." Parker went back to his keys. "That's . . . so stupid I can't even think of a response."

"I don't mean to say she trashed your labs, but what if she was the reason for the break-in? Have you noticed how she hasn't been around lately? What if it wasn't the Pyramid paper?"

"Why not you or me for that matter? Nothing makes any sense."

Jason looked down at the ground and took a deep breath. "Look, I know you like her. I did too—not too long ago. But I . . . I think you should think long and hard about what you're doing."

"Why? Because I'm in a wheelchair?" Parker winced at the anger in his voice.

"Not because of you." Jason looked stung. "It doesn't have any-thing to do with you. It's her I'm worried about." He looked mis-erably at the ground. "Look, I didn't want to say anything. I guess I was hoping she'd prove me wrong. But I don't think you can trust her. Something about her is very, very wrong."

"I don't think we should be having this conversation." Parker turned away from Jason and inserted a key in his door.

"Parker, listen. Do you know where she lives? Do you even have her phone number?"

"Yeah."

"Her *home* phone number?"

Parker sat facing the open door. Darcy was his friend. He should go inside and shut the door, but . . .

"She told me a guy in her lab has been giving her a ride home," Jason said. "That was a lie. He doesn't even have a car. Once she had me drop her off at a building in Oakland. Said it was her apart-ment. I checked it out. It was a warehouse for storing paint. And then, next thing I know, I find out she was out wandering the streets of Berkeley. Doesn't that seem a little odd to you?"

Parker closed his eyes. Darcy was his friend and he trusted her—that was his choice.

"And now the police are following her. That was before Mighty Mouse. Remember? Before John Pyramid."

Parker turned around slowly and faced Jason. "You're right. There's a lot going on that doesn't make any sense. Maybe she knows something we don't. Maybe it's none of our business. I don't know. But I do know that Darcy's my friend. She would never willingly do anything to hurt me. Or you. That much I know for sure."

Jason shrugged. "You're probably right. I hope to God you are. I really like Darcy, but . . . well . . . you're my friend too. I don't want to see you get hurt. Some guys in the department call her the Ice Queen. Did you know that? They tried to warn me away from her too, just like I'm doing for you. I hope you understand it's well-intended."

Parker nodded. "I appreciate it. But I take it you didn't listen to your friends either."

Jason smiled. "I suppose some things you just have to learn the hard way." He stepped toward the door. "Need any help with the injection?"

Parker shook his head. "Actually I'm starting to get pretty good at it. I think my fingers realize how good it is for them."

"Okay . . ." Jason glanced back toward campus. "Still friends?"

"Still friends. All three of us." Parker rolled inside. "I'll be on the phone for a while, searching for Darcy. If she doesn't turn up soon, I'm going out looking for her. You're welcome to join me. We can test-drive my new legs."

"Sure, and in the meantime I'll snoop around and try to find out more about the break-in. Maybe our friend Pyramid left fingerprints."

"Okay." Parker waved and shut the door, locking it behind him.

He shut his eyes and took a deep breath as the darkness, cool and soothing, started to soak into his sun-fried senses. *"Our friend Pyramid left fingerprints."* He crossed the room to the refrigerator and pulled out his serum vial. *"Break-ins . . . Pyramid's lab . . . they call her the Ice Queen."* The words barely registered as he filled a 5cc syringe and injected the drug into his thigh.

CHAPTER 17

DARCY

THANKS A LOT, JASON. Darcy pushed her way through the bird-of-paradise plants and stormed across Parker's lawn. *Way to be a friend.* She limped down the sidewalk, windmilling her arms to work the numbness out of her frozen muscles. She'd waited all night for Parker to get home. All morning. For what? To be stabbed in the back by a sore loser. A pathetic brat whose ego was too fragile to handle not being the center of every girl's universe. *Ice Queen, huh? Well, sorry, guys. Sorry if I don't live down to your standards.*

She stopped in the middle of the sidewalk and looked back at Parker's apartment. Jason had said Parker liked her. And Parker hadn't denied it. He'd even stood up for her. Maybe if she explained . . . She looked at the ground. Explained what? That she'd lied to Jason because she lived in a ceiling? That she had a criminal record? That she'd almost killed a deranged paramilitary loony, and now he was trying to kill her? She turned back to the campus and kept on walking. Parker would love that. A nice Christian guy from a nice Christian family. His parents were doctors of all things. And she was . . . orphan trash. Smart trash, but trash nonetheless.

Trash. The word clunked like a broken pot at the back of her mind. What had Jason said about someone trashing Parker's lab? Last night? When she was attacked? That could only mean one thing. The Dark Man knew about Parker. Knew his address, his phone number. If he had been in his lab during the attack . . .

She stopped again and looked back at Parker's apartment. She shouldn't have let him walk her back, shouldn't have eaten dinner with him. If she had just gone back to Sacramento when she first thought about it, none of this would have happened. But now that Parker was involved . . . shouldn't she at least warn him? Didn't she owe him an explanation?

She turned slowly and limped back to Parker's apartment. Even if he was totally disgusted, at least he would know the truth. At least he'd know enough to look out for the Dark Man. She stared at Parker's door for a long time. Finally, she took a deep breath and rang the bell.

"It's open." Parker's voice sounded through the door.

She ran her fingers through her hair and two leaves fell out. If only she had a mirror. She brushed the mulch off her clothes and used a sleeve to wipe her face. She was running a finger across her teeth when the door opened.

"Darcy! What happened?" The concern in Parker's voice, the look in his eyes. It was too much.

"I . . ." The events of the night came rushing back in a flood of panic and terror. "I . . ." Her voice broke. The world went hazy. Next thing she knew she was in his arms, her face buried in the depths of his sweater.

"Darcy, it's okay. Everything's going to be fine." Her father's voice.

She stood, clinging to Parker, crying out all the pain and pent-up fear of the last eleven years.

"Darcy, it's okay."

"Parker, I . . ." She was looking up into his face. He was standing. The realization washed over her, turning her tears to gasping sobs. Strong arms squeezed her tight. Too tight.

"You're hurt." He brushed a warm hand across her cheek. "And cold as ice. Come in and sit down. I'll make some hot tea." He led her to the sofa. His steps were awkward and a little springy, but he was *walking*. She felt suddenly light-headed. Her legs buckled under her, and she sank down into the sofa. Parker's tender eyes. The delicious warmth of the sofa. He wrapped a blanket around her shoulders, and she dissolved into a fit of shivering. Shutting her eyes. Letting his voice surround her. Before long, the terrors of the night faded into the steamy smell of hot tea.

"Is honey okay?"

She opened her eyes and stared at him. Parker's eyes, deep and rich as mocha. He was so serious. Worried?

"Darcy, are you all right?"

She didn't know how to answer. The nightmares were still there, just below the surface.

"Darcy?"

She nodded.

"Do you want some tea?" He held out a steaming mug. *Harvard Medical School*. A lion with the head of a chicken danced across an auburn crest. *Where the Wild Things Are*—it reminded her of one of the monsters.

Parker set the tea on a table and dug in the pocket of his chair. His phone.

"I'm fine." Darcy leaned forward and placed a hand on his forearm. "Just got a little chilled. The tea should help." She reached out for the mug and cupped it in both hands.

"So what happened?" He slid out of his chair and sat on the floor at her feet. Carefully he rolled up her pant leg. "Your leg's cut up pretty bad. I can't tell from the blood but it might need stitches. I'll get something to clean it up." He bounced into the bathroom.

Darcy stared down at her leg in amazement. When had this happened? She shook her head, trying to clear her mind.

After washing and dressing her wound, Parker reached up and took her by the hand. "Darcy, I'm your friend. You can trust me. Are you in some kind of trouble? I want to help, but I need to know what's going on."

She blinked her eyes. She was *not* going to start crying again. "Jason's right. I'm not . . . who you think I am."

Parker's eyes widened. "He told you?"

"I was out front." She nodded toward the door. "Waiting for you to get home."

"How long were you waiting?" Parker climbed up onto the sofa and settled himself next to her. She felt suddenly self-conscious. He was so close. She'd never realized before what a barrier the wheelchair had been.

"Darcy?"

"I'm sorry, I was just . . ." She turned on the sofa to face him.

"Last night, after you dropped me off at the chemistry building, I went to the gym. When I got back . . ." She shut her eyes and pictured the dark chemistry building. The broken glass. "When I got back to the chemistry building, I was attacked."

Parker's muscles quivered, forming knotted cords beneath his skin. "Do you know who it was?" His face was hard, his voice chiseled out of stone.

"Maybe." She shook her head. "I don't know. There's this guy. Larry Tranter. Everybody calls him the Dark Man. He's one of the regular crazies. Dresses up in dark camouflage and paints his face black. You might have seen him on Telegraph at night—before the rage riots. Anyway, some people say he fought in the Gulf War, but I don't think it's true. He's on some kind of mental disability."

"You said *maybe*. You didn't see him?"

"It was too dark," said Darcy. "At first I thought the power was out, but the elevator buttons were lit. I don't know."

"Did . . ." Parker's eyes churned with emotion. He opened his mouth but couldn't seem to form any words.

"The front door was broken, glass was all over the ground, and he just came out of nowhere. There was this terrible scream. Like an angry animal." Darcy shuddered. "A *big* animal. It chased me up the stairs. I hid on the landing, and it kept going. Up the stairs like it was jumping instead of climbing. I ran back down and hid in the bathroom, but it must have heard me. It went totally nuts. Tore down the bathroom door and smashed apart the stalls. I think it was still smashing the stalls when I escaped. And then I just ran. I thought it was following me. You were the only one I could think of to help."

"So you got away?" Parker's eyes were wild. "You must have been terrified."

She nodded and looked down at her tea.

"You're really amazing, you know that?"

Darcy glanced up at him and looked back down. Something in his expression. She felt like a world-class phony. He still didn't know her. Didn't understand. "Parker, there's something you should know about me. I've been meaning to tell you, but . . ." She took a sip of tea, watching his expression over the rim of the mug. His eyes were full of turmoil. As if he'd already guessed what was coming. "I lied to Jason. I didn't mean to; it's just that . . . I didn't want him to know. Didn't want anybody to know. You see I—"

"It's okay," Parker whispered. "You don't have to tell me if you don't want to. It's not going to change how I feel."

"You don't know that," Darcy snapped. "How can you say that? You don't know a thing about me."

Parker reached out a trembling hand and placed it gently on her shoulder. "I know what I know. That's enough."

Darcy had to look away. She took a deep breath and let it out slowly. "The last semester of my senior year I'd just gotten into the biochem program at Harvard and wanted to celebrate. Some girls I knew invited me to a rave. Invitation only. Supposedly they knew the guys who were putting it on, but I. . . . Anyway, a friend of mine who was graduating had just given me his old scooter. I didn't have a license, but I rode it to the party anyway. Just one time, I thought. What would it hurt?" She looked up at Parker, tried to read his expression. "While I was there someone put a drug in my drink. They say it was probably Rohypnol. I don't know. When I woke up, I was behind the DJ tables." Darcy took another sip of tea, then a big gulp. Drained the mug to the bottom.

"The guys at the table tried to convince me to stay. One of them offered to take me home, but I wouldn't listen. I was upset and scared and . . ." She dropped her eyes. "Ashamed. It was still dark out. Too dark to see a guy with night paint and dark camouflage." Darcy squeezed her eyes shut. The squeal of the tires. The dizzying slide. The sickening thump.

"I tried to stop, but the scooter skidded out of control. I wasn't going that fast, but apparently I hit him just the wrong way."

"And that's why he's after you?" Parker sounded incredulous. "It was an accident."

"Compound fracture of the femur and a broken hip." Darcy hung her head. "I didn't have any money. No parents. Nobody to give me advice. The police said they were willing to testify on my behalf, but I felt so . . . guilty. I could have killed him. As it was I . . ." She shut her eyes, saw the man in the hospital bed, raging and swearing and covering her with abuse. "Sixty thousand dollars. That was the settlement."

Parker shook his head. "But if you didn't have any money . . ."

"Twelve thousand a year for five years. I got off easy, considering . . . what I'd done." Darcy took a deep breath. "I had to say no to Harvard. Had to work out a deal for late admission to Cal. They have a policy about inbreeding, you know. But there was no other way. I couldn't afford to go anywhere else."

"So the department agreed to pay him?" Parker's voice was hushed.

"The department doesn't know. They can't know," Darcy pleaded. "I could get kicked out of school."

"For what? A scooter accident?"

"Actually, there's more." Darcy looked down at her hands. "I live . . . I've been sleeping in Pyramid's lab. I've got a loft in the drop-down ceiling—above the offices."

"Really?" Amazement filled Parker's voice. "Cool."

Darcy studied Parker's face. "You think it's cool?"

"Sure. It's a great idea. That explains why you had Jason drop you off at a warehouse. You've been saving your money to pay that guy off."

Darcy nodded. "Until four months ago. I lost the part-time job I had, and then someone stole my bike and I needed new clothes. And I guess I got behind."

"So the guy's coming after you to collect his money?" Parker spat out the words. Fire kindled in his eyes. "How much do you owe him?"

"I just missed two payments. I paid him last month and this—"

"How much? How much do you still owe him, total?" Parker pushed himself onto his feet and collapsed back down into his wheelchair.

Darcy's mind went blank. "I . . . um . . . started in April so I have sixteen months to go. Sixteen thousand plus the two months I missed."

Parker wheeled around in his chair and rolled into the back room. She stared after him. A drawer slammed shut. The sound of rattling paper. "Parker?" She rose halfway to her feet. Was she supposed to follow him? Was he just angry? Disgusted? Color rose to her cheeks. She'd expected him to react, but not . . . No, she really hadn't had a clue how he'd react.

Footsteps sounded at the bedroom door. Darcy dropped back onto the sofa.

Parker lurched into the room, walking like a circus performer on stilts. "Okay. Here's what you do. First, pay that Dark Man guy off. Then call the police. Tell them everything you told me." He perched on the arm of the sofa and handed her a slip of paper.

At first it didn't register. A line of zeros so long it took her breath away. $18,000.00. A check for eighteen thousand dollars. She couldn't speak. Couldn't breathe. Couldn't take her eyes off the check. *Eighteen thousand dollars!* "Parker, I can't . . ." She let the check slip from her fingers. "I can't take this. It's too much."

"You have to. Consider it a gift." Parker picked up the check and handed it back to her. "This is your life we're talking about."

"But what if it's not him?" She stared at the check. "What if I was just . . . at the wrong place at the wrong time? It could have been anybody really."

"It's still your life. You can't tell me it hasn't been hard for you. Living alone in a lab."

"No!" She looked up into his eyes. Searched them. Poured into them the emotion behind her tangled thoughts. "Don't you see? It can't be you. I can't . . . owe you. Not this much."

"You owe the Dark Man." Parker's voice wasn't unkind, yet the words left a definite sting.

"That's different. Don't you see how that's different? I don't know him. He's crazy."

Parker arched his eyebrows. "That doesn't make any sense."

"Yes, it does. A lot. Don't you see?" Darcy held out the check. How could she make him understand?

"If you had the money and it was me in your situation, wouldn't you give me a check to save my life?"

"But this isn't like that. I just got a little behind."

"If my parents knew you were in need and I didn't help—they'd kill me. By taking the money you're saving *my* life."

"But I don't—"

"Shhh . . ." Parker leaned in close, touched a trembling fingertip to her lips. "If it makes you feel better, you can pay me back. Take as long as you like. I'm in a wheelchair, after all. If I ever decide to come after you, at least you know you'll be able to get away."

Darcy smiled, and a rush of emotion threatened to overwhelm her. He was serious. It was really going to happen. Relief, after so many years. She reached up, placed a hand on his shoulder, and kissed him gently on the cheek. "Thank you." Her whisper barely rose above the sound of her pounding heart.

Parker stared back at her with wide eyes. The room around her was getting hazy. "Okay." When he finally spoke, his voice was husky. "I guess that makes us even."

JASON

One male and one female, both carried briefcases, both wore suits of smudgy drab. *Detectives?* Jason spread the window blinds wider, and a decade of dust and grit shook free into his face. He was too high up to see their faces, and they seemed to be in a hurry. Others had come and gone, but these were the only two with purpose behind their steps. And they carried briefcases. Since when did the police carry briefcases? Jason pressed his face closer to the blinds. They walked past a uniformed cop. No nod, no wave, no sign of any recognition at all. Who were these guys? Feds?

Jason pulled back into the shadow of the darkened lab. A queasy, tingling excitement thrilled up his spine. They were Feds— they had to be—and they were here because of John Pyramid. He could feel the truth of it in his bones. Government agents from a government research lab. He wiped his hands on his khakis and hurried from the room. He had to get to the chemistry building. Had to be there when the feds started asking questions. He raced through the sixth floor hallway of Stanley Hall, bounding down the stairs a half flight at a time. John Pyramid. Twelve labs were doing animal research, but of those twelve, only Pyramid's and Parker's had been touched. The teaching labs were just a red herring. Something to confuse the police. He pushed through the double doors and ran out into the blinding sunlight.

A huge man in black brushed by him, clipping his shoulder and spinning him halfway around. "Sorry." Jason stared up at the man and gasped. His face was a livid mask of scars and blotches.

"No problem." The man's voice was a low, rumbling growl.

Jason followed the man up the sidewalk, slowing his steps to a bored, deliberate pace. *Okay, calm down. Blend. You're a busy guy. Overworked and underpaid. This is just a job. One more detail to attend to before you can break for lunch.* He crossed the street to the chemistry building, watching out of the corner of his eye as the man in black pushed back a couple of gawking students and ducked under the yellow tape. Waving at a uniformed officer, the man then disappeared into the building. What was going on? Was this guy a cop?

"Excuse me." An older man in a shabby tan windbreaker took a step toward Jason, pen and legal pad in hand. Probably a reporter. Too late for the breaking news and too early for the break-in report.

"Sorry." Jason waved him off. He was too busy. Too busy to mess with reporters. He had a job to do.

He quickly ducked under the tape and waved at the officer lolling in the shade of the building.

"Hey!" the officer shouted.

Jason couldn't remember the guy's name, but he'd been talking to a cop named Spence that morning. "Has Spence already taken off?"

The man strightened and brushed at his shirt. "He's on another call."

"Could you tell him Jason Shanahan has some information for him?" Jason kept walking, heading for the open door.

"Information. . . ? What kind of information?"

Jason had to slow down. "About one of the labs that was broken into. The Pyramid lab." He watched the cop for a reaction.

"Okay," the officer responded, a puzzled look on his face. "They're not letting anyone inside yet. Why don't you tell me, and I'll pass it on."

Wonderful, Jason thought. If only he'd kept his big mouth shut, he'd be inside now. "It has to do with a paper Pyramid just published," Jason explained. "The effects of an adrenaline derivative on laboratory mice."

"Okay . . ." The officer brushed at his shirt again. "I'll be sure and tell him."

"Let him know the mice were muscular-dystrophy positive. Tell him it induced a hyperactive response."

"Okay . . ." The man nodded slowly. "Sure . . . got it. . . . It induced. I'll let him know."

"Great, thanks." Jason sighed wearily. "So who was that guy? The one in the Halloween mask?"

"No idea," the officer said.

"Then why did you let him in?"

The officer shrugged. "He seemed to know where he was going.

From the looks of him, I figure he's about a *d* away from dead."

"I know what you mean," agreed Jason. "Did you hear him talk? Sounds like he gargles with battery acid."

Jason turned and retraced his steps back to the yellow tape barrier. The students were gone, but the man in the windbreaker was still there. He was watching him like a starving dog. *Oh well.* Jason walked right up to him. "You the reporter from Reuters?"

The man considered the question. For a second Jason thought he had lucked into the jackpot, but then the man shook his head. "No, I write for the Star newspaper group. Would you mind answering a few questions?"

Jason grinned. Ace reporter, this guy was not. Still, you never knew who might end up seeing the article. *Might as well shake the tree and see what falls out.* "Okay, but all I'm allowed to say about John Pyramid is that he was working with mice with muscular dystrophy."

"John Pyramid?" The man scribbled the name in his notebook.

"The professor whose lab was broken into. You've probably heard the rumors about his breakthrough. It's huge. Bigger than penicillin."

"Really?" The man's face lit up.

"Apparently someone—or some *organization*—was trying to steal his research. Pyramid's so secretive about his work, it's hard to say whether they got anything useful or not." Jason looked around casually, waiting for the next question. Better to let the guy drag it out of him.

The reporter looked up from his notebook. "How do you spell John? Is that with an *h* or not?"

"J-o-h-n." Jason turned so he could watch the entrance of the chemistry building. Something told him this was going to be a long interview.

CHAPTER 18

PARKER WALKED ACROSS THE FLOOR of his bedroom. *Not so springy. Lean forward. Bend at the knees.* He walked back again, watching himself in the mirror hanging on the back of the door. Okay, he wouldn't be going on a walk with Darcy anytime soon. He looked like a cross between Frankenstein's monster and the Easter bunny. But he *was* getting better.

He Franken-hopped closer to the mirror. His face was glowing like a stoplight. It had been stinging all morning, but he hadn't paid it much attention. He pulled down his collar to reveal a sharp delineation between white and pink skin. Sunburn? From just that little bit of exposure this morning? It didn't make sense . . . unless it was another side effect of the drug. That had to be it. Light-sensitivity, both his eyes and his skin. As side effects went, it could have been a lot worse.

A bump sounded inside the bathroom, and the apartment grew suddenly quiet as the rush of the shower subsided. Then a clickety-click rumble and a bump. The sound of the shower door opening. Parker stepped toward the bathroom and started to ask her if she needed anything, but the idea of talking through the thin door made his cheeks burn. Besides, he'd given her a towel, a hair dryer, and a brush. What more could she want?

The image of the mounds of junk covering the counter of his sister's bathroom sprang to his mind. No, that was Jenny. Surely Darcy was more practical than that. He turned his back on the door and hop-walked back to the living room. She was fine. She'd feel a lot better now that she was warm and clean. He'd get a chance to talk to her soon enough.

He sat down on the sofa and tried to get comfortable. Stood back up again. *The Dark Man.* Even the guy's name made him burn. He lurched across the living room floor. The beast had tried to kill her. Darcy. The sweetest, most innocent girl in the world. It was beyond belief. What if he tried again? Before he got the money. What if the money wasn't what he was after? The thought made him sick. He had to do something. Had to do something fast.

He walked back to the bathroom door. "Darcy, are you okay? Is there anything I can get you?"

"I'm fine." The bathroom door opened and Darcy stepped out, wet hair plastered to her head. Her clothes were still ripped and dirty, but she looked a thousand percent better. She was watching him with an intense, wide-eyed expression that made his sunburned face radiate heat. "I still can't get over seeing you standing. It's just so amazing."

"I . . ." Parker hesitated. She seemed so calm now. So normal. Did he really want to remind her of the attack? He hated to do it, but he had to. Some things just couldn't be ignored. Like black-faced lunatics trying to kill you. "I hate to bring this up, but don't you think we ought to call the police now?"

A storm cloud darkened Darcy's face. He could see her recoil as the nightmare played itself over in her mind. "Don't you think we should wait to see what they find on their own? To be honest, I'm not sure I trust the Berkeley police. I for sure don't trust Kelly."

"Trust or not, they have to be told. If this Dark Man guy is guilty, he has to be stopped. Before he hurts someone else."

Darcy bit her lip and stared at the floor. "What if they ask for my address?"

"You don't have to tell them. They'll understand. I wouldn't give out my address either if a crazed lunatic was after me." Parker picked up the phone, dialed the number of the police station, and handed it to Darcy.

She stared at the receiver like it was his dad's cooking, then held it to her ear. "Hello. Yes. My name is Darcy Williams, and I want to report . . . an attack."

Parker walked back and forth across the room as Darcy outlined her story, first to one, then to another officer. Finally, after being transferred what seemed like fifteen times, Darcy hung up the phone.

"Well?" Parker sat down next to her on the sofa. "What'd they say?"

"They're sending a detective to talk to me. I told them I'd meet her at the chemistry building."

"Why not here? I don't mind."

Darcy shook her head. "I don't trust them."

"Come on. This is the police we're talking about."

"I'm serious. If I don't trust them enough to tell them where I live, I'm certainly not going to give them *your* address."

"But nobody's . . ." Parker swallowed his words and studied her expression. Did she realize what she'd just implied?

Darcy turned toward the front door. "Would you mind coming with me? I'd feel a lot better having you there."

"Sure!" Parker winced at the enthusiasm in his voice. Mr. Cool he was not. "Um . . . let me just get some stuff together."

He clomped back to his bedroom and grabbed a pair of sunglasses from the dresser. Then, digging in his closet, he pulled out an old Indiana Jones-style hat and a jacket. That should do it. He slipped the jacket on and put on the hat and glasses before getting into his wheelchair and powering back to the living room.

Darcy laughed when she saw him. "What's the disguise for? Embarrassed to be seen with me?" She looked down at her clothes. "Not that I'd blame you."

"No!" The word exploded out of him before he could stop himself. "I mean, I . . . Actually, I think it's a side effect of the drug."

"The irresistible urge to dress like Walt Whitman?"

"Sensitivity to light." Parker rolled to the door and held it open for her. "The sun was barely up this morning, and I still managed to get a burn."

"I did notice you're a little red." Her eyes lit with a mischievous grin.

"What?"

"Nothing. Just wondering if maybe you'd like to try walking there. You've been getting around pretty well. I could help."

Parker looked up at her. Imagined himself walking arm in arm with her. Leaning on her for balance. He could feel his cheeks burning. "I don't know. . . ." He gripped the arms of his chair tighter. "It's a long way, and we're in a hurry. Don't you think maybe it's a little soon?"

"Maybe." Darcy stepped toward the open door and hesitated. Then, peering cautiously up and down the street, she stepped outside.

A heavy weight settled in Parker's stomach. "Maybe you shouldn't be walking around in plain view." He stopped and pulled out his cell phone. "We could call the police back and have them meet us here."

"Don't be silly." Darcy kept on walking. "Nobody will even notice me. Not with you dressed like the Lone Ranger."

Parker laughed and jammed down on his joystick to catch up with her. "Hi-ho, Silver . . ."

———

"Besides the lobby area and two open labs by the stairs on the second floor, most of the damage seems to have been confined to the third floor. I can take you through, but please don't touch anything." Judy Runyan held the elevator doors open for Darcy and Parker, then stepped in after them. Detective Runyan was a tall, raw-boned woman who looked to be in her late forties. Her voice was severe and gravelly, and her skin had a yellow, leathery texture that suggested a nasty tobacco addiction. But her eyes were kind, and Darcy seemed to trust her. The detective had taken to Darcy immediately and listened to her story with an almost motherly attentiveness.

At first Parker had been worried that reliving the attack was going to be painful for Darcy, but with Judy's encouragement and his outbursts of admiration at her resourcefulness, the exercise seemed to have the opposite effect. By the time Darcy finished walking them through the attack in the bathroom, she was almost back to her normal self. Parker, on the other hand, was almost sick. The broken lights, dented elevators, demolished doors and bathroom stalls. . . . Darcy had said the Dark Man was crazy; but the extent of his insanity hadn't registered with Parker until he'd seen the destruction firsthand. The man was a monster. Darcy wouldn't be safe until he was behind bars. Even that might not be enough. With the possibility of parole and legal loopholes and insanity pleas, she might never be truly safe—not until the Dark Man was dead.

The elevator stopped at the third floor, and Parker darted forward to hold the door for Darcy and the detective. Runyan led the way down the hallway and stopped outside Parker's lab. The door had been torn off its hinges and lay on the floor just outside the lab. Parker sucked in his breath as he pulled forward to look inside. The lab was completely wrecked, the benches tipped over and broken, all the drawers and their contents scattered on the floor. Glass was everywhere.

"Parker, I'm so sorry." Darcy reached down and took Parker by the hand. "I never thought . . . I should have known."

"It's okay." Parker couldn't take his eyes off the carnage. "I guess I'm . . . finished with my research anyway." He tore his eyes away from the lab and caught Detective Runyan frowning at him.

"I take it this was your lab?"

Parker nodded. "I—"

"It's my fault," Darcy interrupted. "I was helping him with his research. Working in his lab. I never thought—"

"So this isn't the lab you normally work in?" Runyan turned to face Darcy, but Parker could still feel her watching him out of the corner of her eye. His hands. She was watching his hands. He gripped the arms of his chair to keep them from trembling.

"No, my lab's in the old part of the building." Darcy escorted them down the hall and stopped at the corridor that led to her lab. A ribbon of police tape hung across her door. Broken glass sparkled on the off-white floor.

"And this is the laboratory you work in?" Runyan sounded irritated.

Darcy nodded. "That's right. Can I go in?" She poked her head inside the door and looked around the room.

"The room in the back was vandalized too," Runyan said. "We think they got out through this door. It was kicked in from the inside." She studied Darcy carefully. "Am I right in assuming the labs were both fine yesterday?"

"Of course." Darcy bit her lip. Her backpack was ripped in half and lying on the floor. "I guess the Dark Man knew where I worked. He must have been . . . watching me."

"I wouldn't be so sure," Runyan said. "This wasn't about money—or animal rights. Your description of the attack rules out activists, and the vandalism pretty much rules out your 'Dark Man.' If the attack was motivated by revenge, he would have attacked long ago, and if it really was about the money, why the unfocused vandalism?"

Darcy turned to Parker, her face a mask of confusion.

"Can you think of anyone else who might be out to get you?" Runyan's eyes were intense. "An enemy from the past. An old boyfriend maybe?" A cold glance at Parker. "Someone with a history of substance abuse?"

"Substance abuse?"

Runyan nodded. "Everything I've seen and heard so far convinces me our perp was flying without a pilot's license. I would have bet my badge it was just a random rage addict off the street, except that your labs seem to have been specifically targeted. It's got to be someone you know."

"Like the Dark Man."

Runyan frowned. "We'll certainly bring him in for questioning, but, from everything you've told me, I doubt it's him. You ran into him how long ago?" Runyan's eyes darted to Parker's hands, and he gripped the arms of his chair tighter.

"Almost four years ago," Darcy replied. "Spring semester of my senior year."

"And you stopped paying him four months ago?" The detective shifted her gaze.

"I didn't stop." Darcy's face flushed. "I just got behind. I had some extra expenses, and I started going out with this guy and needed new clothes."

Started going out with a guy? Jason? Parker looked to Darcy. Her attention was focused on Runyan.

"And the payments were a thousand dollars a month?" Runyan frowned again, motioned to the side with her eyes and head.

"I'm only behind by two payments," Darcy added. "I was going to make them up."

"Sure you were." A deep voice sounded behind Parker. He yanked up on his armrest, breaking off the plastic pad with a loud snap.

"I know what graduate students make." Officer Kelly's voice. "Tell me, how does a student like you afford to make payments of twelve grand a year?"

Parker stared at the broken armrest. He glanced up at Runyan, but her attention was focused on Kelly. Pressing the pad back onto his chair, he turned to face Kelly.

"I'd think about that if I were you, *Detective.*" Kelly finished with a sneer. "I'm just a uniform, but it all sounds awfully fishy to me."

"I'm interviewing a witness," Runyan said stiffly. "I'm going to have to ask you to leave now."

"Hey, no problem." Kelly sauntered down the hall. "Just trying to help. You know, information sharing between the divisions."

When the sound of Kelly's footsteps finally faded, Darcy leaned in close to Runyan and said in a low voice, "Not too long ago, I saw him passing what looked like drugs to glass addicts. He's been after me ever since."

"That doesn't surprise me in the least." Runyan stepped to the corner and checked to make sure the hallway was clear. "Ever since the rage riots, Kelly's been on assignment with the DEA. You'd think he'd been promoted to commissioner the way he struts about the precinct. He's got a bad case of what's known in the force as Chihuahua syndrome. You'd do well to stay away from him."

Darcy quirked an eyebrow, and Parker responded with a shrug.

"So, shall we check to see if anything is missing?" Runyan ducked under the tape and motioned for Darcy to follow. Parker started to roll forward, but Runyan stepped into the doorway to block his way. "Actually, James, if you don't mind, there's a lot of glass on the floor. We'll be able to step over it, but you . . ."

"No problem." Parker backed away from the doorway. Darcy shot him an apologetic look. He shrugged it off with a smile. "I'll be back in a few minutes."

He turned and wheeled down the corridor. As soon as he was around the corner, he halted his chair and flipped over the broken armrest to examine it. The eighth-inch screw that had attached the armrest to the chair had snapped completely in half. Metal fatigue? He flexed his biceps, thrilling to the way they jumped beneath his skin. He felt unusually strong, like maybe he really could break a steel screw. Of course, after being so weak for so long, he was bound to feel that way. To him, even normal strength was superhuman.

Approaching the entrance to his lab, he drove as close as the leaning door allowed. The faint smell of smoke drifted out of the room. It smelled like a fire in a fireplace. He glanced up and down the hall. No one coming. Shoving the door to one side, he held up the tape and drove inside. He jolted to a stop as a piece of glass crushed under one of his wheels. Carefully he pushed himself up onto his feet and stepped gingerly from one clear spot to another, balancing awkwardly on one foot and then the other as he made his way toward the refrigerator. Finally, after what seemed like hours, he reached the fridge. Opening the door with shaky hands, he looked inside. The adrenaline was gone. The Eppendorf trays, his samples, even his case of Cherry Coke. Everything, gone. He searched the lab in a daze. What would the Dark Man want with his drug? After a few minutes of searching, he found the Eppendorf trays in a pile under the door of a broken cabinet, and the Eppendorf tubes and cuvettes were scattered everywhere. His Cherry Cokes were under the dishwashing sink. But he couldn't find the adrenaline anywhere.

Only one place he hadn't looked. He hopscotched across the floor to the bench at the back of the room. As he passed the sink, a black smear at the bottom caught his eye. At first he thought it was just a trash bag, but then, when he got closer, his nose told him differently. Ashes. Lots of them. A marble-backed edge caught his eye. A fan of smoke-tinted white. Part of a lab notebook—a whole pile of them. They'd all been burned.

He started to poke through the ashes when a noise in the hall caught his attention. Footsteps. He vaulted across the floor and pressed himself to the wall next to the dishwashing sink. The large Peg-Board that Ray used to dry glassware blocked his view of the door.

The footsteps stopped. Heavy breathing. The rustle of the tape being lifted aside.

With a start, Parker realized his wheelchair was parked out in the open. Fast as thought, he reached out and dragged it against the wall.

Again, the echo of footsteps. The crunch of broken glass. Through a gap in the drying board Parker caught a glimpse of a red, scarred face. He held his breath and waited as the man turned slowly to look about the room. Then he walked back outside, and his footsteps faded down the hallway.

Parker's arm was trembling. He looked down at the chair. One wheel was lifted off the ground, five maybe six inches. *Impossible.* He lowered the chair to the floor as a cold numbness slowly spread itself throughout his body. He stared down at his chair with wide eyes. Three hundred pounds. The chair weighed almost three hundred pounds. He was sure of it. He reached down and lifted it again, tipping it up on one wheel. Impossible. It was absolutely impossible. He was holding up half the chair with the same effort it used to take him to lift his backpack!

DARCY

Darcy stepped around the fragments of fluorescent light bulbs that littered the floor of her lab. Every light in the room was smashed. A dark gouge had been cut into one of the mottled ceiling tiles next to a light fixture. Someone had used a stick or pole to break the lights. But why?

"See anything?" Detective Runyan's voice was muffled by a white mask. "Anything obvious missing?"

"Not really." Darcy watched as Runyan crouched by the desk, brushing her pictures with a fine black powder. "What a mess. Why would anybody do this?"

Runyan shrugged. "Who knows."

Darcy edged closer to the door into Pyramid's lab and pushed it open with her shoulder. It too was covered with papers and broken glass. She looked casually up at the ceiling. So far so good. The ceiling tiles were undisturbed. Apparently the police hadn't checked the ceiling yet. Hopefully they never would. "How long are you going to keep the labs sealed off?"

"Maybe a day or two. The others are going to want to look things over again when they hear your story. Student activists are one thing, a rage attack quite another."

Darcy stepped into the other lab to hide her disappointment. Another day or two? Where was she going to sleep until then? She stepped over the broken neck of an Erlenmeyer flask and stooped to examine a huge wet spot on the floor. A fine white residue crusted the shards of glass and the floor around the spill. She closed her eyes and tried to picture the lab the way it had been before she had gone to the gym. Had Jason set up a new synthesis? She was almost sure he hadn't. In fact, she distinctly remembered the benches being fairly clean. Jason had just taken a load of dirty dishes over to Parker's lab for Ray to clean.

"Find anything?"

Darcy leaped to her feet and spun around, barely managing to suppress a shriek. "You scared me."

"Really?" Runyan stood in the doorway watching her with narrowed eyes. "What's that on the floor?"

"That's what I was trying to figure out. Something spilled, but I can't remember what. I'll have to ask . . ." Darcy looked back down at the spill and shook her head. The last thing she wanted was to bring Jason into this mess. Runyan was distracted enough as it was. The Dark Man was the one she should be focusing on.

"You'll have to ask? What do you mean?" Runyan stepped toward her.

"I'll have to look it up in my notebook."

Runyan held Darcy with a penetrating gaze. Finally she shrugged and said, "Your friend's back. He says he needs to talk to you."

Darcy squeezed past Runyan and made her way across the cluttered lab. Parker was waiting for her at the door. His face didn't register her approach. He just sat, staring at his hands with a dazed expression on his face. "Parker, what's wrong?"

"I don't think Detective Runyan likes me very much." Parker didn't look up. "I don't know why, but I get the feeling she doesn't trust me."

"What? You mean that crack she made?" Darcy lowered her voice. "She was talking about *old* boyfriends."

Parker looked up sharply, and an amused smile played at the corners of his mouth.

"I mean . . ." Darcy looked back into her lab. "She's just grasping. I don't know why, but she seems to be going out of her way to avoid considering the Dark Man as a suspect."

"As much as I hate to say it, she may have a point." Parker's expression turned suddenly serious. "Why would the Dark Man wait so long? And if it was money he was after, why attack at all? He obviously knows how to work the legal system."

"He's a deranged loony that blackens his face and wanders around in the dark wearing night camouflage." Darcy's voice rose in frustration. "Why doesn't anybody get it? Have you noticed all the lights?" Darcy glanced back over her shoulder. Runyan was working her way along the lab bench, spreading a cloud of black dust as she went. "They're all smashed. Up here and downstairs. Who would do that? Not your typical student activist. It's insane. Insane as the Dark Man. It's practically his calling card."

Parker shifted in his chair. "But why would the Dark Man want to steal—"

Darcy turned to follow Parker's gaze. Detective Runyan was standing right behind her, staring at Parker through narrowed eyes.

"James," Runyan stepped toward him and stooped down. "Would you mind if I looked at your shoes? I noticed something earlier, before you excused yourself."

"Why?" Parker grabbed his joystick. The knuckles of both hands suddenly went white.

"I see they're a bit dirty. You might even say worn, and well, I couldn't help overhearing what Darcy said about the fluorescent lights. It *is* insane. You see the glass is very fine and tends to stick to everything—especially the bottoms of shoes." Runyan took hold of one of Parker's feet and lifted it up to the light. The sole of his shoe sparkled with tiny bits of glass.

JASON

Jason waited behind the wheel of a seventeen-year-old Honda Accord, watching the gated driveway ahead. One of his classmates, Lisa Thomas, had loaned him the car for the afternoon. Make that traded. He'd left her with his new Miata, while she'd given him both her car and, judging from the way it smelled, a sixteen-year-old tuna fish sandwich hidden somewhere inside the glove compartment.

The gate swung silently open, and an old white pickup pulled out of the driveway. *Finally.* Jason looked at his watch. He'd been waiting almost three hours. If Mr. Lee had taken any longer with the pansies, he would have had to try again tomorrow. Courtney, his beloved stepmother, was due back from her historical society meeting in ten minutes. He didn't have much time.

Jason watched in his rearview mirror as the pickup disappeared around the bend. Then, throwing open the door, he slipped out of the car and ran for the gate. With a fluid motion born of many years of practice, he ran up a low stone wall and swung himself over the fence. Dashing across the stone driveway, he cut across the manicured lawn and vaulted the steps up to the front door of the three-story house he'd grown up in. As a precaution, he rang the doorbell. He wasn't worried about the housekeepers. They were all new and could be easily handled. It was Courtney he wanted to avoid. For the past twelve years she'd been systematically eliminating every trace of him and his father from the house and adopting a new woman-about-society life. The last thing she'd want was to help him go through his dad's old papers—assuming she hadn't already found and destroyed them all.

He unlocked the door and climbed the mahogany staircase to the master bedroom. The room had been completely remodeled since he'd last seen it, but the built-in set of drawers in the walk-in closet seemed to be untouched. He walked to the back of the closet, pushing aside the ghosts of his father even as he pushed aside Courtney's froufy gowns. Kneeling on the floor by the back wall of the closet, he traced his fingers across the intricately carved drawers. The smell of the polished wood brought back a flood of memories. Not all of them were good, but even the bad ones brought back the familiar hollow feeling, the awareness that a big part of him was missing. A part he'd never be able to get back.

He pulled out the second drawer from the bottom and laid it aside. It was filled with men's clothes—not his father's, but some other, much softer, prettier man's. No doubt Courtney's latest love-of-her-life-for-a-month. He reached inside the space left by the drawer and pried the cedar panel off the wall. The space was still there!

Plunging his hand inside, he probed the inside walls cautiously, expecting any second to feel the creepy-crawly legs and venomous fangs of a brown recluse spider. His hand closed around something soft and gritty. *Yes!* Carefully he maneuvered his father's old leather briefcase through the narrow opening.

His dad's old research papers. After his dad died, Jason had collected every paper he could find and had hidden them in his dad's secret hiding place. For twelve years they had lain hidden, haunting his dreams, keeping him awake at night, wondering, worrying.

He stared at the dusty case. The tarnished latches on either side of the handle mocked him. Even now the power of the case was overwhelming. Setting it carefully on the floor, he touched one of the latches with his finger. The shock of the cold, gritty metal made him wince. *Not now.* This wasn't the time nor the place. For a second he toyed with the idea of leaving the compartment open. No, it belonged to him and his dad. Courtney might own his dad's house, but she didn't own his secrets. He replaced the cedar panel and shoved the drawer back into place.

Wiping the case on one of Courtney's gowns, he left the bedroom and hurried for the stairs. Halfway to the bottom of the steps, a young Asian woman in a black dress and white, frilly apron stepped into the front hallway.

"Hello there," Jason called down the stairs. "You must be Stephanie."

The woman looked up at him, frowning like she'd just tasted sour milk. "Stephanie left last month. I'm Peggy."

Jason turned at the bottom of the stairs and looked her up and down before speaking. "Well, Peggy, I see why Courtney's been keeping you from me."

Peggy's face hardened. She opened her mouth to speak, but Jason cut her off.

"Tell her I stopped by to see her but then got called away— more business with the North Shore project." He moved to the door and threw it open, then turned and appraised her again with a cocky smile. "I'll try to stop by tomorrow. Maybe, with luck, she won't be here." He winked at her and then slammed the door behind him.

Walking across the lawn at a slow, even pace, Jason hit the button to open the gate and ran back to Lisa's car. He'd just swung around in a wide U-turn when Courtney's black Mercedes pulled up to the gate. With luck he'd embarrassed Peggy enough so that she wouldn't say a word, but even if she did, there was nothing Courtney could do about it. He had the case, and she didn't even know it existed.

The drive back across the bay took over an hour. By the time he got back to Berkeley, the smell of rotten tuna fish had sunk deep into his pores. It was too late to return the old Honda to Lisa. Somehow he didn't think she'd mind keeping his car an extra night. He squeezed the car into the left-hand bay of his garage and carried the briefcase into his study.

Carefully, with an almost spiritual reverence, he opened the case and pulled out the sheaf of papers. He went through each sheet, one by one. They'd been incomprehensible to him when in grade school. All he knew was that they were important. Science with a capital *S*. Halfway through the stack, he found what he was looking for: typewritten notes on the aggression suppressor experiments, complete with a full synthetic protocol and hand-drawn structures.

He sat down at his computer and pulled up *ScienceDirect* in his browser window. He typed the keywords *rage, chemical structure, synthesis, drug* into his computer and searched the entries. Two hours later he still hadn't found a chemical structure for rage, but he wasn't surprised. It was a controlled substance, after all. After the devastation of the rage riots in the Bay Area, they were probably watching the Internet closely.

Time for the big gun. He brought up the Beilstein database and typed in his name and password. Drawing the structure of his dad's molecule with the chemical editor, he hit the Search button and held his breath as the computer transmitted his search request to the Beilstein-database server. Thirty seconds later the search came back empty. He double-checked the structure he'd entered into the system. No mistakes. It was exactly what his dad had drawn.

The Beilstein database contained over ten million chemical structures and reactions. Ten million! Everything in the chemical literature dating back to the nineteenth century. He took a deep breath and tried to force himself to calm down. His mind buzzed with excitement. If Beilstein didn't have his dad's compound, it could only mean one thing—it was a controlled substance. He didn't know for sure which one, but he had a pretty good guess.

CHAPTER 19

"CAN YOU BELIEVE HER?" Parker guided his chair down the campus sidewalk. "She practically accused me of attacking you! I thought she was going to whip out handcuffs then and there."

"Well, you have to admit, it did look pretty suspicious. A guy in a wheelchair with glass on the bottoms of his shoes." Darcy was limping now, favoring her cut leg.

"Hey, she let you in *your* lab." Parker slowed down in order for Darcy to catch up. "I had every right to check out mine."

"You should have told her right off what you were doing," Darcy said. "Now she doesn't believe you. She thinks she saw glass on your shoes *before* you went in your lab."

"If I'd asked permission, she wouldn't have let me in the lab. And then we wouldn't have known about the burned lab notebooks or my missing medicine. Why do you suppose she never mentioned the notebooks?"

Darcy shrugged. "I don't know. Why didn't you tell her you can walk?"

"Because . . ." Parker looked down at the sidewalk. Why hadn't he told her about the drug? It wasn't anything to be ashamed of. "I don't know. I guess I didn't think it was any of her business. It seems so . . . private. Kind of like smiling the first day after getting braces."

"But now she doesn't trust you."

"So?" Parker looked back up at Darcy. "I don't trust her either."

Darcy shot him a sharp look. "So you've handed her one more reason not to arrest the Dark Man. Every little rabbit trail she has to run down is one more chance the Dark Man has to get lucky. He probably burned the notebooks to throw . . ."

Parker slowed down. When she didn't catch up, he turned to see what was wrong. "Darcy?"

She was standing in the middle of the sidewalk, patting her pockets.

"What's the matter?" Parker moved toward her and stopped. She didn't seem to be paying any attention to him.

"Don't turn around. Just listen," she whispered. "There's a man watching us. A guy with a scarred-up face. He's standing just inside the entrance to Campbell, and I think he has a gun."

Parker froze, senses suddenly on the alert. "Dressed in black? Red face—like he's been burned?"

"You know him?"

"He walked in while I was in the lab. I assumed he was with the police."

Darcy shook her head. "Runyan says no. I've seen him before. In the chemistry building, asking for Pyramid."

"Surely he wouldn't try anything here. Look at all the people." He started to turn his head, but she stopped him with a sharp look.

"If I started running, could you keep up with me?"

"No problem. This chair is specially geared, fastest in the line. It'll do—"

Darcy eyes went wide. "He's coming this way. Get ready . . . now!" She spun around and took off down the sidewalk.

Parker jammed down on his joystick, and his chair lunged forward. Footsteps pounded behind him. The guy was gaining on him. He was too fast. Parker pegged the joystick, pushing the chair past his ability to control it. It pitched and rattled beneath him. Gravel. He struggled with the controls, fighting to keep it on the sidewalk.

"Parker, come on!" Darcy had turned. She was waiting for him.

"Darcy, get out of here! Split up!" The footsteps were getting fainter. The man was slowing. Getting tired.

Parker swung the chair to the right and hit a ramp at full speed. The chair bounced and jolted and almost tipped, but he threw his weight to the right and balanced it out. Darcy was out ahead of him, losing herself in a crowd of students. She was going to make it. He couldn't hear his pursuer at all now.

He slowed down to maneuver through the pressing students. Darcy was gone. If he could just find a place to hide.

"Parker!" A hoarse whisper to his right. Darcy standing at the top of a ramp, holding open the door of one of the classroom buildings.

Parker swerved the chair around to the left, then cut hard to the right and guided it up the narrow ramp. Slapping footsteps. Behind him. Darcy yelled for him to hurry as he threaded his chair through the doorway. "Sorry. I wasn't fast enough. Run, get out of here! I'll distract him while you get away." He crossed the lobby and stopped his chair outside one of the two elevators centered on the back wall. The lights at the top showed their progress. One was on the fourth floor, the other on the sixth.

"Not enough time." Darcy plucked the hat from his head and grabbed his sunglasses. "Come on. Stand up."

Parker squinted in the bright light. Soft hands pulled him from the chair and guided him toward the doors they had just entered by.

"He's still coming . . ." Darcy stopped suddenly, and he ran into her. A hand slid behind his neck and pulled his head down to look into her upturned face. For a moment everything else disappeared, everything but soft, luminous skin and tantalizing lips. He felt himself falling, felt her lips pressed to his, a jolt of tingling electricity that dazzled his brain.

Slowly she pulled away. He stood shocked, still . . .

"He's gone." Darcy's whisper sent chills up his spine. "Ran up the stairs."

"He?" Parker nodded dully.

"Sorry if I . . ." Her eyes darted back and forth. She bit her lip, her brow puckered in a look of . . . fear? "I . . . couldn't think of anything else." She took him by the hand and pulled him toward the doors. "I knew he wouldn't recognize you standing up, but me . . . I had to hide my face . . . without being obvious."

"It's okay." Parker stepped out into the daylight and stopped. He felt suddenly dizzy. A tightrope walker struck blind by the sun. "Go on. I'll catch up in a second." He shook her off and headed back into the lobby. Throwing himself into his chair, he spun it around and maneuvered through the doors and outside into the late afternoon sun. Shielding his eyes, he searched up and down the sidewalks.

"Over here!" Darcy waved at him frantically from the entrance of a building on the other side of the walk.

He zigzagged through the crowd and drove through the door she held open for him.

"What were you doing?" She led him into a long hallway and ducked through an open door to her right. "That chair makes you a sitting duck."

"I couldn't leave it." Parker followed her into an empty classroom. "I might need it."

"Why?" She swatted at a light switch, and the room became bearable. "You can walk now. Why do you insist on riding that thing?"

"This *thing*?" Parker felt like he'd just been slapped. He knew he wasn't being fair, but he couldn't help taking her question personally. He followed her across the room to a covered window and watched as she peered through a tiny slit between the blinds. "It's not that easy. I'm not used to walking." He tried to get close enough to the window to see out. "I'm no good at it. It's like David and Goliath. I can't be in a battle with legs I haven't tested. I'm not ready."

Darcy didn't look away from the blinds. She was still breathing, fast and heavy—like she was angry.

"Most of my adult life I've had to fight to get people to see me and not just the chair. But now . . . now that I finally have the chance to break away from it, I just can't. I feel naked without it. When I stand on my own two feet, I have to stand on my own two feet. Know what I mean? There's no place to hide."

"I think I know what you mean." Darcy turned and looked at him with an expression he couldn't read. She turned slowly back to the window. "And I'm sorry. I shouldn't have said anything. I was just scared. So much is happening, and I don't understand . . . any of it."

"It's okay." Parker pushed aside his footrests and stood up next to her. "We'll figure it out. I know we will."

Darcy leaned into him, and he wrapped a protective arm around her. "I think we can eliminate the Dark Man," he said. "There'd be no reason for him to steal my drug *or* burn my notebooks. And no reason for him to be working with that man with the scarred face. Unless . . . The Dark Man's face isn't scarred under the black makeup, is it?"

Darcy shook her head. "I'm pretty sure he's a chemist."

"The Dark Man?"

"No, the guy chasing us. The area around his eyes isn't scarred at all. It's like he was wearing safety glasses when an explosion hit him."

Parker turned and looked down into Darcy's face. "Safety glasses? Are you sure it couldn't have been regular glasses?"

Her eyes lost focus for a second, and then she nodded. "Almost positive. The protected area was too wide at the sides of his face. Kind of like a raccoon's mask."

A chemist. It made sense! Parker opened a slit in the blinds and peered out at the building on the other side of the street, trying to catch sight of the face of each man that went in or out. "What if whoever attacked you wasn't after you at all. What if you just surprised him while he was trying to escape?"

"Escape from what?"

"From the building, after destroying our labs. Stealing my drug."

"But why would he—"

"Remember all those papers we sent out as John Pyramid?" Parker said. "What if one of those chemists was trying to steal our research? What if they stole the adrenaline and burned our notebooks to weaken our claim on it. It makes sense!"

"But why?"

"Money." Parker let the word sink in. "Millions and millions, maybe even billions of dollars."

"For what?" Darcy asked. "You said yourself that only a small number of people have your form of muscular dystrophy. It's not worth the expense of a drug company even developing the drug."

"But what if the drug doesn't just work for people with MD? What if it works for everybody?"

"What are you saying? A drug that makes walking people walk? I hardly think there'd be much of a market for that."

"Jason and Ray gave the drug to control mice too. Remember? They turned into Mightier Mice."

Darcy's eyes went suddenly wide. "You mean one of the chemists we sent the paper to ... You're saying they might think the drug could make humans stronger? That's ridiculous."

"Is it?" Parker looked down at his chair. Suddenly everything seemed to make sense. "Remember, I said your raccoon-faced friend walked in on me while I was in the lab? I didn't want him to see the chair. Without even thinking I dragged it across the floor. I can lift one of the wheels off the floor without even straining."

"Really?" Darcy's voice was double-dipped in skepticism.

"With one hand." He grabbed the chair with his right hand and tipped it onto one wheel.

"Amazing." Darcy looked dazed.

"Just think of the applications.... Athletics. Nursing homes. The military. The possibilities are endless," Parker said. "And let's just say we sent Pyramid's paper to an unscrupulous chemist— maybe someone who's having grant trouble." Parker moved back to the window and searched the walkway for Raccoon Face.

"It's enough money to tempt anybody. Even law enforcement." Darcy was right behind him. He could feel her eyes on his back. "We know for a fact that Kelly's been snooping around. At first it seemed to have been tied to me, but what if he found out about your experiment? It would explain a lot."

"Maybe." Parker shook his head. "We can't rule Kelly out, but I think it's much more likely to be a chemist. Raccoon Face tells us that much."

"So what do we do now?" Darcy stepped closer. He felt a tingle of energy as she stood by him at the window.

"I don't—" Parker held his breath as a man pushed through the doors of the building opposite them and hurried down the stairs. Even from across the street he could see the scarring on the man's face, the patches of light skin around his eyes. A raccoon in reverse. The man searched up and down the street and finally turned up the hill in the direction of the chemistry building. Parker watched him until he disappeared from view behind another building.

"We should go." Parker pulled away from the window and dropped into his chair. "While we still have a good idea of where he is."

"Where?" Darcy left the window and limped for the door. "He

saw us together. If he doesn't already know where you live, he will soon."

Parker followed her through the door. "I've got a friend who lives nearby. We could stay there for now. But after that . . . I don't have a clue what to do. We can't just hide and wait for it to go away. I think we should call the police. Someone we trust."

"That leaves out Kelly and Runyan." Darcy led the way to the other side of the building. "With all that money on the line, we can't trust anyone. And we can't just give Raccoon Face the missing ingredient and expect him to leave us alone either. He'll have to get rid of us to protect his claim. The only thing we can do is beat him to the punch. Patent the drug before he can. Once the patent's secure, we should be safe." She pushed through a metal door, and the hallway was filled with blinding light.

"Can I have my hat back? What did you do with my sunglasses?" Parker blocked the light with his hands. He heard a faint rustle and the click of his glasses as they snapped open.

Darcy slid them onto his face and placed the hat on his head. He opened his eyes to see her smiling back at him. "You know you're doing it again."

"What?"

"Riding in your wheelchair."

Parker drove it through the open door and down a zigzag ramp. "It beats carrying it. Want a ride?"

"Yeah, right. Why not leave it here? You don't need it any-more."

"Do you have any idea how much these things cost?" Parker turned away from the chemistry building. "I've only got one more dose of the drug left in my apartment, and after that . . . nothing. It's back to the chair for me."

"Then we'll just have to synthesize more." Darcy walked along-side Parker. "Without the lab notebooks, we won't be able to prove a date of discovery, so we're going to need a sample of the drug for the patent. Before whoever stole the drug can analyze it and work out the synthesis."

"How?" Parker asked. "The chemistry building is almost sure to be watched."

Darcy smiled. "We'll just have to find another way in. Soon."

DARCY

Darcy leaned back against Parker's chest, felt his encircling arm tight around her waist. Newly planted trees drifted lazily past them. Walking students, looking but not looking. Downcast eyes that paused and looked the other way.

Her leg ached, a dull throbbing pain that sent up red-hot flares at every jounce of Parker's chair. She turned and looked back over Parker's shoulder. It would be getting dark soon. Parker's superman theory was interesting, but what if he was wrong? What if it really was the Dark Man? Just because the drug gave him back his strength, didn't mean it would do anything for anyone else. Of course he felt super strong. After being so weak for so many years, he probably felt invincible. But how hard was it to tip a wheelchair on one wheel? No matter how great he felt, it didn't change the facts—someone had tried to kill her and would probably try again.

"How far away are we?" Darcy turned to face the front. "I thought you said this thing was fast."

Parker pressed harder on the controls. "Just a few more blocks. I don't want to go too fast. If we hit a crack we could—"

Darcy pushed down on his right hand and the chair leaped forward. They went careening down the sidewalk, rattling and bumping over its uneven surface. Pain stabbed up through her leg, but she couldn't help laughing. They hit the ramp at the intersection at full speed, and she almost bounced off, but Parker hauled her back on.

"Sorry about that." He started to ease up on the joystick so Darcy pushed it back down again. "Hey, watch out!"

A car slowed to wait for them. A horn beeped, and a grinning lady waved. Darcy turned to wave back.

"Hey, I can't see." He grabbed her hand and pressed it around the joystick. "If you're going to be that way, you drive."

"Parker!" The chair swerved to the right and then straightened. "I don't know how." She directed the chair to the side of the road and slowed to a crawl.

"That's okay, you're doing fine. Just turn up that driveway and get back onto the sidewalk."

"Sure, give me the hard part. What happens if I run off the edge?"

"Then we both die in an agony of hay fever and grass cuts."

Laughing, Darcy managed to guide the chair up the ramp and onto the sidewalk.

"Darcy?"

"Too close to the edge?" She eased the stick to the right.

"No. You're fine. That's her house—the brown one on the left."

"Her?" She pulled back on the joystick, and the whine of the chair's motor grew quieter.

"My friend. She used to be one of my attendants."

One of his attendants? The tall blonde coming out of his apartment. "Just how close a friend is she?" Darcy ventured to ask.

Parker took over the controls and guided the wheelchair down the walk and up the narrow wheelchair ramp onto a broad trellis-lined porch. "Not nearly as close as you." He stopped the chair outside the weathered door and reached an arm under her knees. A slight tremor ran through his body, and then he was standing, holding her in his arms.

"Parker. . . !" Her voice choked off.

"It's okay. You're so light. So . . ." He stared deep into her eyes. Leaned in closer.

His face went suddenly rigid, and he closed his eyes tight as if in pain.

"What's wrong?" She could feel his muscles starting to shake. "I'm too heavy for you. Put me down."

"No, you're fine." He transferred her weight to one arm and rang the doorbell. "I'm just . . . I guess this was pretty silly. Showing off like a middle-schooler." He lowered her to the stoop and set her lightly on her feet.

Darcy winced as she put weight on her injured leg. "Not silly at all. It was nice."

Another jolt seemed to pass through him. He stared at her with intense eyes, his chest heaving, hands clenching and unclenching at his side.

"Are you sure you're okay?"

Parker closed his eyes, nodded his head. "I'm fine. I just . . ." He turned to the door and knocked. "Rachel? Are you there?" He crouched down without looking at her and pulled a key from a large clay pot with a dead plant in it. Turning the key in the lock, he pushed open the door. "After you." He stood back, avoiding her eyes.

"She won't mind us being here?" Darcy stepped into a nice, antique-filled parlor. Mission furniture, floral prints. An expensive-looking Persian rug was centered on a dark hardwood floor.

"Of course not." Parker crossed the room and picked up a slip of paper from off the coffee table. "She's visiting her mom. Looks like we have the place to ourselves." He crumpled up the note and dropped it in a wastebasket.

"I take it you visit Rachel often."

Parker nodded and looked away. His ears and cheeks were definitely turning pink. "Fairly often," he said. "She's home during the day, and her place is a lot closer to campus than mine."

"And you're sure she won't mind . . . you being here with me?"

"Positive." He fidgeted with his hands. Took a step toward the door. "Her mother lives in San Francisco. She visits all the time. Sometimes she even stays at my parents' house."

"Okay. . . ." Darcy plopped down on the sofa and propped her sore leg up on the coffee table. "So what's next? What do we do now?"

"I . . ." He moved nervously closer to the door. "Why don't you lie down and get some rest? I've got to run and pick something up, but I'll be right back."

"Parker, what's wrong?" She pushed up from the sofa and crossed the room. "I know it's something. Why aren't you looking at me?" She put her hands on his shoulders, and his whole body tensed. Cords of muscle stood out on his neck. He was shaking again.

"Nothing. Really." His voice turned suddenly husky. "Please. I just need to go . . . get some supplies. I'll be right back." He opened the door and tottered down the front steps.

"Okay. But hurry," Darcy called after him. "We need to talk."

Stepping around the wheelchair, he hurried down the sidewalk at a fast, awkward walk. She watched him until he was out of sight. What had just happened? Had it been the note?

She wheeled the chair inside and shut the door behind her. Then, checking the window one more time, she crossed the room and pulled the crumpled note from the trash. *No.* She dropped the note back in the wastebasket. It was Parker's note. If she couldn't trust him . . . She paced the room, wincing at each step. Her leg . . . It felt like it was getting infected. She needed to find some antiseptic. She followed a hallway at the back of the parlor. The door at the end of the hall was open. A large bedroom. Pictures covered the walls. Walking past the bathroom, she stepped into the bedroom and looked around the well-kept room. Photographs of Mount Diablo, the Golden Gate Bridge, a seventies-style picture of a woman dancing with a marine. The next photograph hit her hard. Framed in gold. Sitting on top of the dresser. It was of Parker with his arm around a beautiful woman—a young woman with long blonde hair.

She limped back down the hall and dug the note out of the wastebasket.

Parker,
> *Visiting my mom. Should be back in a couple of weeks. Water my orchids if you get a chance.*

> *Love,*
> *Rachel*

CHAPTER 20

PARKER

A LONELY BUZZ FILLED THE AIR—dull orange streetlights struggling to kindle their flames in the cold damp fog of coming night. Parker leaned into the biting wind and kept walking, pushing through the ache of his protesting muscles. He'd walked around the block five times, observing his apartment from every possible vantage point. No one was watching—from the back or from the front. He was sure of it. Either they were inside one of the other apartment buildings or they were waiting for him inside his apartment, or no one was waiting for him at all. He prayed it was the latter, but even if it wasn't, he still had to go in. He'd never get inside the chemistry building if he had to ride in his wheelchair, and there was no way he was going to let Darcy go on her own. He needed adrenaline.

Avoiding the streetlights, he cut across the narrow lawn that fronted his apartment building, dove behind a stand of bird-of-paradise plants, and made his way to his apartment door. He crouched in front of the door and cupped his hands around a small penlight he'd bought at the 7-Eleven. The deadlock and door handle looked fine. No scratches or bulges in the wood—nothing to indicate anything had been forced. Inserting a key in the lock, he threw open the door and leaped inside.

Nothing. No black-faced veterans, no raccoon-faced men with guns, no monsters under the bed. Feeling a little foolish, he closed the door behind him and bolted both locks. Then, feeling his way through the dark living room, he shut himself inside his bedroom and switched on his penlight. He moved to the bed and pulled his pillow out of its case, then carried the pillowcase to his dresser where he started stuffing it with supplies. A pocketknife, two-way radios, a sweatshirt and jacket Jenny had left long ago. He searched the bottom drawer. Had Jenny left jeans too? Sweats? He left the room and walked to the bathroom. At least he had a new toothbrush for Darcy, even if he didn't have—

A thump sounded at the front door. Parker froze, considering and discarding idea after idea after idea. Setting the penlight on the bathroom counter, he rushed out into the living room. Another crash at the door. The sound of splintering wood. He dove into the kitchen as a final crash shook the apartment—the slam of the door hitting the carpeted floor. Heavy footsteps made their way back to the bathroom where his light was still shining.

A loud crash echoed in the bathroom. The sound of glass breaking. Parker crept to the refrigerator, yanked open the door. Grabbing the adrenaline, he made for the front door. An explosion of footsteps sounded behind him. He ran from the apartment and cut across the lawn. Across a driveway, over a small hedge, onto the sidewalk. His foot caught on a sprinkler head and he went down hard, hitting his head on the cement. Climbing unsteadily to his feet, he searched the night behind him. A dark shadow was coming for him. Billowy and insubstantial, its face a black smear against the haze of gray fog.

Parker blinked his eyes as another shadow drifted against his mind. The smell of burnt rubber. He said he'd protect her. He'd promised. The shadow flickered inside his head. Surrounded him. "No!" Parker screamed. He was running. Slowly. Swimming through a sea of dark molasses, he pushed through the filmy night. *The Dark Man.* A black rage rose up inside him, tightening the muscles in his arms and back. Pain shot down his spine, burrowing under his skin like fiery demons. Pain. His ears rang with the sound of it. His bones were breaking. He could hear them, muffled pops in a sea of quivering muscle.

It was right behind him. Pounding footsteps. Dark images, sinister and strange. Black poles. Dark lines against the night. He was a speeding train. Streetlights sped past him. Wind shrieked in his ears. Telegraph Avenue. That's where the Dark Man lived. With all the freaks and crazies. Telegraph Avenue. He had to run. Faster.

The world churned and twisted around him. Pressing bodies. Staring faces. Cool shadows, sanctuary from the stabbing, burning lights. He had to hide. It was after him. Searching for him. He could feel it soaking through his skin.

Rough planks of paint-flecked wood. A butterfly-shaped chip of paint.

He looked up and a dark shadow rose up before him. Military fatigues. Black and gray. He knew he should run, but he'd forgotten how. He tried to take a step, but the world spun around him with the rush of shrieking wind. Darkness, black and final. A cold shadow groped for him with outstretched hands, a shadow with eyes but not a face.

DARCY

Darcy pounced on the phone before it had emitted half a ring. "Hello, Parker?"

"Darcy, it's me." Parker's voice grated over the phone. "Listen. The batteries in my phone are running out, so I've got to talk fast."

"Parker, where are you? What happened? I've been worried sick."

"I'm in Willard Park—next to Telegraph. On Derby Street."

"Derby Street?" Two blocks from where the Dark Man lived. "Parker, please tell me you weren't going after the Dark Man!"

"I wasn't. I was getting supplies."

"They already got him. Runyan told me last night. I called her to help me look for you."

"The Dark Man? What time?"

"Yesterday afternoon. Right after we left the chem building. She says he didn't do it. Says he needs a walker to get around, but I think he might be faking."

"He's not." A deep voice.

Darcy waited several seconds. "Parker, are you okay?"

"I'm fine. I had another blackout. But I . . . need your help." His voice rung with an edge of desperation.

"Are you sure you're okay?"

"I'm fine. I've got my medicine, but I can't take it without a syringe and needle."

"You've got your medicine? You went back to your apartment?"

"Yeah. I'll tell you about it later, but I need that syringe now."

Darcy bit her lip. Parker didn't sound like himself at all. Did he think someone was listening? Tapping the phone maybe? "Okay, I'll call Jason," she said. "He should be able to pick up some syringes."

"Jason can't go near the chemistry building. They'll be watching for him too."

"He can get Lee-Hong to bring them out. Do you need anything else?"

"Have Jason pick up a cardboard box—a big one. The kind they ship twenty-inch televisions in."

"A television box? What for?"

"Just have him bring it to Rachel's and wait for us there. I'll explain later. Now hurry, and bring my chair. It takes a while for the drug to kick in, and we've got to get started on the synthesis soon. I've only got one dose left."

"Parker, calm down. We'll get the drug synthesized. It's not like you haven't had to be in a wheelchair before, right?"

Silence.

"Parker. Are you there?"

"I'm fine, but the phone's starting to go." A monotone voice.

"Just hold on," Darcy said. "I'll take care of the syringe and box and get your chair. Willard Park. Derby Street. Right?"

"Thanks . . . appreciate it."

"No problem." She felt like she should say something but she didn't know what. "Parker . . ."

"Yeah?"

"Don't worry. I'll be there soon." Darcy hung up the phone and punched in Jason's number. Something was wrong; she could hear it in Parker's voice. She paced back and forth, stretching the phone cord as far as it would go. Finally the phone picked up on the ninth ring.

"Hello?" Jason sounded half asleep.

"Hello? Jason?"

"Darcy?"

"Sorry to be calling so early, but Parker's in trouble. The people that tore up the labs . . . we think they're after Mighty Mouse. He needs syringes and a fresh needle, only we can't go near the chem building. We think they're watching it."

"Parker's in trouble?" A long pause. "What's wrong?"

"No time to explain. Just don't go near the chemistry building, okay? They're probably looking for you too. Call Lee-Hong and have him bring you some 5cc syringes and a pack of needles."

"Are you at Parker's place?"

"No, I'm at Parker's friend's place, at the corner of Dwight and Ellworth. A brown house." Darcy's voice broke. "Jason, please. We need to hurry."

"Okay, what was the intersection again?"

Darcy gave him directions, pacing the floor madly as he wrote it all down. He sounded like he was drunk. More likely he'd been sleeping off a hangover.

"Okay, I'm out the door. Right now. I should be there in five minutes."

"But we also need—"

The phone went dead.

Five minutes? Picking up the syringes and needles at the chemistry building was going to take a lot longer than five minutes. She started to dial Jason's number again, but then decided against it. If he didn't have them when he came, she'd send him out again with clearer instructions. Hopefully he'd be more awake by then. They could pick up the box after they found Parker.

She unplugged Parker's wheelchair and maneuvered it to the door. Then, pacing back and forth at the front windows, she watched for Jason's car.

Sure enough his Miata pulled up after only four minutes. Jason hopped out of the car and staggered up the steps. Eyes puffy, hair tousled, clothes rumbled and stained, he looked like a hangover with a hangover.

Darcy opened the door for him, and he rushed right in.

"Where's Parker?" He turned in a half circle, sweeping the room with blurry eyes.

"He's not here. I need to go get him, but first you need to bring me the syringes. Lee-Hong's number is 1489."

Jason looked confused. "These aren't the right ones?" He held up two 5cc syringes and four packs of needles. "I thought he needed them for the drug."

"Actually, these are fine." Darcy took the packs from Jason and stuffed them in her pockets.

"Need a ride?" Jason looked back at the wheelchair and ran a hand through his hair. "I don't know how we'd carry the chair, but if Parker just needs a ride . . ."

Darcy shrugged. "I don't know. He just said to bring his chair." She went to the phone and punched in Parker's number. His voice mail picked up after three rings. Either his phone was off or his batteries were dead. She took a deep breath and turned back to Jason. "I think the best thing you could do right now would be to go out and try to find a cardboard box."

Jason stared blankly at her.

"I don't know. Parker just said to find a cardboard box big enough to hold a twenty-inch television."

"Tube or plasma?"

Darcy shrugged. "Get both. Parker seemed to think it was important."

"Okay." Jason started for the door. "But my share of the patent just got bigger."

She turned the chair on and steered it awkwardly out the door and down the wheelchair ramp. After running it off the sidewalk twice, she finally resorted to climbing inside and driving it down the sidewalk.

The sidewalks between Rachel's house and Telegraph were choked with students. Darcy smiled and nodded as they swerved off the sidewalk to let her pass, but none of them seemed to notice her. No smiles. No *good mornings*. No one even made eye contact. Everyone could see the chair, but the girl in the chair, the girl who used to run guys into telephone poles with her smile, was invisible. In the chair she was just 'another one of those people.' It made her want to scream. She wanted to reach out, grab them by the throats and make them notice her. Make them understand. Not one of them had seen Parker. Even she had missed him. She had known of his accomplishments, but if he hadn't saved her from the glass-heads, would she ever have noticed *him*? The smartest and best-looking guy in the department, and she'd never even said hi to him.

Red flashing lights interrupted her thoughts. An ambulance at the corner of Telegraph and Dwight. Darcy urged the chair to greater speed. The ambulance was flanked by two police cars and a crowd of silent spectators. Whatever the emergency had been, it wasn't an emergency any longer. She turned onto Telegraph and felt like she was entering a war zone. Four, no seven police cars and three more ambulances lined the streets, all of them with their lights flashing. She felt disoriented, dizzy.

"Rage riot," she heard someone say. Another outbreak.

"Excuse me." Darcy pushed her way through the crowd. If Parker had been caught in a rage riot . . .

She turned onto Derby Street and headed straight for the park. At first she didn't recognize him in his sunglasses and hat. He was sitting on a park bench, watching the police cars as they moved slowly through the crowd. She left the chair on the sidewalk and ran to him. "Parker. Are you okay?"

"I'm fine." His sunglasses were scraped and his face was dirty, but he didn't seem to be in any pain.

"What happened?" Darcy sat down next to him, turning to face him.

"First I should take the drug. It takes a while for it to kick in."

Darcy pulled the syringes and needles from her pockets and set them on the bench.

Parker assembled a syringe and jabbed the needle through the serum vial's septum. "Only enough for one more dose. I wish the supply in the lab hadn't been stolen."

Darcy nodded and watched as he filled the syringe and injected himself in the thigh.

"So? Are you going to tell me what happened, or not?"

"I went by my apartment to pick up supplies." Parker put the cap back on the used syringe and covered it with his hand while a police officer walked by. "I'm almost positive I got in without being seen. But I wasn't there more than a few minutes before someone broke down the door and chased me outside. I think I was starting to black out while I was running away. Everything's kind of a blur. Normally I have thirteen or fourteen hours after taking the drug before I pass out from exhaustion, but last night with all the walking I was doing, I guess I blacked out early."

"You woke up? Here?" Darcy cast a wary glance around the park.

"Close to here. I managed to crawl to this bench without anybody seeing me." He nodded to the police cars cruising up and down Telegraph.

"Do you know what happened?" Darcy wished Parker wasn't

wearing his sunglasses. She wanted to see his eyes.

Parker shook his head. "Whatever it was, I was conked out at the time. The police sirens woke me up." A frown darkened his face, and he looked down at the vial. "If we hurry we can sneak into the chemistry building now, while the police are still occupied."

"Sneak into the chemistry building?"

"If Runyan wasn't lying about taking the Dark Man into custody—and I don't think she was—then we won't be safe until we can synthesize more adrenaline and establish our claim."

"What if we just gave it to them? Let them have the patent?"

"Then they'd kill us to protect *their* claim." Parker's muscles went suddenly rigid. His face turned red. He was shaking from head to toe.

"Parker?"

"I'm . . . okay. We've got thirteen hours. Starting now. After that I won't be able to get us in."

CHAPTER 21

PARKER

PARKER PULLED A BASEBALL CAP low over his eyes so its visor rested on his dark glasses. He crouched down and picked up the television box, holding it carefully under the bottom. Jason had paid for a TV in order to get the box. Two of them actually. A tube television and a flat panel. Apparently it never occurred to him to ask for just the boxes.

Parker walked toward the chemistry building, scanning the area, studying each face. So far so good. He didn't recognize any of the faces he'd seen on his first trip into the building. Of course, they could be watching from a neighboring building. As he neared the entrance, he hoisted the box higher, holding it up so it partially hid his face.

A pretty redhead held the door open for him. "Thanks," he called to her and walked inside. Carrying the box into an elevator, he hit the button for the second floor. The elevator dinged open, and he walked around to the back stairs and then down four flights to the lower basement. Hurrying through the maze of passages, he made his way to the animal room. Three taps on the door and Darcy opened it immediately.

"Any trouble?" she whispered as soon as the door clicked shut behind them.

"None that I saw." Parker set the box down on the floor and started to open it.

"Man!" Jason pushed up through the top of the box and climbed to his feet. "I can't believe you actually did it!" He was practically shaking with excitement.

"You aren't that heavy. I told you that." Parker couldn't help smiling. Jason had been convinced Parker wouldn't be able to pull it off.

"I wasn't worried about me." Jason turned to Darcy with a big grin. "It's her I was worried about."

"Watch it!" Darcy turned on him, holding out a condenser tube like a sword.

Jason ignored her. "Do you realize what we've got here? Think what Mighty Mouse could do for the marines, professional football, the Olympics . . . It could be worth billions!"

"If we live long enough to spend it." Darcy set the condenser on the table.

"Okay, guys." Parker turned to the computer. "We've got five hours before I turn into a pumpkin. We need to get busy."

"One more question," Jason said. "How much can you lift? I'm seeing a fantastic demonstration for the press conference."

"The press conference?" Darcy looked to Parker.

"Jason thinks we should hold a press conference," Parker explained. "Publicize this whole thing. Once we detail every step in the synthesis and tell the world about the guys trying to kill us, it'll be almost impossible for anyone else to jump our claim."

"Not to mention it'd be a great way to drum up interest in the drug." Jason paced the floor. "We'll be rolling in venture capital. Genentech will buy us on the spot!"

"We can worry about that later," Parker said. "First the synthesis." He started connecting the HPLC instrument on the computer table to the PC.

"What about that HPLC?" Jason stood behind him. "Can you lift that?"

Parker couldn't help smiling. "I already did." He hefted the instrument, balancing it on one hand as Jason let out a high-pitched whistle. "Actually, it's not that heavy. Darcy weighs—"

"Watch it!" Darcy raised a hand in warning.

" . . . nothing compared to the HPLC." Parker laughed at her expression.

"Oh, man!" Jason glanced back and forth between Parker and Darcy. "I still can't believe you can lift *her*."

"Okay guys. Enough is enough." Darcy stepped between Parker

and Jason. "Can we talk about something else now? Like maybe how big Darcy's thighs are getting? Or how bad her breath smells?"

"Seriously, Jason," Parker said, "I hate to put a damper on your enthusiasm, but if we don't get this drug synthesized soon, we may not get—"

A thump sounded behind them. Parker spun around and stepped forward to place himself between Darcy and the door. Jason handed him one of the two-by-fours they'd used to reinforce the bottom of the television box. He stood next to Parker, gripping the other board like a baseball bat.

The door swung open, and Ray stepped into the room. "Parker?" Ray stumbled back. He looked like he'd seen a ghost.

Parker lowered the board. "Hi, Ray."

"Dude, it *is* you! Oh man." Ray stepped cautiously inside, the door swinging shut behind him. "Dude! Like, I didn't recognize you at first. Look at you!" He took a couple of steps to the side, keeping a cautious distance from Parker. "You figured it out. The adrenaline's really working. What did you do to make it work?"

"Make it work?"

"You know, our drug made the Mighty Mice go crazy. How'd you fix it?"

"I didn't. It's the same drug you and Jason tested." Parker stepped back and dropped the two-by-four in the box. "I suppose you already saw the lab."

Ray stared back at him like he was a minor deity. "Sorry I didn't call you and tell you myself. Things have been totally off the hinges lately. The police weren't going to let me in, but I told them I had to feed the mice. I think they were worried I was some kind of animal-rights activator. They wrote down my driver's license and everything."

"So the police are back outside?" Jason stepped forward.

"Yeah. They were here yesterday too. I would have come in, but they wouldn't—"

"Ray." Jason stepped closer to Ray, slapping the two-by-four in the palm of his hand. "It's important you don't tell anyone about Parker. Do you understand?" He sounded angry. "No one can know Parker can walk. Okay? Don't tell anyone about the drug."

"Sure, but . . ." Ray looked to Parker, his face a mask of confusion.

"It's okay, Ray." Parker put a hand on Jason's shoulder and

pulled him back. "Just don't tell anyone about us. The guys that trashed the lab might come back if they knew we were down here."

"Okay. . . ." Ray stood there, fumbling with his hands.

"We need your help," Parker said. "If you don't mind. We need you to collect reagents and glassware from around the department. It's best if we're not seen in public."

"No problem, dude."

Parker and Darcy made a list of the materials they would need and sent Ray off on a scavenger hunt throughout the building.

"Do you think we can trust him?" Jason asked as soon as Ray was out the door.

"I don't know," Parker said. "If we can't, I guess we'll find out soon."

DARCY

Darcy swirled a Florence flask in a slurry of dry ice and acetone, leaving it submerged until the solution inside was frozen solid.

"Isn't there something else we can do to speed up the roto-vap step-up?" Parker paced the room like a caged animal. "The synthesis is taking too long. We're running out of time." His last sentence was practically a snarl.

Darcy turned her head in surprise. "Parker, calm down. It's okay."

"I am calm." He stared back at her beneath knotted brows. "Ray should be back by now. I know for a fact that we've got ethanol in the Sinclair lab. He's up to something. I can feel it."

She exchanged glances with Jason, who was weighing out reagents on a top-loading balance. "Ray just left a few minutes ago. He had five items on his list."

"He's stalling. Waiting for *him* to come." Parker turned toward the door. "I'm not waiting anymore."

Jason stepped between Parker and the door. "Waiting for who to come?"

Parker pushed Jason out of the way. "Don't think I'm not on to you. I know what you are." His eyes narrowed and his mouth dropped open in a wolfish leer. "Out of my—" Parker's head cocked to the side. His eyes widened and he took two steps before his legs buckled and he collapsed in a heap on the floor.

"Parker!" Darcy ran to Parker's side and rolled him over onto his back. She checked his breathing and pulse while Jason straightened his legs and moved him away from the door.

"Pumpkin time," Jason muttered.

Darcy nodded. "What do we do now?"

"We get that drug synthesized while he's sleeping it off. He's going to need it in the morning to get us out of here."

"Do you really think the box is necessary?"

"Are you willing to take that chance?" Jason said.

"I guess not."

Jason got up and went back to the balance. "Then get to work. I've made a good start on the patent application, but I need that sample."

"*You've* made a good start?" Darcy was surprised. Parker hadn't said anything about Jason working on the patent application.

"Yeah. Parker got me started on it when he was still at home in recovery. In fact, it was my idea. He hadn't even thought of registering a patent."

Darcy brushed Parker's hair back from his forehead and then climbed to her feet. "Okay, let's get to work." She walked back to the acetone slurry and removed the flask.

"I've already started on the press conference too." Jason grinned. "Parker's still not so sure about it, but going public's absolutely necessary if we're going to beat our competition to the punch. Think you can use your influence to convince him after he wakes up?"

"I'm not sure how much influence I have . . ." Darcy looked back to where Parker was lying and let out a gasp. His eyes were wide open. "Parker!" She hurried to his side as his eyes drifted slowly shut. "Parker?" She shook him gently. "Are you awake?"

Parker's eyes fluttered beneath closed lids. A faint smile touched his lips. He seemed to be sound asleep.

JASON

Jason selected a Zegna tie from his closet and looped it around his neck. After pausing at the mirror to check how it looked with his Armani suit, he raced into his office and checked the window that looked out over his driveway. Parker had cautioned him not to go back to his house, but he had no choice. For something this big, he had to look the part. In the public relations arena, appearances were eleven-tenths of the business.

He went to his desk and searched through the lists of names and phone numbers he'd pulled together for the press conference. There it was: *Susan Lany, CBS News.* He punched in the number and waited.

"News desk, Lany speaking."

"Susan? Jason Turner, University Relations, UC Berkeley." Jason automatically matched Susan Lany's terse speech pattern. "Listen, about the Pyramid press conference. I need to make sure you're not sending more than one camera crew. I just got a call from NBC, and they were planning to bring four. Can you believe it? We're going to be flooded. Standing room only, okay?"

"The Pyramid press conference? Actually . . ." Susan paused. Jason could almost hear the cogs turning. "We were planning to send . . . two crews."

"Sorry. We're at the limit—unless you're willing to station a crew backstage. Pyramid's worried people won't believe their eyes. A backstage crew might help rule out smoke and mirrors."

"Really?" Her voice came alive with sudden interest. "Sounds like it's going to be quite a show."

"Biggest science news since Apollo 11." Jason grimaced. Way too Hollywood. He needed a more concrete hook. "Listen, one more thing. If your crew brings a common household object—a folding chair maybe, or a fireplace poker, something that couldn't possibly be bent by a normal human being—I'll make sure your reporter gets on stage to talk to Pyramid. Just make sure they can verify that the object hasn't been tampered with."

"Okay. But what's this all about? Can you—"

Jason tapped the flash button on his phone, waited a few seconds and tapped it again. "Hello, Susan? I've got an important call on the other line. Can I get back to you?"

"Sure, I—"

"Call you in ten, okay?"

He hung up the phone and checked CBS off his list. That was

the last of the major networks. Now he needed to get to the University Relations office fast, before Susan called.

———————

Jason swept into the University Relations suite and made a beeline for the vice-president's office.

"Excuse me. Can I help you?" A middle-aged admin rose to her feet as Jason hurried past her desk.

"It's okay," he said. "Kohler's expecting me." Jason opened the door without knocking and stepped inside.

A balding man with white, bushy eyebrows looked up from behind an enormous, gray metal desk.

"Robert Kohler? I'm Jason Turner, Shanahan Communications." Jason crossed the room and shook Kohler's hand as he rose from his chair. "John Pyramid hired my firm to set up the press conference. I just wanted to make sure you understood that his decision to go with us wasn't motivated in any way by a lack of faith in your organization. I hope to work with you at every step of the process."

"John Pyramid?" Kohler blinked several times, making his eyebrows waggle like big fluffy fans. "I'm afraid I don't understand. I've gotten several calls about—"

"Sorry, we've had to move fast on this one. Somehow the Pyramid breakthrough has been leaked to the public. His lab was broken into and his research may have been stolen. There have already been two attempts on his life."

"You're kidding me. You mean the animal rights break-in at the chemistry building?"

"That's what we're telling the public—for now. The Pyramid discovery could be worth billions to the university. The patent lawyers are working around the clock on it, but the faster we go to the press, the more secure Pyramid's claim will be."

"I'm not sure I quite understand." Kohler shook his head. "What you're telling me is all very strange."

Jason considered his options. To backpedal now would be an admission of weakness. "I need press packets, parking, an auditorium, security at all entrances. No one can be at the press conference without a pass."

Kohler watched Jason through narrowed lids. Jason could see

the skepticism building in his eyes.

A knock came at the door, and Kohler's admin poked her head into the room. "Bob, I've got a representative from CBS on the phone. The New York office. She wants to talk to a Jason Turner?"

"Sorry about that." Jason jumped to his feet, watching as Kohler's eyes grew round. "Mind if I take the call in here?" Jason didn't wait for a response. "As you can imagine, the information we're giving out is very sensitive."

Kohler stood up suddenly and motioned for Jason to use his desk. He was hooked.

PARKER

"Parker, you look great. Don't worry." Jason pulled a bundle of black material from a plastic shopping bag. "Just put this on with your hat and sunglasses."

"What is it?" Parker unfolded the heavy material. "A blanket?"

"It's a coat. I got it from the drama department. Isn't it great?" He turned it over and helped Parker into the thing.

"You've got to be kidding. I'm not going to wear this." Parker looked at his reflection in the mirror. He looked like a Hollywood stage magician.

"Of course not. Pyramid's going to wear it." Jason straightened it on Parker's shoulders. "Once you tell them who you really are, you can take it off. It gives drama to the transformation."

"But—"

"Trust me." Jason looked him in the eye. "I know what I'm doing. If we're going to make the national news, we've got to go for visuals."

"I look like a buffoon."

"Would you rather look dead?" Jason set Parker's hat on his head and tapped it down in the back. "The press conference isn't worth doing if we don't make a huge splash. The world has to know who invented adrenaline 355. We need to be the talk of the town."

Parker studied his reflection in the mirror. "Well, I can guarantee one thing. If I go out looking like this, I'll definitely be the talk of the town—if they can stop laughing long enough to talk."

DARCY

Darcy looked around the second row of the crowded auditorium in amazement. The place was packed. Television cameras were set up everywhere, along with lights, still cameras, microphones. A reporter stood three feet away from her, bathed in an intense beam of light. She stood with her back to the stage, talking into a microphone about a folding chair she was carrying. Another reporter held a stop sign. Another leaned against a torchiere lamp. CNN, NBC, ABC. It was crazy. A huge multimedia flea market.

She didn't know how Jason had carried it off, but he'd certainly delivered on his promise of a big press conference. It seemed almost too big. She couldn't help wondering if it was even necessary. They'd finished the synthesis without incident. No mysterious watchers. No bogeymen in the stairwells. It had been almost a week and they hadn't seen any sign of Raccoon Face. No sign at all that they were being watched. She was starting to wonder if maybe the break-ins had been animal rights activists after all. The police seemed to think so. They'd been so busy with the fresh outbreak of rage riots that they hadn't even bothered to take down the tape across the door to her lab.

She looked at her watch. 3:35. The press conference should have started five minutes ago. She searched the crowd for Jason or Parker. Professor Sinclair, Parker's major professor, was present and sitting in the front row. Parker's pediatrician and muscular dystrophy doctors were there too. But no sign of Parker.

A murmur went through the crowd as Jason walked across the stage to the podium. Adjusting the microphone, he flashed the crowd a big smile. "Ladies and gentlemen . . ." He waited for the noise to subside. "Ladies and gentlemen, my name is Jason Turner. Before I introduce John Pyramid, I'd like to tell you how deeply this man has touched my life. I grew up with Pyramid in Marin County. And until very recently I'd given up all hope of ever seeing him again. I can't begin to tell you how deeply I've missed him. No matter what he's done, no matter how famous he becomes, the only thing I care about is my being able to talk to him face-to-face." Jason paused and looked out over the audience. What did he think he was doing? Darcy turned and looked up the aisle Parker was supposed to be coming down.

"And now, ladies and gentlemen . . . John Pyramid." Jason held his hand out over the audience like a ringmaster at a three-ring circus.

Parker walked quickly down the aisle, bobbing erratically in his peculiar stiff-legged gait. A long black coat billowed behind him like a superhero's cape. His ridiculous hat was pulled low over his sunglasses. Jason had told Darcy about the coat. She still couldn't believe he'd actually convinced Parker to wear it.

Two-thirds of the way down the aisle Parker jumped, springing six feet into the air. The crowd gasped, and an excited murmur broke out. The auditorium exploded with flashes of light. People started pouring into the aisle. Parker took two quick steps and leaped for the stage, clearing a small crowd of camera people and reporters.

"Ladies and gentlemen, please be seated!" Jason called out over the sound system. "Please return to your seats. There will be plenty of time for questions. But first . . ." Jason signaled to a security guard who escorted the reporter from CBS up onto the stage. The reporter followed Jason to the microphone and handed him a metal folding chair. "This is Susan Lany from CBS news. Susan, can you confirm for us that this is an ordinary folding chair?"

"I brought it here myself from the CBS office in New York."

Jason opened the chair and set it on the stage where everyone could see it. Parker stepped up on the chair and hopped up and down on it, windmilling his arms to maintain his balance. Then, hopping off the chair, he picked it up and crushed it in his hands. Darcy smiled as she watched the faces of the reporters. Jason was right. They'd make every news channel in the country.

Parker dropped the crumpled chair on the stage with a loud metallic *clang*, then stepped behind the podium. "I'm . . . um . . ." He waited for the auditorium to quiet. "I want to apologize for the theatrics. My friend Jason just wanted to get your attention. This isn't the circus, and I'm definitely not a strong man. In fact, I'm a scientist. A scientist who's invented a new drug." He pulled a vial of adrenaline out of his pocket and held it up for everyone to see. "The drug is called—"

A gunshot rang out from the back of the room. Parker spun backward and fell to the floor. Darcy rose to her feet screaming as two more shots sounded over the cries of a mob in full panic.

PART 3

Hyde and Seek

"'If he be Mr. Hyde,' he had thought,
'I shall be Mr. Seek.'"

—ROBERT LOUIS STEVENSON
THE STRANGE CASE OF DR. JEKYLL AND MR. HYDE

CHAPTER 22

PARKER

PARKER SLAMMED INTO THE FLOOR, thunderclaps ripping through his head. Explosion after explosion jolted his body. Burned into his chest, his left arm. *Heart attack.* The words hit his brain like a high-pitched scream, drowning out the roar of the crowd. *Heart attack.* He needed help. A doctor. He tried to push off the floor but his left arm buckled beneath his weight, giving way in a flash of crippling pain. Hot to the touch, wet . . . He pulled back his hand, and a smear of bright red made the auditorium spin. He'd been shot! So much blood. He couldn't believe it.

Darcy! Parker struggled to his knees. Electric blue spots filled his vision as he crawled toward the storm-tossed crowd. Writhing, roiling, it surged toward the left exit, gathered in a dense wave, recoiled and surged to the right. *Darcy.* He caught a glimpse of her, fighting her way against the flow. He slid off the stage, felt his legs give out from under him. He crumpled to the floor in excruciating pain.

"Parker!" Cool hands cradled his face. Soft golden eyes.

The noise of the crowd swelled, rising around him like a tidal wave. Parker shook his head. Tears were running down Darcy's face.

"Darcy, it's okay." Parker tried to sit up, tried to find his strength.

"Your . . . You've been . . ."

"It's just a scratch. See?" He rolled away from her and rose shakily to his knees. "Help me stand up. We've got to get out of here."

"What?"

Parker scanned the crowd. A man in a white shirt and dark tie. A woman with a large canvas bag. "Whoever shot me may still be here."

"Too many people." A wet hand grabbed him around the wrist, and Darcy's head appeared under his arm, hauling him to his feet with surprising force. "They'd never get through this crowd." She pulled him along the stage, pushing against the panicked mob.

His legs felt wobbly at first, but after a few steps he felt his strength come surging back.

Still no police. Where were the police officers he'd seen earlier in the back of the auditorium? Parker searched the crowd for uniforms. "You'd think the police would have taken charge by now," he said.

"Come on!" Darcy dragged him onto the stage and pulled him behind the curtains. Weaving around the bleachers and podiums that filled the backstage area, they pushed through an exit door and burst out into a brightly lit hallway.

Footsteps came from their left. Hushed voices.

"I think I can run now," Parker whispered. "Let's get out of here." Taking Darcy by the hand, he turned right, and they hurried down the hall in an awkward skip-hop-leaping jog. Right at the first corner, left at the next, they made their way through the building's maze of corridors. A steady stream of harried onlookers stopped and stared as Parker and Darcy ran past. Slack jaws. Wide, fearful eyes. The halls behind them buzzed with excited whispers. "Pyramid . . . Blood . . . Someone tried to kill him."

Sirens wailed in the distance. Parker stopped at a steel door under a glowing exit sign. "I can't run anymore," he said. "It's attracting too much attention."

Darcy nodded. "The hat and cloak aren't helping either."

Parker shrugged his right arm out of the coat. Gritting his teeth, he peeled the sleeve from his left arm and dropped it on the floor. He then removed his hat and tossed it on top of the coat. "So what's it going to be? Make a run for it now or go back and take our chances with the police?"

Darcy frowned, her eyes fixed on his arm. "The police in the auditorium—they had guns. Everybody else was searched."

Parker nodded. He'd been thinking the same thing.

"You need to get to a hospital," Darcy said. "You've been . . . I can't believe this is happening! It doesn't make sense."

The sirens were louder now; they didn't seem to be moving.

"I don't need a doctor. It's just a scratch. But the police . . . Maybe they were just fakes. Maybe the real police could take us into protective custody."

"But for how long? You think Raccoon Face will leave us alone after he steals your invention?" Darcy shook her head. "Better to deal with a down-and-out chemist than to be hunted down by a billionaire with unlimited resources." She shoved the door open and poked her head outside.

"See anybody?" Parker stepped closer and peered out over her head.

"Only a few hundred people."

"Good. Maybe we can blend in." Parker followed Darcy out onto a wide, crowded avenue. All around them people were talking in hushed, excited tones. People from the press conference. Parker scanned their faces, searching for someone he recognized. Someone who didn't fit.

Darcy gripped him by the right arm and pulled him into the center of a group of reporters. "Straight ahead." Her voice was a hoarse whisper. "A man in a leather jacket. Standing next to that bench."

Parker looked up without moving his head. The man was watching the crowd, scanning each person who walked by.

Parker led Darcy to the left, maneuvering behind a tall, white-haired man in a navy blazer. Then he noticed another man—on the sidewalk, just opposite the man in the leather coat. The man's arms were folded across his chest with his right hand concealed beneath his jacket.

"Dead end," Parker whispered. "Way dead." Parker slowed his pace, holding his ground as the rushing crowd shouldered their way past them. The man by the bench looked up, eyes flashing in recognition. Parker grabbed Darcy's hand as the man motioned to his partner and the two of them broke into a fast walk, pushing their way through the crowd.

"Run!" Parker spun Darcy around and they took off running. A man's angry cry. Footsteps right behind them. Parker glanced back. The men were running now. The man's hand was out of his coat.

"The creek!" Parker released Darcy's hand and hurdled a low wall to his left. Scrambling down a shallow bank, he wove through a stand of redwoods, leaping from side to side like a slalom skier. A quick glance back. Darcy was right behind him. Where were the men? Climbing up a steep, ivy-covered slope, he made for a tree-shaded building. Almost there. All they had to do was get around the buildings, lose themselves in the tangle of steps and alcoves. A whistling shriek rang in his ear. A hissing cough from behind. The men were running up the bank of the creek. Parker dodged to his left and kept running. Another cough. A spray of dirt and leaves.

"Hurry! The faculty club!" Parker cleared the top of the hill and leaped behind the cover of a shielding wall. Up a set of steps, down a sidewalk, he ran out into a wide clearing. *Great.* The men were still close behind them. He followed the edge of one of the buildings, searching frantically for a place to hide.

"Turn right," Darcy called out.

Parker took off down a narrow alleyway between two buildings. If they could just cut back and get behind the men. He took another right and then stopped at a wall. Dead end. Darcy rounded the corner and slammed into him. He had to wrap his arms around her and hold her to keep her from falling.

"Par—"

"Shhh." He touched a finger to her lips and listened, holding his breath to hear. Men's voices. Parker looked frantically around the tiny alcove. No doors, no windows. Rust-colored stains and a lingering smell marked the space where a Dumpster used to sit. Steam rose up from the gutter like a sputtering ghost.

Footsteps sounded at the back of the building. They could hear heavy breathing—two men panting after a long run. Parker and Darcy pressed themselves against the wall at the back of the alcove. *Father God, please. Please save us.*

Suddenly, like a burglar alarm in the dark of night, Parker's cell phone went off in his pocket.

JASON

Jason sat slumped on a set of backstage bleachers, holding his cell phone to his ear. "Come on, Parker. Come on." The phone picked up on the first ring. "Hello, Parker?"

Nothing. A metallic clang. The faint sound of men's voices. Then the connection switched off. Dial tone.

Jason dialed Parker's number again. Counted off the rings. "Hello, Parker?"

"You have reached the voice mail of James Parker. . . ."

He cocked his hand back to fling the phone across the room. All his planning! How could it have gone so wrong? He went rigid, trembling with the rage that welled up inside. Not yet. He had to hold it together. Had to find Parker. He lowered the phone and hit redial. Still no answer.

Jabbing at the Off button, he slipped the phone into his pocket. He stood up and took a step toward the stage. John Pyramid. It just wasn't possible, was it? He felt like he was going to be sick.

The harsh squawk of a radio sounded ahead of him. Two police officers stepped around the curtains. "Jason Turner?" The taller of the two officers stepped forward. "We'd like to ask you a few questions."

Great. Jason's gut tightened. He never should have agreed to do the introduction. The whole press conference was a bad idea. He raised a hand to his stomach, let his eyes go defocused. "I . . . uh . . ." A long pause. "I . . . I'm Jason."

"Jason, we understand that you've been through a terrible ordeal, but we need you to tell us what happened. While it's still fresh in your mind."

Jason let his eyes drift away from the officer. "I think there were several shots. Gunshots. One of them hit P . . ." Should he tell him about Parker? About Pyramid? Suddenly he wasn't sure—of anything. "Pyramid was shot. I saw him go down. I . . ." Jason held his breath and shut his eyes for a second, then let his breath out in a light hiss. "It's all on film. Is there any way we could talk about this later? I'm not feeling so good."

"If you could just answer one or two more—"

"I'll be right back." Jason stumbled toward the exit near the stage. One of the officers started to follow, but a cameraman close by waved to get their attention.

Jason hit the door and started running. Parker. He'd seen him with Darcy at the base of the stage. A reporter had distracted him for just a few seconds and then, poof, they were gone. Disappeared into the crowd. He ran out onto the street and jumped into his car.

Somehow they'd managed to get away without anyone seeing them. But how? Where? He pulled out in front of a yellow Mercedes and made a tight U-turn. Either Parker was at his apartment or at the hospital. It didn't matter which. But he *would* find them—even if he had to check every hospital in town. And if they were at Darcy's place . . . He'd figure out a way to lure them out. One way or another.

He parked his car outside Parker's apartment and ran to the door. "Parker? Darcy?" He jabbed at the doorbell. "Parker?" He tried his key in the lock, but the key wouldn't turn. What was going on? Had Parker changed the locks?

Taking a step back, he kicked open the door and slipped inside. The place was a wreck. Broken glass on the floor. Ripped furniture. Papers and books everywhere. "Parker?" he called in a low voice. "Anybody?" He checked the bathroom and bedroom. They were torn up even worse. What had happened here?

Walking through the living room, he checked the kitchen one more time. Broken picture frames were scattered on the tile floor. He turned one of the pictures over and froze. Jenny. Parker's sister. He pulled the picture carefully from the broken frame, shaking it to remove any pieces of broken glass. The picture gave him an idea. Parker's dad was a doctor; he'd never risk going to a hospital. He'd go straight to his parents' house.

DARCY

Darcy ran blindly through the darkness, feeling her way along the sweltering, steam-filled tunnel. Her hand jerked back from a burning pipe. Her hip clipped a metal brace. Sweat drenched her clothes. The heat was unbearable. It was a giant steam oven. A torture chamber from the pit of hell.

A gunshot rang out behind them, and Parker's hand tightened suddenly around hers. He'd been hit. She bit her lip to keep from screaming. The shot had been so close. They were catching up. She wasn't going to make it.

"God, please . . . No . . ." Darcy plunged forward, pulling Parker deeper into the boiling darkness. Another metal brace caught her shoulder and spun her around, wrenching Parker's hand from her grip. She felt as if she were falling. Tumbling without a lifeline into a deep, dark sea. Heavy breathing sounded all around her.

An invisible hand seized her by the arm and swung her around. She lashed out with her fists, felt her left hand connect. Again. Again.

A soft voice. "Darcy, it's okay." Strong arms. A tight embrace. "It's me—Parker. It's okay."

Darcy gradually went limp. It was too late; they weren't going to make it. It was her fault.

"Darcy, we've got to keep going. Can you make it?"

"I think so."

The strong arm wrapped around her, guiding her slowly through the tunnel. "We're okay. We just need to find a hiding place." The calmness of his voice soothed through her. "All we need is a—"

Another shot fired behind them. Darcy started to run, but Parker pulled back on her hand, forcing her to slow down. "They're a lot farther away than they sound," Parker whispered. "Listen for their footsteps."

Darcy nodded. A turnoff, that's what they needed. There had to be a turnoff. A passage to route the steam pipes to other buildings.

"Who knows, maybe we can hide in the Red Man's lair. He's probably good friends with your Dark Man. They may even be related; they have the same last name." Parker's upbeat tone sounded a little forced.

"The Red Man?"

"You haven't heard the legend? A homeless guy is supposed to live in the steam tunnels. Red as a beet from all the steam."

"Does he have horns, a pitch fork, and a pointed tail?"

"Shhh." Parker froze in his tracks.

Darcy held her breath and listened. Nothing.

"I think we're okay." Parker started walking again but at a more rapid pace. She could feel herself tensing. Something was wrong. He'd heard something but didn't want to frighten her. Suddenly the wall dropped away from her right hand. She stopped and reached out as far as she could into the void. Nothing. "I think I found a turnoff!"

"Shhh . . ." Parker swung her around to the right. "It's a lot narrower," his whisper was so low she could barely hear him. They felt their way along the walls of the new passage, keeping their hands stretched out in front of their faces. The passage narrowed more until it was hardly wide enough for the two of them to walk side by side. Darcy ducked under Parker's arm and slid an arm around his waist. He pulled her in close, wrapping an arm around her shoulder. The memory of her father's face. Hugs, soft and warm. Contentment. Trust.

Parker stopped, and the two of them turned, arm in arm, to listen. She could hear footsteps now. A whining noise that sounded like static from a radio. The footsteps grew louder and then gradually faded. Darcy leaned into Parker, felt herself being drawn up into a crushing embrace. Her heart pounded. She wanted to shout, scream out for joy. She rose up on her toes, reaching with upturned face.

A strange noise behind them. Were the men coming back? They hurried deeper into the narrow passage. For a long time they walked, stopping occasionally to listen, but the noise was never repeated. She searched the passage ahead. It seemed to be getting lighter. She could see the faint outlines of giant steam pipes, the curve of the passageway.

They inched their way forward. The light was coming from a grate ahead of them. She heard a static buzz coming from directly above them. The closer they got, the more familiar it sounded. A police radio. She could hear the dispatcher's voice. Something about University Avenue. They waited, but the officer didn't seem to be moving. He just stood there. Guarding the exit?

Parker motioned to Darcy, and they crept back in the opposite direction. When they were well out of earshot of the grate, Darcy stopped and stretched up on tiptoe to whisper in Parker's ear. "That was a police radio. The men chasing us had a radio too. I think they were the police."

Parker's cheek brushed up against hers as he nodded. "We've got to get out of here. Soon."

Darcy nodded. "Maybe if we wait here a little while, we—"

"You don't understand. I'm going to turn into a pumpkin any minute now. If I pass out, there's no way you'll be able to drag me out of here. You've got to promise to leave me here and get yourself out. Okay?" Parker sounded desperate.

"Don't you still have a vial of adrenaline? You had it at the press conference."

"It doesn't help. I always pass out, no matter what."

"Then we'll just find a way out of here, before you pass out."

"Just promise me," Parker whispered. "Promise me you'll leave me behind and get out."

"We've got plenty of time." Darcy grabbed Parker's hand and pulled him through the dark passage. When they came to the intersection, they decided to follow it back the way they had come. There had to be another way out—a grate or a manhole or something. The police couldn't be watching all the exits.

Finally, after what seemed like hours, they found another side passage and followed it to a vertical shaft of dim light.

Parker reached up and felt along the ceiling. "It's a manhole cover. It's dark outside, but I think there's a light nearby."

"Listen." Darcy didn't hear a radio, but that didn't mean anything. Somebody could be up there watching, ready to start shooting at the first sign of movement.

"I don't hear anything. I think we just have to chance it." He reached up and fumbled with a crude latch on the underside of the manhole cover.

"Wait. Someone could be up there."

"We don't have time to wait." Parker's voice went suddenly deep. "I can already feel it. It's starting to happen." He slid back the latch and pushed up on the manhole cover. A crescent of soft light shined in, illuminating his features. He pushed the cover to the side and reached down to squeeze Darcy's hand. Silence.

Parker leaned down and whispered in Darcy's ear. "I'll go first. You wait here until you're sure it's safe and then follow me out. If we get separated, we'll meet back at Rachel's house."

Darcy nodded. The picture of Parker with the beautiful blonde flashed before her eyes, but she didn't say anything. Parker's hand was beginning to shake. She had to let him go. "Go on. Hurry." She stretched up and brushed his cheek with her lips.

Parker drew in his breath sharply. He stepped away from her, drinking her in with large, luminous eyes. His jaw quivered, and his eyes darted around like a frightened animal.

"Go," Darcy whispered. "Hurry!"

Parker nodded, climbed up the metal rungs, and disappeared

through the manhole. A few seconds later Darcy followed him up, poking her head outside to watch as he ran toward a cluster of buildings.

A shout sounded behind her, followed by the sharp report of a gun. Darcy whirled around. Three men with flashlights were closing in fast on Parker. "Run!" she cried.

Parker stumbled. He was moving slower. He wasn't going to make it.

"Hey!" Darcy called out to the men. "Over here! I'm the one you want."

The sidewalk near her head erupted in a stinging spray of cement as a muffled shot rang out behind her. Running footsteps. Shouts. Now they were after her!

PARKER

Parker turned at Darcy's shouts. "Look out!" he yelled. He stood frozen in place, watching the scene in horror as the air around him buzzed with invisible death. Darcy's head ducked back into the tunnel. Hoping they would ignore her to chase after him, he ran for the cover of the nearest building. A quick backward glance. Two men were still after him.

Sprinting up a sidewalk, dodging between two buildings, he made his way up the hill. Lights! He dodged around a streetlight, keeping a healthy distance between him and the deadly beams. Crouching in the shadows, he felt a black presence hovering at the edges of his mind. The lights were pursuing him, chasing him up the hill. Jumping out at him, blocking his way. He could hear their pounding footsteps. They lashed out at him, filling the night with bursts of thunder.

Familiar ground. The chemistry building. Blinding light stared down at him, filling him with loathing and dread. The shadow. He could feel it burning in his legs. The agonizing fire that blazed in his left arm. The lights were getting closer. He had to run. Faster.

A young woman stood silhouetted against a glass door. Down he swooped, through the door. He was flying now. Up the stairs. To Darcy.

The door exploded, sending a burst of splinters into his face.

Blood. The red splatter filled him with rage. He leaped up the stairs, stomping out the pain that flared up all around him. Hazy smoke, exploding in blinding bursts of flame. Footsteps. He ran faster. Spinning round and round. Lowering his shoulder, he burst through a locked door. Out into cool, soothing darkness. Shivering stars. A Hollywood moon blushing behind a wash of silk-screen clouds.

Gravel crunching beneath his feet, he ran across the rooftop. It was too late. The shadow was upon him. Its footsteps echoed behind him. It was inside him now, filling his mind with its putrid, oily stain. He had no choice. Racing to the edge of the roof, he leaped out into the void as the shadow closed around him. One by one the rushing stars slowly winked out.

CHAPTER 23

DARCY

Darcy raced through the steam tunnel, pushing through the boiling darkness with hot, blistered hands. Slamming into the end of the corridor, she turned and listened. The men were close behind. Two, maybe three, of them. To the right or to the left? She looked one way, then the other. A bobbing light in the left passage made the decision for her. *To the right!* She ran up the corridor, threading her way between jutting metal braces. Finally, after what seemed an eternity, the corridor seemed to be getting lighter. Strips of faint light against a water-stained wall. She climbed onto a pipe on the side of the wall and pushed up on the grate with all her might. The heavy bars shifted slightly, but she didn't have the strength to lift it.

Ripping a piece of fabric from her already torn sleeve, she pushed up on the grate and wedged the cloth so that it hung down into the corridor. A dim light bobbed up and down along the wall to her left. They were drawing near. She jumped off the pipe and ran down the dark corridor—and into a wall. A dead end. She felt both sides of the passageway. No way out. She was trapped.

"This is the way they got in." The grating voice froze her where she stood. They couldn't be more than thirty feet away.

She moved to the back wall, careful not to splash in the ankle-deep puddle that pooled around her feet.

"Look!" Another, deeper voice. "Think she's already out?"

"Could be a decoy," the first voice said. "Let's keep going."

A jolt of panic shot up Darcy's spine. She felt frantically along the corridor walls, burned her hands on the steam pipe overhead. They were getting closer. She could hear the splashes of at least three sets of feet.

Pulling her sleeves over her hands, she climbed up into the twelve-inch space between the steam pipe and ceiling, gritting her teeth to keep from crying out at the heat that seeped through her clothes. Arching her back and pressing down with her heels, she fought to hold herself off the scalding pipe. The corridor gradually grew brighter. Darcy held her breath, waiting. Flashlight beams crisscrossed the end of the tunnel. Beads of sweat dripped from her face. Her shoulders were burning. They were taking too long. Searching too carefully. She closed her eyes, waiting for the shots, the bullets that would end her life. One more second. One more—

"It's a dead end." The deep voice. "I told you she got out."

Splashing feet. "We couldn't have done nothin' about it anyhow. She's long gone now. Might as well tell Dave." The corridor dimmed as the footsteps receded.

"Might as well tell Dave*?"* What was it about that name? Darcy waited as long as she could. Finally, when she couldn't stand it any longer, she slid off the pipe and dropped to the floor, lying back in the icy coolness of the puddle.

She stood up and waded back to the back of the corridor. They thought she'd gotten away. They'd give up the search soon, then all she had to do was wait it out and sneak back to Rachel's house. Hopefully Parker was there waiting for her. *God, please help him,* she prayed. *Help him to get safely back to the house.* She sat down on the damp floor and leaned back against the wall. After the day she'd had, sitting in a wet, dark sewer was going to be almost pleasant.

Darcy slipped inside Rachel's house and locked the door behind her. "Hello? Parker?" She felt for the light switch and flipped it on. "Parker?" Running down the hallway, she checked the bathroom, bedroom, office. Back to the kitchen. "Parker!" Icy fingers closed around her heart. She couldn't breathe. "Parker!" He hadn't made it. Had he passed out before he could get here? That had to be it.

Cold, exhausted, numb from shock and pain, she sank to the floor. What should she do now? The men might still be looking for her. She couldn't risk going back. Not now. It was too soon.

Jason. She pushed herself to her feet and stumbled to the living room. Scooping up Rachel's phone, she punched in Jason's cell number.

He answered on the first ring. "This is Jason. What'cha got?" He sounded surprisingly awake for—Darcy checked her watch— 2:30 in the morning.

"Jason, it's Darcy. I—"

"Darcy! I've been so worried. Is Parker with you? Is he . . . okay?" She could hear the hum of a car engine in the background.

"I . . . don't know." She fought to keep her voice steady. "There were these men. They tried to kill us. They had guns. We escaped into the steam tunnels, and Parker made a run for it and—"

"Darcy, where are you? Are you at Parker's?"

"Jason, listen. They were shooting at him. He was about to pass out."

"Where are you?"

"I'm . . ." Darcy looked around the room. "We were by Stephens Hall. He was running toward the tower."

"Darcy, calm down. I know this is hard. It's hard for me too. But if I'm going to help, you've got to tell me where you are."

"I'm at a friend's place. Parker's friend."

"The place you were at before?"

"Uh-huh. Parker was supposed to meet me here. But he might have had to hide somewhere else. Maybe the chem building. He has keys and they—"

"Darcy, shut up and listen, okay? I'm in San Francisco now. I should be there in forty minutes, okay? Forty minutes. We can figure everything out when I get there." The phone went dead.

Forty minutes. Darcy hung up the phone. What if Parker didn't have that long? She grabbed a peach and a bottle of water from the refrigerator and crossed the room to look at herself in the mirror. If she went out now she'd stand out like a mud wrestler at a high school prom. She went to Rachel's bedroom and threw open her closet. Shucking off her torn muddy clothes, she searched the closet for something . . . different. Something that didn't look like her. Something nice. She grabbed a black suit. Fancy. Even Parker wouldn't recognize her in this.

She pulled it off the hanger. Rachel wouldn't mind, not if she was really Parker's friend. *Friend.* The word stuck at the back of her mind. She slid on the pants and smiled. Rachel was obviously much taller than herself, but apparently she was bigger in the waist as well. She put the top on, and her smile faded. Okay, maybe she was bigger in other ways too. She knew it shouldn't, but the thought irritated her.

Tying her hair back in a black scrunchy, she examined herself in the mirror. Not bad. She was about as un-Darcy as she could get. She rushed from the house and out into the night. Jason would figure it out. She'd told him where to look. Besides, two of them searching separately would be more efficient than both of them searching together. She slowed to a fast walk when she reached the edge of campus. The streets were deserted. No one in their right mind would be out this late, not with the recent outbreak of rage riots going on. She searched the street. Anyone out now was either up to no good or a very desperate grad student. She tried to act the part as she darted across the street.

Keeping to the shadows, she cut through the alley between the Hearst Gym and the parking garage. Memory of the glass-heads made the hair at the back of her neck tingle. Parker had saved her. He'd already risked his life for her once. Why had she let him go first? If something happened to him, it would be her fault.

She cut across a courtyard, moving from tree to trash can to bench to tree. The faculty club stood across the glade to her right, but she couldn't risk cutting across the open space. Not enough cover. Besides, Parker would have been trying to lose them. He would have stayed away from the clearings.

Crouching low to the ground, she scooted across a short stretch of sidewalk and down a series of steps. Her foot slipped on the last tread. The cement was slick with a black stain. Her stomach tightened as she bent down to examine it. Surely it wasn't . . . She reached out a finger but couldn't force herself to touch it. The sharp scent of iron. The smell of . . . death. Heart pounding, she backed away from the steps. Blood. There was so much of it. Too much. She took a deep breath, spun around to search the night around her.

The stain. Her eyes kept wandering back to it. It seemed to trail away to the north, like something had been dragged through it. Some body?

She followed the trail across the creek and moved in a daze along Gilman to the front of the chemistry building. If Parker was hurt, that's where he'd go. As much as her mind revolted at the thought of him being injured, it all made sense. She forced herself to search the grass on either side of the walk, afraid of what she might see, afraid of what she might miss.

A thud sounded ahead of her. A man, about fifty yards away, shuffling up University Drive. She froze and was about to dive for cover when a flicker of recognition sparked inside her. The shaky, bobbing walk. The way he carried himself, held his arms. Parker? She took a deep breath and held it. They weren't out of danger yet. She couldn't risk a shout.

Running up the paved walkway, she chased after him, waving her arms whenever he seemed to look her way. Sure enough, he was heading toward the chemistry building, covering the ground in awkward leaps and bounds. She was about to call to him when a door clanked open. The *tap-tap* of distant footsteps.

Darcy pushed herself to greater speed. Someone was coming; he was heading right for them. If she shouted, he'd be able to run, but what if it brought the men with guns? She watched silently as a woman appeared at the top of the hill. Most likely a grad student. Nothing to worry—

The woman's scream tore through the night as the figure sprang toward her with a tremendous leap. The woman turned and started to run, but he cleared the distance separating them in another bound. He picked her up. For an instant she was suspended above his head, then he sent her sailing through the air to crash into the windshield of a parked car.

Darcy stopped, too shocked to make a sound. She watched in horror as he advanced on the still form of the woman. She was still alive. Darcy could hear her whimpering. She twisted and turned pathetically as he grabbed hold of her, raised her above his head. . . .

"No!" Darcy found her voice in a high, wavering scream.

He whirled around, dropping the woman on the hood of the car. He advanced on Darcy, crouching low like a wild beast. A low growl rumbled through the darkness. She couldn't breathe, couldn't run. The woman climbed to her feet and limped away, but his gaze remained fixed on Darcy. Dark, alien features. The stealthy movement of an animal.

"Parker? It's me—Darcy."

Another growl, this time louder. He leaped forward, covering in a single bound half the distance between them. Another leap, high into the air.

Darcy scrambled forward, ducking as Parker sailed over her head. Without turning back she took off running. The chemistry building. If she could just get inside. A loud thump. Scraping footsteps behind her. She kept running. *Don't look back, just run!* The footsteps were getting closer, but so were the doors. Twenty more feet . . . Ten more . . . A dagger of realization stabbed through her. He was right behind her. If the doors were locked, she was dead.

PARKER

A soft golden light. Dancing, swaying, leading him deeper and deeper into the shadow. Filling him with a terrible longing. A deep, aching void. Parker chased after it, running, leaping, dodging this way and that. Long interminable hallways, dark classrooms, desolate labs. Stretching out his hands, he cried out, but the figure eluded him, slipping through a wall of shattered glass. He slashed at the wall with ragged talons, tearing out great shards of diamond-bright crystal. Bloodred hands. Sparkling gemstones littered the floor. He couldn't see. She was getting away.

Lowering his head like a battering ram, he dove through the wall. A splash of dazzling color. He was through.

The figure cowered before him. Golden eyes. Soft white skin. Her beauty stunned him. Filled him with a terrible dread. He tried to turn away, but his feet wouldn't listen. Step after step he moved closer, shielding his eyes with twisted, pronated hands. Her eyes, her lips. He couldn't stop. It was too late.

Laughter. The sound of pealing bells. The music of the sun. It burned through him, chasing away the shadows, dissolving the black tendrils twisted around his heart. Anger, rage . . . The taste of it faded from his tongue like a half-remembered dream. Washed away by a bright, rushing sea.

A strong odor filled his nostrils. Eucalyptus! Parker opened his eyes, blinking against the surrounding brightness. No! Not again. Red-hot shame prickled through him. Guilt. *God, please forgive me. The dreams. They're getting worse.*

He tried to lift his face off the ground, but a burning pain stabbed up through his left arm. It felt hot, stiff. His memory came rushing back. Men with guns. He and Darcy in the tunnel. Jumping off the roof. Parker shut his eyes, struggling to remember what had happened next. He'd been running from the men, had tried to jump from the chemistry building, a two-story drop onto Tan Hall. After that, nothing. He couldn't remember. Just the nightmares, dark and terrifying. He squeezed his eyes shut, trying to erase the horrific visions from his mind. They were just dreams. Harmless. He'd feel better soon; he just needed the drug.

Careful not to move his left arm, he wriggled over onto his back and pushed himself into a sitting position. Fifteen minutes. He'd feel better in fifteen minutes. Shielding his eyes from the early morning sun, he searched the area. Redwoods. A grassy field. He was on campus. Somewhere near the creek.

Then he saw the blood. His hands were covered with it. It was on his pants, his shirt. Had Darcy seen him like this? Why hadn't she said anything? He plunged his hand into his pocket and pulled out his medicine and a new syringe. No time for alcohol. He needed the drug now. For Darcy. She'd be worried about him.

Jabbing the needle through his bloody pants, he injected himself in the thigh. The drug burned through his leg, bringing it trembling to life. The quiver of anticipation. The surge of strength. Everything would be okay now. Everything would be just fine. Darcy was safe and sound at Rachel's house. He'd see her in fifteen minutes.

"Darcy!" Parker dug for the key under the dead plant on Rachel's porch. Where was it? Had she taken it inside? He tried the door and the knob turned in his hand. "Darcy, I can't believe you forgot to lock the door." He closed the door behind him and scanned the empty living room. "Darcy?" He hurried back to the hall and stopped. Darcy's muddy clothes littered the floor just inside the bedroom door.

A lump formed in his throat. He stood frozen in the hallway, staring down at the clothes. "Darcy. . . ?" He stepped toward the bedroom. His head spun with the images from his dreams. Darcy could be hurt. She needed his help. He took another step.

No. He averted his eyes and quietly closed the door. Poor thing. She'd probably been up all night worrying about him. After what she'd been through, she deserved a chance to rest. Besides, it would give him a chance to get cleaned up. She'd freak if she saw him like this.

He tiptoed back to the bathroom and carefully peeled off his clothes. His arm and side didn't look so bad once he inspected the damage. And once he'd washed the wounds off in the shower, they looked better still. His side was gouged by an inch-long cut across the rib cage. A small hole that went all the way through the meaty part of his triceps pierced his arm. It hurt like crazy, but it was going to leave an impressive scar. It was almost worth it.

Parker searched in Rachel's medicine cabinet for bandages and applied an old Jar Jar Binks Band-Aid to his ribs and two Queen Amidalas to his arm. Then, selecting clean clothes from the stash he kept in Rachel's linen closet for emergencies, he got dressed, brushed his hair, and inspected himself in the mirror. Not bad— considering. And with all the racket he'd made in the shower, Darcy was sure to be awake.

He stepped out into the hall. The bedroom door was still shut. "Hello, Darcy?" He tapped softly on the door. "Are you awake?"

No answer. He started to turn the knob, but thought better of it. She was probably exhausted. Besides, she wasn't even dressed. He let the bolt slip gently back into place and crept back to the living room.

Pacing back and forth, he tried to make sense of the events of the last couple of days. John Pyramid. Was it him or Pyramid they were after? And why the earlier attack on Darcy? Had she just been at the wrong place at the wrong time? Or were the attacks connected somehow? He had to think they were, but how? And what did Jason have to do with everything? What was with that strange introduction at the press conference?

He collapsed onto the sofa and flicked on the television with the remote. With all the cameramen at the press conference, surely they'd be playing the story on the news. Maybe they'd already captured the gunmen. He flipped through the channels and stopped at a tape showing him dressed as Pyramid jumping down the aisle of the auditorium. He turned up the volume.

" . . . and here we see footage from a security camera mounted outside a building on the UC Berkeley campus." The image changed to a grainy black-and-white night shot of a patio area. Parker gasped as a smudgy shadow entered the screen at the upper left and then leaped out of the picture in a high arching jump.

"This shot was taken five hours after the Pyramid press conference, only minutes before a female graduate student reported being attacked by a, quote, 'tall, super-strong creature that flew through the air like a character in a kung fu movie,' unquote."

Parker sat stunned as the black-and-white image played and replayed in slow motion. This was followed by a side by side, slow-motion comparison with the jump at the press conference. He felt like he was going to throw up. Three students had been attacked. One killed, two seriously injured.

A blurry close-up of his face filled the screen, bright lights reflecting in black sunglasses. John Pyramid. Murderer. One killed. Two seriously injured. "Dear God, no! Please . . ." Parker slumped over onto the floor. "Please, it can't be true. I was asleep. It was just a dream. They were all dreams!" The man in black. He'd had pincers instead of hands. It wasn't real. It had to be a dream. The glowing woman, she was lit up like a lawn Santa on Christmas Eve. It couldn't have been real. She'd been trying to kill him. And Darcy. Golden, glowing Darcy. She'd been flying. A will-o'-the-wisp in a dark wood.

Something deep inside him broke, a chord of recognition. It was true. He'd known it all along. "No!" A sobbing moan escaped his lips. The guilt, the pain, the self-loathing—he'd been trying so hard to suppress it, hoping to convince himself it wasn't real. *God, please* . . . A tremor jolted through his body. "No!" The scream ripped through his vocal cords, burning through his voice until it died in a ragged whisper. He slammed the floor with his fists, and his arm flashed out in pain. He hit the floor again. Again. He deserved pain. He deserved it all.

No, please, no . . . The words repeated over and over in his mind. It was all over. Everything. There was nothing left. Nothing but pain and loss and misery. *God, please forgive me. Please forgive me.* He reached out, begging for comfort, but the heavens were shut off from him. Guarded by a dark and fiery storm. The pain would never go away. He'd been given the choice and he'd chosen to take the drug. He'd gone against everything he knew was right. His choice would haunt him for the rest of his life. However long that might be . . .

When he finally sat up, his eyes were crusty and swollen, his face stiff as cardboard. There was only one thing he could do now: turn himself in to the police. He'd spend the rest of his days in jail, but he could live with that. It would be safer that way—for everyone. But first he had to destroy his drug supply. His notebooks, the laboratory setup, every hint of how to make the drug. He'd have to swear Jason and Ray to secrecy. And Darcy too. A pang stabbed through him, so intense it felt like he was being ripped apart. All his hopes. His dreams. He'd been so close to making them come true. She really seemed to like him. Even when he was in the chair. But now . . . Now it was only prison, maybe even the electric chair. Whether it was his wheelchair or the other electric chair, it made no difference. Without the drug, death would come soon enough either way.

He walked to the hall and looked back to the bedroom. Somewhere, deep inside him, something stirred. He stepped toward her door. Now was his chance. She didn't know yet. He had one last chance to say good-bye. One last chance to stand before her, a man moving under his own power. He turned the doorknob, swung open the door.

What was he doing? He staggered back from the pile of clothes lying on the bedroom floor. The beast was inside him, fighting to come out. It was trying to trick him. He turned and ran down the hall, across the living room, swung open the front door. He had to destroy the drugs, now before it regained control. Already he could feel the hesitation, something deep inside resisting the drug's destruction. Excuses flitted through his mind. He could feel his resolve weakening. The beast was growing stronger. And if he blacked out before he could finish? What then?

He ran back into the living room and grabbed a notepad and pen from off Rachel's desk. Taking a deep breath to control the shaking of his hands, he started writing.

Darcy,

Just made a terrible discovery. Can't explain now, but whatever you do, don't go near the chemistry building until you hear from me again. As soon as you read this, go to a friend's place—someone I don't know—and stay there for at least two days. You've got to trust me. I can't explain, but your life could be in danger.

He bit his lip. How should he end the note? He wanted so much to tell her how he felt, but it would only make things worse, more painful. He took a deep breath and wrote: *Your friend, Parker.*

His hand trembled as he signed his name. If he could just see her one more time. Look in on her. Kiss her hand. Her cheek . . .

No! He ran to the front door and taped the note to the doorknob. Then, locking the door behind him, he stepped outside. There, it was done. He started to turn away but a thought stopped him. His chair. It was still inside. If he went off the drug he would need his chair. Maybe if he just waited there—

"No!" He leaped off the porch and hit the sidewalk running. He had to get away from her, had to get to his lab. The beast was coming back, and he didn't have much time.

CHAPTER 24

DARCY

DARCY LAY HUDDLED IN THE DARKNESS, curled up in a tight ball in the safety of her loft. She could still see the woman crashing into the car's windshield. She cringed at the thought of Parker standing over her, lifting her over his head. *Why? Why is this happening? Why Parker?*

No answers. No comfort. Nothing. Just cold, hard silence. Even her tears were gone. All she could do was remember, remember and wonder why. Over and over she went through the events of the night in her head, trying to make sense of it. There had to be an answer somewhere. The men with the guns. Running through the steam tunnels. One minute Parker had been close to passing out, the next he was attacking women on the street. Attacking *her* too. At least he would have if he'd been able to catch her, if the glass doors hadn't been broken. If she hadn't been able to get inside with all the bright lights.

It had to be the drug. It had to be. It had changed him, just like Alzheimer's had changed her grandmother. Only the drug was much, much worse. Parker was wrong. After all was said and done, chemistry and biology always won out in the end.

She turned and looked out across the grid of light that filtered up through the ceiling tiles beneath her. What if Parker had attacked others too? The police cars and ambulances on Telegraph. It had all happened while Parker was blacked out. People had been . . . killed. It couldn't have been Parker, could it? He'd have to go to jail. Or would he? If it was the drug and Parker didn't know anything about what was happening, could anybody really blame him? It was the drug, not him. He didn't even have a choice. Or did he?

She rolled onto her back and pressed her palms to her eyes. *God, no. It can't be Parker. You wouldn't have allowed it. It wouldn't be fair.* She sat up and crawled to her ceiling tile door. It wasn't Parker. She wouldn't believe it. Couldn't believe it. Maybe it was someone who just looked like Parker. It had been dark. She'd never seen his face. Not really. One of the Dark Man's friends perhaps. Maybe that's why she hadn't seen his face; it had been darkened to blend with the shadows. She climbed down the ladder and tiptoed across the lab.

But Parker was alive. That at least was good news. She stopped in the doorway, realizing the implications of her thoughts. If the beast she had seen wasn't Parker, then she had no reason to believe he was alive. He could be lying wounded somewhere on campus. Trapped somewhere and unable to walk. If she really believed the man she'd seen wasn't Parker, then she'd be out there looking for him, wouldn't she?

She picked up the phone and dialed the number of Rachel's house. Pacing, waiting, letting it ring until the answering machine finally switched on. "Hello, you've reached Rachel's answering machine . . ." A soft, sultry voice sounded over the phone. She hung up the phone and tried again. One more time. Finally she decided to leave a message.

"Hello, Parker. This is Darcy. It's eight o'clock and I'm at my . . . apartment. You know, in my bedroom. Call me back as soon as you get this message. I'm really worried about you. I . . ." She hesitated for a long time, groping for the words that needed to be said. A loud beep sounded in her ear. Too late. She hung up the phone and slumped into her desk chair.

If he wasn't at Rachel's, where could he be? The chemistry building? His lab or maybe the animal room downstairs. She got up and hurried down the hall. She had a key to his lab so she'd search there first. Then, if she didn't find a clue there, she'd try the animal room.

PARKER

All those dreams. Parker lifted the HPLC above his head and smashed it against the concrete wall. Pieces of broken plastic skittered across the floor as the machine slid across the floor and bumped against the rack of mouse cages. The man with pincer hands. The glowing woman. Their faces danced before him. Mocking him. Laughing at his pain. It would be so easy . . . He could take the drug and run. There would be other labs. The chemistry department was full of labs. He couldn't destroy them all. He might as well accept it.

No! Parker swept the computer off the table and grabbed the new lab notebook from the desk. He wouldn't do it. He'd never take the drug again. Grabbing a lighter, he carried the notebook to the sink and lit it on fire. All the notes they'd rewritten from the first set of notebooks. All the mouse data, the synthesis procedures. He watched as the flames darkened and curled one page after another.

The light hurt his sensitive eyes, burning through the dark lenses of his sunglasses. Acid tears streamed down his face. He'd done this before. In his lab upstairs. *He* was the one who had burned the notebooks. Somehow, during one of his blackouts, he'd found a way to resist. It all made sense. He'd burned the notebooks *and* torn up the labs.

Attacked Darcy. Parker staggered back from the flames. "Please, no!" Something caught the back of his leg, and he fell to the floor. He lay on his back, stunned. Everything in his being recoiled at the thought. He couldn't believe it, but it had to be true. Suddenly it all made sense. All the pieces suddenly fit.

He climbed to his feet and looked frantically around the room. He could feel the monster roiling inside him, struggling for control. *Run away! Get away from the police.* The urge was almost overpowering. He took a step toward the door, then hesitated. How could he trust himself? How did he know which thoughts to trust?

Okay, Jammy. Calm down. Think. Something wasn't right. Something about the lab break-ins didn't fit. His mind cleared for an instant like the sun peeking out from behind dark storm clouds.

The drugs ... The answer came to him in a sickening burst of insight. He'd thought the drugs had been stolen, but it had been him all along. The monster. He'd hidden them from himself. He'd known all along he would eventually figure out what was happening and try to destroy them. He was saving them, waiting for a moment of weakness. The moment he started taking control.

Parker flung open the animal room door and made for the stairs. Leaping up the stairs a half flight at a time, he reached the third floor in seconds. How could he have been so stupid? He'd been so busy concentrating on the animal room that he'd forgotten all about the drugs in the refrigerator in his lab. No, not forgotten. He'd been tricked. The monster was getting stronger. Invading his thoughts, clouding his reason.

Footsteps ahead of him. He looked up just as a woman with light brown hair stepped into one of the elevators. "Darcy?" He called after her as the elevator doors dinged shut. No, it couldn't have been. Darcy was asleep at Rachel's house. He unlocked the door to his lab and walked across the room. Something felt wrong. He looked around the lab. The books on his desk. The papers on the counter. Had he left his desk drawers open? His stomach turned flip-flops as he stepped over to the fridge. He reached out his hand but couldn't bring himself to open the door. If he destroyed the drugs now, he'd never know what could have developed with Darcy. It would be good-bye forever. The drugs were his last chance at freedom, at life.

No, that was a lie. Not freedom. Slavery. He had to destroy the drugs. Had to. *God, please. Give me the strength.* He swung open the refrigerator door and looked inside.

The drugs were gone. Across the top shelf, on the tray where the drugs should have been, was the smeared print of a bloody hand.

DARCY

Darcy took the elevator down to the lower basement and stepped out into semidarkness. Some of the lights must have gone out. She inched through the twisting corridors, listening to the echo of her shoes against the painted cement floor. Not bothering with the sterile scrubs in the entrance to the vivarium, she walked back to Parker's animal room.

"Hello, Parker?" She knocked on the door. Nothing. She tried the knob and was surprised to find it wasn't locked. The door opened with a swoosh of escaping air. The acrid smell of smoke blasted her in the face. She stepped inside and stood next to the door, too stunned to move. The room had been ransacked, everything destroyed. The glassware, the HPLC, the roto-vap . . . Everything. And something had been burned. She stepped over to the sink and examined the ashes inside it. Parker's new lab notebooks? Just like what had happened before. Her mind raced. Someone had been here, and recently. Probably the same person who had trashed the labs before. Which meant the person who attacked her earlier wasn't Parker. It couldn't have been. He'd never burn his lab notebooks or trash his labs, even on drugs. Why would he?

So the person she'd seen last night couldn't have been Parker. *Ockham's razor—keep it simple.* It had to be the same person who tried to attack her before, the same person who burned Parker's notebooks. And he'd returned here last night to trash the place and burn the new notebook. It all made sense now.

Which meant Parker was still missing. If he wasn't the one who attacked her, why hadn't he called? Unless . . . She looked down at the floor and a flashlight caught her eye. The steam tunnels. She'd waited so long before going back to Rachel's last night. What if Parker had gone back to the steam tunnels to search for her? He could be there now, too weak to crawl out. She scooped the flashlight off the floor and ran for the door. Her clothes were a little fancy for spelunking, but Rachel would just have to understand.

PARKER

Parker crouched on the roof of the chemistry building, huddled against the cold night wind. He'd been searching the ninth floor ice machines for the missing drugs when a group of strangers stepped out of the elevators. He'd barely had enough time to duck into a vacant lab. Luckily the lab had a window that opened out onto the roof or he would have been discovered immediately. He'd barely gotten out in time.

They'd searched the floor for hours. Surely they were gone now. He poked his head up above the window ledge and looked inside the lab. Empty. Slowly, carefully he slid the window open and crawled inside. The lab was silent except for the rushing of the wind outside. He crept to the door and looked out into the hallway. The coast was clear. Apparently they'd given up and gone home.

He tiptoed around the corner and slipped into the stairwell. His mind raced as he descended the stairs. Where could he have hidden the drugs? He'd searched the whole building. If he didn't find them soon he was going to have to admit defeat and go home. He crept out into the third-floor hallway and made his way back to his lab. Maybe if he looked one more time. He opened the door and stepped inside his lab. But where to start? He'd already searched the lab once.

Suddenly it hit him. He didn't feel the slightest bit of resistance to the idea of searching for the drugs. That's what *it* wanted him to do. He looked up at the clock on the wall. 9:30. The day had flown by. He could black out any minute now. He had to do something. He couldn't let himself . . . kill.

He swept the lab, blinking his eyes in an attempt to penetrate the fog that clouded his brain. *Don't worry,* a voice spoke deep inside him. *You're okay. Just calm down. God will take care of everything.* Parker sat down at his desk, felt himself starting to relax.

How could I be such an idiot? He leaped to his feet. Couldn't he see where this was leading? He couldn't lock himself in his apartment. It wouldn't hold him for a second. *Think, Jammy, think!* His eyes fell on the cabinet where he stored the pH meters and other expensive equipment. He'd had to lock them up months ago when all his equipment started disappearing.

He yanked open the tool drawer and pulled out his electric drill. Good, it still had the screwdriver bit in it. Fingering through the keys on his ring, he tried three keys in the padlock before it finally sprang open. Opening the hasp, he used the drill to back out the seven heavy screws that held it in place.

Two minutes later he was bounding down the stairs. The walls of the animal room were cinder block and reinforced concrete, and the door was massive. If he could just lock himself inside for the night, by the time someone came by to let him out, he'd be harmless.

He raced to the animal room and slammed the heavy door shut behind him. Holding the hasp across the door, he drove the screws into the frame, closed the hasp and inserted the lock. Almost done. He pulled the key off his key ring and slid it under the door. Then the screwdriver bit, his pocketknife, all his change.

Panting like a winded dog, he circled the room, running through scenarios in his mind. He'd thought of everything. Even if he wanted to, there was no way he could get hold of the drug. Let the monster come; he was ready for him.

He sat down on the floor and waited. It was going to happen soon. He could already feel the fatigue, the dark shadow crawling up his spine. His eyes fell on the bank of mouse cages to his right, and a spark of excitement flared to life inside him. What if *he* had hidden the drugs in the animal room? What if *he* had known all along he would lock himself inside? What if it had been *his* idea in the first place?

The room seemed to spin around him. It was too late. *He* was coming. He leaped to his feet and ran for the door. Suddenly the lock struck him as a small and ridiculous thing. He'd been tricked again. The puny lock could have held Parker, but not him. He grabbed the door handle with both hands, braced a foot against the wall, and yanked.

DARCY

Darcy crept up the back stairs of Lewis Hall and slunk through the deserted main hallway. She'd come back from the steam tunnels to find the chemistry complex swarming with a small army of men. She couldn't tell whether they were cops or not, but judging from the way they were moving, they were all concealing weapons. She'd spent the whole afternoon and most of the evening hiding out by the creek, pretending to be engrossed in a enzymology textbook she'd checked out from the undergraduate library.

She crossed through into the chemistry building and took the stairs down to the lower basement. She'd check the animal room first and then Parker's lab before admitting defeat and holing up in her loft for the night. After that she didn't know what she'd do. As much as the prospect of being questioned by Runyan grated on her, she would just have to chance calling the police and telling them everything she knew.

Cracking the door open just enough to determine that the lower basement hallway was empty, she switched on her flashlight and wound her way back to the vivarium. Her wet shoes made a sucking, squishing sound that seemed to come from everywhere at once. She turned suddenly around and shined the light behind her. *What was that?* There it went again. This time it was behind her. It was coming from the vivarium.

Rats. She pushed boldly through the swinging doors and went inside. Rats and mice. The place was full of them. Ahead of her another noise, this time louder. The rattling of a door. The door to Parker's animal room. She crept forward, listening. It was Ray; it had to be. It was feeding time. He was—

The door burst open. Darcy spun around as a tall, shaking fig- ure emerged from the room. She started running, her flashlight beam crisscrossing wildly across the walls.

"Darcy?" Parker's voice. "What are you doing here?" His voice shook. With anger?

She stopped and turned around. "Parker? I . . ."

Parker lumbered toward her, outstretched hands blocking the light. "I told you to stay away. You've got to go. Now!" He collapsed to his knees, burying his face in his hands.

Darcy took a step backward, stunned at the tone of his voice. "Parker, what's wrong?" She backed away from him, unable to take her eyes off him. She couldn't leave him. He needed her. It wouldn't be right.

"I'm changing. I can feel it." His words slurred together. "I can't control it any longer. Run!"

"I can't leave you!"

"I said, run!" He looked up at her with wide, fearful eyes. "Now! I don't want to . . . hurt you."

Darcy backed through the swinging doors, stumbled into the dark corridor beyond. *"Don't want to hurt you. I'm changing."* Could it really be true? She ran through the corridors, all the way back to the stairwell. Flinging the door open, she pounded up the steps, burst out into the lobby, and out into the night.

The rage riots, the girl outside the chem building. It was all Parker. The drug was turning him into a monster, and he'd known it all along.

CHAPTER 25

A SHAFT OF SUNLIGHT PIERCED THE CLOUDS. Crystal dewdrops clung to translucent blades of grass, dazzling with rainbow bursts of brightness. A fat bee, black and yellow, its legs impossibly burdened with sacs of golden pollen. Its buzzing grew louder, more insistent.

"Is he breathing?" Voices broke through the drone. "Careful. You sure you should touch him?" An unseen hand poked him. He felt himself falling. Burning light blasted his face. He raised his hands to his eyes and felt the warm touch of a human hand.

"Are you okay? Can you hear me?" A soft, feminine voice. "Do you want us to call an ambulance?"

"No. Please . . ." Parker squinted in the sunlight. Silky black hair and chocolate skin. Lustrous brown eyes. "I'm okay. I just have these . . . fainting spells."

"Do you need help?" Another face crowded in. Golden hair, backlit by the morning sun.

Parker pressed his hands to his face as the reality of his nightmare came crashing down on him. He'd left the chemistry building. The monster had come back—while he was with Darcy. Horrible guilt flooded over him. He was a murderer. It was a reality he could never escape, no matter how hard he tried.

"Are you okay? What's wrong?" Soft hands pulled his arms from his face.

Parker looked up into warm brown eyes, felt a stirring deep within. A strangled groan escaped his lips. "Get away. Please. It's not safe."

The girl drew back, her eyes wide with surprise.

"Please. Leave me alone. You don't know me."

The girl opened her mouth and glanced at her companion, who shrugged and looked away.

"I'll be okay." Parker coaxed. "Please, just leave."

"We were just trying to help." The girl rose out of view. "Try to be friendly these days and you get your head bit off."

Parker propped his head up with his hands and watched as the girls made their way back across the grass. When they were finally out of sight, he flipped over onto his stomach and army-crawled across the dew-drenched lawn. The road was about thirty yards away. If he could just reach it, maybe he could get a taxi to take him to Rachel's house to pick up his wheelchair. And once he had his chair . . .

Then what? The only thing he wanted, the only thing he cared about at all was being with Darcy. Life in a wheelchair had been tolerable until she came along. It had been good. But now . . . An image floated before his mind, a vial of the drug sitting in his apartment refrigerator. The monster . . . Had he made it that easy to find the drugs? All he had to do was get back to his apartment and destroy them. Then he'd be done with the whole thing. No more risk. No more temptation.

Of course if he locked himself away at night . . . The cold room had a thick metal door. Or maybe he could install metal bars across the door to his bedroom. He could still work things out. Maybe he could find a way to live with the drug *and* Darcy.

He pulled out his cell phone and dialed the number for the East Bay Paratransit van. Thirty minutes later and a fifty dollar tip poorer and he was guiding his chair down the wheelchair ramp in front of Rachel's house, waving good-bye to the overly inquisitive attendant.

He waited until the van was completely out of sight before striking out for his apartment. The morning was warm and bright. A flock of cedar waxwings squawked from a stand of berry bushes across the street. A white-haired lady in baggy pink sweats looked up from digging in a flower bed. She smiled at him and nodded as he waved back. Everything seemed so normal. Peaceful. If he'd really gone berserk and killed people, wouldn't he feel guiltier? What if the reporters had gotten it all wrong? What if it hadn't been him? The murderer had been identified as John Pyramid, but

Pyramid didn't even exist. He'd left his cape and hat at the auditorium. What if someone else had been wearing them?

The more Parker thought about it, the better he felt. He'd been with Darcy last night as he was changing—blacking out. He'd left the building and nothing had happened. To Darcy or anyone else. Didn't that prove he wasn't a monster? Maybe it was the men with the guns. That made a lot more sense than monsters.

He pushed down on the joystick, and his chair lunged forward. He needed to find Darcy. Together, the two of them could talk to Runyan. But first, before he did anything else, he needed his medicine.

DARCY

Darcy awoke with a start. She was lying on an old slipcovered couch in a cluttered room with no windows. She sat up and turned toward the sound of a television. Beth Dolan, a friend from back when they were both first-years, was standing over a steaming pot on an avocado-colored gas stove.

"Good morning." Beth smiled at her from the kitchen. "Sorry about the noise, but I've got to get to work. I hope you slept okay?" She looked at Darcy pointedly, her eyebrows raised in a silent question. Darcy had burst in on Beth in the middle of the night. All she'd been able to explain was that she was in trouble and needed a place to stay. Beth had been kind enough not to pepper her with questions, but she was obviously curious.

"Thanks for letting me stay the night." Darcy looked down at her hands, wondering how much she should say. "I know this is going to sound strange, but remember a couple of weeks ago when the chemistry building was broken into?"

Beth nodded. "It was broken into the night before last too."

"Well, the same person who did it may be trying to kill me."

Beth's eyes went wide. "Why?"

"I don't know. I thought he was coming after me last night. I couldn't stay at my place."

Beth walked from the kitchen and crouched down beside Darcy. "Did you call the police?"

Darcy shook her head. "It's kind of complicated. I don't know how much I can say without putting you or some of my other friends in danger."

Beth looked away for a couple of seconds. Darcy could tell she was choosing her words carefully. "This wouldn't have anything to do with a certain visiting chem professor, would it?"

Darcy didn't get the connection. "I don't think so. Actually there's this guy—"

"James Parker."

Darcy looked up in surprise. "How'd you know?"

"I heard you were working on a collaboration with him. Jason told me. He didn't seem too happy about it."

"Yeah." Darcy looked down at the floor. Just thinking about Parker made her sick to her stomach. She couldn't believe he'd kept on taking the drug, especially after he realized what it was doing to him.

"So last night . . ." Beth bit her lip. "Were you actually there when it happened?"

"When what happened?" Darcy wasn't sure she wanted to know.

"A man and his wife were attacked. They're saying it was Professor Pyramid. Nobody seems to know anything about him."

"Pyramid?"

"Don't tell me you haven't heard. You can't turn on the TV without seeing footage from the press conference. Apparently he's invented a drug that turns him into the Incredible Hulk. He's been hopping around the city attacking everything that moves."

Darcy shook her head. It couldn't be Parker. It just couldn't. He'd never hurt anyone. It just wasn't possible. "So when did . . . the attack happen? Did they say?"

Beth shrugged. "Sometime late last night—early this morning. They were on their way home from the airport. Just a few blocks from here on Dwight Way."

Dwight Way. Darcy closed her eyes and collapsed back onto the sofa. The street Parker lived on.

PARKER

Parker turned in front of his apartment and wheeled down the sidewalk toward the front door. His whole body tingled in anticipation of the medicine that would give him back his strength. Soon he would see Darcy, gather her up in his arms. He'd tell her about the nightmares, all the coincidences that made him think he was turning into a monster. They'd have a good laugh over it, and then they'd go to the police and report the attempts on their lives. The police would be able to help them. He and Darcy might even be put into protective custody. Together, just the two of them. It would be great. They'd finally be able to talk about something besides research and break-ins and staying alive.

He snaked his key ring out of his pocket and reached for the door. His door . . . The world twisted suddenly on its side. A chunk of wood was missing from the edge of the door; the deadbolt and knob were turned at a funny angle. What had happened? His landlord had said he'd fixed the door. Had his apartment been broken into again? Suddenly the whole apartment felt sinister, evil. He backed away from it. Something was wrong. Why was he so certain his medicine was in the fridge? He hadn't put it there; the medicine had been stolen from his lab. How would he know it was in his apartment, unless . . .

Spinning his chair in a tight one-eighty, he flew down the sidewalk. He whipped out his cell phone and dialed with his left hand. "Hello. East Bay Paratransit? This is James Parker, the muscular dystrophy client you picked up this morning. This is an emergency. I need a pick-up at the corner of Dwight and Ellsworth as soon as you can get there. I need a ride to the Oakland airport."

Parker looked up at the flight information posted above the check-in gate. America West Flight 536 to Phoenix, Arizona, departing at 11:50 A.M. Only five minutes before preboarding. He hit the redial on his phone one more time. "You've reached the Channing lab. Aggie, Mita, and Darcy are not able to come to the phone right now. . . ." Parker hung up the phone. Where was she? It was almost noon. He hadn't intended for her to hide forever.

He punched Jason's number into the phone and hit Send.

"Talk to me." Jason's voice was almost drowned out by the hum of traffic.

"Hello, Jason, this is Parker. I need—"

"Parker, where are you? I've been searching all over."

"Jason, listen. I don't have much time. I need you to tell Darcy that I'm going away for a while. Tell her the drug's been changing me into something I'm not. She'll understand."

"What? Parker, slow down. What are you talking about? Where's Darcy? I thought she was with you."

"She'll go back to her lab eventually. Tell her it's okay to tell the police. I'm going to turn myself in as soon as I get where I'm going."

An announcement came over the loudspeaker. They were already starting to preboard.

"Jason, I've got to go. Please make sure Darcy goes to the police, okay?"

"Parker, where are you? It sounds like you're in an airport."

"I'm counting on you to look after her, Jason."

"I don't even know where she is. She doesn't tell me anything."

Parker considered for a second. He didn't want to break Darcy's trust, but he didn't want her facing this alone either. "You know the lab that connects to hers?"

"Pyramid's lab?"

"Yeah, Pyramid's lab. She's been sleeping in the false ceiling above the old cold room. I don't have time to explain now."

An airline attendant walked up to Parker. "Excuse me, sir, but I need to get you boarded now."

"Parker, stay right there. I need to talk to you. I can be right over, just tell me where you are."

"Bye, Jason." Parker nodded to the attendant and held up his index finger. "Tell Darcy that I . . . I wish things could have been different."

He hung up and stuffed the phone in his pocket. The attendant then wheeled him down a ramp and transferred him to a narrow wheelchair with the help of another flight attendant.

"Sir, we've got to prep the batteries on this thing before we check it, but I'll make sure it gets on the plane. Another attendant will bring it to you when you land in Phoenix."

"Thanks." Parker pulled out his wallet and handed the man every bill it contained. "Could you do me another favor?"

"Sir, what's that?" The man stared down at the fistful of cash with bulging eyes.

One by one Parker pulled out his credit cards. "Could you cut these into pieces for me? I've got a one-way ticket, and I want to make sure it stays that way."

JASON

"Come on!" Jason slammed his cell phone down on the passenger seat of his Miata, sending the back cover and battery skittering onto the floor. "Fifteen minutes!" Fifteen more minutes and he would have had him. He stomped on the brakes and yanked hard on the steering wheel, sliding the car around into a squealing U-turn at the entrance to the airport.

Fifteen minutes! He gunned the engine as the oncoming traffic bore down on him. So close. To get the call from Parker when he was only five blocks from the airport and still end up missing him. If it wasn't so infuriating, it would be comical. He'd been searching for Parker and Darcy nonstop since the press conference fiasco. Parker's parents' house, the chemistry building, every hospital and doctor's office in the city. His whole life was spinning out of control, and he couldn't seem to do a thing to stop it. Parker was gone and Darcy would be next, if he didn't get to her fast enough. At least he knew where she was staying. The false ceiling above the lab. He should have known. It all fit together like a perfect three-dimensional puzzle. She'd always joked about living in the lab. When would he learn to take her at her word?

He pulled off Hegenberger and onto the freeway. *Union Street. . . .* He counted off the exits. There it was, the Fifth Street exit. He pulled off the freeway and navigated to Union. His heart pounded in his ears as he stopped in a weedy spot between two vacant warehouses. He'd never intended things to go this far. Never. Things had gotten so crazy. Reaching under his seat, his hand closed around the comforting handgrip of his Colt .45 semiautomatic. Flipping the safety off with his thumb, he turned the gun handle forward so he could get to it in a hurry.

Okay . . . He looked at his watch. 12:35. Five more minutes and it was show time. He leaned back in his seat and shut his eyes, listening to the noises of the city. An odd rattling noise sounded behind him. It was getting louder. He fought the urge to turn around. Finally, when the sound had drawn almost even with him, he turned and looked out the window. An old, toothless, homeless guy stood staring at him over the top of a rusty shopping cart heaped with bulging garbage bags.

"Give me some money." The old man rapped with swollen knuckles against Jason's window.

Jason stared back at the man, searching his expression for a nod, a wink, any sign that he was part of the game. He decided to go along with it. Either the homeless man was extremely unlucky in his sense of timing, or he was the best cover Jason had ever seen. "I've got two." He pulled two dollars from his wallet, cracked his window open a fraction of an inch, and slid the bills out to the man.

The man snatched at the money greedily without taking his eyes off Jason. "Give me the money." The man's tone didn't change, but his expression sharpened just enough to make his meaning known.

"Show me the trash first." Jason's voice was smooth as silk.

The man reached his hand deep into one of the trash bags and pulled out a tiny ziplock bag full of white powder. Jason noticed that his other hand was buried in another bag where he couldn't see it.

The man's face contorted into a toothless grin. "Go anywhere near that gun under the seat and I blow your head off."

"Do I look stupid to you?" Jason stared back at him with ice-cold eyes.

"Stupid enough to come to a drop in a brand-new Miata."

"Proved I wasn't a cop, didn't it?" Jason lowered the window further and held out a bulky white envelope. "Two thousand dollars. You can count it if you want."

The man grinned and tossed the bag into Jason's lap. "Wouldn't dream of it. Smart Miata boy like you's bound to know he wouldn't get fifty feet if he crossed *us*." The man glanced up at the warehouses that lined both sides of the street.

"Of course." Jason raised the window and nodded to the man. Then, keeping his movements smooth and slow, he pulled the car onto the rutted road and drove slowly to the next intersection.

Checking his rearview mirror as he drove, he fingered the bag of white powder and held it up to the afternoon sun. One hundred percent pure uncut rage. Now all he needed to do was to find Darcy.

CHAPTER 26

DARCY HIT THE PLAY BUTTON on her answering machine one more time.

"Hi, Darcy. It's Parker. I'm sorry, I didn't know. You've got to believe me. I had no idea it was me. It's like I'm turning into a totally different person. Dr. Jekyll and Mr. Hyde." An odd-sounding voice echoed in the background. She thought she heard the rush of a train. It sounded like he was calling from a BART station. "I think Hyde stole my supply of the drug and hid it somewhere. In my apartment, I'm pretty sure. Probably somewhere else too. He wants me to find it and take it again, but I won't. I'm off it for good. And to make sure I stay off it, I'm going someplace far away. Someplace I can trust the police. Someplace I'll never be able to hurt you again." A long pause. "I'm back in my chair now, and it isn't so bad. The only thing I'm really going to miss is you. You're the most . . . wonderful person I've ever known. I love . . . the time I got to spend with you. I'm going to miss you." The message clicked off.

Dr. Jekyll and Mr. Hyde. Darcy slumped back in her chair. *God, why? Why does it always have to happen this way? Everybody I've ever loved. Where's the good in that? If you really loved me . . .* She stood up and walked across the lab. If He really loved her, what? What would happen? What was she supposed to do? This time she wasn't the one running. It wasn't her fault. Parker was trying to protect her. She tried to believe it. Tried to remember the agony in his voice. He really did care for her. She had to believe it.

"*Someplace far away.*" Her grandmother's voice came to her. Maybe Mama Macy was right. Maybe Darcy really was being punished. She collapsed back onto her desk chair. It was probably just as well that Parker left when he did. It was going to happen sooner or later anyway.

No. Darcy stood and started pacing the room, shaking her head to clear her mind. That was Mama Macy's Alzheimer's talking. Parker was a good person. He really was trying to protect her. She had to take him at his word. He'd almost said he loved her. Deep down in her heart she knew it was true. She'd always known it, from the very beginning. Parker was just that way—the kind of guy who loved people. Even people like her.

Parker loved her and she loved him. She wasn't going to let that get away. Not this time. If she could just find him . . . . She went to her answering machine and skipped forward to the last message.

"Darcy? Jason here. I've been looking all over for you. We need to talk. It's important. Life and death. I have an important message from Parker, but I can't talk about it over the phone. Call me as soon as you get this. You have my number. Bye."

Picking up the phone, she dialed Jason's cell phone one more time. A half ring followed by a click, then nothing. She slammed down the phone and went back to pacing. Where could Parker have gone? Not his parents' house or Rachel's. She'd already tried both places. Was it possible he was with Jason? Maybe that's why Jason wasn't answering his phone. The thought made her uneasy. Jason's whole involvement in the Mighty Mouse experiment didn't sit right with her. First he didn't want to have anything to do with the project, and then, next thing she knew, he was Parker's right-hand man. What had happened? Was it the money? Not for a drug that only helped a handful of people. He couldn't have known about the drug's more universal effect. Could he?

Nothing made sense. There was much more going on than just Parker taking the Mighty Mouse drug. They hadn't even discovered the drug when Kelly started following her. And her lab had been searched too. And Raccoon Face—he'd turned up way before Parker started taking the drug. He'd been looking for Pyramid. Everybody was looking for Pyramid. In fact, Parker wasn't even the one that got shot; Pyramid was. The men with guns had been chasing Pyramid, not Parker. But why? Pyramid was just a name Jason had made up, wasn't it?

Jason. Darcy headed out the door and jogged down the hall to the elevators. Jason had said something when he introduced Pyramid at the press conference. What was it? Something strange, something that didn't quite fit. He'd known Pyramid for a long time? He wanted to talk to him in person? There was more. What was it? She stepped into the elevator and punched in Jason's floor. Jason definitely knew more about Pyramid than he was letting on. He was the one who came up with the idea in the first place. Sending the e-mail under Pyramid's name, taking over the hot room, the press conference . . . It had all been Jason's idea. She'd thought it all unnecessary at the time, but Jason had insisted. Why?

She stepped out of the elevator and walked back toward Jason's office. Pyramid was the key. Why was everyone so interested in him? It was almost as though Jason had planned it from the start. She pushed Jason's door open and walked into the old lab that served as his office. No one around. She moved to his desk and thumbed through an old lab notebook. According to the dates, he'd had the notebook since he started at Cal, but almost every page was blank. Every page but the first one. Didn't he do any work? She pulled back on his top desk drawer, but it was locked. The bottom drawers too. They were all locked.

Weird. Whoever heard of a grad student locking a desk drawer? She slid the chair out and crawled under the desk to have a look at the locking mechanism. Nothing visible. She was about to give up when a red ice bucket and a small cardboard box under the desk caught her eye. She lifted the top of the bucket. Nothing but water—cold water. Sliding the box out, she opened it and looked inside. NMR tubes, plastic cuvettes, a stoppered flask half-filled with a clear solution. What was Jason working on? She pulled a stack of NMR spectra out from under the glassware. Whatever it was, it wasn't adrenaline 355. She traced a cluster of high-field methyl peaks with her finger. It was similar yet not quite the same. Some kind of derivative?

She put the spectra in the box and sealed it back up. As she was sliding it back into place, she noticed something else. The corner of a white sheet of paper poking out from the back of Jason's middle drawer. She pulled out the sheet, and her name jumped out at her. It looked like a page from her grad school application. Where had Jason gotten hold of her application? Why?

A creak sounded at the back of the lab. Darcy turned around. Nothing. She cast a nervous glance toward the door. Time to stop snooping and get back to her loft. She reached under the desk and tried to stuff the paper back into the drawer, but something was in the way. She ran her hand along the back of the drawer and felt something soft and slick. It came away with the sound of ripping masking tape.

She stared down at the plastic baggie that lay in her open hand. It was filled with fluffy white powder. Glass?

Her hands trembled as she taped the powder back behind the drawer. She had to get out of here. Had to get out of the building. The city. Jason knew her too well. She wasn't safe. If he caught her . . .

Pushing Jason's chair back under his desk, Darcy fled the room. Into the stairwell, down the stairs, she raced back to her lab, slamming and locking the door behind her.

A loud ring made her jump. Her telephone. She stared at the phone. *Jason?* What would she say if it was him? But what if it was Parker? She grabbed the phone and held it to her ear, waiting for the caller to speak first.

"Hello?" Jason's voice.

She hesitated, started to hang up the phone.

"Hello? Darcy, is that you? It's Jason. We've got to talk. It's about Parker. I think he might be in danger."

Might be in danger? What gave you the first clue, scumbag? The fact that people are shooting at him? Darcy pressed her fist to her mouth to keep from screaming.

"Come on, Darcy. I know you're there." The slam of a car door. A revving engine. "Say something. Parker asked me to give you a message. It's important."

"First, where are you?" Darcy blurted out.

"Darcy, finally! Stay where you are. I'll be right there."

"Tell me where you are or I hang up right now." Darcy didn't try to hide her anger.

"What? What's gotten into you?"

"Where—are—you?"

"I'm in my car, backing down my driveway. I'll be there in ten minutes. Just don't go anywhere."

"You'd better not be lying."

"What are you talking about? Why would I—"

"Where's Parker?" Darcy raised her voice.

"I don't know. He didn't say."

"I don't believe you."

"Look, I'm just as worried as you are. I've been checking with the airport. I've pretty much got it narrowed down to LA, Phoenix, or Las Vegas."

"I still don't believe you."

"Why not? I know a lot of scary stuff has been happening, but I don't know any more about it than you do, I swear."

"Really . . ." Darcy let the sarcasm flow. "You're the one who invented John Pyramid. You pushed it hard, even when Parker and I wanted to back out. And you're the only one who wanted to hold a press conference. You set the whole thing up yourself—including the security arrangements. Then you insisted Parker dress up in that ridiculous costume. And that bogus introduction, what was up with that? It was so obviously a hidden message."

"Hidden message? That's crazy! Darcy, I was just working the crowd. Playing at the biggest practical joke since Nicolas Bourbaki."

"And it was just a coincidence that everyone and their grand-mother wants Pyramid dead? Know what I think? I think you knew all along they would come after Pyramid. I think you wanted Parker to get killed. That's why you set up the press conference in the first place. That's why you insisted he dress up."

"I . . . can't believe this. I can't believe you're actually saying it." Jason sounded genuinely outraged. "Why? Why would I do that? It doesn't make sense."

"Jason, I . . ." She was about to apologize, but something stopped her. The sound of the engine in the background. It was steady as a rock. His voice showed emotion, but he hadn't trans-ferred an ounce of emotion to his driving. She knew Jason. He always sped when he was upset. Had he really been trying to get Parker killed? The implication stunned her.

"I'll tell you why. There could be lots of reasons." The words tumbled out of her like cubes from an ice machine. "You knew what the drug was worth. Maybe you wanted a bigger share of the patent. Maybe your father didn't invent John Pyramid. Maybe John Pyramid *is* your father."

"What? That's the stupidest thing I ever heard!"

"Is it?" Darcy's voice came out tight and shrill. "If you could convince everyone it was your father who invented the drug, and then your father was shot, who would inherit the money?"

"Darcy, calm down." Jason took on a soothing tone. "If you'd just think a second, you'd see how ridiculous that is. My father died when I was thirteen. If Parker was killed, they'd do an autopsy. They couldn't help but figure out who he was. Hundreds of people could identify him."

"But what about the glass? I found it under your desk. And my grad school application too. You've been spying on me."

"Glass? I don't—" Jason fell silent. "I get it. Is that what this is all about? Darcy, that's not glass, it's rage."

"Rage?" Darcy backed toward her loft. "And that's supposed to make me feel better?"

"It's not for me; it's for Jenny."

"Jenny? Parker's sister?" Darcy felt suddenly unsure of herself. She'd expected him to deny having the drug. Why was he admitting to possession of rage?

"I needed to synthesize more drug for her, but when the lab got trashed again, all the raw materials disappeared. Rage is really close in structure to adrenaline 355, so I've been using it as a starting point to make more drug."

"For Jenny." Darcy felt like an idiot. How had she managed to forget about Jenny? "What about my grad school application?"

"I'm really sorry about that." Jason sounded uneasy. "When I found out you didn't live at the Mel-coat warehouse, I guess I just . . . let my curiosity get the best of me. I tricked Dolores into giving me your file. That's how I knew about Diane."

"Jason, I . . ." Darcy could feel her face burning. She felt light-headed. Dizzy. "Jason, I'm so sorry. I don't know what got into me. I was just so upset about Parker leaving and getting shot and—"

"Darcy, it's okay. I understand," Jason soothed. "We've both got a lot to talk about. I'll be right there. Just stay put. Okay?"

"Okay. I really do feel terrible . . . about everything I said." Darcy sat down at her desk. "See you when you get here. Bye." She hung up the phone and buried her face in her hands.

I can't believe I actually accused him. Of all the stupid things. Her cheeks still burned at the thought. It was too much. She was finally cracking. Pushing herself up from her chair, she moved back to the hot room. She needed a good strong dose of Extra Strength Tylenol. Tylenol and a double Dr. Pepper.

Climbing up the ladder, she lifted the ceiling tile and crawled up into her loft. Reaching out to turn on her lamp, her hand closed on empty air. Something was wrong. She switched on her flashlight and gasped. Her microwave, clothes, dishes, books, everything she owned was dumped in a pile in the center of her sleeping deck.

They'd finally found her. She no longer had a place to hide.

PARKER

Parker hooked a hand around the heavy police station door. Slowly pulling back with his chair, the door cracked open. A little more. More . . . The door hit his footrest and slipped out of his grasp.

No. He drove forward and grabbed at the door again. His hands were stronger than before the drug, but without the neurotransmitters to control them, they might as well be the same twisted hands he was used to. He yanked back on the door again, and this time he got it most of the way open. Easing his chair forward, he angled his footrest into the door and . . . Still not enough. His hand slipped and the door slammed shut.

Wonderful. He couldn't even break into a stinking police station. They wouldn't need to send him to prison, he *was* a prison.

He swung his chair around and waited by the door. *God, why? Why are you doing this to me? I never meant to hurt anyone. I thought I was doing the right thing. Why didn't you direct my steps? Because I have wheels?* He slumped in the hot sun, waiting. Waiting for answers. Waiting for someone to come by and open the stupid door.

But nobody came. Finally he was forced to take shelter under a covered walkway with picnic tables and vending machines. A newspaper stand displayed the grainy picture of a dark figure bounding across a dimly lit patio. *Great.* He couldn't even get away from it in a desert. He turned away from the papers and stared at a ketchup-blackened picnic table. He didn't get it. How could he have fouled up so badly when his motives were so good? He'd been certain he was supposed to work on a cure. Sometimes that confidence was the only thing that kept him going. Had he been wrong about the whole thing? Had he been wrong about God?

His eyes wandered back to the newspaper and the headline jumped out at him. *Pyramid Strikes Again.* Parker turned to the newspaper stand and started reading. *A Berkeley man was shot last night by an assailant he later identified as John Pyramid. Thirty-year-old Berkeley native, Kevin Buchanan, was investigating what he described as suspicious activity at his next door neighbor's house when a cloaked figure leaped out of nowhere, threw him to the ground, and shot him in the shoulder as he tried to get up.*

"Yes!" Parker spun around in his chair. The paper said it happened last night. He double-checked the date on the newspaper just to be sure. "Yes!" That proved it. It couldn't be him! He had been safe and sound in Phoenix when it happened.

He turned back to the article and continued reading. *Police confirm that the residence at 2219 Dwight Way had been broken into and that the personal effects of two prime suspects in the Pyramid case were found inside.*

"2219 Dwight Way?" Parker slumped back in his chair. There had to be some mistake. That was Rachel's address. What would Pyramid be doing there? Nobody knew about Rachel but his parents. His parents and Jenny and Darcy and . . . *Jason.*

Parker stared at the grainy photo. What did he even know about Jason? Besides the fact that he was a mercenary, money-grubbing, scheming hustler. How had he ever managed to insinuate himself into Parker's confidence? It was so obvious now. The whole Pyramid scheme was his idea. And the press conference with his stupid costume and secret-message introduction. It all made sense. And that phone call at the airport. Why had Jason been so desperate to find him and . . . Darcy.

"No!" Parker wheeled around and sped back to the door of the police station. A police officer was just leaving the station. Parker started to call out to him, but something made him hesitate. The press conference. The police officers at the back. Jason had brought them all in. He'd organized the whole thing. What if the police really were trying to kill him? For all he knew, Jason and the Berkeley police were working together.

He swerved away from the door and sped through the parking lot. He had to get back to Berkeley. If something happened to Darcy, he'd never forgive himself. Why had he left her in the first place? He was such a coward, running away from temptation when he should have stood up to it and dealt with it head on. Well, he was through with running, and he was through with the drug. Darcy's life was on the line. No way was he going to give in to temptation.

Plunging a hand in his wheelchair pocket, he brought out his cell phone and dialed his parents' number.

"Hello." His heart leaped at his mother's voice. He was making the right decision. He knew it.

"Hello, Mom? This is James. I don't have time to explain but I'm in Phoenix now, and I need a ticket home. Right away."

CHAPTER 27

DARCY

FOOTSTEPS, SOFT AND LONELY, hung on the chill night air. Darcy stepped around a tree, pressing her back against its shaggy trunk. The footsteps were getting closer, twenty, maybe thirty yards to her right. She circled slowly around the tree, timing her steps to coincide with those of the unseen stranger. It was probably just a student, a foolhardy scientist making a mad dash home through the faculty glade. She froze when the footsteps stopped. Had he forgotten something? A lab notebook maybe? Keys?

She held her breath, waiting for the footsteps to resume. It couldn't be one of those men with the guns. Not here. They couldn't have known she'd be cutting across campus. Could they? No. She hadn't known herself until a few minutes ago. But what if they'd seen her sneaking out of the gym? She'd spent the entire afternoon holed up in the women's locker room, pretending to stretch, cooling down, taking shower after shower till her hands were wrinkly prunes. It was the perfect hiding place. No one had even seen her face.

The footsteps sounded again, moving in the opposite direction now. The faint smell of cigarette smoke. Whoever it was, they didn't have a clue about the mechanism of carcinogenesis. Probably a humanities student. . . .

Darcy crept out from behind the tree and followed the deep, sheltered creek bed toward the east edge of campus. If she had just waited in her lab for five more minutes, she wouldn't be in this mess. But the realization that her hiding place had been discovered had totally freaked her out. She'd fled her lab in a blind panic, running straight for the safety of the gym. And now, if she was to have any hope at all of finding Parker, she had to find Jason.

She climbed a steep bank to a dark, silent road and set off at a slow jog. A tap sounded behind her. A rustle to her left. The closer she got to the chemistry complex, the closer the darkness pursued her. The chemistry building loomed above her like a dark, silent tombstone. What if Raccoon Face was there right now, waiting for her in her lab? He knew her secret. He'd be expecting her to return. What if he'd stationed his men around the buildings?

But Jason said he knew where Parker was. He'd said he had a message from Parker—a matter of life and death. She couldn't just pack up her bags and leave. Not without knowing. She climbed an ivy-covered hill and peered down into a brightly lit parking garage. She knew it! Jason's Miata was in its normal parking space, right by the exit. He was still waiting for her. She'd been trying to get in touch with him all afternoon, but he wasn't at home and his cell phone wasn't working. Half a ring and a click—that's all she got. It wasn't even transferring to his voice mail.

Making her way back down the hill, she darted across the street and scrambled over a group of large boulders to a dark, sheltered path that paralleled the road. She knew the chemistry complex better than anybody. She'd be in and out before they knew it. Besides, all her valuables were still in her loft. Her mom and dad's wedding picture. The picture of her mom holding her when she was a baby. She couldn't leave town without her pictures. It wasn't even an option. And she had to leave town tonight. Ph.D. or no Ph.D. Things had gotten way out of control. She was out of Berkeley for good. Once she found Jason, they could talk in the car—all the way to Sacramento if he was willing to drive her. And if he wasn't, they could talk at the bus station in Walnut Creek. The Berkeley bus station wasn't an option either. Not anymore.

Darcy skirted around the chemistry building and headed for the back of Lewis Hall. Entering through the shipping and receiving bay, she ran up the stairs to the fourth floor and walked the length of the building to the narrow hallway that connected Lewis with the chem building. Jason's office was to her left. If she was lucky she wouldn't even have to go to her own lab. If Jason was in his office, she could send him to collect her valuables. Nobody seemed to be after Jason, just her and Parker.

Something rumbled overhead. Somewhere on the fifth floor. Maybe the sixth. She waited for several seconds before tiptoeing down the hallway to Jason's office. The door was shut, the gap under the door dark. She tried the knob just in case. Locked.

Great. She'd been afraid of this. He was probably waiting in her lab. If he was there, that probably meant the coast was clear. He'd notice if someone suspicious was hanging around. Probably.

She hurried down the hallway and stopped outside the stairwell door to listen. Nothing. She pushed the door open and slipped inside. Step, step, listen. She worked her way carefully down the stairs, stopping at the third-floor landing. If anybody was looking for her, they'd be on the third floor. She opened the door a tiny crack and peered up and down the corridor. Nobody. She slipped through the door and crept down the hall, stopping to check each intersection. Almost there. It would only take a few seconds. She'd just get her pictures and get out, Jason or no Jason.

She tiptoed down the last corridor and froze, chill bumps prickling at the back of her neck. Silence. In your face, screaming at the top of its lungs silence. Taking a deep breath, she poked her head around the corner and . . . nothing. The door to her lab was closed, its opaque window dark. Everything seemed to be in order.

Holding her keys in her fist to keep them from jingling, she turned the lock and pushed the door open. *So far, so good.* She shut the door behind her and locked it with the deadbolt before turning on the lights. Everything looked the same as when she left it. She grabbed the jacket from her desk and hurried back to the hot room. Quick, in and out. Just the pictures and a few clothes.

The crunch of broken glass. A hoarse whisper, somewhere out in the hallway.

The lab went dark with a shuddering groan. The high-pitched hiss of air compressors faded to silence. Total and absolute.

Darcy felt her way through the dark lab, reaching for her ladder with outstretched arms. *Boom!* A jolt rattled through the floor. The door to her lab?

She hit the ladder as a wood-splintering crash filled the room. Pounding footsteps. Breaking glass. Another boom. Pyramid's door slamming into the wall.

Up the ladder, through the gap in the ceiling, Darcy pushed blindly through the darkness. A crash sounded below her. Heavy, scrabbling steps. The rumble of heavy breathing. She crouched in the darkness, fighting to control her trembling muscles. Someone was down there. Some . . . *thing*. Something not human.

A tremor vibrated through the wall next to her. The creak of straining wood. Slowly, a dark form rose up through the ceiling behind her. A low, rumbling growl . . .

Darcy leaped away as a flurry of motion rattled through the ceiling. Scrambling to the edge of her plywood platform, she stretched herself out, distributing her weight to her arms and legs as she crawled out across the flimsy metal grid that supported the false ceiling. Another crash. Right behind her. The whole ceiling was shaking, swaying back and forth like a flimsy rope bridge. She crawled faster, slithering in and out between the wire supports. It was right behind her; she could hear it breathing.

The shriek of twisting metal struts. A hand slashed across her ankle as the ceiling behind her caved in, filling the room below with a bellowing roar. Half human, half beast, the cries sent her scampering on across the undulating ceiling. *Oh, God. Oh, God.* She called out for help with each panting breath. A heavy board smashed up through a ceiling tile to her right. Again it tore through the ceiling—right in front of her. She could feel the grid buckling. She was going to fall.

Lunging forward, she hooked an arm around an insulated pipe as the false ceiling gave way beneath her. One more lunge and she had both arms around it, both legs. The room boiled beneath her as she scooted along the pipe. There was an opening ahead, a hole in the wall for the pipes to pass through. She'd seen it from her loft.

Ceiling tiles smashed all around her as she tried to escape. The pipe rang out like a fractured bell. Right behind her. She stretched out as far as she could and pulled herself forward. *Smack!* Her head hit a cement wall. A rough edge cut into her arm as she wormed her way through the opening. Almost through. Almost through. Everything but her legs . . .

A heavy blow smashed her foot. The ceiling gave way beneath her, and she fell. Darkness rushed past her for a dizzying second before she slammed into the floor.

Yellow and red lights. Hot flashes of pain. She struggled to catch her breath as dust and debris settled over her like rain. She waited for the roar, the tearing pounce that would end her life, but the crashes and roars continued to shake the room next door. She couldn't believe it. They were still in Pyramid's lab. She struggled to her feet and felt her way to the door of her own lab. Her heart surged. She was going to make it. She was going to—

Pyramid's door slammed open behind her. Shuffling steps. She ran for her door as a high-pitched whine sounded in the hallway beyond. Flashing lights. The whine was getting louder.

"Freeze! This is the police!"

Darcy's heart stood still. *Parker?*

An inhuman roar sounded behind her. Scrambling feet.

She plunged through the doorway and out into the hall. "Parker, get out of here!" She squinted her eyes against the blinking lights. Then she was past him, running as fast as she could.

"Darcy, thank God!" he called out from behind her. "Get the police. I'll hold him off."

"Him?" Darcy skidded to a stop. "Parker, run! There are too many of them." She watched in terror as Parker spun around and raced after her, pursued by a mob of dark forms. "To your lab!" She turned and the whine of his chair chased her down the hall. Stopping at his door, she fumbled with her keys in the lock. Heavy footsteps shook the floor. Lurching shadows.

"Got it!" She shouldered her way into the lab and stood aside to let Parker follow, then, throwing her shoulder against the door, she slammed it shut and turned the lock. *Crunch!* An explosion of force knocked her away from the door. "It's not going to hold!" she shouted. "I think they're on Mighty Mouse."

"I knew it!" Parker raced to the back of the lab and pushed against the shield of the fume hood. "Help me get this open. I've got two bottles of sulfuric acid in here."

Darcy crossed the room and threw open the Plexiglas shield. A floor-shaking crash sounded behind her.

"I've got flasks on the shelf and stoppers in that drawer." Parker pointed to a narrow drawer under one of the benches. "Fill the flasks with acid and stopper them tight. We'll need a good supply to hold them off."

Darcy grabbed a handful of 500 ml. flasks and began filling

them with the fuming acid. "Acid grenades. Right?" She stumbled to the drawer and brought back a handful of stoppers. "What about you? What are you doing?"

"Thermite." Parker wheeled back and forth, dumping reagents in a big pile on one of the benches. "Mighty Mouse repellent. Just a few more minutes and—"

The door burst open, and a tangle of shadows entered the room. Darcy hurled a flask at a rushing figure, but the flask went wide, crashing against the wall in a shower of broken glass. She threw another flask and it burst with a sizzling spray. No screams. No cries of anguish. The shadow melted back into the darkness and two others took its place.

"Parker, hurry!" She launched another flask. Another. Acrid fumes filled the room, burning her eyes and throat. "Parker . . . I'm . . . out!" She forced out the words between gasping coughs.

"Almost there!" Parker was coughing as well.

Sudden movement caught her eye. A soft flutter like the flapping of leathery wings. Darcy threw herself to the floor as a crash shook the fume hood behind her. A heavy body fell across her legs. Whirling, grasping.

"Parker!" A wave of revulsion overwhelmed her reason. She lay on the floor kicking, twisting, scrambling to get away.

Then a hissing roar cut through the darkness. The room was filled with a blinding light. She was free.

"Run!" yelled Parker. An electric whine cut across the room.

"Parker!" Darcy climbed to her feet, crashed into a metal stool. Color-blasted streaks blurred her vision. Light-edged shadows stumbled away from a sparking light, hands thrown up in front of unseen faces. Something was burning on the bench. She stumbled past a shadow, dodged to the left, stepped to the right. Then she saw the door. A rectangle of black against a shimmering curtain of tears. Pushing past the flailing, grasping shadows, she ran out into the hallway, followed the flashing lights. Parker was waiting by the elevators.

"Power's out!" she called out over the pursuing footsteps. "Get to the stairs."

"Just this floor," he said. "The rest of the building has power."

"What?" Darcy slowed to a stop as the elevator doors slid open. She stood for an instant, confused by the light, but then, as a rumble of footsteps sounded behind them, she followed Parker into the elevator and jabbed at the button to close the doors.

Whump! The doors bent inward. She could feel herself falling as the elevator descended.

"Hey, you dumb uglies!" Parker was shouting at the doors. "We're in here. That's right. Come and get us!"

"Parker! What are you doing?" She wiped at her burning eyes with her sleeve.

"The longer they work at that door, the longer we'll have at the bottom."

A heart-stopping jolt shook the elevator. A plastic panel broke loose from the ceiling and hit Darcy on the head. She struggled with the panel, knocking it back against the wall. A pounding, scratching sound, just above her head. The sound of cracking plastic. A hand reached down from the ceiling, groping for Darcy with outstretched fingers.

"These guys are serious! What did you do to them?" Parker's casual tone sent a wave of fury through her.

"What did I do?" She ducked beneath the hand just as the elevator came to a stop. Lunging for the doors, she tried to pry them open with her fingers. Finally the doors opened and she took off across the lobby. Where was Parker? She turned back to search for him. He was still back at the elevator, punching madly at the buttons inside.

"Parker!" She watched from across the lobby as a man dropped headfirst into the elevator. Echoing booms sounded from the stairwell.

Parker backed out, and the elevator closed. He zipped across the lobby and maneuvered through the door. "Need a lift?"

Darcy hopped into his lap, felt his arm encircle her waist. The chair lurched forward and whined its way out onto the sidewalk. Up the hill, around the auditorium, they sped down the dark deserted streets, putting more and more distance between themselves and the monsters that pursued them.

She shut her eyes and let the night glide past her. The comforting sound of the electric wheelchair. The soothing tone of Parker's voice. "It's okay now. Everything's all right. We lost them back at the chem building. The guys on the elevator are still on their tour of every floor in the building."

Darcy nodded absently. A black cloud of despair was settling around her heart. She could feel its weight crushing down on her. It wasn't going to end; they would keep coming and coming until she and Parker were dead. It was just a matter of time. They had to get away. Away from the university, away from the Bay Area, away from California. Even then, she wondered if it would be far enough. She could still hear Jason's voice. Billions and billions of dollars. It was a lot of reasons for someone to want them dead.

"You came back. Why?" The sound of her voice shocked her. She sounded so fragile, like a frightened child.

Parker's chest expanded and contracted in a long sigh. "I was worried. I heard about the attack at Rachel's house and thought maybe . . . I was worried Jason might . . . try to hurt you."

"Jason? Why would he do that? He already knows how to make the drug. Besides, if he wanted to hurt us, he could have done it a long time ago. He's had plenty of chances."

"I know. I was an idiot." Parker shook his head. "It's just that I was so worried. I wanted to be here for you, to protect you."

"So why leave in the first place?"

Parker looked away. When he looked back at her, his eyes were haunted, etched with pain. "The drug was turning me into a monster, just like those guys back at the lab. I didn't want to believe it at first. I kept telling myself that God wouldn't lead me to invent a drug that would do that. But then I saw the news reports. All those people getting hurt—"

"But don't you see? It wasn't you. It was those other guys. Someone must have stolen the formula—the same person that burned the notebooks."

"You can't know that." Parker turned on her with fiery eyes. "You saw what they were like. They were obviously on adrenaline 355. So was I. As soon as I realized what was happening I went back to the lab to destroy the drug, but it was gone. I thought I'd hidden it from myself . . . when I was a monster. That's why I was in such a hurry to get away. I didn't trust myself, especially with you around. I kept having these awful nightmares. I had to get away."

Especially with me around? Darcy's heart stood still. "Why didn't you trust yourself with me around?"

"For one thing I was afraid I'd hurt you. The thought that I might have been the one who attacked . . . I've never been so miserable in my life."

Darcy bit her lip. "And second?"

Parker was silent for a long minute. "I guess I was afraid I'd be tempted to keep on taking the drug. Things have been so . . . wonderful. Being with you. I didn't want it to stop."

Darcy turned to look at the road behind them. "So you just left? Without bothering to say good-bye? Without—" She snapped her mouth shut, trying to keep her bitterness from spilling out in a flood.

"I'm sorry." Parker sounded miserable. "If I'd had any idea of the danger I was putting you in—" He stopped the chair suddenly, spun around and moved into the shadow of an old apartment building.

Darcy turned and swept the street with frightened eyes. Someone was approaching from the top of the hill. They watched in silence, shrinking back against a large leafy bush as the shadow approached at an awkward, stiff-legged, hop-shuffling gate.

CHAPTER 28

PARKER

A BLACK-AND-WHITE POLICE CAR rolled slowly through the neighborhood, playing the beam of a powerful spotlight back and forth along both sides of the street. Parker slid down further in his chair as the spotlight lit the slat-board fence and garbage cans he and Darcy were hiding behind. He sucked in his breath as the beam held the fence in its white-knuckled embrace. Finally, the car moved on.

Parker breathed a sigh of relief. That was the second police car in the last half hour. And they'd already seen three separate groups of men searching on foot, most of them on adrenaline. He'd recognize the Franken-hopping walk anywhere. But there were others too. Men who swaggered up the streets with the poised, eager hands of Wild West gunslingers. Men with earphones who murmured to themselves as they searched from yard to yard. Three times he and Darcy had managed to elude the searching men, but he knew it was just a matter of time. His wheelchair was a big neon target attached permanently to the seat of his pants. As long as Darcy stayed with him, she was going to be in the line of fire.

"I think we should split up," Parker whispered to the shadow crouching behind a recycling bin. "You'll be able to move a lot faster without me."

She moved closer to whisper in his ear, "Nice try, but you're not getting rid of me that easily—not without an army of glass-heads and an extra-strength flea collar."

"Darcy, I'm serious." He pushed himself up with his elbows in an effort to see over the cans. "It's me they're after, John Pyramid. There's no reason for you to even be here."

"I'm John Pyramid too, remember?"

"No one has to know that." He searched her face, but it was too dark to make out her expression. "You could go back to Sacramento for a while. Hang out with friends until this whole thing blows over."

"While you do what?" she demanded. "Stay here and hang out with Mr. and Mrs. Recyclables Only?"

Parker sighed again. He didn't want an argument. He just wanted her to be safe, out of harm's way. It wasn't her fault doped-up monsters were roaming the streets. It wasn't her fault people were being attacked. Murdered. A trembling queasiness stole over him. The fault was all his. If only he hadn't tried adrenaline out on himself. If only he hadn't sent out the paper for review . . . What had he been thinking? He'd known it was wrong. The whole John Pyramid thing. Everything was wrong. A lie here. A made-up scientist there. Bypassing drug testing procedures. No wonder they were in such a mess.

A car crept across the right-hand intersection at a snail's pace. He couldn't see whether it was a police car or not, but it obviously wasn't a normal commuter, not at 4:00 in the morning.

Half a block away. He was tempted to chase after the car. To turn himself in and be done with it. People were dying. He had to do something. It was his moral duty to go to the police, to tell them everything he knew.

But not with Darcy. She was right about one thing: the police weren't to be trusted, at least not the Berkeley police. He already knew of two bad apples in the bunch. With billions of dollars worth of incentives, it wasn't hard to imagine the rot spreading rapidly through the whole barrel. If he could just get her to see reason. Get her out of town for a few weeks . . . Then he could go to the Oakland police, or the San Francisco police maybe. If he talked to someone near the top, a police chief or commissioner or district attorney. They couldn't all be corrupt.

Something scraped against the sidewalk. Footsteps, less than a half block away. Parker looked around for a better hiding place. Someplace big enough for his chair. But the footsteps were right on top of them. It was too late to move; his chair would make too much noise. He motioned for Darcy to run, but she shook her head at him.

The searcher stopped about fifteen feet away from them. In the distance Parker could hear more footsteps. Someone running.

"Hey, Kareem." A man's wheezy voice carried over the breeze. "Dino got someone that say he saw wheelchair boy riding down Telegraph. Pyramid wants us to check it out."

"Telegraph? You sure it wasn't some other cripple?"

"That's what I say, but Dino think he's doubled back."

"What's Pyramid say?"

"Says he's doubling the stakes. Wants us to check it out."

A litany of obscenities floated above the sound of shuffling feet. The men were leaving.

Parker stared at Darcy as the *slap, slap* of running feet faded into the distance. She leaned closer. Breathed a single word, "Pyramid?" The name buzzed in Parker's brain. *Someone named Pyramid? Searching for us? It doesn't make sense.*

"Come on!" He backed his chair out from between the trash cans and out onto the sidewalk.

Darcy ran out ahead of him to check the cross street at the next intersection.

"This way." Parker turned left, gliding across the street and looping around to a nearby driveway to get to the sidewalk again.

Darcy caught up and paced him for several yards. "Where are you going?" she whispered.

"To the BART station. Trains start running at four o'clock. I can call Rachel and have her pick us up at the San Francisco station."

"Rachel?" Darcy straightened suddenly and fell behind.

Parker spun his chair around. She was standing in the middle of the sidewalk, watching him with overcast eyes. He rolled back to where she was standing and said, "She's visiting her mom in San Francisco, remember? No one will think to look for us there."

Darcy shook her head. "I don't know. I wouldn't feel right."

"It's okay. She won't mind; she's used to it."

Darcy frowned, looked up and down the street. "I don't want to impose on Rachel—or her mom. Couldn't we just go to your parents' house?"

"Too easy to trace. Rachel's mom's house is perfect, and you'll

really like Rachel. She's wonderful." Parker turned back up the
sidewalk, but Darcy didn't follow. What was wrong with her? Why
wasn't she. . . ? Suddenly it hit him. He hadn't even asked her what
she wanted to do. What if she didn't want to go with him? What if
she wanted to be with someone else? Jason maybe.

"Darcy, I . . ." He spun around and drove back to where she was
standing. "I'm sorry. I didn't mean to assume . . . I mean, we don't
both have to go to the same place. I could go to Rachel's mom's
and you could, you know, go somewhere else if—"

Darcy's head shot up and she turned her back on him.

Nice going, Jammy. Open mouth, insert wheel.

DARCY

Darcy slumped against the wall of the BART train, letting her
head rattle against the scratched Plexiglas window. Her ears and
sinuses felt like they were going to cave in, but she was too tired to
even yawn. Everything was coming at her too hard, too fast. Whiz-
zing by in a blur, streaking lights in the dark tunnel that was her
life.

The train's banshee wail dropped a half octave, and the emergency lights in the tunnel started to slow. Three blasts of its horn
and the train burst into an underground station. Embarcadero.
Darcy looked across the aisle to Parker, who was watching her with
an apologetic lift to his eyebrows. He shook his head and held up
four fingers. Four more stops.

She turned back to the window. She knew she was being petty.
It wasn't his fault he loved someone else. She should have recognized the signs. But somehow, in all the excitement, she'd managed
to convince herself he really cared for her—beyond just friendship.

"You'll really like Rachel. She's wonderful." She could still hear the
singsong emotion in his voice. How had she been so blind? Sure he
treated her nice. He treated everyone nice. That was the way he
was. But it didn't mean he was in love with her. What was wrong
with her? When would she ever learn?

"You could, you know, go somewhere else." She closed her eyes, tried
to figure out someplace she could go, besides Berkeley and Sacramento. For all his protests to the contrary, it was obvious Parker

wanted to be alone with Rachel. And here she was tagging along like a stray dog. He'd called Rachel up from the Lake Merritt BART station. Woke her up at 4:00 A.M. and she didn't even seem to mind. The voice coming over the phone sounded just as sweet and bright and cheerful as an angel. An angel with beautiful blue eyes and a dazzling smile.

The train started forward with a buzzing hum. It picked up speed through the deserted station and plunged back into the darkness. She knew she should say something. She should be cheerful and happy and bright, but she'd just been attacked by superhuman monster men and hunted by men with guns working for a scientist that didn't exist. If that didn't entitle her to a little grumpiness, what did? She leaned her head back against the window and watched as another station opened up around her. Another.

She wished they were going to Parker's parents' house. She rolled her head across the window and snuck a peek at Parker. Did he really think the men would track them to his parents' house, or was it all just an excuse to visit Rachel? And how could all those men be working for John Pyramid? Whoever he was, he was the key to the whole puzzle. Jason definitely knew more than he was letting on. That much was obvious. If they could just talk to Jason, maybe he could give them a better idea of what they were dealing with.

The train finally coasted into the fourth station. Darcy stood up and followed Parker to the doors, scanning the deserted platform as they slowed to a stop. The doors opened with a hiss, and Darcy stepped outside. Two women were running hand-in-hand across the station. Darcy caught her breath as she recognized the tall, willowy blonde. *Rachel.* She was even more beautiful in person than she was in the photograph. The other woman was almost as tall. Gray hair, matronly. Darcy recognized her from the photographs in Rachel's bedroom.

"Jammy!" The blonde flew by Darcy and threw her arms around Parker before he was halfway through the door of the train. "I've been worried sick. Jason said you were shot."

"It's okay now. Everything's okay," Parker's voice was a husky whisper. Tears shimmered in his eyes.

Darcy felt sick as she watched the couple embrace. She turned awkwardly to search the far end of the station, shuffling her feet to relieve the tension of the embarrassing silence.

The electric whine of Parker's chair. "Darcy, I want you to—"

Beep-beep-beep. The driver of the train signaled for them to move away from the doors.

Parker rolled forward, clinging to Rachel's hand like a dream that was about to slip away.

Darcy looked back at the train. Slashed a sleeve across her eyes. She couldn't do it. Not now. They were so . . .

Beep-beep-beep. Darcy leaped back onto the train, turning sideways to slip through the doors as they snapped shut with a *whoosh.* The train jerked forward, tipping her into an upright bar. Clinging to the bar, she lowered herself into a seat by the door, keeping her back to the flickering windows. The train plunged back into the tunnel and a wave of black despair crashed down on her like wind-driven breakers under a lightning-streaked sky. There was no going back. She was on her own. The only person who could help her now was . . . Jason.

JASON

Jason marched through the deserted train station. As far as he knew, neither Parker nor Darcy could drive. If they were going to get out of town, they would almost certainly take the BART. They'd been conditioned by too many years of miserly grad student living to even consider the expense of a long taxi ride, and buses were too wheelchair hostile. Even if Parker was walking now, which he seriously doubted, he wouldn't take a bus. He probably didn't even know how. It had to be the BART.

He strode up to a glassed-in booth to the left of the admission gates. A lone attendant sat slumped in a chair with her back to him. Jason rapped sharply on the Plexiglas. "Hello."

The attendant's head snapped back, and her hands flew up in a starburst of fluttering fingers. Swiveling in her seat, her eyes widened as they locked onto Jason. For a second he considered the flirtatious approach, but he abandoned the thought when she looked down and started brushing imaginary crumbs from her jacket. This was going to be a tough one. Too old to play games and too game to play old. He was going to have to strong-arm her.

"Excuse me." He waited for her to look him in the eye. "Sorry to wake you, but did you happen to see a guy in an electric wheel-chair come through here this morning?"

"Lotta people come by." The attendant rolled her eyes and pulled a black notebook from a stack of papers on her desk.

"This is urgent. Life and death," he continued in a louder voice. "Was anyone working here earlier—someone who was awake?"

She just sat there, pretending to read the notebook.

"That's okay. Don't worry about it. If I were you, I'd have been sleeping too." Jason brought out his cell phone and punched in a number. "Hello? Information? . . . Yes, could you give me the number of the main BART office? . . . Yes, ma'am. The Lake Merritt station. I need to talk to the supervisor."

"Did he have dark hair?" The attendant had put the book down and was looking at him now. "Nice looking?"

Yes! He was still in the chair and therefore trackable. Jason forced his features to relax into an expression of skepticism and hung up the phone. "Maybe. Was he with anyone?"

"Kind of a pretty girl." The attendant's eyes drifted to the left, and her mouth puckered like she'd just bit into a lemon. "I don't recollect what she looked like exactly, just that she was pretty. Pretty enough they could have been a couple."

Jason moved closer to the window. "Do you remember what time they came through here?"

"It was right after the station opened. Four o'clock, maybe four-thirty."

Jason glanced at his watch. 5:30. Missed them by an hour. "Thanks." He flashed her a smile. "You've been a big help."

He turned and jogged through the station, running up the bro-ken escalator three steps at a time. Even if they'd gotten on the train as late as four-thirty, they had too much of a lead for him to catch them getting off. But if he hurried, he'd probably be able to identify the BART station. And if he knew the station, he could identify their destination within a matter of hours. His cell phone was dead, so he'd have to call from home, but a quick chat with Parker's parents would give him everything he needed to know. Since Thanksgiving he'd been careful to maintain a relationship with them, and his forethought was finally going to pay off—though not exactly in the way he had originally intended.

He dashed across the street and slowed to a walk when a slow-moving police car caught his eye. Keeping his steps slow and unhurried, he let his eyes wander to the rising sun. The officer in the car watched him suspiciously. Jason held his breath and angled his body to keep his left side turned away from the cop. Jumping over the low-slung chain that separated the sidewalk from the parking lot, he fished in his pocket for his keys. He could feel the cop's eyes on his back, trailing him to his blue Miata.

The police car turned into the parking lot. Jason calmly opened his car door and slid inside. Shutting the door, he started the engine and reached around for his seat belt while his left hand snaked a pistol out of his belt and carefully placed it under the front seat. Then, slowly shifting the car into reverse, he looked up at the rearview mirror and backed the car out of its spot. The police car was gone.

DARCY

Darcy searched the lines of waiting commuters as her train burst into the Berkeley station. She'd passed through the station twice before and both times she'd spotted a suspicious-looking man wearing an oversized army jacket, watching the passengers as they got off the train. This time she didn't see him anywhere, but she couldn't be sure. The station was busier now, and he could easily be hiding in the crowd.

Three passengers walked past her and stood in a clump at the doors. Two businessmen and a woman who looked as if she might be a street person. Darcy left her seat and moved in close behind the larger of the two men. The crowd could work in her favor too. All she had to do was get off the train and over to the escalator without being spotted.

The doors opened, and she followed the man out, shuffling her feet to keep from trampling on his heels. A line of commuters filed past her on their way to the train. She ducked around the businessman, using his bulk as a shield. Matching his speed, she walked to the escalator, the entire time keeping him between her and the rest of the station. She let her face sag and her eyes glaze over as she rode the escalator up to the concourse level. No rush, no interest in her surroundings. She tried to withdraw from the world around her. She was a seasoned commuter. Disinterested, half-awake, still clinging to the dreams that had been snatched away from her by the hard-edged alarm clock of reality.

She was following the flow of traffic toward the ticket gates when she saw him—the man in the army jacket. He was watching the passengers as they filed in and out through the gates. Veering gradually to her right, Darcy ducked into a nearby women's rest room. Flattening her back against the wall, she waited with pounding heart just inside the door.

Several minutes passed. No sign of the man. Either he didn't see her, or he was waiting for her outside. She went to the nearest sink and turned on the hot water. Bending over and turning sideways to work her head under the faucet, she soaked her hair, raking it back with her fingers to wet it down to the scalp. Then, using a wad of paper towels to squeeze the excess water out of it, she pulled it back into a tight ponytail and held it in place with one hand. There. Her hair looked darker now, almost black. And the ponytail made her face look thinner. Releasing her hair, she dabbed at her face with a wet paper towel, wiping away most of her eye makeup. Even better. If the guy in the army coat had only seen a picture of her, he'd be searching for her more by hair color than anything else. Maybe.

She pulled her key chain from a pocket and used the jagged edge of her lab key to hack a two-inch strip from the bottom of her shirt. Tying her hair back with the ragged strip of cloth, she pushed her sleeves up on her forearms and inspected herself once more in the mirror before cracking open the rest room door and peeking outside. A new wave of commuters was just coming up the escalator. She waited until a line had formed at the gates and then pushed boldly out into the crowd.

She stopped at the back of the line and waited with exaggerated impatience. Hand on hip, chin in the air, she dared the whole world to notice her. This guy had to know she was a scientist. A scientist on the run, no less. The last thing she wanted was to look like she was hiding. She strutted forward. She could feel the man's eyes boring into her, but he didn't seem to recognize her face. In fact, he didn't seem to be looking at her face at all. She reached out, and the portal sucked in her ticket with the pneumatic hiss of opening gates. Grabbing the ticket on the far side of the gates, she walked with long, confident steps, thrusting her hips forward, letting them swing with the abandon of a fashion model on a strobe-lit runway. The man in the army jacket leered at her, but she was used to being stared at. She ignored him, focusing instead on the escalator that led to the street above.

The back of her neck burned as she stepped onto the escalator. He was coming after her. She could almost hear his footsteps, feel the gun pointing at her back. Fighting the urge to look behind her, she strode out onto the sidewalk and scanned Shattuck Avenue. A taxi sat parked next to the curb, its dome light illuminating the features of an elderly driver reading a newspaper.

Darcy ran to the cab and threw open the front door. The driver jumped, pressing his newspaper against the steering wheel.

"I'm sorry," Darcy pushed aside a pile of papers and slid onto the seat. "Can you take me to Hill Road?" She slammed the door, searching the sidewalk behind her.

The taxi driver nodded and pulled the cab out onto the empty street. "You okay?"

Darcy watched as the BART station disappeared behind them. She knew she should say something but her mind was a blank. All she could think about was the man in the army coat.

"Hey. You okay?"

She turned and looked at the driver. He frowned at her from beneath bushy eyebrows. She should say something. Anything.

"You cold? You're shaking like a leaf." He reached to the dash and the heater blasted out a torrent of warm air.

"I'm fine." Darcy cast an uneasy glance behind them. "It's just . . . A man in the subway—I thought he was after me."

"And you need to get to Hill Road?"

Darcy nodded, trying to remember Jason's address. "In the hills, overlooking the city." She leaned back in the seat and dug a wad of bills out of her pocket. "I only have seven dollars. Is that going to be enough?"

"Should be." The driver pushed down on the gas, and the taxi shot forward. "This your first time in a cab?"

Darcy nodded. "I'm a student at the university. I usually walk or take BART."

The driver chuckled and gunned the engine as they approached a yellow light. Darcy braced a hand against the dash, looking both ways as they sped through the intersection.

"Whereabouts on Hill Road?" the driver asked.

"I don't remember the street number. It's somewhere near the top of the hill. I'm sure I'll recognize the house."

"This man that was after you—you worried he'll try to follow you there?"

Darcy shrugged. "I don't think so." She turned and faced the road ahead, wishing the driver would do the same.

"Someone you know? I could call the police."

She waited several seconds before shaking her head. She never should have said anything. Maybe if she kept quiet, he'd stop asking so many questions.

"Just trying to help." Again he turned to look at her. "Just say the word, and I'll mind my own business."

"I'm sorry." Darcy noticed the meter. $6.80. "I don't have enough money. You can just stop here and let me out. I can walk the rest of the way."

"I said I'd get you there." The driver reached out and pressed a button on the meter. "If there's anything I take pride in, it's being a man of my word. And I ain't never abandoned a woman in distress neither."

"Thanks." Darcy turned a smile of gratitude on the driver. "I really appreciate this."

He glanced back at her with an exaggerated wink and turned left onto Hill Road.

Darcy sat back and tried to relax. Almost there. The closer they got to Jason's house, the better she felt. He'd know exactly what to do. His talent for getting out of scrapes was only exceeded by his talent for getting into them. She'd be able to rest soon. She could just see the faint blush of dawn peering out over the peaks of the hill.

"Right there." She pointed to a high-roofed house clinging to the hill below the road. Bright lights shined through high, vaulted windows, giving the house a warm, inviting look. Perfect. Jason was already awake.

The driver stopped the car, and Darcy handed him all her money. "Thank you so much. I wish I had more."

"That's all right." The driver regarded her with a fatherly smile.

"You ever in need of help, just call on Jack T. Burnley and it's Yellow Cab to the rescue."

"Thanks again, Jack." Darcy climbed out of the cab and stood off to the side of the road as Jack turned the car around and headed back in the direction they had come. She waved good-bye, then walked down the sloped driveway to the decorative gate that guarded the path to the front door.

A loud slap sounded from the driveway behind her. Darcy spun around to face a shadowy figure as two more shadows leaped into view on either side of her. She let out a shriek and bolted for the front door, but a bobbing man stepped from the house and advanced on her with a menacing snarl. She was surrounded.

CHAPTER 29

JASON

CAPTAIN JAMES W. NIENHAUSER pushed his way through a crowded hallway. Shoulders pulled back, arms held out from his body, he reminded Jason of a baby sumo wrestler stepping into the sand ring. Jason sidestepped to let two uniformed officers pass. Even at 6:00 A.M. the police department was crawling with cops. Sweat was beginning to soak through his shirt. He pulled his sports jacket closed and buttoned the top button as he walked. This was a bad idea. He could already feel his control starting to crumble. Nienhauser might come across as a Dudley Do-right, but he was still a cop. Skepticism was his job. The guy couldn't be conned.

Unfortunately Jason was fresh out of choices. Nobody in the entire BART system could remember seeing a guy in a wheelchair leaving a station. Nobody. Either he'd taken the drug and walked out, or he'd figured out another way to get off without attracting attention. Either way was bad news for Jason. He hadn't been able to reach Parker's parents either. He was completely blocked. The police were the only way.

Nienhauser stopped at an open door and motioned Jason inside. "Have a seat. Want a cup of coffee? Donut?"

Jason could barely hold back a smile at the cliché. "No, thanks." He stepped inside and stretched himself out on the chair facing a massive oak desk. He waited with steepled fingers while Nienhauser grabbed a box of Krispy Kremes and plopped into a frayed fabric chair.

"I've been here since five A.M. with another rage incident. This is breakfast." Nienhauser shrugged and pulled out a glazed donut. "Are you sure you don't want one?"

Jason allowed himself a smile. "No, thanks. Really."

"So—" Nienhauser took a big bite and brushed the crumbs on his desk off onto the floor—"what makes you think you can't talk to our detectives?" His words were a slurry of professionalism and Krispy Kreme.

"Actually, I have several reasons," Jason replied.

The desk phone emitted an ear-piercing ring. "I'm sorry." Nienhauser cast an apologetic look at Jason and picked up the phone. "Nienhauser." His expression went from Do-right to Whiplash in two seconds flat. "Did you look at the card? Did it say who they were from? . . . I don't know any Samuel Katib, and even if I did, he certainly wouldn't be sending me flowers. No, wait. Don't do anything till I get there." He hung up the phone and rose to his feet. "I'm sorry. Someone just left a vase of flowers with my name on it down in the station room. I need to check them out pronto, before someone gets trigger-happy and calls in the bomb squad."

"No problem." Jason didn't get up. "Mind if I help myself to a donut while I wait?"

"Changed your mind, eh? Go right ahead." Nienhauser slid the box across the desk as he walked to the door. "I'll be right back."

Jason counted off twenty seconds before grabbing the phone and punching in Officer Kelly's office number. *Come on. Pick up the phone!* Kelly had been in his cubicle not fifteen minutes ago. Jason had checked—right before dropping off the flowers.

"Hello?" A drowsy voice sounded over the phone.

"Dave Kelly? This is Michael Turner from ADO. I need you up in Captain Nienhauser's office right away."

"Nienhauser's office?"

"That's right. James Nienhauser's office. Right away." Jason hung up the phone and took a big breath. Might as well enjoy himself because he was committed now. He picked up the phone again and dialed the UC Berkeley automated course registration system. Then, settling back in Nienhauser's chair, he selected a plain glazed donut from the box.

A knock sounded at the door.

"Just a second. That should be him now," Jason informed the

computer-controlled voice on the phone. "Come in."

A beefy cop with a blotchy pink face opened the door and stepped timidly into the room. Still listening to the recorded message, Jason motioned Kelly to take a seat in the chair he'd just abandoned. "Aw right. Good. He's here right now. I'll get back to you in five minutes . . . Good . . . Okay. Bye." Jason rolled his eyes and hung up the phone.

Kelly shifted in his chair while Jason sized him up. So this was the guy Parker and Darcy had been so worried about. He'd looked a lot more formidable from three floors up.

"So . . . Dave." Jason leaned back in the chair and braced himself for the fireworks. "I understand you've got a nice little glass distribution system worked out."

"Yes, sir. Almost ten kilos a week."

Jason took a bite of the donut to mask his surprise. He'd been prepared for a denial, hostility, threats, but certainly not a confession. Something was wrong.

"I know what you're thinking, but these latest outbreaks aren't rage." Kelly's eyes were lit with the passion of conviction. "It's something new. Something completely different. The glass distribution plan is working. The rage network is out of business. Permanent. We completely buried it. And the market's gone too. The addicts aren't going back. All they want is glass. Our agents haven't even been able to give rage away. You can check the reports."

Jason raised an eyebrow and took another bite of the donut. The police were distributing glass? It didn't make sense. His mind raced in and out of a hundred rabbit holes. He couldn't stay silent much longer. At the same time he couldn't risk talking until he figured out what he was talking about.

"The only problem with the glass program, sir, is that someone's figured out how to modify the stuff—to make it less . . . zombifying. But I'm this close to tracking down the one that's doing it." He indicated a half-inch gap between his thumb and index finger. "I tracked it to a female grad student in the UC chemistry department. She's got the equipment, the materials, the motive, unexplainable income, and I practically caught her red-handed with the souped-up glass addicts she was peddling to. All I need is a little more evidence and the manpower to track her down."

Darcy. The man was talking about Darcy. Time for a different tack. "So let me see if I've got this straight." Jason sat up in his chair and leaned forward over the desk. "Your department has been trying to squash the rage trade by handing out glass on the cheap, but someone's modifying the glass and reselling it on the open market?"

Kelly nodded cautiously. His eyelids lowered slightly, and he looked at Jason as if seeing him for the first time.

Jason didn't miss the cue. Time for another zag. "And Darcy Williams and James Parker are your primary suspects."

Kelly's mouth dropped open. "How did you—"

"Mr. Kelly." Jason pushed himself out of the chair and stepped toward the door of the office. "I haven't been completely honest with you. Can we go back to your work area?"

Jason didn't wait for an answer. He headed out into the hall as Kelly's chair scraped the floor. The door slammed, and floor-shaking footsteps caught up with Jason. Flustered, Kelly appeared at Jason's side.

"Mr. Kelly, I came here to accuse you of drug dealing and maybe worse." He pulled his cell phone out of his breast pocket and pretended to switch it off. "This was dialed in to an off-site answering machine, but I see now I won't be needing it."

Kelly looked to Jason with slack-jawed confusion.

Perfect. Almost there. "I'm Jason Shanahan, a friend of Darcy's and Parker's. I'm sure you've heard of the press conference with John Pyramid."

Kelly's eyes lit with sudden recognition. "That's it. That's where I've seen you before." Kelly started to turn left toward the main office area, but Jason took him by the arm and guided him through the glass doors that led outside.

"I know what you think you saw." He drew Kelly to the side of a small cement patio and looked him in the eye. "You thought you saw me introducing a scientist named John Pyramid. But Pyramid doesn't exist. Parker and Darcy *are* John Pyramid. They created him—along with a more practical invention. Something worth billions to the first pharmaceutical company that gets its hands on it."

"Billions?" Kelly's brow puckered in confusion. "What did they—"

"An estimated sixty billion in the first three years." The number was bogus, of course, but it didn't matter. Jason had him hooked.

He could see it in his face. "I understand you met Parker once. He was in a wheelchair, right?"

Kelly nodded.

"Well, the last I saw him he was leaping six feet into the air and bending steel chairs with his bare hands." Jason paused for effect. "Right before he was shot on live television with over sixty million witnesses."

"So . . . John Pyramid. That was James Parker?"

"That's why I need your help." Jason put a hand on Kelly's shoulder and turned him to face away from the doors. "I have reason to believe at least one of the men after Pyramid is a police officer. Maybe a government agent. Do you know of an agent whose face is entirely scarred over except for a goggle-shaped band around his eyes?" Jason studied Kelly's face carefully for any sign of recognition.

Kelly wrinkled his brow and shook his head slowly. "Not that I remember. Maybe if I saw a picture . . ."

He was telling the truth. Jason was sure of it. "Don't worry about it. But promise me. You can't say anything about this to anybody. Okay?"

Kelly seemed hesitant.

"Not the captain, not your fellow officers, nobody. You know how things work around here. We're talking sixty billion dollars. Enough to corrupt even the incorruptible."

"So why come to me with this? What do you want from me?"

"I bet you don't even know where Darcy Williams lives, do you? Well, I know where they live, what they like to eat, who their friends are. Like I said, Darcy and Parker are my friends. I'm the only one who knows them well enough to figure out where they're hiding. But I need your help."

"So . . ."

"So we work together. I tell you what I know; you tell me what you know. Simple as that. What do you say?"

"I'm still going to take them in—for questioning."

"Fine. All I ask is that you let me know the second you find them."

A slow grin spread itself over Kelly's face. "When do we start?"

DARCY

A shadow man leaped into the air, long coat flapping behind him like the wings of a bat. Darcy threw herself to the ground. At the last second she tried to tuck her shoulder and roll, but her impact with the ground stopped her cold. A pincerlike hand clamped around her arm, yanking her into the air like a puppet on a string. Body twisting, feet kicking, she connected with something solid and wrenched her arm free. For an instant she was free, suspended in soft, rushing darkness. Then she hit the ground with a chest-deflating *thud*.

The shadow beasts surrounded her, sucking the wind out of her. She could hear their hissing breath. The swish of their footsteps. Getting closer. Just above her.

Snapping her knees to her chest, she rolled backward down the steeply sloping lawn. Feet barely touching the ground, she rolled again and again until finally a thorny bush stopped her, flopping her over onto her side. Still gasping for breath, she struggled to her feet and stumbled away from the wheezing shadows still pursuing her.

Another beast was working its way up the slope, hopping and skipping toward her like a hobbled stallion. Darcy took a faltering step down the slope. Another.

Then she started to run, angling away from the nearest pursuer. Step, step, leap . . . Step, step, leap . . . The night air whipped around her as she dropped like an avalanche down the slope. Her pursuer was right beside her, ten feet to her right, but he couldn't seem to turn.

Darcy's feet slid out from under her as she hit a patch of loose rock. Pushing herself back onto her feet, she tried to put on the brakes, but she kept going, faster and faster, skittering across the gravel like a barefoot water-skier. She had to slow down. Any faster and she wouldn't be able to—

Suddenly the slope dropped away from her.

Heart-stopping silence.

She hit the ground with the slash of snapping branches. Pain erupted all around her. Consuming her, drawing her in. Deeper and deeper until she was a tiny spark of fire in a calm and tranquil sea. Sinking. She just had to relax. Let herself go.

A torrent of sand and gravel rained down on her head. They were coming for her. Something pelted her on the forehead with a sharp rap. She tried to roll over but some force was holding her down. The shadows . . .

Darcy threw herself to the side, kicking and punching with her fists. Scratchy branches lashed out at her. She twisted around and once more pushed up onto her feet.

Footsteps sounded close by, the scrape of unsteady feet on rocky ground. She fought her way free of the entangling branches just as a crouching form came into view from around the curve of the slope. In a single leap he cleared the ten feet that separated them and wrapped his arms around her in a rib-crushing bear hug.

"Stop! You're hurting me!" Darcy could barely gasp out the words.

The man's wheezing breath felt hot on her face. He squeezed tighter as gurgling spasms erupted from his chest. His lips parted in the hideous mockery of a smile.

Cascading pebbles. More footsteps. The fiend whipped Darcy around to face the sound. Her head pounded with nauseating pain. She felt herself choking. They were all around her now.

"Put—her—down." A woman's voice rang like a bell through the gray haze. "Now!"

A rattling jolt passed through the body of her captor.

"I mean it. Put her down!"

Darcy strained to trace the voice to its source. The shadow men were slinking into the darkness. At first she thought they were leaving for good, but they stopped not far away. Then Darcy saw her. Bending down to pick up the trunk of a fallen sapling. Blonde hair. Blue eyes. She stood with the branch, tall and slender. Impossibly beautiful. Darcy recognized her from the BART station. It was Rachel.

"Where's Parker?" Darcy gasped. "You've got to get out of here."

"Looking for you." Rachel looked warily from one crouching figure to the next. "On campus. He refused to take the drug."

Just then, one of the men charged. Quick as lightning, Rachel met the man's charge with the root end of the small tree. The man's feet shot out from under him as he was knocked backward onto the ground.

Stunned silence. Then, as if responding to a silent command, the men all charged at once. *Whack! Whack!* The tree spun around twice before Rachel was knocked off her feet.

Darcy closed her eyes as one of the men pounced on her prostrate form. *Dear God, please help her! Please* . . . She could hear the beating of flailing limbs. A melon-hollow *thunk.* The snap of what could only be bone. *God, no. . . !* Darcy twisted in her captor's grip, kicking wildly in an attempt to throw him off balance.

"I told you. Put—her—down!"

Darcy opened her eyes, blinked through tears. Rachel had her arms around one of the men, pinning his arms to his sides. His feet were flailing in the air as she spun him around and threw him into an outcropping of rock. He stood groggily to his feet and moved toward her, but by then she'd retrieved the club end of her broken tree. He squinted at her dumbly for five thick-as-a-brick seconds, then turned and stumbled away at a limping trot.

Rachel swung back around and advanced on Darcy's captor, gripping the tree like a baseball bat. "What's it going to be, softball brain?"

Her captor stepped backward, dragging Darcy with him.

"Not too smart, are they?" She smiled at Darcy and took a practice swing with her club. "The drug seems to turn their brains to mush."

The man dragged Darcy five or six steps backward, but Rachel cleared the distance in a single, graceful hop.

"You're on it too?" Darcy's head was swimming. Did Parker know she was taking it? Had he given it to others as well?

"Yeah, but it doesn't seem to have the same effect on me." She jumped again.

The man snapped Darcy around. Suddenly she was flying through the air, crashing into a weedy bank. She lay still, listening to the man's scrambling flight.

"Are you okay?" A soft gentle voice. Strong, trembling hands eased Darcy to a sitting position. Rachel was crouching in front of her, tears streaming down her cheeks.

Darcy reached out and pulled her close. Tears soaked into the fabric of Rachel's shirt. Parker's Rachel. She'd been so petty, so hateful and selfish in her jealousy. If she really loved Parker, she should be happy for him. Rachel had stood by him long before there was even hope of him walking. She deserved him.

Rachel pulled back slowly. "I'm so sorry." Tears were still flowing down her face.

"Sorry?" Darcy didn't understand. "Why?"

"For ignoring you . . . at the BART station," she said. "It's just that I'd been so worried about Jammy."

"It's okay. I understand. You—"Darcy took a deep breath—"love him."

Rachel nodded. "But why? Why did you get back on the BART? Jammy was so worried."

Darcy looked down at the ground. "I don't know." She could feel her cheeks burning. "I guess I thought you and he . . . you know. Three's a crowd, and I didn't want to be in the way."

"In the way?" Rachel's brow crinkled. "You do know, don't you, that Jammy's in love with you?" Her voice was a mixture of disbelief and amusement. "Tell me this isn't news."

"With me?" Darcy felt light-headed. "I thought . . . The way he was looking at you . . . I thought he was in love with you."

The woman screwed up her face. "My brother?"

"Your brother? What!" The world did a one-eighty around Darcy and clicked suddenly into place again. *Jenny.* Parker's sister. The girl in the hospital, under the knitted hat and breathing mask. "But Parker said we were meeting Rachel at the BART. I heard him talking to her on the phone."

"I was spending the night at Rachel's mom's house when he called. I insisted she bring me along."

"Then the lady at the BART station, the older lady with gray hair?"

"That was Rachel."

Darcy laughed aloud and pulled the woman—Jenny—into another hug.

CHAPTER 30

PARKER

PARKER GUIDED HIS CHAIR down the cement drive of Jason's house, staring up at the high, glassed-in gable that crowned the natural wood structure. A stone fireplace, two-car garage, landscaped lawn—it certainly didn't look like a grad student's house. Even a grad student who drove around in a brand-new Miata. He checked the street number again. *1243 Hill Road.* This was the place all right. And even if it wasn't Jason's house, it was the address he'd given Jenny. He'd told her to wait here whether she found Darcy or not.

"Jenny? Darcy?" He called out and waited, looking at his watch. The Paratransit van had taken forever to pick him up. They probably got tired of waiting and were talking to Jason inside the house.

He followed a stone path around a freshly mulched flower bed. Amazing. When did Jason find the time for gardening? A section of crushed alyssum caught his eye. Fresh boot prints creased the damp soil. The broken plants were still green; the flowers hadn't even wilted yet. Parker pressed harder on the chair's joystick. Muddy footprints on the walk. Turned up divots in the lawn. He stopped at a splintered wooden gate. A dark red splotch stained the bright surface at a break in the wood.

"Jenny! Darcy!" Pushing through the gate, Parker followed the path onto a triangular front porch. The door into the house stood wide open. "Jenny!" He picked up speed and bounced over the step-up into the door. Nobody in the living room. He checked the kitchen, the bedrooms, the study, the bathrooms. Nobody. "Jenny!

Darcy!" He sped back to the living room, searching frantically for a note. Nothing. What had happened?

He'd gotten here later than expected, but not that much later. Was it possible they'd tired of waiting and gone off to look for him? No, Jenny knew he was planning to stop by the chemistry building. She couldn't have known it was being watched. He'd made up a lot of time there. He hadn't even let the Paratransit driver slow down. They just kept on driving past the entrance and straight to Jason's. The detour had lasted less than five minutes. Maybe Jenny was late. Maybe her taxi ran out of gas or had a flat tire.

He rolled outside and followed the sidewalk all the way around the house. No sign of the girls—or Jason. A more thorough search of the gate revealed more signs of struggle. Gouges in the lawn, trampled flowers, more blood. Parker was moving back to the trampled flower bed when a flash of silver caught his eye. A set of keys lying in the grass. Darcy's keys!

"Darcy!" Parker shouted at the top of his lungs. "Darcy!" He rolled back into the house, picked up the phone, slammed it back down. They had Darcy. He drove back and forth across the kitchen floor. They had Darcy, and he couldn't do a thing about it. But why? Who were they? What did they want? How was he supposed to find her? He didn't know anything.

He grabbed the phone again and dialed Jason's cell number. Still not working. What if they'd caught Darcy and Jenny *and* Jason? He retraced his route back through the house, searching for something, anything. The door had been left open, which meant they'd almost certainly been inside. They couldn't have left without a trace.

A handwritten note lay on Jason's desk. Grabbing it up, he held it to the light coming in from the window. Not Jenny's handwriting, or Darcy's. It didn't look like Jason's either. He was about to put it down when he noticed a sketch of a molecular structure. At first he thought it was adrenaline 355, then as he studied it more carefully, he noticed a few subtle differences. It had the same adrenaline moiety, but one of the side chains was completely different. What was going on? What did Jason know that he didn't know? Had he figured out who was trying to kill them?

Parker picked up a stack of papers on the desk. The handwriting was the same, the paper the same too. Faded, yellowing around the edges. It looked ancient. He flipped through the hand-written pages. It was the draft of some kind of research article. A synthesis for a drug, an experiment to explore aggression in mice.

He searched the rest of the stacks. More research papers, all of them handwritten on old yellowed paper. A folded sheet of new white computer paper jumped out at him. Jason's uneven scrawl covered the sheet. A long list of physico-chemical properties. At the top of the list was written one word, printed in bold block letters: *RAGE.*

Rage? What did rage have to do with adrenaline 355? Jason was definitely on to something. But what? Parker searched some more but didn't find any answers—just more questions. Jason had definitely figured something out. He just hadn't written it down. The only way to find Darcy, it seemed, was to find Jason. But what if Jason had been taken too? How could he find the bad guys if he didn't even know who they were?

The chemistry building. The answer hit him like a punch in the face. He didn't have to search for the bad guys. He knew exactly where they were. They were searching for him at the chemistry building. All he had to do was let them find him.

He ran back to the kitchen and scrawled a quick note on a sticky pad.

Jenny,
    Darcy's been captured. Went back to chem building to

He paused to choose his words. The last thing he wanted was for Jenny to worry. If she thought he was in danger, there was no way she'd be willing to wait at Jason's house.

    look for Jason. He may have a clue to help find her.
    Stay here.
               Jammy

He stuck the note to the floor inside the door and fumbled in the pocket of his chair. Three syringes and a serum vial, Jenny had forced them on him at the BART station.

"God, please, strengthen me just this one time." He drew out a syringe with trembling hands and filled it with the clear solution. "Please . . . I don't have a choice. They've got Darcy."

He jabbed the needle into his thigh and injected himself with the drug.

This time it was okay. He didn't have to worry about blacking out. He wasn't planning to last nearly that long.

DARCY

"Come on. Hurry." Jenny reached a hand down to Darcy and pulled her up the steep bank. "If Parker makes it to Jason's place before we get back, he's going to be worried."

"And if our doped-up friends get back with reinforcements, we'll have something to worry about too!" Darcy said. "The guys they're working with are straight, and *they* have guns."

"And you say they all work for John Pyramid—the scientist you and Jammy made up?"

"A guy calling himself Pyramid, anyway." Darcy was out of breath, but she kept on climbing. They were getting closer. The hill was starting to level off.

Jenny dragged her forward. They were back in Jason's yard now. Just a few more seconds and she could rest.

"I think Jammy's here!" Jenny exclaimed. "The door was open when I got here."

Darcy looked up at the closed door. The monster men had been hiding in Jason's house. Why? She ran across the porch and hesitated.

Jenny opened the door. "Jammy?" His empty wheelchair was sitting just inside the door, a used syringe lying on the seat. Jenny bent over and peeled a sticky note from the floor. "He was already here. For some reason he thinks the bad guys have you." Jenny handed the note to Darcy. "He's gone back to the chemistry building to look for Jason."

Darcy read the note. "I thought he'd just searched the chem building."

"That was the plan."

"Come on." Darcy ran back to the kitchen, picked up the phone and dialed Jason's cell phone number. Nothing.

"Are you calling a cab?" Jenny was right behind her. "We've got to get out of here. They'll be back with reinforcements soon."

"First I've got to check on something." Darcy looked down at Jason's answering machine. A bright red five was blinking off and on. She hit the Play button.

The first four messages were from her and Parker. She skipped forward, and a familiar voice sounded over the machine.

"Hello, Jason. Dave Kelly. Just wanted to let you know your tip was right on the money. Runyan and I went over to the university and spotted a dozen men watching the chemistry building. Don't worry, they didn't see us. We left a man to keep an eye on them. Call me if you have anything else. I haven't been able to get through to your cell phone."

Jason working with Kelly? Darcy's insides turned suddenly to ice. "I can't believe this," she said. "Parker's walking right into a trap. We've got to warn him."

"A dozen men . . ." Jenny was watching her with large, frightened eyes.

"And those are the ones he could see. There are probably more." Darcy picked up the phone and dialed information. "How much money do you have?"

"Me? Sixty or seventy dollars. Why?"

"We need to get down to the campus. Now."

PARKER

Parker strode down the center of the sidewalk, fists clenched, head held high. He was through with skulking around. The scumbags had Darcy; now they were going to get him. He burst through the doors of the mining building and headed for the stairs. Leaping up the stairs a half flight at a time, he climbed all the way to the top where a rusty door with lock and metal chain barred his way to the roof. A hard kick buckled the door. One more kick and the door burst open, chain, lock, and broken hasp swinging like a medieval morning star.

He stepped out onto the graveled roof and looked across to the next building. It was at least fifteen feet away, maybe more. Fortunately it was a good fifteen feet lower as well. He backed up to the opposite edge of the roof and started running. Faster, faster, a step onto the low wall and a huge leap . . . Wind rushing, rooftops blur-

ring, a great abyss opened beneath him like the jaws of a giant pred-
ator. He hit the deck hard, his momentum rolling him over and
over across the biting, gravel-covered roof. Heart still pounding, he
climbed shakily to his feet and brushed himself off.

He took a step and winced. The landing had hurt him worse
than he'd expected. He was lucky he hadn't broken a bone. Just
because his muscles were stronger, didn't mean his bones were
stronger too. He had to be careful.

He walked gingerly to the roof access door and tested the lock.
Good, it was open. He limped down the stairs and navigated the
maze of hallways to another set of stairs. Two more flights and he
was on the fifth floor. The man with binoculars was stationed on
the south face of the building, two windows from the corner. Circling to his left, Parker came to an office door. Gray light filtered
through its opaque window. A hazy shadow moved against the light.
Someone was definitely home.

Parker kicked open the door and took the room in with a
glance. A skeletal man spun around to face him, dropping the binoculars as he turned. Parker cleared the room with a leap and
pinned the man's arms at his sides.

"Hey! What—"

Parker lifted him up and slammed his back against the wall.
"Where's the girl?" He channeled all his anger into his voice.
"Where is she?" He squeezed the man's upper arms until the
muscle gave way to bone.

White lines creased the man's face. His eyes looked as though
they were going to pop out of his head.

"Darcy Williams. Where is she?" Parker gave the man a shake.

The man shook his head frantically. "You got the wrong guy!
I'm just . . . bird-watching. Leggo and I'll—"

Parker swung him around and shoved him up against the window. "Imagine me pushing you through this window and letting
you dangle over a sixty-foot drop. Imagine it real Hollywood. Lots
of broken glass, lots of blood. Okay? You got a good imagination?"

The man nodded. Tears were running down the creases in his
face.

"Good. Now imagine what you're telling me when I ask you *one
more time*. Where's the girl? Where's Pyramid holding her?"

"I don't know. I swear. I'm just a lookout. Don't nobody tell me nothin'. If they got her—"

"Who's they?" Parker lowered the man to the floor but kept a tight grip on his arms.

"I don't know. This is just a one-time job. My supplier got it for me. He's the one with the connections. I swear. His name is Biggie Dee. Hangs out at the Club Verde on Forty-third Street. Just don't tell him I ratted. He'd kill me."

Parker let go of an arm, searched the man's pockets, and took his wallet and phone. "Where's your gun?"

"Gun? You think I'm stupid?"

Parker released him, and the man sank to the floor, hugging his arms to his chest. "They gave you a number to call. What's the number?"

"It's written on the picture." The man nodded to a nearby desk.

Parker backed to the desk and picked up an eight-by-ten glossy. A glance revealed a grainy photo of Darcy and himself coming out of the chemistry building. He was in his chair and Darcy was holding the door. A local phone number was scrawled across the bottom in black ink. Parker folded the photo and stuck it in his pocket. Then, rifling through the man's wallet, he came up with his driver's license.

"Well, Roland." He studied the license to make sure it wasn't a fake. "I'd advise you to lay low for a while. I'm going to visit your friends, and if I get any idea at all they knew I was coming, I'll let them know who gave me the nice photograph. Understand?"

Roland stared up at him with wide eyes.

"Do you understand?"

An eager nod.

"Good. So, do you have any more friends out there I should know about?"

Roland started to shake his head, but Parker took a menacing step toward him and Roland jerked back against the wall.

"Okay, one guy downstairs and one, maybe two outside the building. But I think they left about an hour ago. That's all I know about, I swear."

"Thanks, Roland." Parker held up the license. "I'll just keep this if you don't mind. If everything turns out okay, I may send it back to you. Otherwise it goes to the police. We understand each other, don't we, Roland?"

Roland nodded.

"Good." Parker turned and ran through the broken door. Roland probably wouldn't rat on him, still he needed to move fast, just in case. He pounded down the stairs and burst into the lobby with the bang of a slamming door.

A punk with a scraggly beard and long, stringy hair took a step backward and turned to flee. Parker pounced on him, driving him to the floor. "Who hired you? You've got five seconds!"

"I don't know what you're—"

Parker yanked him off the ground by an arm, raised him over his head. "Two seconds."

"I never saw him! Just a voice on the phone. A guy I know set it up. They didn't tell me anything. Just gave me a picture. I—"

Parker slammed him back down on his feet, and a cell phone clattered to the floor. He stomped on the phone and then squeezed the punk around the triceps. "Friendly advice. You have no idea what you've gotten yourself mixed up in. Don't make any calls, don't call out for help, just run like crazy. It's your one and only chance of getting out of this alive."

Without waiting for a response, Parker flung him into the wall and dashed for the door. He was wasting time. Whoever Pyramid was, he wasn't going to trust his business to a bunch of drug addicts. The guys on the front lines wouldn't know anything. He had to get to an officer. One of the men with guns.

He crossed the street and circled below the chemistry complex, scanning the street for unstudent-looking students. The place was deserted, but even if they spotted him, it would take several minutes for them to figure out what he was doing. He had the home-turf advantage. By the time they figured it out, he'd be in and out of Jason's office and halfway across campus.

He ducked into the back door of Gilman and pounded up the stairs to the second floor. Running the length of the building, he pushed through the doors and ran across the open bridge that connected Gilman to Tan. Another two flights of stairs and he was racing through the chem building. Past the chemistry office, around the corner, he pushed into Jason's makeshift office.

"Parker!"

Parker jumped backward, slamming his back hard against the wall. He couldn't believe his eyes.

"Parker, are you okay?" Darcy ran to him. She clung to him with encircling arms.

Parker held her close, buried his face in her silky hair. The smell of sage, fresh and outdoorsy. "I . . . can't believe it." He stroked the back of her head with his hand. "I thought they'd kidnapped you."

Darcy looked up at him, eyes sparkling like a cut topaz. "It was Jenny. She rescued me. I wish you could have seen her. It was just like a kung fu movie." She pulled away and turned back to the room.

"Jenny!" Parker exclaimed. She was sitting at Jason's desk, watching them with a mischievous grin. "What are you two doing here? I thought—"

"Sorry to break up the reunion, but there are over a dozen men watching this building. We should get going."

"A dozen men?" Parker looked down at Darcy. "How'd you get in?"

"The basement passage through Hildebrand." Darcy stepped toward the door. "If anyone spotted you, this place will soon be crawling with monster men. We've got to—"

The door in front of Darcy exploded inward. "Freeze! This is the police!" Two uniformed men with guns pressed into the room. Kelly and Runyan moved in right behind them, guns drawn and pointed at Parker's chest.

"Kelly." Parker lifted his hands in the air and stepped forward to place himself between Darcy and the officers.

Officer Kelly pushed by the two officers and squared his shoulders to face Parker, his face blossoming into a florid pattern of splotches. "Mr. Parker, we've been looking for you."

"What do you want, Kelly?" Parker reached back with a hand to make sure Darcy was still behind him.

"What does every good cop want? To lock up the guilty and protect the innocent."

"Is that why you're dealing glass?"

Runyan shot Kelly a questioning look.

"I'm doing that to save lives." Kelly returned Runyan's glare. "It's called the rage Contravention Program. Look it up. It's not public knowledge, but it's not a secret neither. By handing glass out to addicts, we've completely destroyed the market for rage. It's called dumping. Good old-fashioned economics. They get their high; we get docile, easy-to-manage addicts. The program has saved thousands of lives."

"Right. Now we've got glass-head murderers instead of rage murderers. Nice program," said Parker.

"That's not our fault." Kelly's face turned a purplish shade of red. *"Someone . . ."* Kelly looked past Parker to Darcy. "Someone in the chemistry department has been modifying the glass we're handing out. Selling it on the street for a profit. It's the modified glass that makes addicts violent."

"So you're the one." Darcy stepped forward. "You're the one who searched my lab. You searched Pyramid's lab too, didn't you?"

"Everything was by the book. I had a warrant. Probable cause."

"And you didn't find anything, did you?" Runyan interjected. "Unless I miss my guess, all this violence has to do with the drug he's taking—not the modified glass."

Kelly nodded. "Way ahead of you. That's why me and some of the guys have been keeping an eye on this place. That's how I knew you were here."

"If you saw us coming, so did the bad guys." Parker took a step toward the door. "We've got to get out of here."

Kelly shook his head. "Got it all taken care of. We rounded up the goons watching this place before moving in. All eight of them."

"I got the two in Stanley," Parker said. "I doubt they'll call in the cavalry."

"Really." Kelly cocked his head to the side. A new light seemed to shine in his eyes. "I was wondering what happened to that door. Impressive."

"We can get each other's autographs in a more secure location." Runyan put a hand on Darcy's shoulder and guided her toward the door.

"Wait a minute. Jenny." Parker looked back over his shoulder. Jenny was sitting at Jason's desk with a glazed look on her face. "Jenny, come on."

Her head swung around slowly. A befuddled smile lifted her otherwise slack features.

"Oh no!" Parker rushed over to her.

"Parker, what's . . ." Darcy's voice sounded across the room. She rushed over and knelt by his side. "Jenny? Are you okay?"

"The drug's wearing off." Parker took Jenny by the hand and shook it lightly. "She's not going to make it."

"What's going on?" Runyan marched back into the room. "We've got to get—"

"She's crashing." Parker pulled out the desk chair and lifted Jenny in his arms. "The drug only lasts thirteen or fourteen hours. She'll be out for at least nine." Following close behind Runyan, he carried his sister from the room. Kelly followed at a distance.

Darcy hovered at Parker's shoulder, holding Jenny's head steady and smoothing back her hair. "Do you trust him?" she whispered, nodding back toward Kelly.

"I don't think we have a choice," Parker whispered back. "His story makes sense. The glass-heads that attacked you couldn't have been on normal glass. I could see how he'd think—" Parker fell silent as they reached the elevators.

"You're not straining at all, are you?" Kelly asked Parker. He held the door of the elevator to let Darcy and Parker step inside. Runyan had put her gun away, but Kelly was still holding his.

"She's actually pretty light," Parker said.

"So how much can you lift?" Kelly's eyes were narrow slits. "Could you lift me?"

"*She* could lift you." Darcy swept a tendril of hair out of Jenny's face. "I saw her fight off four guys, all of them twice her size."

"And she was just like you? In a wheelchair?" Kelly looked surprised.

Parker nodded as the elevator doors slid open.

"That's just amazing. Flat out amazing," Kelly said, holding the door and standing back to let everyone out. "Your friend was right. I didn't believe it at first, but I can see how someone might want to steal an invention like this."

"My friend?" Parker followed Runyan across the lobby and out onto University Drive.

"Jason Shanahan?" Kelly's eyes narrowed. "He *is* your friend, isn't he?"

Parker nodded. "Jason told you about the drug?"

"Came to my office first thing this morning. Wouldn't trust anyone but me. Which reminds me." Kelly pulled a cell phone from off his hip and punched in a number from a glossy black business card. He listened a few seconds, then punched in another number. "Hello, Jason? Dave Kelly."

Parker leaned closer to Kelly, hoping to listen in on their conversation.

"Just now," said Kelly. "We'll be at the police station in fifteen minutes." He listened for a few moments. "On the campus," Kelly continued. "It doesn't matter, just meet us at the station."

Parker moved even closer and heard, ". . . three minutes, okay?" He thought he heard the word *Pyramid* before Kelly glanced at him and stepped off the curb out into the street.

Kelly spoke into the phone, "Why can't you tell me now? . . . University Drive near the main entrance, okay? They'll be fine. See you at the station." With a huff, Kelly snapped the phone shut and clipped it to his side. He stepped back up onto the sidewalk and looked over at Parker. "Your friend doesn't know when to quit, does he?"

Parker shook his head. "What did he say about Pyramid?"

"Said he had important information, so important it couldn't wait fifteen minutes." Kelly quickened his pace. Runyan was leading Darcy to a black Crown Victoria.

Squealing tires sounded in the distance. Roaring engines. Two huge SUVs skidded around a curve and barreled up the road toward them.

"Get to the car!" Kelly grabbed Parker by the arm and started pulling him forward.

Parker shook off his hand and ran for the car, hugging Jenny's limp form to his chest. A gunshot rang out. A high-pitched scream. He dove onto the grassy median as a fusillade of shots ripped through the air. He crawled toward the car, dragging Jenny behind him. Darcy was crouching with her back against the passenger-side front tire, her arms covering her head as a spray of glass rained down on her. Kelly, gun in hand, was stretched out on the grass behind her.

"There's too many of them," Parker shouted over the blasts. "Call for help. Get Darcy out of here!"

Kelly didn't move. Parker stretched out and grabbed Kelly's wrist and the gun fell out of his hand. Parker then turned to Runyan, and a chill ran up his spine. Runyan was lying motionless on the street side of the car.

He and Darcy were on their own.

CHAPTER 31

DARCY

DARCY PRESSED HER HANDS TIGHTER to her ears as blast after blast rang through her head. Glass pelted her like rain. Cut cubes of crystal brightness. Shouting voices. Squealing brakes. A cloud of burnt powder closed around her, filling her with the metallic stench of death. She pressed her face to her knees, huddling against the storm as the thunderclaps faded to the rush of her own frantic breathing.

"Hold it!" an angry voice cried out. "One more move and she's dead!"

Darcy turned in the direction of the voice. A balding man stood at the back of the car aiming a pistol straight at her.

"I'm dropping the gun. Just don't hurt the girl." Parker's voice. The thud of a heavy object hitting the ground.

The gunman's hands were shaking. Darcy didn't dare turn around. It wouldn't take much to make him pull the trigger. She stared up at him, and a strange sense of calmness spread through her. She knew she was going to die, but she was okay with it. The thought made her smile.

"Now get in the back of the truck," another man ordered. "No tricks, Hercules, or Manny there shoots the girl."

Darcy stood slowly and watched as three men with guns herded Parker cautiously toward a white SUV. They obviously knew what he could do.

Parker stopped outside the door and turned to face Darcy. "Darcy, I'm—"

"Get in the truck!" the balding man bellowed. "You too!" He motioned Darcy to the second SUV.

She walked slowly to the truck, looking back to Jenny's still form on the sidewalk. She was all right, she was just unconscious, she had to be—

"Get in!" her bald captor snapped. "Slide all the way over."

Darcy climbed into the truck and the SUV leaped forward, pushing her back against the seat.

"We're on the radio with the other truck. Do anything stupid and we'll blow your boyfriend away. Got it?"

Boyfriend. The word made her smile.

"I'm warning you. Whatever you're thinking, try it and he's dead."

Darcy bit her lip. No matter what she said, it would only make things worse. She turned to sit straight in her seat, and a flash of familiar blue caught her eye. In the rearview mirror, two cars back, she thought she had glimpsed a blue Miata. *Jason?* She tried not to let her excitement show. No, it couldn't be. How would he know where they were?

She glanced at the mirror again, but the Miata was gone.

They wove in and out of traffic, turning left and right through the rutted Oakland surface streets. Graffiti-covered warehouses sped by them. Mounds of machinery and rusty metal. *Jason?* Another flash of blue in the rearview mirror. It was too far away to be sure. A street sign flashed past her. Maybe she could . . .

It suddenly occurred to her that the men weren't making any effort to conceal their whereabouts from her. They didn't seem to mind her seeing their faces either. She put the thought out of her mind. *"Happily ever after."* Jason was following them—she had to believe it. She and Parker were going to be all right. One way or another.

PARKER

Parker's SUV stopped at the garage-style door of an old boarded-up warehouse. The man in the front passenger seat spoke into his headset, and the door opened before them.

"Okay, the door's open. We're going in." The man had been narrating the whole trip, like an NFL colorman at a zero-to-zero game. "Okay, we're in. Hercules is being a good boy, but keep your distance. We don't want him trying anything."

Parker looked at the guy sitting next to him and rolled his eyes. He smiled at Parker and shook his head. As he did so, his gun hand dropped another inch so that the barrel was now pointing at the driver's kneecap. Parker wasn't about to do anything to put Darcy's life at risk, but he'd been working on this guy the entire trip. From the running commentary, Parker had learned his name was Jake and he seemed to have nothing but contempt for the man with the headset. Parker didn't blame him.

"Okay, we are getting out of the truck. I'm getting out first, then Sweeney, and then Jake with Hercules." Headset opened the door and stepped out.

"Houston, I am out of the truck," Parker whispered to Jake.

"I am out of the car . . ."

Jake snorted and nodded to Parker, motioning for him to climb out of the car before the driver.

"Hercules is out before Sweeney. Hercules is out before Sweeney."

"Knock it off, Juju." Jake hopped out of the truck and led Parker across the shipping room with exaggerated swagger. Parker turned as the second SUV pulled in beside the first. Jake pulled back on his arm, indicating that he should wait.

"What do you think of my girlfriend?" Parker turned to Jake with what he hoped looked like a *one of the guys* smirk.

"Nice." Jake's voice was a throaty growl. "Definitely nice."

Parker stole a look at Darcy while Jake watched her get out of the truck. She smiled at him. Her shoulders were back, her chin held high. He mouthed the word *sorry* and then shifted his attention back to Jake. "You gotta girlfriend?"

"Three of 'em," Jake answered matter-of-factly. He turned and led Parker down a dark corridor. "But not as nice as that."

"Three of them." It was all he could think to say. He had to move on to another subject, one that would force Jake to think of him as a human being. "You know I was in a wheelchair until just a few weeks ago. Just when I get a girlfriend and it looks like I'll finally be able to get out of school, then this happens."

They turned into another corridor that opened into a high-ceilinged, sky-lit room. Jake motioned him toward a set of rusty metal stairs that led up to a paper-covered office door. Dim electric light leaked through black spray-painted windows.

"Hold up." Jake turned and raised a hand. "We better wait for the others."

"What do you think is going to happen to us?" Parker asked.

Jake shrugged and looked down at the floor.

Parker nodded. At least Jake wasn't happy about it. That was progress. Maybe he'd hesitate to pull the trigger if . . .

Sweeney and the one they called Juju walked into the chamber, followed by Darcy and three men with guns.

"Are you okay? Have they hurt you?" Parker resisted while Jake tried to force him up the stairs.

"I'm fine," said Darcy. "Good but *not gorgeous.*" She nodded slightly as she spoke.

What did she mean by *not gorgeous*? Parker wondered. She was obviously trying to tell him something.

"No more talk." The guy behind Darcy, the one with the shaved head, seemed nervous. "Come on, what's the holdup? Move!"

Parker gave in and followed Jake up the stairs. When they reached the door at the top, Jake stepped behind Parker and shoved his gun into Parker's back.

"Go in," Jake said. "The boss is waiting."

Parker opened the door and stepped inside, with Jake and his gun close behind. An old heavyset man in ill-fitting, thrift-store clothes was sitting at a large desk.

"Ah. Mr. Parker. Miss Williams. Glad you could join us." The man smiled a mostly toothless smile. "My partner is eager to talk to you."

"Your partner?" Parker let Jake drag him farther away from Darcy.

"Yes. I understand he's a colleague of yours. And yours too, Miss Williams." The toothless man stood up behind the desk and nodded to Darcy. "Quite a brilliant scientist. John Pyramid, they call him."

Parker wasn't surprised. "And your name is. . . ?"

"Unimportant." Toothless smiled smugly. "Invisible men don't require names. All we require are answers. My associate has some questions for you."

"Okay."

Footsteps sounded on the stairs outside the office, and Toothless looked eagerly to the door. Whoever it was, Parker could tell by the man's expression that he and Darcy weren't going to be happy to see him. The door opened slowly, and into the room stepped . . .

"Ray?" Darcy gasped. "How could. . . ?"

"I'm, like, really sorry." Ray looked at Parker with dark, haunted eyes. "I never meant it to turn out like this. I really didn't."

Toothless walked over to Ray and put a hand on his shoulder. "None of us did, Ray. None of us did. But business is business, and we businessmen have to protect our secrets."

Darcy turned on Ray. "It was you all along? You're the one who attacked me? You wrecked the labs?"

"Totally by accident," Ray said. "I was just testing out the drug and, like, got the dosage too high." He backed away from Darcy and leaned against the desk. "It totally screwed me up. I didn't even know I'd done anything. Now we know to keep the dosage real low. They're not as strong, but at least they can, like, think better."

"That night outside the chem building. It was you, wasn't it? I can't believe I didn't recognize you."

"But why?" Parker shook his head in disbelief. "Why take the drug in the first place?"

"You saw the mice. They were like super mice! That stuff is way better than glass. Better than rage, even."

"The glass-heads! That was you too, wasn't it?" Darcy started toward Ray, but the bald guy held her back. "Kelly said someone in the chem department was modifying glass and reselling it on the street. It was you the whole time."

"That's why he was always working late," Parker said. "I thought it was strange at the time. I can't believe I never made the connection."

"With his lab technique," Darcy added, "it's a wonder he didn't poison someone!"

Ray pushed off the desk and stepped toward Darcy, his face flushed. "For your information, I—"

"I hate to break up this happy reunion," Toothless stepped in front of Ray, "but maybe you would like to ask Pyramid's question."

Ray shifted his feet, eyes darting all over the room—everywhere but at Parker.

"Ray?"

"If you'd just told me earlier, none of this would have had to happen." Ray finally turned his gaze on Parker. "But no . . . You had to keep it a big secret. Even though I was the one that invented adrenaline. If it weren't for me, you wouldn't be *standing* here right now."

"What are you talking about?" Parker demanded. "What secret?"

"What did you do to modify the drug?"

"Modify the drug?"

"No more games." Ray's eyes flashed. "I know you're doing something. We wouldn't be having this conversation if you weren't."

"Do you know what he's taking about?" Parker turned to Toothless. "Because if you do, I need you to explain it to me."

"Simple logic." Toothless stepped forward. "You're walking, so you're obviously on adrenaline. And yet you're not a raging monster. Meaning you've obviously figured out a way to modify the drug—in much the same way Ray here has been altering glass."

"I know it's not methylation," said Ray. "That was the first thing I tried."

"The choice facing you is a simple one." Toothless nodded to the bald man, who then wrapped an arm around Darcy's neck and put a gun to her head. "Tell us how to modify the drug or watch your girlfriend die."

"Don't tell him!" Darcy pulled her captor off-balance and pierced Parker with a desperate look. "They're going to kill us anyway or else they wouldn't have—"

The bald man jerked Darcy backward and pressed his gun to her face.

"Well, Mr. Parker? Your decision," Toothless said. "How easy do you want Miss Williams to die?"

Parker's mind raced. What was Darcy trying to tell him? There wasn't any secret to tell. It sounded like everybody that took adrenaline turned into a beast right away. Maybe it was the enzyme he and Jenny were missing in their neurotransmitter pathway. Jenny had never had any problems with the drug at all.

"Okay. Here's the deal." Parker let his words slur together ever so slightly. If he wasn't dead on, this wasn't going to work. "I'll give you the formula—but on one condition: you have to let Darcy go free."

"No way!" Ray protested. "You know—"

Toothless held up his hand, and Ray sat back down on the desk. "And?"

"And I'll tell you everything I know. I'll even show you how to do the synthesis. But first you have to let her go. I'm not saying anything until I see her get in a car and drive away. If I see any sign of a double cross, you'll just have to kill me, because I won't talk."

"And suppose we just torture the information out of you?" Toothless asked. "Suppose we were to torture her?"

"I'm sorry." Parker looked into Darcy's eyes. "This is the way it has to be." He took a deep breath and looked Toothless in the eye. "If you hurt her in any way, I give you my word as a follower of Christ that I'll die before giving you what you want." He crossed his arms and stared defiantly at the men in the room.

Toothless looked pointedly at Ray, who just shrugged.

"Okay." Toothless's lips parted in a hideous smile. "In that case I guess we have no choice." He turned to Juju, who was still wearing the headset. "Go prepare a car for her. Make sure it's clean and everything is . . . in order."

Parker didn't miss the hidden command. He had no illusions about the men letting her go, but at least he'd just bought them some time. *Not gorgeous.* Darcy had been trying to tell him something. Where had he heard that expression before? Jenny? He glanced at Darcy out of the corner of his eye, but she wasn't paying attention. She was staring off into space, probably working out plans and backup plans, and backups to the backups.

"Everything's all set," Juju announced as he burst through the door less than ten minutes after he left. Parker noticed the question in Toothless's eyes and Juju's answering nod.

Ten minutes. Parker exchanged glances with Darcy and looked down suggestively at his watch. She smiled and gave an almost imperceptible nod. Ten minutes wasn't enough time to prepare anything too elaborate. Even so, Toothless didn't seem worried. Parker studied Juju as they all walked back toward the shipping bay. No whispers, no glances, no communication of any kind. Whatever Juju had set up, Toothless already seemed to know what it would be. They'd obviously done this before—or something similar.

An old beat-up Camaro sat parked in the bay. The two SUVs were gone.

"Nice ride," Darcy said, snapping out of her daze. "I would have preferred one of the SUVs, though. Or maybe a nice sporty *Miata*. But a Camaro is *excellent*."

Again the slight nod. The emphasis on the name Miata. Darcy was trying to tell him something about Jason. But what?

The bald man led Darcy to the car, where Juju handed her a single key. "Could we have three minutes alone—to say goodbye?" Darcy looked hopefully at Toothless.

"Don't push it." Ray stepped menacingly toward Darcy.

"Just *three* minutes." Darcy looked to Parker. "Three minutes . . ."

Jason! Had he arrived at the university in time to see the gunmen? Parker wanted to shout. Instead he pretended to stumble, letting his knees go all rubbery for a full second before catching himself. *Jason!* He kept his face expressionless. Jason had definitely said something about three minutes when he was talking to Kelly on the phone. If he had followed them . . . Was it possible?

"Mr. Parker, you mentioned you wanted to watch her drive away?" Toothless nodded to Jake, who escorted Parker to the corner of the garage.

"Parker. . . ?" Darcy said.

Parker tripped over his feet as he turned, breaking free of Jake's grip.

"I love you." Darcy's voice.

"I love you too." Parker blinked to clear his vision. "I'll always love you."

She got into the Camaro, and the bald man slammed the door shut behind her and stepped to the side, gun still leveled at her head. Darcy smiled bravely, then turned in her seat to start the car. After a few false starts, the engine finally turned over. The car rolled backward a few inches and stalled with a wheezing cough. She started the car again and revved the engine, put it in gear. Swinging the car around slowly, she stopped and revved the engine again. The car then took off with the squeal of tires and a cloud of blue smoke. Parker swayed on his feet as she raced down the street and turned away from the warehouse at the first intersection.

"Sorry, but I . . ." He stumbled into Jake, staggered away, and fell over backward, smacking his head on the crumbling asphalt.

DARCY

Darcy jammed the gas pedal to the floor and gripped the steering wheel with both hands in a frantic effort to keep the Camaro from swerving off the road. She'd been worried she wouldn't remember how to drive, but it was just like drivers ed. Only the final exam would be a whole lot more final if she didn't figure out what the bad guys were up to. She glanced down at the fuel gauge. Sure enough, the needle was resting on empty. That, at least, was a good sign. They wouldn't have bothered to siphon the tank if they'd planted a bomb. At least she had a better idea of what to expect. She reached up and adjusted the rearview mirror, swiveling it so that it angled down and toward the windshield.

The turn was coming up fast. Once she went around the corner, she'd be out of Parker's sight. Ducking down in the seat so she could barely see over the dash, she hit the brakes and swung the car into a screeching turn. No oncoming traffic. She slid onto the floor, leaning her head against the seat to see the reflection of the roadside in the outward facing mirror. If they were planning to shoot—

The car windows shattered, showering her in a hail storm of broken glass. Another shot. Another. The car was pounded by a barrage of echoing blasts. The windshield, the sides, the back. Glass was everywhere. She couldn't see.

The steering wheel pulled suddenly to the side, and the car started to vibrate wildly. *God please, let it be a soft landing.* Darcy yanked the wheel hard to the left and then slid all the way onto the floor. The Camaro bounced beneath her and jolted to a bone-jarring crash.

She lay dazed and shaken in semidarkness as metallic bangs and pings sounded above her. Something was falling on the car. She reached up and felt a slick fabric above her. A deflating airbag.

Shouting voices cried out in the distance. They were coming for her. She tried to sit up, but her head was trapped beneath the seat, her knees wedged under the dash. She had to get off her back, but she was jammed in too tight to turn over. More voices, getting closer.

Darcy snaked her left arm under the deflated airbag and felt the door for the handle. Got it. She pulled on the latch and pushed open the door. She could hear footsteps now. Hollow-sounding voices. They were at the car. She yanked her arm back under the airbag and held her breath.

"She's not in the car!" a voice called from outside the open door. "Fan out and check the building. She couldn't have gone far."

A confusion of pounding footsteps. More voices. It sounded like at least six or seven, maybe even a dozen men.

" . . . knew this was a bad idea. He's going to . . ."

" . . . upstairs. I'll check the back. . . ."

Darcy lay on her back listening as the footsteps passed her by. She counted out sixty seconds. Paused and listened. Counted another sixty. Eventually the police would come. Any minute now. Unless . . . What if she was in a private complex? She'd seen several chain-link fences from the SUV. What if nobody came until it was too late? Parker might be running out of time.

She pushed herself to the side, squirming around to get her head out from under the seat. Then, forcing herself onto her elbows, she managed to get her head far enough up to see out the door. The car was halfway inside some kind of warehouse. Apparently the whole building was in an advanced state of dry rot. Pieces of wood were still falling from the hole she'd made in the crumbling wall. If she hadn't hit a stack of old crates, she might have driven straight through the building without even slowing down.

Scanning the dimly lit room, she squirmed through the car door and rolled onto her knees. Dusty light filtered in through the car-sized hole. The soft murmur of voices. Harsh laughter. Following the body of the car back to the hole in the wall, she leaned carefully over the trunk to peek outside.

A blue convertible Miata was parked on the side of the road. Jason was leaning against it, talking to a group of men. She gasped aloud when she recognized them. The bald man and the driver of Parker's SUV. One of them turned and pointed straight at her. She jerked away from the edge of the hole and dropped down to the dust-carpeted floor.

Jason was one of *them?* She couldn't believe it. No, it couldn't be. He was her friend. Maybe he'd been captured. A burst of laughter sounded outside on the street. She got up again and peered outside. Jason was reaching inside his car, the others still laughing as he pulled a large handgun out from under his seat. He motioned with the gun toward the end of the street, and the two men lumbered off in that direction. Then slamming the door of his car, he turned to Darcy's hiding place and sauntered across the road.

Darcy's throat felt suddenly tight. She pulled away from the hole. Stumbled backward. Running blindly across the room, she leaped and dodged the contents of a dozen gutted boxes. *Jason.* It had been him all along.

She ducked through a door and ran down a dark corridor.

Why hadn't she realized it before? His transformation. He'd been so jealous at first, then poof. All of a sudden he and Parker were the best of friends. Just after they'd discovered the drug. He'd even started injecting the mice, running experiments. Jason and Ray had been inseparable.

And then there were the drugs she found under his desk. Rage no less. It's not like you could just pick the stuff up at a local drugstore. Using rage to synthesize adrenaline for Jenny . . . How could she have fallen for such a ridiculous story? Rage was a protected substance, its chemical structure classified. Even if he knew the structure, it would take months to work out a synthesis. Why not just express order reagents from Sigma?

The corridor opened out into a cavernous chamber. Heavy footsteps sounded right behind her. She spun around and dove behind a stack of moldering pallets. If he came upon her from the wrong direction . . . She rolled herself into a tight ball, pressing herself against the pallets, trying to blend into the bolts of cloth that littered the floor.

Echoing voices. A shout. Footsteps running across the chamber. The voices grew softer. Were they moving on to search someplace else? Maybe Pyramid had called off the search.

Pyramid. The whole thing had been Jason's idea. Especially the name. He'd sent out the paper under the name, set up a lab and an e-mail account, held a press conference. A lightning bolt of realization struck her then. If the rights to adrenaline 355 were ever disputed, John Pyramid would get the credit. It all made sense. When the man in ragged clothes mentioned his partner, she'd assumed he meant Ray, but what if he'd been talking about Jason? What if Jason *was* John Pyramid?

But why have Parker dress up at the press conference? Why have a press conference at all? Unless the whole thing was just for show. Jason got to mug for the cameras while Parker got gunned down in cold blood. Faceless and anonymous. It was the perfect alibi. And with Parker dead, Jason could take full credit for the discovery. He was the scientist, and Parker was the poor test subject.

A tap sounded close by. The swish of fabric brushing fabric. Darcy's muscles tightened. He was right on top of her. Her nerve endings were on fire. She had to look up. How could she fight if she couldn't see. . . ?

"Found her!"

The stranger's shout released her like a coiled spring. She jumped to her feet, spinning in the air. A savage kick cut her feet out from under her, and she crashed onto her back. She started to sit up, but a large handgun pressed into her forehead.

"Hey, Sweeney! I got her. Do I kill her now or what?"

CHAPTER 32

PARKER LAY ON HIS BACK on the cold cement floor, listening to Jake's shoes scraping back and forth near his throbbing head. Hot pain stabbed through his body with every breath he took, but he kept his eyes closed and his face relaxed. They'd kicked him twice in the ribs before Ray could convince them that blackouts were a natural side effect of the drug. If he hadn't been half unconscious from hitting his head in the fall, he probably wouldn't have been able to hold still. As it was he had a terrible headache. Still he was grateful. Grateful to be alive and, most of all, grateful Darcy had gotten away.

An urgent message had come five minutes after she'd left, and all the thugs but Jake were ordered to join in the search. Whatever they'd prepared for her had obviously gone wrong. She'd been gone at least a half hour now. More than enough time to find a phone and call the police. So why weren't they more worried? Why weren't they evacuating the warehouse?

That was what worried Parker most. Toothless was too calm. Too sure of himself. Like he had a foolproof backup plan. A hand so full of trump cards he didn't even need to pay attention to the game.

Jake paused near the door and turned back toward Parker. They were finally alone. Now was the ideal time. *Come on. Just a little closer.*

No! Jake turned back and resumed his restless pacing. Time was running out. They'd be coming to get him any minute now. If they were going to evacuate, now was the time to do it.

Parker went suddenly rigid, twitching his arms and legs. The sound of Jake's pacing stopped. He was coming closer. Parker stopped twitching and started breathing heavier, tightening his face as if he were having a bad dream. Another step closer. A shadow fell across Parker's face.

Parker swung out with his right hand, putting everything he had into the awkward punch. His fist struck a glancing blow to the side of Jake's jaw. *Not good.* Lunging upward, he swiped at Jake's gun hand, missed, and fell crashing to the floor. The room dimmed as flashes of burning pain short-circuited his brain. He lay still, waiting for the bullet that would usher him into the presence of God. The room was completely silent. Nothing stirred.

Pushing himself up off the floor, he turned slowly, blinking his eyes against the electric blue dot that blocked his sight. At first he didn't see him. Then, slowly his eyes were drawn to a dark blur on the floor. Jake, lying in a heap, his fingers curled loosely around his gun.

Jake's hand twitched as Parker reached for the gun. Too risky. Heaving himself onto his feet, Parker braced himself against the wall to steady himself. The electric fireball was getting bigger. He could hear it whistling in his ears. He staggered along the wall. Were those footsteps he heard? Throwing open the door, he pushed out into a dark hallway. His legs were stiff, wooden. The welt on the back of his head throbbed, filled his mind with fire. The corridor was too long. He wasn't going to make it. Once they discovered Jake, they'd seal off the whole building.

A metallic squeal sounded just ahead of him. He was about to turn around when a bright light swept across the wall ahead of him. Sunlight! So close. He pressed himself against the wall. Footsteps heading his way. Only one man between him and freedom. He tiptoed to the intersection and waited, preparing to spring. Then, just as a shadowy form stepped into view, he leaped through the air, driving the man to the floor in a flying tackle.

His head exploded in nauseating pain as the blue spot expanded to fill his vision. Brighter. More electric. He could feel blackness closing in all around him. Sweeping his hands across the floor, he tried to hold on. There'd been a gun. He'd heard it clatter to the floor. But his head hurt so badly. He was so tired.

His hand closed around something metal. Something heavy, solid. The force of its presence traveled up his arm. A soft groan came from behind him. He pushed himself to his knees, turned to face the struggling man. Gripping the gun in both hands, Parker pointed the weapon at the man's chest and said, "Make a sound and I pull the trigger."

"Parker?" The voice sounded strangely familiar. "It's me, Jason."

"Jason?" The name finally registered. "What are you doing here?"

"I'm . . ." Jason rose to his feet with a groan. "We . . . They've got Darcy. I saw them take her inside. In here. I tried to call the police, but my phone isn't working."

Parker steadied himself against the wall as he climbed to his feet.

"Parker, give me the gun. We've got to go after her. I heard them talking. They're going to kill her."

"No." Parker stumbled forward. "No, they're not." He pushed past Jason and headed back into the building.

"You're hurt. Give me the gun." Jason followed at Parker's side. "I know how to use it."

"Stay back," Parker whispered. "I don't want you getting hurt."

Jason dropped back but only a couple of feet. They came to an intersection, and Parker took a left.

"The other way," Jason whispered at his shoulder. "I think I heard voices back in the other direction."

Parker nodded and turned around. He followed the corridor until it opened into a large chamber. Metal stairs leading up to a glassed-in office. Toothless's office.

"Give me the gun," Jason urged. "You're on Mighty Mouse. You don't need it."

Parker shook his head and motioned up the stairs to the office. "Not your fight." He stumbled across the room and led the way silently up the stairs. He could hear voices inside. Darcy's voice. She was still alive! They paused at the top of the stairs. Parker could make out Toothless's voice, Ray's voice too. He couldn't tell if anybody else was inside or not. The others didn't say much when Toothless was around. There could be twenty of them or none at all.

Jason reached for the gun. Parker considered for a second. He might be able to leap across the room and take out the man holding Darcy while Jason focused on everybody else. But Jason didn't know about Ray. He didn't know about Toothless, the lay of the room. Better to hold on to the gun himself. His head might not be able to handle another jump.

He motioned for Jason to stand back. Then, on a count of three, he kicked in the door and leaped into the room.

"Parker! Glad you could join us. We've been expecting you." Toothless was holding Darcy in front of him like a shield. He was pointing a gun to her head. "I trust you had a nice nap."

"Drop the gun." Ray pointed a gun at Parker's chest. "Drop it now or we shoot the girl."

"Don't do it, Parker," Darcy called out. "Shoot him while—"

Toothless slapped her across the face with the barrel of his gun. Furious, Parker glared at Toothless.

"Drop the gun. Now!" Ray shouted.

Parker didn't have a choice. He let his hand drop to his side and released the gun so that its momentum carried it behind him, clattering out onto the stair landing. It was all up to Jason now.

"The deal was for you to let Darcy go!" Parker let his fury seep into his voice.

"The deal . . ." Toothless smiled hideously, "was for you to tell me how you modified the drug."

"And if I tell you now?"

"If you don't tell us, the girl dies right now. Slowly. One piece at a time."

Parker looked at the floor, formulating a new plan. "It's a transesterification reaction." He tossed out the first thing that came to his mind. "It's very simple. All you need is ethanol, benzoic acid, and phenol."

"Does that mean anything to you?" Toothless looked over at Ray.

Ray shrugged. "I'd have to look it up. I'm pretty sure we have all those ingredients."

"You're not going to find it in any textbooks," Parker said. "It's specific to the adrenaline compound." He took a step toward Darcy. "Take us back to my lab and I'll show you how to make it myself."

"We'll do better than that." Toothless nodded to Ray. "We'll bring your lab to you."

Ray motioned with his gun toward a door at the back of the office. "Come on. This way."

Parker frowned and led the way back into a large, window-lit room. A row of long wooden tables laden with glassware and lab equipment divided the room in half.

"Hey, those are my pH meters . . . and my missing top loader." Parker walked along the tables doing a quick inventory of potential assets. Toothless remained alone in the office with Darcy. Now was the time for Jason to strike. He might not get a better opportunity.

"Okay. Get going." Using the barrel of his gun, Ray shoved Parker toward one of the tables. "You've got five minutes. Try anything funny and it's over for the girl."

"Darcy." Parker picked up an Erlenmeyer flask and filled it with ethanol. "You used to call her Darcy. Remember, Ray? Back when we were friends?"

"I remember her talking down to me. The same way you all talked down to me. I remember being read the riot act for being sick."

"Ray, you didn't show up to work for days at a time. You didn't even call. I should have fired you." Parker clamped the flask to a ring stand and walked to the end of the table where he'd seen a propane torch. What was Jason waiting for? The password and secret handshake?

"Ah. How's our master chef?"

Parker spun around. Toothless stood inside the doorway with one arm around Darcy's neck. Blood oozed from a gash on her cheek. Another spot on the side of her head also seemed to be bleeding. She appeared dazed and pale, like she might be going into shock.

"What did you do to her?" Parker's muscles were quivering. It was all he could do to keep from charging Toothless and tearing him apart with his bare hands.

"Consider it a down payment." Toothless dragged Darcy across the lab to stand next to Ray. "I'm growing bored with these games, Mr. Parker. If I don't see some real results in the next few minutes . . ." He pressed the gun to Darcy's cheek.

"Tell him I'm working as fast as I can." Parker looked to Ray.

"I think he's stalling." Ray walked over to the bench and inspected the flask Parker had set up. "All he's done so far is set up an alcohol bath."

Parker returned to the flask setup with the torch and a friction lighter. He couldn't light it now. Ray was too close. He set the torch under the flask and examined the lighter.

"See, I told you he's stalling!" Ray shoved Parker aside, lit the torch and placed it under the ethanol.

"I'll weigh out the benzoic acid." Parker crossed the room casually and dropped a weighing boat onto the top-loading balance. "Ray, could you get me a thermometer?"

"Get it yourself," Ray growled. "I'm not your slave anymore. This is *my* lab." He leaned back against the lab bench only a few feet away from the torch.

"Ray, I'm serious. Get that thermometer. Now!"

"You—"

The beaker of ethanol exploded, engulfing Ray in a ball of flames. Parker leaped across the floor as an agonizing scream filled the room. He hit Toothless square in the back, knocking him and Darcy to the floor.

Parker scrambled to his hands and knees and tried to stand up, but his vision blurred at the edges. Electric blue fireballs. Intense pain. Smoke. The crackle of burning wood mingled with hideous screams. Darcy was on the floor in front of him. Blood was flowing freely from the side of her head. She looked dazed.

Furtive motion, slow and steady at the corner of Parker's eye. Toothless was crawling toward a gun that lay on the floor just inches from his outstretched hand. Parker gathered his feet beneath him as Toothless's hand closed around the weapon. He lunged.

A shot rang out. Parker's hands closed around Toothless's wrist before he could get off another shot. Wrenching upward and twisting hard, the gun flew through the air and landed in a rapidly expanding circle of flames.

Parker yanked Toothless to his feet and hurled him across the room. Stooping beside Darcy, he lifted her gently off the floor, cradled her in his arms. Her eyes were open, but she was limp as a wet tissue.

"Darcy, can you hear me?" Parker backed away from the fire. "Are you okay?"

Darcy nodded, but he still couldn't tell if she understood what he was saying or not. He had to get her out of here. Fast. It was getting harder and harder to breath. The fire had spread to the walls.

He turned to the door and caught a glimpse of Toothless slipping from the room. A crash sounded over the roar of the fire. A loud shout. It sounded like Jason.

Parker was carrying Darcy across the room when an inhuman scream sounded behind him. Turning, he saw a grotesque figure sail high above the dancing flames and land on all fours right in front of him. It rose up on quivering, pulsing legs, roaring like a wild beast. Shirt hanging in smoldering tatters, its right shoulder blackened and charred, the crinkled roots of what had once been long greasy hair blackened the right side of a bloodred skull.

Parker leaned over to set Darcy down as Ray leaped again. The full force of his jump smashed into Parker's chest, driving him to the floor. A heavy blow caught him in the shoulder and the back of the head. Clawlike hands groped for his neck. Ray was on top of him, trying to kill him.

Parker grabbed his wrists, but Ray was too strong. His arm muscles popped and twitched, pressing down on him like a jackhammer. Adrenaline. He must have taken a massive overdose. Blackened fingers inched closer and closer to Parker's neck. He had to do something—fast.

"Darcy, get out of here!" Parker shouted.

"Not without you." Darcy was leaning over Ray, trying to pry him off Parker.

"Darcy, please!"

An arm reached in and pulled Darcy off. "Jason!" Parker gasped as Ray's fingertips reached his neck. "Get her out of here. Now!"

"Let go of me!" Darcy shrieked as Jason struggled to drag her away. "Parker, he's one of them. John . . . Pyramid!"

A burning timber crashed down into the makeshift lab. The floor shuddered as hot sparks settled around them. Parker couldn't breathe; his lungs were on fire. He tried to work his knees between his body and Ray's, but his strength was fading. The room was getting darker.

DARCY

"Let me go!" Darcy threw her weight to the side, knocking Jason off-balance. She drove an elbow into his gut and he stumbled back into a wall.

"Ow!" Jason lifted her off her feet and spun her around. "What's wrong with you? I'm trying to rescue you."

"Let me go then! I don't need rescuing."

"Don't worry about Parker. He's fine. He's on Mighty Mouse."

"Like you even care." She lunged out with her foot and kicked off the wall, tipping Jason backward.

"Of course I care. What are you talking about?"

"I saw you with those men!" She twisted around. All she needed was to make contact with one good knee.

"What? Those guys on the street?" His voice took on an innocent tone. "I was just pretending. You know, pumping them for information."

Right. And a gun just happened to be in your hand and they just happened to be in the habit of taking orders from you. "Really?" She stopped struggling and let her muscles go limp. "So you aren't working for Pyramid?" Her most gullible airhead voice.

"Of course not. What gave you that ridiculous idea?"

She took a deep breath and forced herself to relax. Good. His grip was loosening. "Those guys just seemed to know you so well."

"I was just playing them. Pretending to be the new guy on the team. You know how I am. I can convince people of anything."

"Exactly!" Darcy spun suddenly around with her elbow and caught Jason in the side of the head. Wriggling out of his grasp, she turned and ran back down the empty corridor.

A blast of hot air hit her in the face. The smell of black smoke. She kept on running. Jason was right behind her. She could hear his pounding footsteps. Turning to the left, she plunged into a smoke-filled chamber. A loud crash sounded ahead of her. The crackling roar of spreading flames.

Dropping to her knees, she wadded up the lower half of her shirt and placed it over her mouth and nose.

"Darcy!" Jason was right behind her. It was either him or the fire.

Breathing through her shirt, she crawled forward, deeper into the warehouse.

CHAPTER 33

PARKER

PULSING FINGERS TIGHTENED AROUND Parker's neck. He couldn't breathe. The room was getting fuzzier.

Thrusting hard with both feet, Parker sent Ray sailing through the air, ripping his hands from Parker's throat. A sickening thud. Ray crashing to the floor.

Gasping for breath, Parker rolled over onto his knees. Climbing to his feet, he staggered into Toothless's office. The door. He was going to make it. If he could just . . .

He turned back to face the burning room. Ray was still in there. He couldn't just leave him to die.

A loud shriek sounded over the roar of the fire. Was it Darcy? He couldn't be sure. He turned back toward the stairs, then hesitated again. *God, please . . . keep Darcy safe.* He plunged back into the smoke-filled room and found Ray crawling across the floor.

Parker lifted him to his feet and threw him across his shoulder. Running back through the office, he pounded down the metal stairs. The smoke-filled chamber shuddered and dimmed every time he coughed. Deep, wrenching coughs. His lungs were on fire. He couldn't breathe.

He staggered out into a corridor, guided by the wail of distant sirens. Help was on the way. Ambulances.

"Darcy!" His shout was drowned out by a shuddering crash. The building was starting to collapse. "Darcy!" He spun around, searching up and down the passage. A tremor passed through Ray's frame. A gurgling cough.

He turned toward the sirens and stumbled down the corridor through a cloud of swirling smoke. Flickering orange flames. Flashing blue lights. Masked faces.

Parker collapsed under Ray's weight as the faces reached up and caught him, bearing him up on the weightless hands of blessed unconsciousness.

DARCY

"Darcy, come on! It's—" Jason's shouts were cut short by a string of explosive coughs. "It's me, Jason."

Darcy crawled deeper under a steel table, pressing herself against a wall. The smoke was starting to thicken. Why didn't Jason just give up?

"Darcy!" Jason's voice was louder now.

What was wrong with him? What could be so important that it was worth risking his life? Sudden doubt assailed her. What if he really was trying to rescue her? She could have been all wrong about him. He really could have been pretending to be a bad guy. Maybe they just let him borrow one of their guns.

"She's inside!" Jason's shout cut her like a lashing whip. He was talking to someone. Barking out orders. "Inside . . . help me search . . . know she's in there . . ." Pyramid's gang. They were organizing a search.

A hazy figure stumbled by, not twenty feet from where she was hiding. Another figure, following close behind the first. She blinked her eyes, dabbed them with her shirt. Jason and someone else. A big man. There was something about him. Something . . . She caught her breath as he turned. *Raccoon Face!*

The man staggered by her hiding place. She pressed her face to the floor, snatching breaths from the eddies of cool air that swept the room. Tendrils of smoke curled around her, burning her eyes, her face, her lungs. Dante's Inferno. Hell. An image dark and terrifying rose up like a thunderhead. The Dark Man hobbling on crutches. Crashing music. Gyrating bodies. A drug-induced haze.

She never should have been there. She'd known it all along. So stupid. She could have killed him.

Whatever happened to her, she deserved it. "Happily ever after" only applied to the good guys. Like Parker. He came back for her—even after she'd run away. She could still see him. Triumphant. Radiant. Eyes flashing with excitement, lighting up the dark corners of her life. Even in his chair he was running, leaping, laughing.

While she lay writhing in agony.

"Happily ever after." Parker's words tugged at the back of her mind. Was she doing it again? Running away?

The voices were receding. She tried to move, to push up onto her hands and knees, but a fiery wave crashed over her. Her head was spinning, the blackness whirling around her.

Running from happiness—from God? How long had she been doing it? Running from the wrong people.

"Jason?" Her voice burned at the back of her throat. "Jason! Help me!" A spasm of wrenching coughs. "God, please. Help me!"

Footsteps rumbled through the storm. Shouting voices. Grasping hands. She felt herself being dragged across the floor. Lifted up. A red, scarred face. Jason bending double, coughing.

The room lurched to the side, and they crashed to the floor in a tangle of flailing arms and legs. Raccoon Face pulled her to her feet and shouted something in her ear. Leaning on each other for support, they staggered through a smoke-filled hallway. Light up ahead. A shadow moving in a doorway.

Darcy tried to run, but Jason stumbled, dragging her down. They were so close. If they could just—

The ceiling ahead of them collapsed, sending up a cloud of smoke and sparks. Darcy felt herself spinning. The air was too hot. She couldn't breathe. Wiping her eyes, she squinted through the smoke. The hall in front of them was blocked by burning debris. They were trapped.

PARKER

Parker looked at his watch. It was already 5:30. Where were Jason and Darcy? He left Ray with the paramedics and ran back to the burning warehouse. A mob of police officers was stationed at the door, swarming every man that stumbled outside. A police van sat about fifty feet away, as well as two police cars, all of them full of men.

One of the officers turned at Parker's approach. He was a short, powerfully built man with a bushy mustache.

"Have you seen a girl?" Parker stopped right in front of him. "About five-foot-six. Light brown hair, golden brown eyes?"

The officer eyed Parker suspiciously. "Sorry, sir, but I'm going to have to ask to see some ID."

Parker handed him his wallet. "I'm James Parker. I was the one who got kidnapped. Darcy Williams too. She was in the building when the fire started. Have you seen her? She should have been with a Jason Shanahan."

The officer motioned to the other men. "This fella here says he's James Parker, the guy Kelly was with when he was gunned down."

The men stared hard at him. He could almost feel their anger.

"I'm looking for Darcy Williams," Parker repeated. "Has she come out of the building? You couldn't miss her. She's about five-foot-six with light brown—"

"Mr. Parker." A policeman with hard eyes and gray thinning hair stepped forward. "I'm going to have to ask you a few questions." He motioned to two officers, and they moved to Parker's side, each taking him by an arm.

Parker swayed on his feet, feeling suddenly dizzy. Tired. "Um . . . fine. I'll answer your questions, but first we need to find Darcy. She may still be in the building." He tugged with his arms, but the men at his side held on tighter. Several others stepped forward. "You've got to let me go! If she's not out here, that means she's still in the warehouse."

"Mr. Parker, I'll inform the fire fighters about Ms. Williams, but right now I'd like to ask you to—"

"Listen, I'm sorry but I've got to go find Darcy. I'll be right back. I promise." He wrenched up on his arms and twisted them free. Then, spinning around, he broke through the cluster of circling police officers and dodged to his right around them. Two men stepped in front of the door to block his way, but a powerful leap sent him sailing over their heads.

He hit the ground running and slipped through the open door. Hot smoke blasted him in the face. The walls doubled and danced around him. He felt light-headed, like he was going to pass out. What? After just a few seconds inside? What was going on? Fumes from the chemicals in the lab?

He checked his watch again. Its hands stretched and bent, making it difficult to tell for sure, but it looked like 7:15. He ran deeper into the building, trying to remember when he'd taken the drug. Then it hit him. He'd been at Jason's house. It must have been about 6:30. Almost thirteen hours. Soon it would be pumpkin time.

DARCY

Darcy looked up through the smoky haze as a dark blur arced through the air. Over the flames, it swooped down on them like a giant bird of prey, hitting the floor with a resounding smack.

"Parker?"

"Darcy, are you okay?" He lifted her off the floor and crushed her to his chest, cradling her in his arms.

"I think so. I—"

"Listen to me. We don't have much time. The drug's starting to wear off." A jolt passed through Parker's frame. A series of muffled booms. Suddenly, he was kicking a hole in the corridor wall. Jason was on his knees tearing chunks of broken drywall from the dark opening.

Parker crouched low and set Darcy on the floor next to Raccoon Face, who appeared to have passed out. "Think you can make it?"

"No problem." Darcy turned to Jason who was coughing and sputtering at the opening. "Go on through. We'll pass this guy in to you."

Parker grabbed the heavy man and started to shove him through.

"Wait a second!" Darcy reached into his jacket and pulled out a heavy gun. "Okay. Now." She flung it down the hallway. When she turned back, Raccoon Face's legs were just disappearing through the hole.

"Go ahead. Hurry!" Parker grabbed Darcy around the waist

and pushed her through the opening into a dark room. Cool fresh air tingled in her lungs, triggering a fit of convulsive coughing. She felt her way to a door and crawled out into another hallway. Jason was dragging Raccoon Face to a pair of back-lit steel doors. Dim sunlight!

Darcy turned to wait for Parker. "Parker?" She crawled back inside the dark room. Parker lay on his face, halfway through the opening. He wasn't moving.

"Parker?" She crouched beside him, pushing on his shoulder. "Jason!" She shouted over the roar of the fire. "Jason, get back here! It's Parker. He's passed out." She tugged at Parker's arms, trying to drag him through the hole. Smoke was pouring in around him. Yellow light reflected off the walls.

Jason appeared at her side and grabbed one of Parker's arms. Together they dragged him through the room and to the doors at the end of the hall.

"They're locked!" Jason slammed his shoulder into the doors. A heavy, padlocked chain rattled between two metal handles.

Darcy threw herself against the doors. "Hello? Anybody out there?" She pounded with her fists. "Let us out of here. Help!"

Jason moved Parker to the side and kicked at the doors. "Help! Let us out of here!" He kicked them again and again.

A loud crash sent a cloud of black smoke billowing toward them. The flicker of orange sparks. Darcy staggered into the left door and slid down its face with a metallic squeak. She lay on the floor coughing, her face pressed to the band of sunlight beneath the door.

"I know," Jason gasped. "This guy had a gun!"

When Darcy looked up Jason was crouching over Raccoon Face, patting down his pockets.

"Too late," Darcy said. "I already got it."

Jason moved to Parker and started checking his pockets. "Parker might have picked up—" He went suddenly tense.

"Jason, what's wrong?" Darcy sat up and looked over his shoulder. He was holding a plastic bag full of syringes, alcohol-soaked cotton balls, and a serum vial. Adrenaline 355. "Jason, no! You can't. It would turn you into a monster."

"Not me." He turned on Darcy, eyes glowing like two burning coals. "You."

"Me? I can't. What if I hurt you?" Images of the Dark Man

flooded her mind. The squeal of brakes. The sickening crunch of bone against asphalt.

"You'll be fine." Jason pulled a syringe out of the plastic bag. "It might not even affect women in the same way. Jenny never had any of the side effects Parker had. Besides, you've never lost your temper a day in your life."

"That's not true. I used to be a little terror." She closed her eyes. She could still remember the tantrums, the feeling of being totally out of control. "Sorry, I can't! I just can't."

"But you're not a terror now. You can control it. I know you can. Just take the drug and break the door down. I'll help you."

"Jason, it's chemistry. Action, reaction. It can't be controlled." She could still hear her grandmother's screams. She'd been the sweetest person on the face of the earth, but even she couldn't control the chemistry of Alzheimer's.

"No," Jason said firmly. "You don't believe that. I know you. Besides, we don't have a choice." He nodded in the direction of the long hallway. A flickering orange glow lit the black smoke.

Darcy closed her eyes and nodded. At least if it didn't work, she wouldn't have long to be haunted by the ghosts.

When she opened her eyes, Jason was filling a syringe. He dabbed her arm with a wet cotton ball. "Wouldn't want you to get an infection after you save our lives." He jabbed the needle into her arm and injected her with the drug.

God, help me. Don't let me do anything wrong. Please. Darcy didn't feel anything for almost a minute. Then a spreading burning sensation. Her muscles started to twitch. She felt it creeping up her spine. More twitching. Pops and jumps. It was getting more and more intense. She couldn't control it; it was taking over. *God, please . . . help me. Help—*

A tidal wave of anger washed through her. Blind rage. Power! It surged through her body. Wave upon wave of crushing strength, pulsing energy. Freedom! Absolute and complete. She leaped to her feet, flying up through the gathering smoke. Bright light dazzled her senses. Dancing flames. The fire. It was attacking her!

No! She turned from the light and tried to run, but a massive door barred her way. Dancing orange highlights against dull, battleship gray. She hammered on the door with her fists. Screamed out her anger.

A voice sounded nearby, soft and menacing. She spun around, shielding her eyes against the attacking light. A face filtered through the glare. He was yelling at her. Something about the doors. *Jason?* The name bubbled up through her mind. The ghost of a memory. *Jason.* He was trying to kill her.

A surge of power flowed through her. An answering roar. She crept toward Jason slowly, savoring the look of panic on his face. He was afraid. Let him tremble. She was invincible. Powerful beyond belief. She crouched low, preparing to pounce.

A hand. Inches away from her foot. She whirled around with a roar, slashing the air with death-dealing hands. The body didn't move. She bent low on pulsing legs, poised like a compressed spring. The face. So familiar. *Parker.* Had Jason dared to attack him too? He would pay for this. He would pay!

Darcy threw back her head and cried out her anger. She turned, spotted Jason frozen against the swirling smoke. A running step and she leaped through the air. Fiery flames snapped around her as she hit him full in the chest and drove him to the ground. Ignoring his flailing fists, she reached out and clamped steel fingers around his neck.

Jason had killed Parker. He would die!

She willed herself to squeeze, but something held her back. A silent voice screaming through her head. *Evil.* What she was doing was wrong.

Sickening revulsion spread through her like a foul scent. Hot prickling shame. Her arms went limp. She rolled off of Jason. Lifted him to his feet like a rag doll. He was talking to her, pointing to the doors.

The doors! She took off down the hall and leaped into the air. Feet first, she hurtled toward the doors. An explosive kick sent her tumbling backward, gray light filled the room. *Parker.* She rolled onto her hands and knees and groped along the ground in the blinding sunlight. Her hand brushed the soft fabric of his shirt. *Parker.* She wrapped her arms around him, pressed her face to his chest. He wasn't moving. It was too late. She gathered her feet beneath her and lifted him shakily from the ground. Carrying him through the open doorway, she stepped out into the coolness beyond.

Stacks of metal barrels. A blast of ice-cold air. She threaded her way through a serpentine passageway and kicked open a gate in a chain-link fence. Wailing sirens. A dazzle of red and blue lights. She turned from the lights and ran, deeper into the protecting darkness. The cool air burned her lungs, setting off a cascade of ragged coughs, but still she carried him. She wouldn't let them hurt him. She'd keep him safe.

She wound her way through a maze of rusted-out cars and laid Parker down next to a mountain of mud-splashed pallets.

"Don't worry, Parker." A ragged voice croaked in her ears. "I'm not going to leave you again. Not now." She stroked his cheek with quivering, trembling fingers. "Not ever."

Darcy sighed. Warm, luxurious softness surrounded her. Comforting voices, serene and ordinary.

"Darcy? Are you awake?"

Her eyes drifted open. Parker's smiling face. A warm hand curled around her cheek.

"Parker?" She started to sit up.

"Shhh . . . It's okay." He eased her back onto the pillow with a touch. "You're at the hospital. The doctors say you need to rest."

"The hospital?" Her mind raced. The booming of guns, flying glass, smoke-filled corridors. "Jason." She looked around the room. "There was a fire. I think I tried to kill him."

"Jason's fine," Parker soothed. "We're all fine thanks to you."

Darcy shut her eyes, trying to make sense of the fragmented images that swirled in her head. "I took the drug, didn't I?"

"To save us from the fire."

"I remember being so angry. Is that what it's like for you?"

Parker shook his head. "I don't think so. I had these really terrible nightmares when I was asleep, but nothing like that when I was awake."

Was? Darcy looked over at Parker. "Why are you still in your wheelchair? Did you run out of adrenaline?"

"I've stopped taking it." He looked down at the controls of his chair and raised his seat back. I know I wasn't the one who hurt all those people, but that still doesn't mean I'm supposed to keep taking the drug. Some of the dreams I've had are pretty . . . disturbing.

Dad thinks it's the hormones and that they will balance out, but I want to make sure . . ."

"But if you stop taking it"—Darcy searched Parker's eyes—"doesn't that mean you'll. . . ?"

"Eventually." Parker nodded his head somberly. "It's an important decision. I don't want to enter into it lightly. But first and foremost I want to do what's right. There are a lot more important things than long life."

Darcy opened her mouth to protest, but the look of determination on Parker's face was unmistakable. She took a deep breath. "Whatever you decide, I want you to know that I'll be here for you. No matter what. You're not going to get rid of me that easily."

Parker stared into her eyes for a long minute. "Thanks, I—"

"Hey, it's Rip Van Winkle!" Jason burst into the room. "Why didn't you tell me she was up?"

"Shouldn't you be in jail or something?" Darcy shot him an exasperated look.

"Not this again!" Jason sighed and rolled his eyes at Parker. "Did I tell you she decked me while I was trying to save her life?"

Parker shook his head. "She was on the drug at the time. You have to make allowances for—"

"No she wasn't," Jason exclaimed. "She hit me way before that. I was—"

"I saw him giving orders to Pyramid's men. What was I supposed to think?"

"I already told you. I was conning them."

"Right." Darcy sat up in the bed, pulling the sheet around her. "And you just happened to have a gun with you."

"The gun was my father's." Jason sat down at the foot of the bed. "I started carrying it after the press conference. With all the bogeymen searching for us, I thought it was a good idea to have a little protection."

"Some protection." Parker swiveled in his chair to face Jason. "Why didn't you come in with the gun when Darcy and I were in Toothless's office? I threw it out to you."

"Threw it right off the stairs and into the room below, you mean. I had to dig through a pile of empty boxes to find it." Jason shrugged. "By the time I got back, you'd already set the place on fire."

"And what about the press conference?" Parker asked. "What was the deal with that introduction? It sounded like you were sending coded messages to Pyramid."

"And what about the rage?" Darcy interjected. "You don't still expect us to believe you were making adrenaline from it."

"Okay, okay. I admit it." Jason held up his hands. "I lied about the rage. So shoot me. I was a little paranoid."

"Paranoid about what?" Darcy asked. "Pyramid?"

"Like I said, Pyramid's just a practical joke my father pulled when I was a kid. When I suggested the name, that's all I knew. But then I found one of my dad's research papers. It was published five years after his death. It could've just been one of his grad students finishing up his thesis work, but I couldn't help wondering if maybe my father was still alive. The paper was on controlling aggression in mice. Aggression—as in rage. I know it sounds crazy, but at the time I thought my father might have been the one that invented rage. I started wondering, what if he wasn't dead? What if he'd gone underground?"

"So that's what the press conference was all about? Sending a message to your father?"

Jason nodded. "There was a chemical structure in his notes. After the press conference I went out and bought some rage just to see if it matched. It didn't, but that doesn't mean anything. If he was a drug lord, he'd be crazy to leave the structure of rage lying around."

"What?" Darcy's mind reeled. "Your father a drug lord? The homeless-looking guy Ray was working for?"

Parker shook his head. "The toothless guy is the real drug lord. Jeremy says the DEA has been after him for years. He confirmed that Jason's father died in a lab fire. He was just a normal scientist who happened to enjoy practical jokes."

"Jeremy?" Darcy looked back and forth between Jason and Parker. "Who's Jeremy?"

"Jeremy LaGrange, the man with the scarred up face," Parker said. "He dropped by a few hours ago to check on you, but you were still asleep. He's a chemist with the DEA. Protected substances division."

"A *d* away from *dead*!" Jason stood up suddenly, his eyes lit with a strange light. "A cop told me Jeremy was a 'd away from dead.'

Get it? D-E-A. I don't know why I didn't figure it out. I kept thinking basketball. You know, like the game of horse."

Darcy turned back to Parker. "So, all that time we thought Raccoon Face was after us, and he was really after Ray?"

"Actually, he was looking for Pyramid," Parker said. "Apparently the paper we sent out contained the synthesis information for one of the precursors to rage."

Darcy shut her eyes, trying to pull together all the puzzle pieces that floated in her head. "All I want to know is, are we safe or not? Is anyone besides Jason still trying to kill us?"

"Define safe," Parker said. "Pyramid is back to being non-existent, but Toothless escaped. Apparently the cops thought he was a homeless man and let him go."

"The *invisible man*," Darcy said. "Isn't that what he called himself?"

Parker nodded. "Most of his gang has been rounded up. Some of them are in this hospital."

Jason grinned, "Runyan and Kelly are here too. They're on the second floor and your friend Ray is on the fourth. Does that make you feel any safer?"

"That depends," Darcy said. "What floor am I on?"

"The third." Parker's eyes sparkled as he reached out and took her by the hand.

"Good!" Darcy squeezed his hand and plopped back on her pillow. "Things are finally starting to look up!"

EPILOGUE

PARKER

"**OKAY, I'VE GOT THE REST.**" Darcy threw her cards facedown onto the center of the kitchen table.

"Wait a second," Parker said, glancing from his dad to his mom. "We've got six cards left. We can still set her, can't we?"

"Don't look at me. I'm just the dummy." His mom aimed a mysterious, girls-only smile at Darcy and walked back to stir a pot on the stove. "I didn't even have any support for her. I just bid up her suit so I could finish supper."

Parker looked down at the ace, king, and queen of spades in his hand. "You're void in spades, aren't you."

Darcy grinned at him. "And the jack of diamonds won't do you any good either. I've got the queen."

"Okay, that does it." Parker's dad threw in his hand. "Darcy, next time you're my partner. This worthless boyfriend of yours hasn't had a decent hand all afternoon."

"I wouldn't say worthless." Darcy gathered the cards together in a stack and started shuffling. "Once his drug makes it through clinical trials, he stands to make ten, twenty, maybe even thirty dollars. He'll be able to pay for a copy of his thesis."

Parker reached across the table and took Darcy's hand. She beamed at him. He loved seeing her so happy. She glowed when she was with his family, drinking in every nuance like a starving child at her first Christmas dinner.

And his family just adored her. As far as they were concerned, she was already part of the family. In fact, with him busy finishing up his thesis, she spent more time with his parents than he did.

The doorbell chimed from the foyer.

"I'll get it." Parker's mom hurried across the kitchen and stopped at the door. She looked back and motioned to his dad. "It's probably Jenny's date. Don't you want to meet him?"

He shrugged.

"Darcy, please excuse *us*," his mom said. "We're very curious about this mystery date of Jenny's. Aren't we, Bruce?"

"Oh, right." He jumped up and grinned at Parker. "It might take a while to give this guy the third degree—more than enough time for any questions you might need to ask Darcy."

"Dad, would you cut it out?" Parker looked at Darcy. "Don't laugh. You'll just encourage him."

"Okay, we're going," his dad called out from the dining room. "Already in the living room. Can't hear a thing now."

Parker shook his head and stared back at Darcy. She was so beautiful. His chest tightened. His heart felt like it was going to explode.

"So. . . ?" She smiled at him mischievously. "What *was* it you wanted to ask me?"

"Right. At the kitchen table over a game of bridge with my parents. Real romantic."

"I don't know. I think a one-diamond opening bid is kind of nice." She sighed. "And I love your parents. I couldn't have asked for better."

"Don't worry. I've already got the perfect occasion planned. But you have to promise to act surprised, okay? Can you wait just a few more days?"

"Okay . . ." She pooched out her lower lip. "But not too long. Your father's about ready to get down on one knee and ask me himself."

"He's too old for you, and besides"—Parker watched her expectantly—"he's just an ordinary MD. I'm going to be an assistant professor."

"What?" Her eyes went wide. "You already heard?"

"Remember the phone call I got during the last hand? It was Jack Dolan from Stanford. They're offering me the position."

"Parker, that's wonderful!" Darcy threw her arms around his

neck. He stood up and folded her in his arms, pressing his lips to the top of her head.

"Wait a minute." She pushed away from him. "You're going to be a professor at SSSSSSSStanford?" She crossed her fingers and made the Stanford hiss.

"Either that or endure the bitter cold winters at Yale. Stanford *is* a lot closer to my parents."

"Hmmm. Fraternizing with the enemy. I suppose . . ." Her eyes danced. "But at the big game we're sitting on the Cal side. Agreed?"

"Agreed." He caught her up in his arms and spun her around.

"Hey, you two. What's going on?" Jason poked his head into the kitchen.

"Jason! What are you doing here?" Parker set Darcy back on her feet and took a deep breath to clear his head. "Did Dad ask you over for a game of bridge? He's been trying to find a new partner all afternoon."

"Actually I'm here to see Jenny." Jason sauntered into the kitchen. "Didn't she tell you? We're going out tonight."

"No way!" Parker shook his head. "Jenny has higher standards than that."

"I think she's trying to reform me." Jason's eyes drifted to the floor, and a hint of color rose to his cheeks. "She's taking me to a party at your church."

"Careful," Parker said with a grin, "that could wreck your gangster reputation."

"My reputation's already wrecked," Jason said. "If I spent any more time at the police station, they'd have to give me my own desk."

"Any news on Ray?"

"Kelly gets out of the hospital tomorrow, but it's going to be a long, painful recovery for Ray. It'll be months before he can stand trial."

Parker nodded. As far as he was concerned, Ray had already suffered enough. He hoped the prosecutor would go easy on him. One of the gunmen had testified that Ray had tried to talk Toothless out of having Parker shot at the press conference, but Toothless had been convinced that Parker would reveal the formula for adrenaline. All he cared about was his monopoly.

"What about Toothless?" Darcy asked. "Any new leads?"

"They're saying he's long gone by now. Doing his homeless man act in L.A. or New York."

The *clack, clack* of footsteps sounded in the dining room. "Sorry I took so long." Jenny breezed into the kitchen and gave Darcy a quick hug. Jason jumped to his feet. His face actually seemed to pale as he took Jenny in. He seemed to have trouble swallowing.

"Ready to go?" Jenny glided to Jason's side and slipped a hand inside the crook of his arm. She turned and winked at Parker.

"Ready as I'll ever be." Jason walked her self-consciously across the kitchen floor.

Parker grinned, enjoying his friend's discomfort. Jason, the master of every situation. It was good to finally see him rattled. "Have fun, you two. And Jason"—he deepened his voice just a tad—"you be good to my favorite sister."

"Like I have a choice!" Jason laughed. "Your favorite sister can lift me over her head and pile-drive me into the ground."

"And don't you forget it." Jenny pulled him from the room, leaving Darcy and Parker alone.

"Jenny and Jason," Darcy wrinkled her nose. "I just can't see it."

Parker stepped toward her, and she slipped back into his arms. "How about us? Can you see us?"

"Most of the time. But sometimes . . ." Her face clouded. "Sometimes it seems . . . too good to last."

"That's why it will." Parker held her tighter. "In the end, *too good to last* is the only thing that can last. Everything else is temporary."

Darcy's eyes drifted shut. "Happily ever after," she breathed, leaning her head against his chest. "I know it in my head. It's just so hard to believe."

"All it takes is practice," Parker whispered. "And this I promise you: I'm going to give you plenty of that."

"Okay, heading back to the kitchen now!" His dad's voice called out from the dining room. "Almost there."

Parker let Darcy go and brushed a strand of hair out of her face.

"So . . . Anything happen while we were gone?" His dad took Darcy by the left hand and shook his head in disappointment. "Okay," he called back to the dining room, "false alarm. Everyone back to the foyer. We'll give them ten more minutes!"

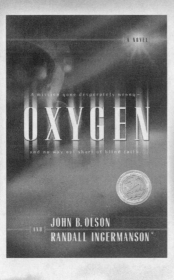